THE FENIAN

Love, hate...and a second chance

To Tom

PLEASE ENJOY

Mike Kean

JULY 2023

THE FENIAN

MIKE KERNAN

JBM19
BOOKS

COVER DESIGN: Ryan McGinness

www.mikekernan.co.uk

JBM19

BOOKS

TO MARGARET

CAST LIST

THE GIRLS

Lorna	Pocahontas
Kirsty	Penelope Pitstop
Wee Mary	Star of Hai Karate TV ads
Karen	Cleopatra
Jo	Barbara (The Good Life)
Fiona	Princess Anne

THE GUYS

Robert	David Cassidy
Big Paddy	Baloo
Cammy	Mowgli
Ross	Hutch (Starsky & Hutch)
Cookie	Joe 90

Chapter 1

March 18, 1975
Make Me Smile – Steve Harley & Cockney Rebel

EVEN by Mum's warped standards, this was mental.
'Heh Lorna,' she croaked weakly as I passed her open bedroom door on the way to the loo. 'Gonnae let us smash an egg over your head?'
'What?'
I had heard. I just didn't get it.
'Mere a minute,' she said. 'I just want to crack an egg over your head. Just the one. You can do one back to me.'
'That'll be chocolate,' I replied, but I went into her room all the same.
Mum was sitting up in bed. That was the first odd thing about that morning. Oh, apart from the egg question of course.
For days she had lain mostly flat out, prone apart from the occasional gasping and twitching. Now, propped up by pillows, the strain of hauling herself to that position was etched in her face. Her hollow, worn-out face, as if she'd just run the marathon at the Olympics.
By her bedside, a ten-packet of Regal, unopened, still sealed. Waste of a good twenty pence, my Dad would have moaned. That was the second odd thing about that day. She was too weak even to smoke, like it was her final surrender. It was about quarter past eight. A Tuesday, a school day, a work day, a normal day. I'd just had my Sugar Smacks with Noel Edmonds. Dad would have left about an hour earlier. Up until a few days ago, the ashtray would have clocked on by this time. It would be well into its shift, already holding the corpses of three or four fags. But it was still empty that morning. Mum's dressing gown was draped around her shoulders, which were thin and frail as the backs of our rickety old kitchen chairs. Nothing odd about that. These days she would still be in her dressing gown when I got home

1

about half four or five. Sometimes I imagined she got up and got dressed after I left for school. I tried to convince myself she did normal Mum things when I was away then changed back into her dressing gown and went back to bed before I got home. But deep down – fine, not even that deep down – I knew it didn't happen.

That morning, her face was white. No, that's not quite right. Not white. Off-white, kind of cement-coloured. Nothing odd about that either, not any more.

Mum hacked but staved off another cough. It went into reverse gear, gurgled back into her lungs, stirred around in there, angrily, a snake tossed back into its pit. She swallowed the pain and spoke again in her gruff, cigarette growl.

'Naw, I'm serious pet. About the eggs.' Her eyes had already told me that. Unnecessarily, she added: 'I know, I know, sounds a wee bit mad.'

'Aye, just a wee bit,' I said.

She persisted. 'It's just...it's just something I've always wanted to do, hen. To see what it feels like. To do it and have it done back to me.'

'Mum, you're crazy. And I'm going to school in a minute. Look, I've got my stuff on.'

'Bugger the school,' she said. 'It'll still be there the morn. Go on hen, just do it, eh? For your old maw. I'll even say please. Away you down the stairs and get the eggs. *Please.* I got your dad to bring in half a dozen special. Told him I fancied an omelette for my tea. Believe anything so he would.'

That was the moment. The exact moment when I knew. When I really, really understood, that my Mum was going to die. She was going to be dead, like my Papa. But this was my Mum and she really was going to die. Very soon.

I went to fetch the eggs.

***

Wait. This really happened. Honest to God, it happened like this, exactly the way I'm telling it.

I've told this story, the story of my Mum's last day, to what, five or six people over the years? I've told it to my husbands. (*Yes, husbands, plural. Just two, though. Don't get the idea I'm a serial wife.*) I've told it to a handful of friends. Friends who have drifted in and out of my life. Mostly friends of my husbands if I'm honest. I told it to Wee Mary of course, the truest friend I ever had. The one I really shouldn't have let slip through my fingers.

Each time I tell it, the reaction is the same. There it is. I catch it, just for an instant. An eyebrow drops a fraction or lips purse for half a second. They

THE FENIAN

don't believe it. I know they don't. I feel it and each time I sense what they're thinking. *It's just not believable. A woman so close to death? She'd be too far gone. Where would she have found the strength?* What can I say? I was there and it's what happened. Really. I can't explain how the candle flickered that one last time before it was snuffed out. I'm not a doctor. I can offer no medical explanation.

But surely I wouldn't revise and edit? Not about that day, not about my Mum. Would I?

Wait again. I'm trying to be completely honest here. Most times I *did* edit. Most times I missed out the last bit when I told this story. The important bit. The bit *after* the eggs. But not this time. I'll get to that.

Bill (my first husband) tried to rationalise it, tried to convince me that I'd got the timescale mixed up, that this must have happened some other time – days before she died, weeks maybe. Sorry Bill, but you're wrong. Just this once, you're wrong.

Not that I can trust myself, not completely, not with timescales, I mean. Because back then, the business of my Mum's dying felt so long and drawn out. Never-ending. But now that I figure it out logically, it took just a few weeks. I know for certain she was home that Christmas, and New Year too. So, it must have been January at the earliest when she went into the hospital for the last time. The cancer hospital, I've heard it called. The Western in Glasgow.

I remember, so clearly, her defiance the night before, insisting on making plans, nagging my Dad, telling him not to forget to book up for the Fair.

'Usual digs in Millport,' she nipped at him.

Then Dad brought her back from hospital a few days later, this withered mockery of my real Mum. They trudged home, the pair of them, deflated and defeated. Like football fans who had just seen their team relegated with six games still to go, praying for a miracle but knowing the game was up because there weren't enough points left to play for. She wasn't even forty years old.

Even the features that had made her so unusual and striking turned on her. People used to say she had a faintly Oriental look about her and sometimes, when my Dad had taken his brave pills, he'd taunt her by calling her Chinky. In his defence, not only was the concept of political correctness still some decades away, he wasn't even being that accurate. I saw in my Mum more a hint of the fleeing women of the Korean War (fourth year history) or maybe even a trace of Apache or Sioux (Westerns at Saturday morning pictures). My aunties reckoned I was a bit like her, though I didn't see it till much later, probably my mid-twenties, when an unexpected reflection in a shop window

3

or a car mirror would summon up an old black and white snapshot. When she came home from hospital that time, that last time, the flattish face and high cheekbones that had once turned heads now seemed stretched and gaunt, almost skeletal. Mum, never slow to take the mick out of herself, shrieked in mock fright when Dad held up his shaving mirror for her to tidy her hair in bed one evening.

'Jesus man, who let Catweazle in?'

She retreated, a hermit into her cave. Lay down to waste away in her bed, beaten and done and fragile as a dried-up twig. Dad slept on the settee in the living room, as if waiting for her to leave.

I hated that room, her bedroom. I hated going in there. It was winter and in my memory the room is always dark and gloomy, the air faintly rotting.

My snobby Aunt Irene gave Mum a telly for the room. This was in the days when folk only had the one telly, or at least folk round our bit. She and Uncle Tommy had just bought their first colour set so they gave Mum their old black and white. She didn't watch it much but when she did, it gave us a flash of old Mum, real Mum. The old, devilish flippancy. She'd call Dad or me in to switch it off or turn it over, and she'd say: 'Pfff, no point me watching anything with a follow-up, eh?'

I'd pretend I hadn't heard or didn't understand.

Mum still smoked, even then. Right up to the final few days, in fact, and she paid heavily for it in gruesome retching for each straining draw of each fag, hammering nails upon nails. The glass ashtray was basted grey on the bedside table, a testament in grime to her slow-motion, forty-a-day suicide. Once a day she'd make Dad or me hide the fags and the ashtray. Make us open the windows wide in a vain bid to get rid of the cigarette smell.

'Better get some fresh air in here afore the school monitor comes,' she would say.

The 'school monitor' was Morag, the tubby, friendly nurse. She came in each day, just after teatime. Back then I thought her second name was Macmillan because of the wee tag on her breast pocket. That was before I knew about the cancer nurses. Morag hummed Rudolf the Red-Nosed Reindeer on a loop, even after Christmas was well by. She was cheery and unfussy. Not in a callous way, mind, just her way of coping with death as a job, I suppose. Sometimes she'd lug an oxygen cylinder upstairs and shut the bedroom door behind her. I tried not to imagine what she was doing in there, to my Mum. Sometimes, when Morag was done with her, she'd drop used syringes in our kitchen bin and tell us to let her sleep. When she left, the smell changed and Mum's room turned fresh and antiseptic. But the cleansed

4

air fought a losing battle. The decay would not be held at bay. It seeped out of her skin to reclaim the room.

These vastly contrasting smells haunt me still. They take me back there, to that room. Smells like the chlorine sting of the swimming baths, or the cloying, smothering hygiene of the dentist's waiting room. Or, in contrast, the stale Monday morning breath of my supervisor when he leans in too close, or the time I left a pot of soup on the cooker for a whole week while we were away on holiday and Mark (my other husband) gagged when he lifted the lid.

Early on in those last few weeks, Mum would have the odd good day when she'd dredge up strength and will from some hidden place. When she'd wrench herself from her bed and make the pilgrimage to the kitchen to sip tea and puff on fags with Big Paddy's Mum, her best pal. But these days grew rare and faded altogether before that final morning.

The morning when she sent me to the kitchen for eggs. Whether it sounds credible or not, it's true. It really happened. I know. I was there, it's imprinted on me.

With a painful effort, Mum sat up properly and I perched close to her on the bed. We smashed eggs on each other's heads, then I left her alone to die by herself.

***

Back up a little. The bit after the eggs. I did say I wouldn't miss it out this time.

OK then. Mum and me. We laughed so hard on that morning. That final morning. Tears choking us, we went through four eggs – two each – then the last couple just for the finale.

(For the record, and maybe I am stalling, I should point that I discovered it's not that easy to crack an egg on someone's head – and having it done to you is actually quite sore.)

I'd changed out of my school blouse into an old T-shirt. I'd raided the back of the airing cupboard for the older towels that were hardly used anymore and spread them over Mum and her bed. But it still went everywhere. Yolk, gunge, fragments of shell all over us. Through our hair, down the back of our necks, but we didn't care. We hugged, we huddled, faces streaming, giggles racing out of control. Sneakily, one of us would pick up another egg. Splat! We'd rub yolk in some more.

Finally, still laughing, it was over. I gathered up the towels and went downstairs and dumped them in the kitchen sink. I rinsed my hair in the bathroom then took a basin through and cleaned up Mum the best I could. But she was long past bothering about appearances.

It was already after nine and I wanted to stay home, to be with her. But she did a U-turn and insisted I had to go to school.

And that was it. Goodbye. We both knew it.

I will never forget her smiles and her joy through the coughing and the choking. A silly, giggly, messy, gungy, yellow, yolky parting. But Mum had something to say before I went. Before she went.

'Lorna hen. School and that,' she started, trying to switch the mood. 'You know what I've always said...'

Don't do this Mum. Don't spoil it. Let's pretend it's a normal day. I'll be home at half four, you'll be making my tea.

'I'm doing fine, Mum.'

'Naw. I mean, it doesn't matter, all that stuff. No' really.'

'Honestly Mum, I'm doing OK at the school.'

She persisted. She had to get this out. She knew she wouldn't get another chance.

'You're no' listening, hen. I just want you to know. I'm no' bothered about O Grades or uni or none of that. No' really. And I don't want you caring either. Living's what it's all about. Just go out there and do stuff. Go travelling if you like, meet folk, enjoy yourself. Make the most of it.'

Salt stung the back of my eyes but I grimly did my best to hold the tears at bay. I recognised a farewell speech and I couldn't face it. School was the escape route.

'I've got to go Mum. I'll see you later, OK?'

Hoping against hope that I would, but not believing it.

'All right then pet, all right,' she said. 'But one more thing, eh? Promise us one wee thing before you go. Just the one.'

'Mum...' I tried not to sound exasperated.

'Will you do it Lorna? Will you make us a promise?'

Did I have a choice? *Did I?*

'Right-oh Mum,' I sighed. 'What's the big promise then?'

She wouldn't look at me but she spoke, softly.

'Promise us you'll never go with a Fenian.'

'What? What are you on about Mum? A Fenian?'

She found a spot on the bed cover to stare down at.

'Catholics and that, know? Promise us you'll never get serious with one of them. That you'll never marry one.'

'Catholics?' I echoed, completely knocked off balance. 'What's wrong with Catholics, Mum?'

THE FENIAN

She still refused to meet my eyes.

'Och, hen,' she sighed. 'It's no' really me, it's your father. More the family actually. Break their hearts, so it would, if you ended up with a Catholic. Married and that, I mean. Will you promise us? I'll never ask you anything again.'

She knew fine she wouldn't ask me anything again. I was reeling. Religion? It had never been an issue, it had never really come up. But it hit me right away.

Catholics. A Catholic. Robert.

Mum galloped on. She was on a mission and time was running out. She had to get this done.

'Look hen,' she continued. 'I've got nothing against them. No' really. Most of them are all right. But it just doesn't work. Letting them in and that, I mean, to the family. They're no' the same as us. It's just, well, they…they think they're something.'

They think they're something?

I know the facts now, of course. I've made it my business to know. I've done the reading.

I know about the centuries of bitter divide. The twisted, spewing bigotry. Civil war, neighbours starving and killing neighbours, families ripped from their roots. Imported, senseless, tribal crap. Ghettoes and disease. Innocent five-year-olds split into separate playgrounds. Flutes and incense, funny handshakes, job interviews where the first question is which school did you go to, wink, wink. Wee favours from your chapel pal on the council. Rangers and Celtic, up to my knees in Fenian blood and are you watching Orange scum. Bombs and blood. That overloaded cargo of retarded, casualty-strewn history, reduced to a petulant, Primary Three playground jibe from a woman on her deathbed.

They think they're something.

Mum didn't have long. She raced on, finishing line in sight.

'Listen pet, you'll maybe no' understand the now. Just promise us, eh? Just this one wee thing. Please?'

Damn right, Mum. I DIDN'T understand. I still don't understand. I wanted to protest. I wanted to grab her and shake her cancer-riddled, useless body. I wanted to scream. I wanted to talk about my friends from the Catholic school. I wanted to explain about this boy I loved and the goodness I saw in him. But Mum's pleading, crumpled face gagged me, threw up a barrier to my words. Or is that just me trying to absolve myself, to justify my weakness and my failure from the distance of decades?

I looked at her for the very last time, her tortured eyes branding the plea into my soul, daring me to deny her mind this final peace. How could I deny her anything? What did it mean anyway? It was only words, it was only me giving into her one last time, it was only me allowing us to part on good terms. There were no witnesses. Surely I couldn't be held to it?

'OK Mum,' I sighed, finally. 'It's a promise. All right?'

She looked at me fondly, gratefully, perhaps a tiny trace of shame. Then she tried to release me from her death with a smile. She tried to lighten the load for both of us.

She said: 'Cross your heart, hacket features?'

Chapter 2

July 2001
There You'll Be – Faith Hill

HEADS were shaking, Pat clicked her tongue. We'd been discussing the story on the news about some MP and his wife being charged with a sex attack and opinions were divided.

'That's your Tories for you,' said Kath, who didn't need subtleties like evidence or juries to make up her mind. 'Filthy snobby bastards. I mean, using a banana...'

'No Kath, you picked it up wrong.' Honest to God, I'm miles from being a Tory fan but I felt obliged to correct her. 'The wife said if it got as far as court, she's a banana...'

'Don't you tell me I'm wrong. That's just what she's saying now to wriggle out of it.'

Pat was clearly becoming more wound up.

'You can't say that. It's not right. Innocent till proved guilty. You of all people should know that, working here.'

'I'll say what I like,' snapped Kath. 'Typical you taking their side.'

Our lunchtime table in the canteen rarely got this heated so Shirley, as usual, decided it was her job to lighten the mood and once she got going, she barely stopped for a breath.

'Listen to this one, ladies,' she started. 'I was on it again last night and I found this guy in my class who was always going on about becoming a priest. Paul White, his name was. Well, turns out he did. Starts by telling you he got ordained in 1980 and all these parishes round Glasgow he was at blah-de-blah. All holy-holy stuff. Baptisms and pulpits and shaking hands with the bishop and that. Then all of a sudden he goes, *In 1993, my life shifted direction a little. Now managing a betting shop and living with my SECOND wife Beth.* Shifted direction a little?'

9

Genuine giggles and wows all round. My pal Shirley hadn't long got her first home computer. The internet had become her new obsession and now she had discovered Friends Reunited. It had taken over our lunch break chat for the last few days, even relegating who had shot Phil Mitchell, which had been top of the agenda all summer.

My other work pal, Kath, grabbed the baton.

'Aw, I love Friends Reunited. First time I was on it I found this guy from my old school in Greenock. This was a year or so back when it first started, mind?' Typical Kath, reminding Shirley – and the rest of us – of her one-step-ahead credentials. 'Greenock's where we stayed when I was wee, well, till I was about seventeen actually. Jim Templeton. Big Jim. Didn't half fancy himself. Tell you the truth, we all fancied him rotten and all. Must have gave half the fourth and fifth year their first shag.'

Prim Pat shuddered at the sh** word. Half the time I reckoned Kath only talked like that to wind her up.

'Fifth year?' Shirley grinned. 'He must have been putting it about in the primary if you were one of his conquests.'

Kath, never shy about keeping us up to date with her rampant sex life – often with an unnecessary level of lurid detail – acknowledged the good-natured dig and continued.

'I wish, Shirley. Built like a horse apparently. Anyway, this Jim, he's down in London now, working in the music business. Produces this one and that one. Big buddy of Robbie Williams, so he says.'

Kath switched her accent from medium-hard Glasgow to her estimation of London posh and told the next bit in Jim's own words.

'*Divide my time between a penthouse in Kensington and a villa in Ibiza. I'm a big sports car fan and currently have a Lotus Elise and a Porsche 911.*'

Kath's accent switched back to native. 'Poor soul, eh? Getting up in the morning and having to worry about choosing between the flash motors. And there's me feeling sorry for myself having to run for the bus if my Colin's Escort's clapped out again.'

I smiled, Shirley laughed. Prim Pat spotted an opening.

'I went on Friends Reunited and found a girl who...'

Kath headed her off at the pass.

'No, hold the bus,' she said, firmly. 'I haven't got to the best bit yet. There's big gorgeous Jim down in London, and I'm telling you ladies, big ride he was. Anyway, there he is, fancy motor, fancy house, going for cappuccinos with Robbie Williams. And I'm thinking to myself, he'll have his pick of the talent down there. But then, right at the end, he goes, *Currently sharing my life with my same-sex partner.*'

10

THE FENIAN

Kath leaned back in her chair, her winning hand dealt. We were all impressed with her story, even Pat.

Once the hoots finally died down, Pat said: 'Did you ever try it, Lorna?'

I didn't get a chance to reply. Kath cut in again.

'What, a same sex partner?' She nodded at me. 'See if you have by the way, Lorna Maxwell, that's the last time I go into the showers with you after the gym.'

'I'm talking about Friends Reunited,' said Pat, earnestly. She didn't want to be hijacked again. 'You ever been on it, Lorna?'

No point trying to bluff it out.

'I haven't Pat, no,' I confessed. 'I remember seeing bits about it in the paper but that's as much as I know about it to be honest.'

Shirley leapt in. 'Our Lorna, at the cutting edge of technology yet again.'

'Ach, you know me,' I said, happy to play along. 'I'm still trying to figure out my remote control. So anyway, how does it work then, Pat?'

'Dead easy,' Kath barged her way in again, our self-appointed leader. 'You just get on to internet explorer and type in friendsreunited – all one word – dot com.'

'Dot co dot uk,' corrected Pat. 'Or you can use Google to find it.'

'Dot whatever, Mrs Expert,' sighed Kath, glowering at Pat. 'They ask you your name.'

'Who asks you?' I asked.

Shirley took over. 'No one. It's just like a form you fill in on the screen. You put in your name. Not your married name – whatever your name was when you left the school. And you give the name of your school and what year you left.'

Kath smirked. 'Christ, there'll hardly be anybody left alive never mind knows how to work a computer from when Lorna left the school.'

I am forty-three, hardly decrepit, but the oldest of the four of us who have palled up here at the fiscal's office. I'm only a year or two older than Kath but she never misses an opening and I'm quite content to slip into the role.

'Yeah, yeah. Maybe I'll try zimmers reunited then. What happens next Kath?'

'That's it,' she replied. 'You give them your details then a list comes up with the names of all the folk from your year at school who've signed on. There's loads of people on it. You've got to try it. It's a brilliant laugh. Me and Colin used to spend hours on it when it first started. We still check it regular because there's new folk joining all the time.'

'Better be careful,' said Shirley. 'It'll give your Colin ideas. He'll be on at you to dig out your old school uniform next.'

11

Sounded quite interesting. Not the uniform bit. I had another thought.

'But a couple of my friends left the year before me, and one or two stayed on after.'

'That's OK, Lorna. We can solve that one for you,' said Pat.

In her early thirties, she is the baby of our canteen quartet but sometimes she speaks to us like that big Tory woman. What's her name again? Ann Widdi-something. Sometimes Pat acts like she is our Mum. *If I had a Mum.* But I'm being unfair, she was only trying to be helpful. As things turned out, it might have been better if I'd never asked.

'You can call up a list of all the other years as well as your own,' continued Pat. 'Just click on whatever year you want, and all the names from that year will come up.'

For the briefest instant, I saw Shirley's face darken. Kath caught it too, and cackled. 'God Shirl, you never knew you could look up other years, did you?'

'Course I did,' said Shirley, defiantly, but she fooled no one. She was trapped between embarrassment and the anticipation of an extension to this world of trivial scandal that had spiced up her life.

Pat played Primary One teacher again.

'Now, you can also look through other school lists Lorna, like if you had pals at a different school in your town. Or even do a name search.'

Then she got a little risqué, by her standards anyway.

'You might even find an old boyfriend,' she smiled.

Old boyfriend? Hmm, maybe best not bother.

Chapter 3

February 1973-December 1974
The In Crowd – Bryan Ferry

RELIGION was never on the agenda. Not really. Not in our gang. Boys. Girls. Who fancied who. Who had got off with who. Who had chucked who. The last party. The next party. Records. Telly. Adverts. Films. School. Tyrant teachers. Dumb parents. Dumber brothers and sisters. Clothes. Hair. Plooks. The future. The past.

That was the important stuff. But religion? Who cared?

There were eleven of us. Eight Proddy dogs (eat the frogs). Three Cathy cats (eat the rats). That meant there was a split between 9am and 4pm, of course. Most of us walked to Cumbride High at the bottom of our scheme, or Hun High as Big Paddy called it in his more eloquent moments. The others had to bus it to St Joseph's on the other side of town.

Robert used to say he'd happily switch religions if Proddy maths was any easier than Tim maths because trigonometry made his head explode and what the hell use were cosines and tangents ever going to be in his life? Karen's take on the whole religion issue was that she was relieved Cookie wasn't a Catholic because neither of them would be able to bear being apart all day.

Robert, Big Paddy and Fiona, the Catholics, still went to the Chapel, though Fiona would get a little miffed at us calling it the Chapel. She called it the Church, same as we called ours. Huh, *ours* – as if we were all regulars or something. Fiona went to Mass with her Mum and Dad every Sunday. Robert and Big Paddy went together but they said it was boring and they used to sneak out before the end. Sometimes, if they were feeling really brave, they skipped Mass altogether and furtively hung about with us instead.

'You wicked Proddy heathens,' Big Paddy would say, shaking his head. 'Leading us from the path of Godliness and righteousness.'

13

Despite their bravado, they were always afraid on those occasions when they dogged Mass. Scared in case they got spotted by brothers or sisters and shopped to their parents. Robert told us his Dad sometimes got suspicious and would interrogate him to check if he had been.

'He asks me what colour the priest's vestments were and what the Gospel was. I always say green and the ten lepers – same answer every time. And he says, *that's OK then, just as well*. Some attention he pays, eh?'

Little Jo wasn't a Catholic but she went to Mass with Fiona once to see what it was like and reported back that the biggest problem was all the kneeling because she was so tiny.

'I couldn't see what was happening,' she complained. 'Up on the stage I mean. And I kept thinking I was going to fall off the kneeler thing and get stuck under the next row.'

The other big difference Jo noticed was Communion. One or two of our lot still went to church sometimes, or the Kirk as our more staunch and upright relatives called it. Karen dragged Cookie along with her parents most Sundays. Wee Mary still went some Sundays and attended Bible Class for a while till she got fed up and chucked it, calling it *Holy Jackanory*. Wee Mary and Karen said they only ever got Communion at the Kirk on special occasions, like Christmas and Easter. But Fiona told us they had Holy Communion every Sunday because it was the most important part of Mass. They had these strict rules about taking Communion, she said. You had to be in a state of supernatural grace for a start.

Supernatural grace. Such a gorgeous phrase that always stuck in my head.

Fiona also told us you weren't allowed to eat anything for ages before you went to Mass, and there was a strict rule about not touching the Communion host with your teeth because it was supposedly transformed into the body of Jesus during the service.

Big Paddy did this terrible thing once that appalled Fiona. He came to the shelter straight from Mass one Sunday and took a little round, white object about the size of a 10p from his pocket.

'This is it folks,' he said, holding it up with two hands like he was pointing it at the sun. 'The Holy Communion. Brought it to show you pagan savages. I've been carrying God's body round in my pocket. Must have been a midget, eh?'

Tiny Jo scowled at Big Paddy. I was uneasy too, though almost certainly not for the same reason as her. It felt wrong, taking the piss out of God and the Chapel and everything. But Big Paddy went even further.

'Watch this,' he said. 'I'm going to bite Jesus's leg off.'

He snapped the little wafer between his teeth, chewed and swallowed. Then he took another bite.

'Oops, there goes his head.'

Grinning, Big Paddy stuck the remainder of the host back into his pocket and said: 'I'm keeping a wee bit for the big dug next door. See if it makes him holy and improves his temperament.'

Robert shrieked in mock horror. 'Ooooh, burny burny, Paddy. Bad fire for you boy.'

That was as serious as religion got with our lot. The shelter gang, I mean. Truth is, we didn't think about it much. It was just the way it was. We were pals. Red and white ties, blue and white ties. Made no real difference.

I suppose I started it, the shelter gang, though I don't think any of us ever thought of ourselves as a gang, either with a capital G or a small g, and we certainly never referred to ourselves that way. It was others, folk at school, parents, people who lived near where we gathered, who called us a gang. Truth is, we were just a bunch of teenagers who drifted together and without any specific intention, formed a bond, a unit. Whatever we called ourselves – if anything – I started it because I became best pals with Kirsty in third year. Sexy Kirsty, even at fourteen. She stayed a couple of streets away but she started coming round to my bit after school. We began spying on Big Paddy. Robert too, at a push, but mainly Big Paddy. He was our age but he was six foot-plus already and growing like he was planted in fertiliser. Big Paddy lived a few doors from me in Cardrum, one of the big housing schemes in Cumbride new town, and I'd known him since I was small. Our mothers were great pals. Anyway, Big Paddy and Robert got the bus home from St Joseph's every day and got off at a stop just up from my house. Kirsty decided she fancied Big Paddy and got me to carry the message. He had never really noticed Kirsty, wasn't even sure what she looked like, and it's doubtful if the concept of a girlfriend had ever crossed his mind. But he said *Yes* all the same. Dead fussy was our Paddy.

Ha, dirty Kirsty's first question, trying on sexy for size. She ran her gaze down him from top to bottom, pausing briefly at a spot just south of his blazer and asked: 'So Paddy, you built in proportion then?'

Beetroot face. Big Paddy hadn't mastered instant comebacks, not yet anyway. Robert had though, and doubled his pal's red neck.

'I've seen Paddy in the showers at PE,' he told Kirsty with a serious face. 'If he was built in proportion, he'd be one foot nine.'

From then on, Big Paddy and Robert would get off their bus after school and kind of saunter over to us casually. They'd hang about for half an hour or so in their blazers or their duffel coats (according to the season) and their red and white ties. Kirsty would lure Big Paddy to the underpass along the road for kissing lessons and, to pass the time, Robert and I would talk about telly. Kung Fu and Kojak and clunk-click every trip. He would crack rubbish jokes until he ran out or repeated himself, and sometimes tell me horrible, dark stories.

The one that sticks in my head was about a boy Robert called *the dafty*, who had supposedly gone missing a few years before. He was a teenager who wasn't quite right, anything from fourteen to seventeen depending on who you heard it from. Folk said he was known to hang about with younger kids, but it all felt more like folklore and no one was sure if he had really existed, never mind disappeared. But Robert knew, or so he told me.

'Mind he was last seen at the building site behind the Afden Road patios?'

You always had to specify building sites because there were so many in Cumbride, and that fitted the narrative because boys were always playing on them. They would do reckless stuff, like climb into flats with no floors, and they'd bring back lumps of putty in their pockets – adult plasticine, Robert called it.

'Turns out he climbed down one of they manholes playing one-man hunt,' he continued. 'But a couple of workies put the lid on without checking.'

'Oh God, that's awful,' I said. 'But how did they find out?'

'It wasn't till months later, when they finished the flats and people moved in. Apparently, they would flush their bogs and sometimes bits of hair and eyes and toes and stuff would come up.'

As Kirsty and Big Paddy walked back to us, Robert would nod in their direction, remove an imaginary lollipop from his mouth and, as if it was a fresh piece of wit each time, say: 'Who loves ya, Paddy?'

Then Wee Mary joined up, another pal from our school. Wee Mary wasn't really that wee. She was about the same height as me, and I would have been five one or two then. Her nickname went all the way back to Primary Two when she started at Cardrum Primary. She was given a seat next to a girl who was also called Mary and was lanky so we gave them nicknames to tell them apart. Wee Mary and Big Mary. With Wee Mary, it stuck.

When you looked at Wee Mary at first, you thought she was a little on the dumpy side. But it was just that she had already grown all the right bits in advance of the rest of us, and even back then, her bits were fighting for space in her school uniform. In those departments, Wee Mary was anything but wee.

So now we were five, and Robert decided he fancied Wee Mary. Probably felt he was lagging behind Big Paddy in those half-four to five o' clock romances. Then came Spring, the clocks changed and the light nights arrived. Hibernation was over and Big Paddy and Robert's football season started.

THE FENIAN

Two or three-a-side games after tea at the swing park with football tops stretched over jumpers – Celtic, Rangers, Man United. It was the swing park some folk called the monkey bars after the boxy steel climbing frame just about everybody had fallen off at some point and ripped open knees or elbows.

We drifted along, Kirsty, Wee Mary and me, and sat in the shelter just up from the swings next to the big open space that was their football pitch. We pretended to watch and Big Paddy and Robert granted us five-minute audiences between games. Gradually, the half-time breaks got longer.

Ross began coming over to the shelter with them. He stayed just along from Robert. Ross had been in my class at primary and was in my year at the high school but we weren't in any of the same classes so our paths rarely crossed. He wasn't the little boy I remembered any more. Not that he was particularly tall – probably about average for a fifteen-year-old, same as Robert – but, as with Wee Mary, there was more of him. He was kind of bulky and tough and hard. He was also blond and probably the first boy I noticed as good looking. Pretty soon he asked me to *go* with him. It felt only fair and anyway, I did fancy him a bit. Besides, it balanced things up.

Wee Cammy appeared next, another footballer. I remembered him from primary too, but we'd lost contact at high school. A weedy little lost soul at first glance, but kind of cute. There was no one spare for him just yet.

Cookie arrived on the scene next, a ginger, and inevitably Karen, dark and shrill, tagged along. She was Cookie's girlfriend. Cookie's *long-term* girlfriend, she emphasised from the start. First time I'd ever heard the phrase. She hung around to keep a tight grip on her property. Then came Karen's best pal, Fiona, who went to the Catholic school, a redhead like Cookie and taller than the boys apart from Big Paddy. In contrast to Wee Mary, Fiona was desperately waiting for any bits to start arriving so she could stop feeling like a bus stop. (Her words, I'm not that cruel.)

That was fine. Ten of us, five-a-side, nice and even. Then a little bit after that, Jo suddenly appeared among us. She was a mystery who seemed to come out of nowhere. I was pretty sure she hadn't been at our primary but I had seen her around at Cumbride High during third year, so tiny you couldn't miss her. But she hadn't been pals with any of us. She just turned up at the shelter one evening, jabbering and chattering, and we kind of took her in. She became our little doll and without a thought, we adopted her.

That really was it. Eleven of us, a unit, a team growing up together. After Jo, we allowed no more intruders. We had the complete cast for our own little soap, the daily/nightly drama that would run for the best part of three years.

Sometimes we had uninvited guests, kind of semi-pals from school who would hear us talk in the dinner hall about our lot and drift along. They'd try and attach themselves and see what it was all about but we were not gracious hosts, it has to be said. We offered them only silence and dirty looks. We froze them out. They usually got the message pretty swiftly.

There was the odd raiding party, other boys from different parts of the Cardrum scheme. Our guys would play them at football and they would stick around after to see what kind of pickings were on offer and work out if they could stage a coup. Big Paddy was usually enough to scare them off. No one tangled with Big Paddy, though I never once saw him actually fight anybody. Ross was the back-up deterrent, Big Paddy's second-in-command. He wasn't that big, but he was hard, and he had a growing reputation. Bigger guys thought they could probably just about take Ross in a square-go, but they sussed they would suffer too much in the process to make it worth the grief. Like a Pyrrhic victory, Robert said about fourteen times, till he finally got the message that no one knew what he was on about or cared enough to ask him to explain. Cookie was big, nearly as tall as Paddy, but Ross quickly marked him down as a shitebag when it mattered. Ross said Cookie was only any good as a decoy, to make the enemy think you had more troops than you really did. Ross said Cammy was game, but not much use. Robert didn't do fighting. Somehow that was never questioned.

The shelter at the swing park was our domain and gradually the boys-girls thing shifted until it was mostly five-minute football for the guys between hanging out with us.

We had our own, regular mini-dramas. Karen and Cookie rowed and she stormed off in a huff. Robert chucked Wee Mary and moved on to Fiona. Big Paddy swapped Kirsty for Jo but it didn't last. Ross confessed to me he fancied Wee Mary, so I traded him in for Cammy. Karen and Cookie reconciled. And on and on. The never-ending partner swap but more pass-the-parcel than free love. Silly, so silly, but big, big stuff at the time.

Karen had the first party in the late spring, just before Jo appeared, except we didn't call it a party, it was a Record Session. No, that's really what we called it, cringe, cringe. Her Mum stayed in the kitchen in voluntary confinement but her presence was enough to keep us in line.

We played daft wee games, like *Hands,* which wasn't nearly as daring as it sounds. Girls stood in a line, boys walked round them, flicking the girls' fingers. The music stopped and you kissed the person whose hand you were touching. Innocent stuff at first – a peck on the cheek, for the daring, a brief brushing of lips.

Karen, she of the long-term relationship, would sneer at the guys.

THE FENIAN

'Don't you lot know *anything*? You're supposed to kiss with your mouth *open*.'

The boys would look blank and disbelieving. Open your mouth? *Boak!* But we were quick learners. *Hands* became *Chairs*. (Titles by Creative Game Names Inc.) The boys sat while we trotted round chairs and sofas. The music stopped, the lights went out, we sat on the nearest knee or snuggled in beside them and kissed while David Essex and Suzi Quatro got us stirred up. You winched the guy unless it was someone you really didn't fancy or had just broken up with. Mostly we cheated with signals and nods to the pal at the record player. The lights came back on, we stood up and started circling again.

A few parties – sorry, record sessions – down the line, we had progressed. When the lights came back on, furtive hands were occasionally withdrawn from under tops. Well, from under dirty Kirsty's top mainly. Kirsty was always ahead of the game. First to hold hands with a boy, first to let one have a feel, first to get walked home for an after-party snogging session at the sheds in the primary school grounds.

When I think of those days, those childish, innocent days, I hear the music again. We all do this, surely. We keep the songs, the singers, the groups from our time. They are planted forever in our heads. Slade and Roxy Music and David Bowie and T. Rex and The Sweet and yes, even the name you daren't say out loud these days – Gary (whisper it) Glitter. Sure, it was only throwaway chart fodder, but they were carving out our soundtrack. Get it On and Band of Gold and All Right Now and Ballroom Blitz and Jet and Street Life and for God sake even Tie a Yellow bloody Ribbon. You can treasure the memories of those songs or they can make you wince but you can't wipe them out, you can't change them. These were the first theme songs of our generation.

It's the same with the clothes. You look back and shudder at the disasters. The flares like yacht sails, the tank tops, the cheese-cloth tops. But back then they were adventures. The boys were a bit unluckier, I think. *I hope.* When our parties started, they hadn't quite got to the dress-themselves stage. I mean, they probably had some minor input but surely they didn't choose those shirts themselves? The floaty, busy, sunglasses-compulsory printed shirts with the giant loops and swirls. And cravats. Honest! Our guys actually wore cravats with little gold scarf rings. *Designer psychedelic relics for today's trendy little man.* Take Big Paddy, for Christ sake. I remember this hulking bruiser prancing about in a black shirt covered in huge orange flowers. I'm talking chrysanthemums.

At some point in late third year, that amazing invention – the mirror – must have finally made its way from Tomorrow's World to Cumbride new town and the guys turned the lights down a bit. I suppose it went hand in hand with the shifts, the first signs of maturity, in our musical tastes. It was still all the fun, chart hits at parties, some of it even a year or two out of date for us. But the rest of the time we got into more serious, heavier stuff – Neil Young, Led Zep, Floyd, The Doors, Genesis – and with that, the guys kind of mellowed into simpler, more muted colours. Well, apart from Ross's brief flirtation with Levi Sta-Press and short-sleeved khaki shirt, complete with Bay City Roller tartan.

Sometimes I wished I'd carried a camera at those parties so that when we were grown up, I could embarrass all those friends, the friends I was absolutely, definitely going to keep all my life.

That same camera might have captured my shimmering gold hot-pants, Karen's mustard kaftan, Wee Mary's dazzling green mini with the *real* metallic stripes, the enormous pink platforms we feared tiny Jo would break her neck on.

Then quiet little Cammy, who had never shown an ounce of fashion interest never mind sense, amazed us all one Sunday by turning up at the shelter engulfed in a massive Afghan coat, all fleecy with wool trim. Once the laughter died down, the baas started up from the guys until he had no choice but to join in himself.

But what the hell, you looked great Cammy. I thought we all looked great. OK, I'm exaggerating, but it was part of what we were, when we were and who we were and the style police hadn't taken the Seventies into custody, not yet anyway.

That extra girl thing. Six of *us,* only five of *them.* It fed the boys' egos. There was always a girl too many, always one of us left out. One girl who had to stay out of the snogging games, one girl to stop the music and do lights duty at parties, and that meant it was always girls who had to compete, to avoid being the spare part.

The guys did have their own protocol though. Robert called it Rule One, though there really was only one rule for the guys. They NEVER moved in on a pal's girlfriend. Inevitably, relationships got stale. The initial rush of romance and excitement waned – usually after a week at most. A fortnight-long fling was heavy duty and anything longer was seen as leave-the-Kays-catalogue-open-at-the-engagement-rings stuff. But when the boys felt it was time to move on, they could only go after two categories of girl: the unattached spare or one who had just split up with a boyfriend. Then there was a strict ritual to follow. A boy could never come straight out and tell a girl she was dumped. He had to tell one of the other guys, who told *his* girlfriend, who told dumpee. The boys also displayed what they saw as their own kind of respect for us – they would wait a full day before trying the next girl in line. I suppose they reckoned they were being thoughtful, giving their ex plenty of time to get over it. Then the process would start again. Boy tells pal who he fancies, pal to girlfriend, girlfriend to intended, and the answer would be relayed back in reverse order.

Mind, we weren't just subservient chattels waiting to be summoned, waiting to do the next heart-throb's bidding. The process could work exactly the other way round – with one concession to male pride. We never actually did the asking. We passed the message along, let it be known we *might* be interested, and possibly available, then we'd wait to see if they would bite. They invariably did.

I've used the word rule but, of course, it was never as formal as that. Even Robert's Rule One line was nicked from an old Monty Python. No, it was just a way of doing things that we fell into casually and anyway, it didn't take much for the whole process to be subverted.

The transfer from one boyfriend or girlfriend to another took about a day and a half on average, but the ritual was relaxed at parties where we adopted a kind of amnesty that would enable a relationship swap to be completed in about ten minutes. It wasn't unusual for me to go to a party as one boy's girlfriend, and be walked home by someone else entirely. Sometimes I used to get ready for a party and stop. I'd have to make a serious, conscious effort to remember who I was supposed to be going with that night.

All incredibly immoral? Incredibly immature more like. But back then it didn't feel tawdry, or childish. It was just the way we did things and it was fun, pure and simple, especially that first glorious year. The explorations, the discoveries, the gossip, the rows, the plotting, the questions. Who was the best kisser? The most mature, the most immature? Which of the guys had started shaving? Which of them had ripped open his face *trying* to start shaving? Who had let their hands wander? Who had let them?

Ross was my kind of go-to boyfriend in those early days. I must have had about half a dozen little flings with him. Cammy a couple of times. Even Cookie. Just the once though and only for about three hours. Karen, his keeper, was away at her gran's one Saturday so our grand affair lasted till she got home at teatime and reclaimed her property. Cookie didn't protest and I didn't either. I had a thing with every one of the guys during that first year after we all got together. Well, every one of them except Robert. He never once asked me, or got a pal etc etc, and I didn't send out any declarations of interest in him either.

But Robert and me, we discovered something else. Something that became just ours. It happened one night as our second summer approached, towards the end of fourth year. I had nipped over to Karen's to borrow a James Taylor record and passed the shelter on my way back home. I found Robert hanging about on his own.

'Forgot my ball,' he said, nonchalantly. 'Walk you up the road.'

It wasn't a question and it didn't require an answer. It was one of those warm, hazy nights in early June when it never really gets properly dark. We sat on the low wall round the back of my house and we talked. Just talked. In a strange way, it felt like the first proper, serious conversation I'd ever had. We talked about the others, analysed them, discussed why they drove us mad and why we loved them. It seemed so weird, the first time I'd ever heard a boy using the word *love* in relation to his pals. But when Robert said it, the way he said it, it sounded OK, as if it was just a natural way to talk. We spoke about our dreams, our fears. I talked about my Mum, how she seemed to be unwell all the time and how worried about her I was becoming. I had never spoken to anyone about her and her illness, the C word that we all knew was going to be confirmed any day but no one wanted to say out loud. I had never felt so open, so exposed. I'd never felt so close to anyone outside of my family.

Still Robert made no moves, still I sent out no signals, but we found excuses to repeat our end-of-the-night meetings at the wall. We made it happen again about a week later and soon it was every other night. We would wait till all of the others finally drifted home, or we'd make an excuse and nip back to the shelter, or even occasionally, get home then slip back out again. Once or twice I walked home with Big Paddy either because it was one of the very rare times when we were an item or simply because we were close neighbours. We'd say goodnight and after he went in, I would hang back for a few minutes and wander round the back of my house, to the wall, which had become *our* wall. Usually Robert would be there already, waiting for me. It was our secret, or so we thought. It never got beyond words back then, hand on heart. But a kind of unspoken code was established. It was like, *Look, we're young, let's have our fun. This, our private thing, it's bigger than all that kids' stuff. Let's be patient, let all this run its course, wait till it's all over then we'll see what happens.*

We both understood that, I think. I know *I* understood it because that is when it was born – the gradual realisation that what I felt for Robert was on a different scale to my feelings for the rest of our crowd. That was when it began to scare me, how important I'd let him become. How much I'd allowed him to infiltrate the private me, to share and even own my thoughts. It scared me because I got to thinking how empty my life would feel without

THE FENIAN

Robert. Back then life seemed so full of fears. Big exams coming up and my inability to get my head into studying. Rumours that my favourite group, Free, were splitting up, though if pushed I'd admit my fandom was more about a massive crush on the singer than their music. Then there was all the horrible stuff on the news – bombs, other explosions killing folk, plane crashes – though they were just vague background worries because I didn't really pay much attention. Then there was Dad saying he'd be out of a job soon because no one would be able to afford a car if petrol went above 50p a gallon.

And the biggest worry of all: Mum. I wasn't stupid, I wasn't naïve though I tried hard to be. Mum's cough had become as regular as the kitchen clock. She had always been thin but she got thinner. She was always feeling *lousy* or *wabbit* – her words. She was shrinking and fading before my eyes. The hospital visits started towards the end of the summer, just before fifth year. Mum and Dad were always so vague about it, always trying to reassure me. *It's just tests, pet. Don't worry.* Then Dad began taking days off his work which was unheard of. They would get the first bus to Glasgow in the morning and it would be, *Get your own tea, hen. Here's money for the chippie. Key's under the mat.* They wouldn't get home until after six and Mum would collapse on to the settee and sit there in silence. She'd look wasted, like a burst balloon, lips a thin, purple smear, eyes dead, hair lank and patchy.

I should have paid more attention. I should have stayed home and spent more time with her. I should have realised precious time was running out. But I was too busy, with swing park life, with my friends, with those nights at the wall with Robert.

I despised myself because of the thought that sneaked up on me. It made me feel sick and depraved and ashamed and guilty. The question that crept into my head sometimes when I lay in bed at night. I tried to hammer it out of my mind and in a fit of self-loathing I would toss and turn and sob and shake and bury my face hard into the pillow. But the question wouldn't go away no matter how I tried. It resurfaced, slowly and insidiously. *Who's more important to you, who could you least live without? Robert or your Mum?*

Chapter 4

August 2001
Eternal Flame – Atomic Kitten

WE were not supposed to go on the internet at work, not for personal use anyway. But Martin, our supervisor, didn't mind. He was an OK guy, even if he was the last person on the planet who still thought it was hilarious to go for the whole, deep-throated *Whassup* when you went to him with a query. He turned a blind eye to us doing bits and pieces on the web, so long as we didn't overdo it. There were slack, quiet spells at the fiscal's office. Some days you got all your work done half an hour before the end of your shifts, all the reports typed up and keyed in, and you had a wee bit of time to kill. The girls all said the internet was great. Kath and Pat and now Shirley all had computers at home, or PCs as they were apparently called these days. They kept telling me I had to get one, but I could never find a reason. I just didn't know what I'd use it for, what I'd look up on the internet of an evening. Occasionally, very occasionally, I'd go *online* – as the other girls called it – at work, like if I was looking for a cheap holiday, though it's hard to find good deals when you travel alone, or ideas for a birthday present for one of my cousin's kids.

That Tuesday, about twenty to five. It had been a busy day with an overload of cases. It could be like that sometimes, then you would suddenly hit a point where you found you had got ahead of yourself. My inbox was empty and I could see the others were winding down too. I heard my phone beep in my handbag. A text from Kath.

U ever try Friends Reunited? Find anybody interesting?

I thought, why not? I didn't reply to Kath. I typed in www.friendsreunited.co.uk on the top line of my computer screen then watched the egg timer spin until the website unfolded on to my screen. The others were right, dead easy to follow. I typed: Lorna Ferguson. Cumbride

24

THE FENIAN

High School. 1975. I added my work email address, then I was asked to give a password so I used ANGELA, my Mum's name. That's what I always use for passwords. Then I was asked if I wanted to submit a profile message. Hold on, did that mean other people could read this? Quickly, I clicked Exit, picked up my phone and texted Kath. She replied right away.

No, u don't have 2 if u don't want 2. Just leave it blank. U can always go back and do it l8r.

I started again. What kind of message could I have left anyway? I definitely didn't have a same-sex partner to astound the world with and no, I hadn't been a nun for a while then started a wild new life. How about, *Living on my own, no kids, two dismal attempts at marriage, no current relationship. Stay in most nights, watch a lot of telly, feel really sorry for myself.* I left it blank and clicked *Proceed*.

It didn't take long. Less than a minute, then a message flashed up. Welcome to friendsreunited blah blah blah. Then beneath that, like a time machine, there it was. My God, Cumbride High School, 1975.

Wow, there was my name. How did they get hold of that? Duh! Then deflation, none of the others were there. I saw a few names I recognised but none of our lot. Three had been at the Catholic school of course – Big Paddy, Fiona and *him*. Maybe check that later. Disappointing about the rest though.

I noticed that some of the names on the list had little envelopes next to them. I quickly discovered that meant they had posted their potted history. I clicked on one name I vaguely remembered.

Janice Scott. 22 years happily married to Tom (Kelly). Still living in sunny Cumbride. Two kids, Rhona age 19, and Tom Junior age 15, who we couldn't be prouder of. Work part-time up the ASDA, usually in cheese and cold meats. Life is great. A great big Hi to anyone who remembers me. It would be great to hear from you.

Well bloody bully for you and your happy bloody marriage and your great great great bloody life, Janice Scott. OK, I remember you, but don't hold your breath among the cheese and cold meats. Bitter? Me? Never!

Rewind a year. I tried 1974 and felt a lurch. Jo was there. Joanna Stevens. Of course, she left school the year before me. Twenty-odd years vanished in an instant and I pictured her as I saw her for the very first time. Tiny, with nice features. Our little doll, we used to call her. So funny and noisy, always buzzing about. I saw bright red cords, tie-dye top, pink platforms, tight dirty blonde curls. We all wanted to protect tiny Jo but she wouldn't let us. She made endless cracks about her size before anyone else could. She used to introduce herself as Bridget the Midget and said her parents should have christened her Bashful, though she was anything but. Insisted she was the lucky one because she would always have her pick of jobs. *I could be an air hostess for Airfix or Barbie's hairdresser.* Yeah, Jo hated being so short.

I've seen her a handful of times over the years. In fact, I caught sight of her in Debenham's in Glasgow just a couple of months back. She was going down an escalator and I was going up another one. I doubled back, tried to find her in the throng of shoppers but she quickly disappeared in the crowd. So, what had she written in her entry? I was curious then disappointed. There was no little envelope, no message. What did people have to hide?

Then, brilliant, another familiar name. Simon Cooke. Cookie. But surely he had left school the same year as me? Unless he'd got it wrong, or I had. Never mind, it was just great to see another name I knew. There was an envelope too – and a little camera. Did that mean a photo? Fantastic. I was already starting to get what my workmates saw in this Friends Reunited thing. I clicked on Cookie's name.

Great big G-Day to all those lucky folk out there who remember me. Look – bet you wish you knew my secret of eternal youth.

At the bottom of the screen was a tiny snapshot. He still wore the trademark specs but most of his wild red hair had gone. I looked for the Cookie I remembered, but all I saw was his Dad. Eternal youth? Nice try Cookie. I went back to his message.

While you lot are freezing your butts off in Scotland, I'm sizzling in Sydney. I'm a personal lifestyle adviser and run my own company.

A personal what? You were going to be an engineer. You were going to build stuff.

I'm currently married to Wend.

Currently?

She's Number Four...and she's for evermore.

Get a grip Cookie.

But wow, Number Four! Hope Karen never reads this. *She was Number One, but that was soon undone.* I basked in my own smartness until Cookie reached out through thousands of miles and two decades plus and slapped me. Hard.

Love to hear from all the gang back in Scumbride – Paddy, Ross, Robert, Jo, Wee Mary, Kirsty, Fiona.

No Karen, obviously, and no Cammy. But no Lorna? Was I that forgettable? What had I ever done to him?

Hey, get over it. What does it matter anyway? It's ancient history, it's only some bald git on the other side of the world. Some bald git who can't hang on to a wife. Worse than me even. I've only failed twice. Ha, pass me a saucer of milk!

My thoughts turned to Cammy for a moment, but only for a moment because my eyes were fixed on that other name that jumped out at me from Cookie's message. *His* name. *Robert.* What was it Pat had said? You can check other schools, not just your own.

I tried to convince myself. Robert won't be there, he's way above all that. Why would he bother? So if he's not there, what's the harm in checking? I might find Big Paddy, or Fiona, or some other peripheral folk from my schooldays. Think for a minute. Robert stayed on for sixth year. He left school a year after me, so that would be 1976.

It didn't take long to find St Joseph's and suddenly, it leapt off the screen at me. I didn't even have to scan the list. Robbie Kane. *Robbie?* Who the hell is Robbie? Maybe it's not him. Course it's him. But when did he become a Robbie? Please, don't let there be a message. Shit, I spotted the little envelope. Don't click on it. Go on, click on it, click on it.

'Whassup, Lorna? Found an old lover?'

I jumped and spun round. It was Martin, our supervisor. He grinned and pointed at my screen.

'Great fun that, isn't it?'

I hauled myself back to the here and now and told a small lie.

'Yeah, it's all right I suppose. Didn't see anybody I knew.'

I clicked X for Exit and got the hell out of there. Who needs this crap?

Chapter 5

March 18, 1975. Later
Reach Out (I'll Be There) – Gloria Gaynor

T HEY came for me just before two o' clock. I was in fifth year French. I had been willing my period to stay away, even for a day or so, just so I didn't have that to cope with as well.

That day in school. It had been like that dentist's waiting room I mentioned, dreading my name being called, dreading the pain, but desperate at the same time to get it over and done with. To suffer the pain so it would end.

Oh Christ, here it comes. The headmaster walks into the class and instinctively, I know he's here for me. I can't go through with this. If I keep my head down, maybe he won't see me, maybe he'll go away and my Mum might be OK. On her feet, making the dinner, smoking a bastard fag, tutting when a bit of ash drops into the totties. *Bastard, bastard fags.*

But the headmaster, Mr Downie, scans the class and catches my eye. He whispers to the teacher, Miss Castle. Her face tightens, then it sags. She looks at me in a kindly way. Miss Castle. Miss. Huh, must be fifty. Never kissed, never touched, or at least that's what we all say behind her back. She is usually tight and anxious with us, never gives an inch, but now she looks almost human. Careful Miss Castle, almost a hint of emotion there.

I hear my name. NO. NO. NO. Don't let it be my name. Let someone else's mother be dead. Oh God, sorry, I don't mean that, but please. Now Miss Castle is standing over me. Don't look up. If I don't look up, it might not be happening. But Miss Castle has placed her hand on my shoulder.

'Lorna, I'm awful sorry. You have to go with Mr Downie.'

NO!

I won't go. I'm not moving. *Fucking, fucking, bastard fags.* But without knowing how, I'm on my feet. *Mum, why do you have to smoke? Please don't smoke any more. Those bastard fags are killing you.*

28

THE FENIAN

Now I'm picking up my schoolbag but Miss Castle is telling me to leave it, not to worry about it. But I need it, my schoolbag. What if my period comes? I need my things but I can't tell her that.

I'm in the corridor. Mr Downie's face is the colour of ash. A bit like Mum's, now I come to think of it. I wonder if Mr Downie smokes. My Mum doesn't smoke any more though, or do they have Regal in Heaven?

Mr Downie has got his hand on the back of my elbow now. It doesn't feel right. Mr Downie doesn't do that kind of thing. He doesn't touch you gently as if he cares about you.

We are in his office. My Dad is there. He is standing up, still in his overalls. Blue, smeared with oil and grease. They must have found him at the garage and brought him here. *They? Who?* His hands are black, black right into the creases. His fingernails are black. His face looks kind of folded in on itself like when he takes his teeth out. All I can hear is Mr Downie's voice. *Sorry. Sorry. Sorry. Sorry.* What are YOU sorry for, Mr Downie? You didn't make my Mum smoke. You didn't force those bastard fags on her. You don't even know her. Now Mr Downie is offering to drive us home but Dad says *No, we can walk. It's only ten minutes, it's not a bad day.* Not a bad day Dad? Is it a good day then? Is my Mum still alive? Tell me what a bad day is Dad.

My Dad tells Mr Downie he doesn't want to get his nice car dirty and points at his overalls. Mr Downie says it doesn't matter, it's only a car, but he doesn't press it.

We're out in the street but it's like I'm in a dream, a daze. No one has mentioned my Mum. Dad hasn't said a word about her. No one has actually told me yet, officially. Does that mean I don't have to believe it? My period is about to start. I can tell. So Miss Castle lied, said I wouldn't need my bag. I want to tell my Dad I have to go back for it, but I can't get my voice to work.

I wish Robert was here. I want him to be with me. He would know what to do. He hasn't long turned seventeen, just a few months older than me. But he knows how to talk to people, to adults. He would find the right person to ask, about my Mum I mean. He would know the right questions. Robert would tell me what to do. Robert would tell me how to feel.

He has only been my boyfriend for three months. In fact, it's not quite our three-month anniversary yet. Eleven and a half weeks. The best eleven and a half weeks of my life.

Until my Mum used her dying breaths to split us up.

We walked back from school quietly, Dad and me. As soon as we got to the house he began falling apart, slowly and quietly. He didn't know what to do with himself, from the most basic action of whether to stay standing or sit in his chair. He didn't seem to know if he should take off his work anorak. I broke the silence which had lasted since we left the school.

'Where is she?'

Dad just stared, not knowing what to say to me, or perhaps not actually knowing the answer himself. Then Big Paddy's Mum came through from our kitchen. Mrs Allan, as I had always known her. They lived a couple of doors along from us. It didn't come as a surprise that she was in our house. It felt like she and my Mum spent half their lives in and out of each other's houses. I only found out later that Mrs Allan had been with my Mum at the end. So appropriate yet so inappropriate at the same time, given our final conversation.

When Dad and I got home, she was brilliant. No messing about, she just took charge. She told my Dad to go and have a bath, to get himself cleaned up and changed.

'Put on something smart,' she instructed, all business, but not harsh.

Then she turned to me and put her hand on my cheek, soft and warm.

'Your Mum's up the stairs. They'll come for her later.'

Upstairs. Having a lie down? In her own bed? Would she be under the covers? Dad would have to go in there to get a change of clothes, unless Big Paddy's Mum had thought of that too and laid stuff out in the bathroom for him. Would Dad still go into the room if he didn't have to? To see his newly dead wife?

And they? Who are they who will come for my Mum? Where will they take her? What will they do with her?

Dad left the room, relieved to have orders, something to do with himself. Big Paddy's Mum spoke softly. Sixth-sense.

'Do you need anything pet?'

I touched my stomach. You didn't really talk about your period, well, apart from with your Mum.

'I'm a wee bit sore,' I managed to say.

'Have you got something OK?' She understood right away.

I shook my head and she fished a hand into the front of her apron.

'Take my key. Linen basket in our room. The one with the double bed. Lie down for a wee while if you like, in there or on the settee. Nobody else'll be in till nearly five.'

'It's OK,' I said. 'I'll be back in a minute. Thanks, Mrs Allan.'

I turned to go but she spoke again. 'Lorna. When you get back, don't be frightened to go into the room up there and sit with her. Talk to her if you like. It's just your Mum. If you've got anything you need to say to her, now's the time.'

THE FENIAN

See, that's a big part of the puzzle right there. Big Paddy's Mum, Mrs Allan, she was a Catholic. She and my Mum were such good pals they were like Siamese twins a lot of the time. Now, I know religion was never an issue with my pals, but what about at home? To be honest, I don't remember it coming up much, or maybe I just didn't notice. I know my Mum's Dad, my Papa, was in what they called the Lodge at one time. Orange sash, bowler hat, white gloves, the full bit. I know my Dad used to go on the Walks sometimes. Just an excuse for a bevvy, I heard my Mum say more than once. When I was wee, I had an idea this was all somehow connected to a picture we had of a man high up on a white horse. I liked the horse. The picture used to hang up on a wall just when you came in the door but I think this must have been when we lived in Glasgow because I don't remember seeing it after we flitted to Cumbride.

I moved to Cumbride the same week as Big Paddy. Our families each found their little boxes close by in the concrete maze that was the Cardrum scheme. My Mum thought she had arrived in a kind of paradise after our damp, scabby old four-in-a-block in Pollok. The first big difference we noticed was that there was no one else living upstairs, no feet clumping about above you, and you could see hills from any window at the back of the house.

Right from the off, they practically cohabited in each other's kitchens, my Mum and Big Paddy's Mum. They drank each other's tea, they smoked each other's bastard fags and as far as I know, never talked about that difference between them. The Sash and the Rosary. Maybe it was a new town thing. A fresh start with no more religious enclaves. No more Govans or Parkheads, no more Bridgetons or Toryglens. All pioneers together with the old barriers torn down.

So, what was all that about? *Never go with a Fenian.* I'd heard the word before but only in one of Dad's rare and not very funny jokes. It was about that Greek singer on the telly, her with the big glasses. Whenever she came on with her backing group, my Dad would say: 'There she is. Nana Mouskouri and The Fenians.'

I wanted Mum to explain it properly. *Never go with a Fenian.* But I couldn't ask her any more, and now she couldn't take it back.

Seems strange now to think that even so soon after her death, it was the Fenian thing that was snagging at me. She was still lying upstairs and already it felt so wrong. In the years to come, that promise would be what I most connected with my mother's death. I know I tried to move it into a compartment, to be opened and dealt with later but her words, that promise, festered, like an echo in my head. It stayed there after Big Paddy's Mum had gone home and the house began to fill up with relatives.

31

My snobby Aunt Irene arrived, Dad's older sister. She assumed charge right away. The Queen is dead etc. Uncle Tommy was there too. He had brought a bottle of whisky. Then my Nana came, then Mum's brother, my nice Uncle John, and his wife, my Auntie Betty and in tow, assorted cousins. Aunt Irene knew how to deal with this kind of situation: Don't talk about it.

'Nae point in upsetting yourself, Andy. Life goes on.'

Life goes on. If she said that one more time…

Andy, that was my Dad. He was shrinking, disappearing, melting like a wax dummy on a bonfire with his whisky anaesthetic. The family huddled around him, as if their closeness and normality would draw the pain from him like a poultice. I felt outside of them, excluded. More likely I excluded myself. To me, this moment was so big, so important. I'd just lost my mother for God's sake. How much bigger can a moment get? Yet all around me, the conversation was trivial. How long the bus took from Glasgow to Cumbride these days. *Flaming nuisance, stops at every wee village.* They talked of how Uncle John's job wasn't safe. *Nothing's been the same since that bloody three-day week.* They nodded sagely to each other and that got Aunt Irene started. *Thank the good Lord they troops came in to clear away all that stinking rubbish. They binmen going on strike, they should get shot so they should.* They talked about the new Tory woman. Thatcher, the Milk Snatcher. A woman Prime Minister? *Yeah right,* said somebody, *sure and that'll happen the day after I book a fortnight's holiday in the Vatican.* They talked about *what an awfy winter* it had been. *Aye,* my Nana said, *and just you watch, it's maybe March but it's no by yet. Wonder I don't freeze to death, the price of coal these days.* Uncle Tommy and Uncle John went into a huddle. I heard Rangers and Celtic mentioned a few times. I heard one of them say, *Might as well cut your wrists open if they Fenians get their ten in a bucking row.*

There it was, that word again, twice in the one day. Mum's pleading was back in my head again. The promise. Fenians. Catholics. Cross your heart. Had I lived in this family for nearly seventeen years with my hands over my eyes and cotton wool in my ears?

One of my little cousins asked if it was OK to put the telly on. Aunt Irene decided the question was meant for her.

'Aye, all right,' she said. 'But keep it down.' She pointed up at the ceiling.

Why keep it down, Auntie Irene? It's not going to disturb her, or wake her up. Tell her Dad, stand up to her, just this once. Tell your big sister it's your house, the telly's not going on, not tonight. Aw Dad, tell them to switch it off, please Dad. This can't be right. There's folk laughing on the telly, in our living room. Morecambe and Wise are acting the clown and people around me are in hysterics while my Mum's lying upstairs, on her own.

My cheeks were on fire, the words and the faces around me blurred. Then there was a knock at the door.

'That'll be them come for poor Angela,' someone said.

I was drowning, confused, no idea how I was supposed to handle all this. As it turned out, I had been right. Robert did know how to deal with it, my Mum's death. God knows how at his age. Nothing had equipped him for this. Nothing had equipped me for it.

All I knew was that I had to get out the house. I didn't ask anyone's permission and no one tried to stop me. I grabbed my anorak off the hook in the hall and squeezed past a man who was coming in our front door, dressed in a black coat and wearing black leather gloves. He had a thin straight line where his mouth should be and he looked at a spot just above my left shoulder. Another man was behind him. Invasion of the body-snatchers.

There was only one place I could go, the shelter in the swing park where our crowd hung out. It was only five minutes away but I don't remember walking there. It was March so it must have been dark and cold but I honestly don't remember how I got from the house to there. They all knew. Big Paddy must have told them. The girls were in a wee huddle in the shelter, a witches' coven cooried in next to the bench at the back. The guys scuffled around outside and kind of hopped, one foot, then the other, like expectant dads in the waiting room at the maternity but preparing for news of a death instead of a birth. They looked unsure of themselves, a bit scared, like they were embarrassed to see me. Karen appointed herself head of the sympathy committee. She approached me, arms outstretched.

'Aw Lorna,' she wailed. 'C'mere.'

I took a step backwards, staying out of her reach.

'I'm all right,' I mumbled.

No one knew what to say to me and I didn't know what to say to them. Why should they? Why should I? We were only kids. We didn't know anything. We thought we did but we didn't, not really. We only played at big, grown-up emotions. Robert kept looking over at me. I tried to avoid his eyes.

Jo said: 'You know, it's really weird. My Mum's not been very well either.'

Kirsty took it a step further. 'Wish it had been mine. Hate the bitch's guts.'

It had been a mistake coming here but where else to go? I felt my face go hot again. A shaking started somewhere deep inside, my legs were in danger of buckling.

Suddenly he was at my side. Robert.

'I'm starving, going for a single sausage,' he said casually. 'Any danger of you walking me up the chippie?'

Just as flippantly, I replied: 'Aye, OK then.'

33

We turned the corner out of the park, just the two of us. No one tried to follow. The second we were out of sight, Robert said: 'Mind your Mum and that bottle of Cherry Brandy?'

'No,' I lied. 'What happened again?'

I remembered fine and he knew I did. I just wanted to hear his voice tell me the tale, because Robert was our storyteller, the keeper of our chronicles, if that doesn't sound too much like one of his boring, endless proggy albums.

Sometimes we would all wait for the magical moment when a lull fell over our conversations and he would fill it with, 'Heh, do you all remember that time…?'

We loved it. We would give him the stage and he would weave us an odyssey out of some incident, any minor event that had been just a little out of the ordinary. It could be from last week or last month or last year. Robert would add in bits and colour in other parts. There would be times when some of us hadn't been involved in an episode, but Robert would faithfully give each of us a cameo role. We understood Robert's stories weren't completely factual but there was always enough that was recognisable – events, places, things we had said. Robert was inventing our history as we went along, making it more special than it really was. His stories, the way he told them, made us feel good, like listening to a choir at Christmas. We were so captivated it's a wonder we didn't sit cross-legged in front of him. No one ever challenged a word. We didn't always believe in Robert's version entirely, but we always accepted it.

So I played the game and pretended once more. I let him tell me the story of my Mum and the Cherry Brandy.

Chapter 6

August 2001
Can't Get You Out of My Head – Kylie Minogue

WHO the hell is *Robbie*? I couldn't stop thinking about it that night after seeing the name on that stupid bloody Friends Reunited thing. When did he become a Robbie? I remember him making a big deal about people not shortening his name to Bob or Bobby. Had she christened him Robbie? His wife, I mean. She was on the telly, like him. She interrogated people on the late news on BBC2. It's not a programme I watch ordinarily because it's usually kind of boring and often it's my cue for going to bed. But occasionally, if I turn over and she is on, I find myself sticking with it, just for the connection and the curious fascination, I suppose. Masochists Are Us. Sad, eh? There is no getting away from it. She was, is, very beautiful with possibly a trace of Spanish in there somewhere. Dark, sultry and intellectual. She, she, she. *Come on Lorna, she's got a name and you know what it is.* Ruth. Ruth Wilkie, not Ruth Kane. She doesn't use his surname. Maybe she hadn't changed her name when they got married, or just kept her own for the telly. Which reminds me, she probably doesn't even call him by his proper first name. Robert, Robbie. Damn!

Ruth flirts with politicians and other important folk on telly – big businessmen, union leaders, police chiefs. I've seen her do it. The way she sucks them in, smiling, then puts the boot in hard night after night. But it's like they never see it coming. They let her charm them then double over, a kind of Bambi surprise on their faces, as she squashes their testicles. *The stunner with the steel toe-caps.* Someone wrote that about Ruth in the paper once.

But what was she like as a wife, what were they like as a couple? Doubtless they would have high-powered friends to go with their high-powered life. I remember the photo in the paper when they got married – not a big story or anything, just a picture with a couple of lines below it. It must have been a year or two later when I read she'd had a baby, a little boy. Another bullet. She was back on telly soon after, right enough. I bet they had a nanny, and a big house in London where they'd have flash parties with important people. Maybe Robert would know that guy Kath found on Friends Reunited, him with the same-sex partner. Maybe *Robbie* was pals with that other Robbie too. Robbie Williams.

I was desperate to read it and dreading it at the same time, what Robbie had posted. No! What Robert had posted. I thought about it a dozen times or more that night, trying to imagine what he might have written...

Twenty wonderful years with Ruth. Three beautiful children. A glittering career in television. Don't ever give a passing thought to a single one of the little people I used to know.

Damn you, Robert. Damn you, Mum. Do either of you think this warped, lonely saddo is the person I want to be? Sitting here on my own making up stuff to twist the knife into myself. Pathetic.

I couldn't concentrate on telly even though I'd been desperate for the latest on the Corrie kidnap. Instead, my thoughts drifted from Robert to the others. Were any of them alone, like me, and where were they? I counted them off, tried to place them.

Cookie: Sounded like a tube. A tube in Australia who'd been married more times than me.

Jo: I had seen her a few times down the years and I was pretty sure she was still working at her Mum's – the hairdressers near my Dad's in Cardrum scheme. Or maybe it was her place now. Whatever, she was definitely around, happily married – as far as I knew – and we were on nodding terms.

Big Paddy: The only one of the old gang I was still kind of in touch with. Saw him just a few days ago in fact which is a big part of why I'm in this state about Robert. But I'll get to that. Paddy was still in Cumbride or, to be accurate, he had returned to Cumbride, like me. I knew he lived in Glasgow, years ago, but he had been back for a good while now. He was stationed here, at the main police office in the town centre.

I was surprised, shocked even, when I heard about Big Paddy the PC all those years ago. This hulking brute I'd known as a boy, scary on the outside, gentle as a puppy when you peeled back the layers. But Paddy Allan a cop? His Mum, Mrs Allan, still lived in the same house just along from my Dad. I still visited Dad every Friday with a fish supper and usually popped into Mrs Allan's for five minutes, just to say Hello. Occasionally I would meet Big Paddy on his way in or out.

How you doing, Paddy? Not bad. Still at the fiscal's, Lorna? *Yeah, how's the kids?* Fine thanks. Your Dad OK? Blah, blah. All trivial politeness – until the last time. That was different, and unsettling, and that's an understatement.

So that was Cookie, Jo and Paddy accounted for. The rest? Ross, Karen, Kirsty, Fiona, Wee Mary? No idea. Didn't even know if they were alive or dead. Hadn't seen or heard from them in years. So sad, Wee Mary especially, best friend I ever had. It was my fault we hadn't stayed in touch. I answered the first couple of letters she sent then I let it slide. Too busy getting on with my life but yup, a massive regret. The last I heard of Ross, he had gone down south, but that was donkeys ago. I seemed to remember Big Paddy telling me once that Karen worked in the main library up the town centre. I've never seen her, but then I've only been in there a handful of times. Not much of a reader.

I knew about Cammy of course. Poor Cammy. Always last to get the joke, always in bother at school, always in scrapes, always in plaster with the stookie that seemed to move around from limb to limb. He didn't get on any better when he left school. Had a hard time getting a job and when he did, an even harder time keeping one. But all the while, he played the poor lamb to perfection and girls loved it, to a point at least. They felt sorry for him, they smothered him. Cammy had this pitiful face that he could produce virtually on demand. It worked until girls realised it wasn't an act and discovered he really was a loser.

Huh, a loser. Who am I to talk?

I tried to picture them, one by one, our Seventies shelter gang. Except, it wasn't their faces I saw, it was the stars from our Cast List. This was something Robert and I dreamed up – Robert, not Robbie!! – after we became close, during our nights at the wall. It was one of our precious secrets. We'd talk about the others and try to match them up with people off TV shows and films, or characters from comics and cartoons. It was Robert who called it the Cast List. It was never too precise, admittedly, but that didn't really matter. It was more an image or an idea. Sometimes the Cast List changed or got bitchy, usually when someone had annoyed one of us. Sometimes we couldn't agree plus, Robert had this in-bred macho thing that stopped him matching any of his pals to good-looking male stars. So no, it was never too exact but here I was, all those years later, remembering not the people, not the real faces, but our Cast List.

KAREN. Pretty or gruesome depending on whether she was being Sugary Karen or Smug Karen. In generous moments, she was Audrey Hepburn, on bad days, Daphne from The Broons. Our compromise was Betty – Barney Rubble's missus.

ROSS. We had the biggest rows over Ross. He was the best-looking guy of our bunch, no question. Blond, fair-skinned and hunky – what you'd called ripped nowadays. So Robert zeroed in on the one tiny flaw he could find to poke fun at – the little tuft of hair that was always sticking up at the front, the bit Ross could never get to lie flat. Robert called him Oor Wullie at first, then Quackers after the duck that used to be on telly with that horrible puppet, Tich. I told him he was just jealous and went for Illya Kuryakin, the sexy Russian one in The Man From Uncle. For a while I switched to Blue from The High Chapparal, then the flashy red car with the white stripe roared on to our tellies and overnight, Ross was rechristened Hutch.

JO. Without a second thought, Robert labelled her Zebedee, but that was more about her energy, the way she bounced and buzzed all the time. Shame on me but I nicked Oor Wullie for Jo. Then The Good Life started and it was sorted. Jo was a ringer for Barbara, the wee cute one with the bum Robert said was like two apples in a hanky.

COOKIE. We got him right away, both of us. It was easy, so easy it took the fun out of it. We tried alternatives. I suggested Blakey from On The Buses. Nah, quite good, but too old. Robert said that without the specs, Cookie could be Shaggy out of Scooby Doo. But Cookie kind of was his specs, especially when he got his new Elton John ones. We were stuck with it. Even though it was something we'd watched as little kids, he was forever Joe 90.

KIRSTY. She started out as the girl from I Dream of Jeannie – just the right mix of dumb and smart and blonde and sexy and cunning. Then Wacky Races became the big cult cartoon and we spotted Kirsty right away, tearing up the circuit in her Compact Pussycat. The never-ending legs clinched it. Kirsty was Penelope Pitstop.

FIONA. Oh Robert, too cruel. I wasn't having Mr Ed. We considered Jo's pal, sorry, Barbara's pal – Margo from The Good Life. But Robert couldn't shake the horsy thing and as a compromise we settled on Fiona as Princess Anne.

WEE MARY. We found the face right away but the body took a bit longer. She reminded us of Aquamarina from Stingray especially on party nights, when Wee Mary – or maybe Wee Mary's Mum – used just the right make-up to emphasise her big round eyes. Usually we just went on faces but with Wee Mary there was more, much more. Just like Cammy, it annoyed us. Then one Sunday night, Robert phoned me and said: 'Quick, put on STV – I've just spotted Wee Mary, on the Hai Karate advert. The face is pretty good as well.' I was too late but I clocked the ad a couple of nights later, featuring an actress who I don't think I ever saw in anything else. I only found out years later her name was Valerie Leon, best known for her two outstanding features.

BIG PADDY and CAMMY. We were spoiled for choice with Big Paddy because there were so many obvious ones. He was Lurch, Bluto, King Kong, Tarzan, Fred Flintstone, Cyberman. We stuck with Lurch for ages and even went back to it sometimes. Cammy was the opposite. We struggled for months on end, then I went to see Jungle Book with my Auntie and my little nephews and spotted Cammy right away. I couldn't wait to get back and tell Robert. 'I found Cammy,' I yelled. 'He's Mowgli.' Robert loved it, then spotted a double act. 'Perfect,' he said. 'And Baloo, that's Big Paddy.' Brilliant.

One night at the wall, I got daring and took a chance.

'So, Robert, the Cast List. What about me then?'

He was too quick.

'Geronimo's daughter.'

'Who?'

'That's not like, the actual name or anything,' he said, trying for casual so I wouldn't know he'd thought it through. 'It's just, you know…those soppy cowboy films you get sometimes with the goody-goody guy from the cavalry who tries to sook in with the Injuns. He always ends up doing the big romantic bit in the moonlight with the chief's beautiful daughter with the long black hair. And that causes all kinds of bother because there's some jealous Apache that's had his eye on her since they were weans.'

He saw I was blushing and stopped in his tracks. Was Robert calling me beautiful? Guys didn't say things like that, not to your face anyway, and definitely not unless they were trying to sweet-talk their way inside your jumper. He reddened too and tried to bluff his way out of it.

'Heh Lorna,' he said. 'I wasn't actually saying any of that shite out loud, right?'

'Saying what?' I played along. 'Never heard nothing.'

'Thank Christ. Anyway, I know who you really are,' he said, trying to get himself as far off the hook as possible. 'Morticia. Know who I mean? The scary wummin. What about me then?'

I'd always seen Robert as David Cassidy in our Cast List. You know, the guy out The Partridge Family who became a teeny-bopper heart-throb for about five seconds. Just a bit too much cutey-cutey sweet-face little-boy going on, but I couldn't risk more blushing so I went for ridiculous.

'Dead easy,' I said. 'Plug!'

'Huh.' Kid-on huff. 'I was kind of hoping for Lord Snooty myself.'

I wondered if anyone had ever done that with Robert. I mean, told a bloke he looked like that Robert Kane off the telly. *You know, the guy on the news.* Because he was our very own star. The one we always thought would be somebody and who actually proved us right. He was always the confident one, the clever one, the one who stayed on longest at school. Well, him and Fiona. We all assumed Robert would go to university but he surprised everybody by going straight into a job. It was kind of a thrill at first, seeing his name in the local paper and reading his stories, even if it was only golden weddings and garden fetes. Then the trap opened and the greyhound hurtled out. To the big papers, Glasgow first, then London. We had all drifted apart long before that, well, certainly Robert and I had drifted apart. Or I had shoved him away, if I'm being honest. I got the odd update at a distance for a bit, either from Big Paddy or his Mum. But once I moved away, I lost track of him completely.

I saw nothing of him for a few years then one night, wham, his face, instantly familiar, on TV. I was married by then, to Bill. I can't remember what the story was, maybe the Queen opening a big theatre or something. I was too mesmerised to pay attention because it was Robert, my Robert, on the news, on the telly, right there in my living room.

Just in case there was any doubt, the main newsreader – Richard Baker, from memory – confirmed it.

'Our reporter, Robert Kane, in Central London.'

That was the only part I remembered that first time. Then, it seemed, he was everywhere. The Falklands in a flak jacket. Florida in shirt sleeves for the Space Shuttle launch. Dressed like a Jehovah's Witness in a boring suit chatting to fans as my old idol Freddie got set to smash Live Aid.

Still my storyteller from the monkey bars, but now explaining the world to me. As I watched him, transfixed, on those nights, I used to wonder, do you still make up bits, Robert?

Chapter 7

March 1974 & January 1, 1975
Devil Gate Drive – Suzi Quatro

BOOZE and fags. Fags and booze. It would be hash and E now, I suppose, or worse, heroin even, because each generation finds its own forbidden fruit. Perhaps we were lucky. We were up and away just in time, before drugs took a serious grip. Before the streets of Cumbride were like the rest of Scotland – awash with drugs. At least, that's what they say, don't they, in the papers and on the news. Personally, I don't come into contact with drugs. Huh, not much – only in about every second crime sheet I type into the computer at work.

Back then, in Cumbride new town in the Seventies, even cannabis was little more than a fable. Sure, you heard stories occasionally, like when Big Paddy told us a boy in their fourth year was a pothead. Smoked a joint in the school toilets one lunchtime and was out of his head the rest of the day. Big Paddy told us the guy sat in technical-drawing staring into space and muttering about how his ears had become detached and were floating around the room. Apparently, he took something Big Paddy called *a whitey* in the toilets in the afternoon break. Robert claimed that meant he was technically dead for a short time. Always had a sense of the dramatic, did our Robert.

Cammy had tried sniffing glue once with some other boys down the Black Woods. Cookie, who had been there too but sensibly crapped out of it, told us Cammy had misunderstood the instructions and finished up with fragments of Cheese and Onion lodged up his nostrils, though he did say he felt like he had wheels on his feet for a wee while.

Fags aren't quite the same, at least I don't think so. Not that I'd know because I've never smoked and it wouldn't take a psychiatrists' convention to work out why. But I don't think people smoke ciggies to get a buzz or anything, do they? Hmm, what do I know? As for why kids take up smoking, there is no mystery. Always been the same, I suppose – a fast track to being grown up, so you can catch big, grown-up illnesses. Not that I ever preached or anything.

Ross was the first of our lot to start on the fags which was crazy, because he was the one with the most to lose. Ross was an athlete, a muscleman, our male model. He had a great body and he knew it. He was forever stretching and lifting things, lifting us if we let him. According to the other guys, he was brilliant at football. Big Paddy called Ross *a pure genius* and reckoned he could make it as a player, as in a serious player, for a proper team and everything. Scouts had come to watch him and another player in our school team. I once heard Big Paddy warn Ross that if he ever ended up playing for Rangers and scored against Celtic, he would hunt him down and chop his legs off.

Kirsty was next. She made a loud hissing noise when she inhaled and only ever smoked halfway down a fag before tossing it away. Jo took up smoking for a while. Yes, tiny Jo. Big Paddy never got fed up telling her it would stunt her growth.

Cookie felt left out. He *wanted* to be a smoker and he would shout *first onners* and grab the leftovers – the wee stump Ross chucked away with a tiny bit of white left glowing above the filter. But Cookie was terrified of being caught – not so much by his parents, but by Karen because she deeply disapproved. Cookie never picked up Kirsty's half-smoked fags just in case he got her lipstick smudged on his upper lip. *Christ, try explaining that to Karen.* He would get into a huge panic if he'd nicked a couple of puffs from Ross's fag-end then saw Karen approaching. He would whine miserably if no one had a Polo, fan his hands in front of his face wildly then try staying side on to Karen in a vain attempt to stop her smelling the ciggie reek off him.

Ross was our first boozer too. Alcohol was like some kind of fever that hit overnight and infected everyone simultaneously. One day we were quite content with Irn-Bru and American Cream Soda, then the next everyone was talking about drinking. Suddenly, being a booze virgin was the worst, most shameful insult you could suffer. There was a mad rush to establish credentials, to come up with a story. It had to be authentic, of course. You needed witnesses and it had to involve getting wrecked, falling down, passing out or being sick with at least two out of four compulsory. Pretty soon, it seemed like almost everyone had a tale to tell.

Ross claimed he helped himself to slugs of his Dad's whisky on a regular basis and got us to sniff his breath to prove it.

Wee Mary told us some older guy had bought her and Jo a bottle of cheap wine one night on the hazy prospect of *going down the fields* with him. They'd scarpered and necked the booze. Wee Mary staggered home drunk and plonked herself down in her living-room where her Mum was doing the ironing. Her Mum asked her what she was doing and Wee Mary mumbled that she was watching TV.

'Might be an idea to switch it on then,' her Mum said. 'Better still, get yourself off to your bed before your father gets home.'

The next day, Jo told us her Mum was raging with her because she had drunk half of the wine then gone home and spewed on her bedroom carpet – the brand-new-that-day bedroom carpet. Months later the stain was still visible.

'Like the shape of they wee aliens in the advert,' she said, then broke into song. 'For mash get smashed.'

Cammy bumped into a couple of other guys from school one night and mooched share of a bottle of Eldorado and a few cans. He somehow found his way home and crawled into bed without taking off his famous Afghan coat.

'I woke up at four in the morning soaked in my own sweat, sick and pish, so I did,' he reported.

We were so grateful to Cammy for sharing that.

Kirsty got herself sent home from the school dance after failing the breath test at the door. Mr Mahon, our fearsome history teacher, took one sniff, shook his head and pointed at the door. Eye-witnesses told later how Kirsty reduced him to jelly by running her finger down his chest, winking, and purring: 'Heh big boy, you not want to do a strip search as well?'

Big Paddy took it a stage further and claimed the first-to-get-served bragging rights. He told us he'd strolled into the big hotel up the town centre, marched up to the bar, ordered a pint of heavy, downed it in about five seconds and marched back out. Unlike Kirsty, he had no witnesses but then he did look that much older than the rest of us and I don't think anyone doubted his story.

So, who did that leave as booze virgins on the day of the Cherry Brandy? OK, I own up, me for one and Fiona almost certainly. Pretty sure Karen and Cookie were too. Oh, and probably Robert, though he insisted otherwise.

***

My Mum and the Cherry Brandy. A drama in two parts.

The way Robert told it, as we drifted vaguely in the direction of the chip shop on the night my Mum died, we were all there for Act One. That definitely wasn't right but it was his story now so no point in letting little things like facts get in the way.

43

It was a wet Sunday, round about February or March the previous year, and my Mum and Dad were visiting my Nana, so I had an empty. We were sitting around listening to a Neil Young record Ross had just bought. Can't remember the name of it – the one with the cover that looked like plain cardboard.

It was a so-so kind of a day and Big Paddy was restless. He broke off from his painful, howling accompaniment to Heart of Gold and said: 'Haw Lorna, any booze loose in the hoose?'

We were all up for it but I didn't dare let them touch the obvious stuff, like the whisky and gin in the living room cabinet or my Dad's two cans in the fridge. So we piled into the kitchen and raked through cupboards. It was Cammy who found the Cherry Brandy.

'Ya dancer! What's this?' He pulled out the dusty, long-necked bottle then, with a whoop of delight and a girly giggle, added: 'Look, it's called Bols, so it is.'

'That's been there for donkeys,' I said. 'My Dad won it at a raffle in Millport last year or the year before.'

'Sake, get a move on and get the bastard open,' ordered Ross.

We all got caught up in the excitement of the moment. I admit, I was nervous. This was my house so it was risky, but bravado ruled. We found a corkscrew and half-mutilated the bottle top before Big Paddy figured out that it screwed off.

'He's smarter than the average bear,' came the compliment from Yogi/Jo.

For a few minutes we let it just sit there on the worktop. It was like the bottle was daring us: *Come ahead. Who's first? Who's big enough?* Naturally, it had to be Ross, the hardened boozer. He grabbed the bottle, took a huge gulp, spluttered and passed it to Cookie, then Robert, then Cammy. The bottle made its way along to Big Paddy but he put up a hand and rebuked the other guys.

'Where's your manners? Here ladies, be my guest.'

It tasted horrible, like cough medicine with a kick. We sipped timidly. It burned but we tried not to show it. We passed it back to the guys and didn't stop until the bottle was empty. It was no big deal really. The Cherry Brandy was probably only twenty proof or something...between seven or eight of us. (Or eleven, according to Robert's enhanced version.) But we kind of decided we were drunk and let ourselves be silly. We put on a show of giggling and falling about and carrying on and feeling sick, just like proper grown-ups.

A couple of hours passed like this, a few of us relieved to have literally lost our booze cherries, but we were sensible enough to start clearing up well before my parents were due home.

Then Cookie spoiled the mood by asking: 'What you going do about the brandy, Lorna? What if your Da's ever looking for it?'

'Aw relax,' said Big Paddy, never one to go looking for a problem. 'Lorna says it's been lying there a couple of year. What's the chances?'

But I was worried now.

'Maybe Cookie's right though. What if my Mum notices it's not there? Like, when she's cleaning out the cupboards and stuff.'

No problem. Ross had the solution.

'Sake, fill it up with cold tea. That's what I do with my old boy's whisky. Then I stick it back in the cupboard. Never notices. They're adults, they've fuck all brain cells left. Come on, somebody find the top and straighten it out.'

Brilliant, a bonus adventure. I boiled the kettle and Cammy ripped open a packet of Brooke Bond. It burst, showering tea leaves all over the kitchen floor. We all got down on our hands and knees, giggling as we picked up tea leaves one at a time.

Then we had a whip-round, gathered our loose change together and Robert nipped to the Mace along the road and came back with another packet. We made a pot of tea and sat it in the fridge to let it cool down. That was old-hand Ross's touch. Then we filled up the brandy bottle. Mission accomplished, end of story.

Until Act Two. Hogmanay, nine months later…

It was a big night for us. A couple of our lot, Ross and Big Paddy, were already seventeen, the rest of us not far behind. It felt like our first real New Year, the first one when we were being allowed out on our own. Apart from Fiona, we'd all got passes from our parents on condition we didn't go daft and checked in now and again.

We had bought a carry-out earlier. Big Paddy had been getting served at the off-licence for ages by this time so we chipped in for a couple of dozen Carlsbergs and two bottles of wine. We had made plans. We'd muck about for a while and all go back to our own homes for the Bells, then meet up again at mine about half twelve, go back out and tan the booze we'd planked in the jaggy bushes at the back of the shelter. After that, we would go wandering and just see what the night would bring.

Cammy was the last to arrive, as usual. Didn't get to my house till about ten to one. We were all dutifully drinking Coke or Irn-Bru or Lemonade out of respect for my parents, desperate to get going.

My Mum was sitting in the corner, a glass in one hand, fag in the other. She was worn out most of the time these days but she was in good form that night. I wasn't to know it would be her last New Year. Big Paddy's Mum and

Dad were already there and more neighbours would probably drop by later. Or maybe, if Mum was up to it, she and Dad and Big Paddy's parents would go round the houses, clinking bottles in hand, a welcome at every unlocked, raucous door. It was the one night when the folk in our street turned into the friends and neighbours they'd liked to have been all year round.

We were all on our best behaviour, but growing impatient. We passed signals that it was time to get moving and almost made it too, but my Mum ambushed us. She turned to my Dad.

'You know what I fancy Andy?'

'Aye, I can guess,' he replied. 'But you'll have to wait till the weans go out and the visitors go home.'

Dad cracked up at his rubbish wit. Life and soul of his own party.

'Aye right son, you'll be lucky,' Mum cackled. 'But tell you what, I could fair go a drop of that Cherry Brandy. Is that old bottle still in the cupboard?'

'Er, aye sure Angie,' said Dad. 'Should be.'

He went off to the kitchen. I didn't give it a thought, then Big Paddy leaned over and whispered in my ear. I froze. *Oh shite.* Panic spread quickly as the news filtered down the ranks. Karen looked ready to burst into tears. Cammy looked set to bolt till Ross gripped his arm and held him back. One for all and all that. Dad came back through, handed Mum a glass and she took a sip. For a split second, her face creased, then a calm smile.

'Ah, lovely,' she said. 'There's nothing I like better than a taste of Cherry Brandy. Apart from maybe a wee drop of cold sour tea.'

We watched as she put the glass down and sharpened the guillotine.

'Tell you what, Andy,' she said, pointing around at us. 'This lot aren't weans any more, sitting there with their Coca-bloody-Cola. They're near seventeen most of them and it's the Bells. Time they had a proper drink to bring in the New Year.'

Dad frowned.

'I don't know. No' that I mind myself, but it's no' my place to be giving them alcohol if their parents don't know about it.'

'Och, don't be daft,' said Mum. 'They want to behave like adults, we'll treat like them adults. Tell you what. Get them all a glass and we'll give them a taste of that Cherry Brandy. It's no' strong. It'll no' hurt them.'

'Smells kind of funny,' said Dad, wrinkling his nose as he poured for us.

She'd outflanked us, well and truly. We had no choice. We tossed back the foul, stale nine-month-old cold tea. Disgusting. Ross retched, little Jo's eyes watered.

Mum grinned wickedly.

'Did youse all enjoy that?'

THE FENIAN

She kissed us on the cheek one by one as we trooped out, me last. Mum leaned in close and whispered: 'Clean the pan after your father for a fortnight and he's none the wiser. Deal?'

***

Robert finished the story. We had walked and walked, putting distance between me and my newly dead Mum. I didn't have a clue where we were. We laughed at the recollection, then I stopped laughing and thought about another memory of that same Hogmanay night. Robert and me, our first kiss.

It happened not long after we left my house. We were wandering, all of us high as jets, the Cherry Brandy incident already turning from ordeal to heroic mythology. We were heading for the shelter, as usual. *Our* shelter. Big Paddy and Ross were gagging to fire into the bevvy we had stashed. We were in a rag-tag crocodile, Robert and me dawdling at the rear, maybe half a minute or so behind the others. I sensed it was going to happen. There was no build-up, no following correct protocol. We weren't boyfriend and girlfriend, never had been. He just turned to me and cupped my cheeks in his hands. The heat on my cold face was intense. He kissed me, slow and serious, and I responded. It grew fierce, like nothing existed outside of that kiss.

It was a major moment, a defining moment, and it was wrecked by hand-clapping and sarcastic cheers. We broke off and turned. The whole crowd of them, horrible sods, were applauding, led by Big Paddy of course. He was grinning, face happy as a wee kid's birthday.

Little Jo, our resident Mike Yarwood, crooned: 'And they called it...Puppy Lo-o-o-ove.'

But that was it. We were together and it felt superior, grown-up, a big, adult love affair. We had broken the schoolkids' dating ritual – no formal approach, no go-between, no testing the water first. We just let it happen and it felt like love, real love.

But what the hell was I doing, thinking about a kiss on this of all nights? My Mum had just died. I pictured her lying there in her room as life, and laughter on the telly, went on around her. I thought about those men coming for her. They would have taken her by now, to do whatever they had to do to her.

I starting shaking and it rippled right through me. Somewhere deep inside my chest, everything burst and I sobbed for my Mum. Great gushing tears, so loud, so violent. I was shuddering, I couldn't control it, it felt like I was drowning in my own tears and I could barely breathe.

Robert was ready. He had anticipated the moment. He gathered me up and

MIKE KERNAN

I buried myself deep into him until it felt like we were one body and I wanted him to never let me go. Sorry Mum, but that stupid promise could go and jump.

Chapter 8

August 2001
Hidden Place – Björk

I DON'T have that much in my life but it's fine, because I don't need that much. But I own my head, my little bits of time, my quiet evenings, my solitude. I own them, damn it, they are mine. So why are you back, Robert Kane? Why have I let you back in and why can't I stop thinking about you?

It wasn't just seeing his name on Friends Reunited – that was just half of it. Mind you, it would probably have been enough even if the first bit hadn't happened. I couldn't stop thinking of his name. Robbie, Robert. Seeing it there on that page. Wondering what he had written, wondering if I had the nerve to read it, or the nerve not to.

Christ! What was my problem? I haven't seen him since we were schoolkids. OK, yes, sure, I've seen him on the telly, loads of times. But you know what I mean, not *really* seen him, not so as I could reach out and touch him.

I've had a whole life since then or, at least, something that passes for a life. Two marriages and two marriage break-ups by the time I was thirty, a handful of family christenings and funerals. Two homes, walked out of both of them and made a third, just for myself. Went back to college in my thirties and for once got the timing just right. Got myself a diploma in basic IT skills just as computers were taking off and found a decent job as a result, which I've kept ever since and where, unless I really screw up, I'll probably work till I retire.

Here's a confession and a half. I haven't slept with a man in five years. Actually, dear God, now that I count, it's more like seven or eight and even then it was no more than the cliché of a drunken fumble with a colleague in a budget hotel after an office Christmas party. Ha, slept-with was probably accurate for once because we were both so out of it, I was never sure if we'd actually done the deed. Up and off our separate ways before the prepaid breakfast so we didn't have to compare notes over the bacon and sausages to check if it had really happened.

Other than that, there was a half-hearted thing a few years ago with Kath's hubby's older brother who was nice enough, if a little on the forlorn and lethargic side. In the end I got fed up having to remind him there was more to a relationship than holding hands on the sofa while we shared a pizza and watched that week's special from Blockbusters – and I wasn't just talking about sex. Anyway, that fizzled out after a few months and chances are I might never get involved with anyone again – short or long term. Do I miss it? The sex, OK, yes, but it's more the comfort of regular physical contact and plain company that is less easy to do without. Overall though, it probably wouldn't bother me that much if it never happened again. Not really. I tell myself I'm just not interested any more.

(OK, a confession. I'm not being entirely honest here. About never getting involved again, I mean. There is a possibility, only a possibility, of something else going on in the background, but it's too hazy and confusing and complicated to go into right now. I'll add it to the stuff I've promised to get back to. Maybe.)

But the Robert business. What is going on here? A daft teenage romance. Yeah, right, because if that is all it really was, why is it in my head every bloody minute. PISS OFF OUT OF MY HEAD. It's been years since my last bout of Robert Kane sickness and I thought I'd buried him deeply enough last time. So why am I letting this happen again? I'm forty-three, for Christ sake. I am not a kid. *Grow up, Lorna. Please. It's long past time to let it all go.*

Blame Paddy. Big Paddy. Because I might have kept this where it belonged, this Robert thing. Way back there in that locked box where it has been stored for years, marked *Fragile. Not To Be Opened Under Any Circumstances.* I might have left it there, might never have been tempted to seek out his name on Friends flaming Reunited. Not if Big Paddy hadn't stepped in and messed around with my head. I'd bumped into him the previous Friday when I nipped in to say a quick Hello to his Mum before I paid my regular visit to my Dad. Big Paddy was coming out and at first it was the usual polite chit-chat. If only that's all it had been.

'Heh, Lorna, you all right?' His gentle tone never quite matched the outward appearance of the bear that was Big Paddy.

'Good Paddy. You?'

'Aye, great. Coincidence seeing you...just talking about you last night. And by the way, how about this weather, know? Getting the barbecue out the night.'

'Oh, lovely.' I smiled.

'How it's been for you, the summer and that?'

'Ach, you know, quiet.'

Quiet? Don't exaggerate, Lorna, just get off the subject fast. Big Paddy doesn't need to know the closest I ever come to a barbecue is when I get adventurous choosing crisp flavours.

Big Paddy called it a coincidence but it isn't that unusual for our paths to cross at his Mum's front door on a Friday teatime. It was different this time, though. Our meetings usually last about thirty seconds – just enough time to get the same old routine questions out of the way. Usually we are passing ships on his Mum's doorstep, but this time he shouted *See you Mum*, and shut the door behind him, deliberately, and started with the inane summer weather patter.

If you didn't know Big Paddy, he'd scare you and you would tell yourself your fear was justified because he looks fearsome, intimidating. But he doesn't frighten me. I have seen inside him. Big Paddy is probably what they used to call a decent, old-fashioned bobby. The kind of cop who would never make Chief Constable, the kind you thought should be riding around a village on a bike too small for him. If I had to guess, I'd say his role model was a toss-up between PC Murdoch and Dixon of Dock Green, either of which puts Big Paddy about forty or fifty years out of date. I guess he probably doesn't crack too many cases or break many arrest records but you can't imagine many people messing with him.

Where was I? Oh yes, last Friday, outside his Mum's house, when I'd established he was going home to fire up the barbecue in the evening sunshine, but also suspected he had something else to say first.

'You not want to know who was talking about you behind your back then?'

Oh yeah, that. Big Paddy towered over me, but he has this trick where he drops his hips into a crouch with his hands on his knees so he can keep you at eye level. I wonder how many wee neds he has stared out like this.

'Go on,' I said. 'Surprise me, Paddy.'

But for some reason I couldn't explain, I knew what he was going to say.

'Remember Robert? Robert Kane.' So cool, as if he had just asked, *Think this weather might break and it'll rain the morn?*

I had no breath. My mouth dried up. Did Big Paddy notice? Big Paddy, the trained observer. How good a cop was he? I struggled, wrestled back control, for a moment anyway.

'Robert who?' Honestly, I should join the amateur dramatics. 'Oh yeah, right, that Robert. God, that's a blast from the past. Where did you see him?'

'We were out for a drink last night,' said Big Paddy, still cool. 'Up the town,

Glasgow. He was asking for you.'

My mind went into overdrive but I tried hard not to let it show. *How come, Paddy? Just happen to bump into each other by chance?* But I didn't ask him that. Instead, trying to match his cool, I said: 'Oh, that's right, you and him were big pals, weren't you? So how did you get back in touch after all these years?'

Good girl, keep it casual. But he blew me away.

'Get back in touch?' Big Paddy's wide pudding smile didn't alter as he echoed me but then threw a low blow. 'We've never been out of touch.'

I was doing fine too, on the outside anyway. But inside, I was churning. Full spin cycle.

'How do you mean?' I asked. 'You saying you two have been pals all this time?'

'Aye, sure,' he said, still so nonchalant but seeing he had to expand and explain. 'Yeah, I see Robert maybe half a dozen times a year. Me and the wife's been going down to London for yonks, usually for the New Year and sometimes a few days in the summer as well with the weans. Course, Robert still comes up for the big Celtic games. Cup Finals, Rangers and that.'

'Oh right,' I muttered, disbelieving but making a massive effort not to show it.

Unbelievable. Un-bloody-believable. There's me spent my entire adult life thinking Robert's away on some distant planet and all this time he's only ever been one person away.

'Anyway,' Big Paddy went on. 'We were talking about some of the old days last night and I happened to mention I bump in to you every so often, so Robert says to tell you he's asking for you.'

Questions were trying to form an orderly queue in my head then they abandoned order and jostled each other to get to the front.

But all I said was: 'Oh, that's nice.'

Then Big Paddy was away.

'Heh listen, got to shoot, get the burgers and that, know? See you later, eh?'

THAT'S NICE? THAT'S BLOODY NICE???

Christ. Was that my best shot? There's this ghost that has been haunting me forever then out of the blue I get a chance, an opportunity to talk about him, maybe find out a few things, finally. And what do I come up with?

That's nice.

Way to go, Lorna.

Chapter 9

May-August 1969
Nobody's Child – Karen Young

THE day Cammy was crucified. That was when I began feeling sorry for him. After that it was always difficult to stop myself feeling sorry for him, same as everybody else, I guess.

I think he kind of liked it. People feeling sorry for him, I mean. Or maybe he just got used to it. At any rate, he grew into it, he cultivated it. You got the impression he worked hard at being helpless, making people pity him, making others feel as if they owed him something, as if they had something they had to make up to him.

He used it…

No, stop, think, try to remember. Try harder. Get this right.

He used it. Is that fair? Did Cammy use it, that helplessness of his? Did he sit down and work it out one day? Did he really construct himself, like some faulty Meccano set, into a pathetic, snivelling, shambling wreck? Did he find a way to stop himself growing? To stay small on purpose, and useless, and pitiful. Was it really a conscious thing with Cammy? Did he know what he was doing and did he keep on doing it because he discovered it paid off?

It worked with pals…

I'll never get this across properly. Did Cammy actually have pals back in those primary school days, or were they just classmates paying off debts they hadn't remembered acquiring?

It's so difficult. Like with Robert. Trying to figure out Cammy. Who he was, what he was.

Start again.

Whatever it was Cammy did, or Cammy was, it worked on other kids. It worked on other boys who played football every lunchtime in the playground at Cardrum Primary. The boys in our class would gather in a bunch, like casual labourers waiting for the foreman's nod, while the two best players went toe to toe. Usually Ross and some other boy. They'd play Giant Steps for first pick, working their way down through the other players according to ability or friendship. The crowd would diminish quickly as the teams were formed until, inevitably, Cammy stood alone, too small and too puny and too shrivelled for Ross or the other self-appointed team captain to even notice. Then someone would shout, *Right, that's fair sides,* and they would go off to their playground game leaving him marooned. Not moving, standing there alone, waiting in vain for someone to pick him, or to notice him even.

No one would care about Cammy or even remember him – for all of about three minutes. Then he would somehow infect the minds of the big guys in the class – the best players, the best fighters, the hardest ones. Unconsciously, they would start thinking about Cammy. He would niggle at them like a tongue probing a bad tooth, haunting them till they'd find themselves forced to seek him out. He would still be standing there on the same spot, alone, forlorn, staring dolefully at the ground. A low cloud would have moved in, a solitary gunmetal cloud settling over his head and raining on him, just him, plastering his dank, greasy hair flat. A finger would start rubbing, worrying at a nerve in the head of one of those big guys and pretty soon, they would crack.

'Haw, Cameron! You come in our team. They can have a backsie. Away you out on the left wing. Keep out everybody's road.'

What Cammy did, what Cammy was, it worked on girls too, because back when he first appeared at our school, he quickly became a bone for any dog who needed one to chew on. Easy pickings for any boy who needed to prove himself.

Cumbride was one of Scotland's post-war new towns, so we were always getting a fresh intake of kids in our school as more and more pioneer families rolled up. We got new boys who knew the law of this new little jungle, who knew they had to establish themselves by giving a demonstration of their hard little feet and their hard little fists. Just the once, that was usually enough, and Cammy was convenient, because it was like he carried a banner around everywhere he went. A banner with huge letters on it, spelling out PUNCH-BAG. New boys would find excuses to bang into him in the corridor or the playground. They'd wave their hands in front of their noses and say *I smell shite* whenever Cammy walked past or sat near them in class. New boys would compete to call Cammy ever more horrible names. Fart Face. Pongo. Human Jobby. Pish Pants. Beggar. Stank Boy. Minger. New boys would tell Cammy stories about his mother. How you could go to Cammy's house at lunchtime, give his Mum a threepenny bit and she would show you her big diddies, sixpence to see her hairy fanny. New boys would run out of ideas to try and get Cammy to claim them, so eventually they'd just tell him, *I'm fighting you, after the bell, big shed.* That was that. Cammy would follow orders and turn up every time. He'd stand there clutching his tattered schoolbag, waiting to accept his punishment inside a circle of little savages chanting, *Fight! Fight! Fight!*

And not once did any of them ever lay a finger on him. Because one of us would stop it. Me, or Wee Mary, or one of the other girls in our class. What we saw was a puppy about to be stomped to death so we would elbow our way through, shoving the baying horde aside. We would threaten them, those brave little mobsters. Threaten them with anything. Hold their collective nerve to ransom.

Touch him and we'll hate you forever.

Or. *You'll have to get past us first then we'll tell everybody you battered a lassie.*

Or, my favourite. *Batter him and we'll pray to God you catch a horrible disease and die. We'll keep praying every night till it happens.*

After a few minutes, they would slouch away. They would disperse, mumbling and scowling, looking for someone to demand their money back from. Cammy wouldn't budge or speak. He would just stand there, face tripping him as usual, not showing any gratitude at the reprieve, no change in his expression. He'd stand there until we decided our work there was done and the other boys weren't hanging around waiting to ambush him. Then we would go, leaving Cammy to shuffle off home on his own.

I own up, I was as bad as the rest. I shunned Cammy when he first came to our school. It was one morning near the end of Primary Six when he kind of slithered into the class, small and grubby, a bit ragged, little round National Health specs that looked like they were made of wire. He was in sannies, not as any kind of fashion statement, mind, because this was decades before the Nike generation. Our Primary Six teacher, Miss McAllister, looked Cammy up and down. She sort of sniffed and created a ghetto, just for him. There were other seats available – double-desks with a vacancy for a co-pilot – but Miss McAllister sat Cammy on his own, in a corner at the back, next to the window.

This new classmate, this oddity, seemed to melt into the wooden desk and pretty soon we forgot about him until later that first day. He must have wet himself, too mired in his new misery, too cocooned to move, or raise his hand, or speak. The classroom was warm and he gave off a smell like wet cat, stinging our nostrils and catching our throats. Cammy gave us a reason to steer clear right from the start.

Then the school holidays came and I pretty much forgot about the new boy, forgot he existed. No one knew where he lived, no one thought about him.

There was one incident that summer. I didn't know about this at the time. Wee Mary told me years later when Cammy became part of our shelter crew and she wound him up about it. It had happened one day during the holidays when she was walking home on her own from my bit. It was only a couple of streets, three or four-minute walk at the most. She was going through a square. There were loads of little squares surrounded by rows of houses in Cardrum, the scheme where we lived in Cumbride. A solitary figure was sitting very still on the edge of a kiddies' sandpit. Wee Mary must have scuffed her shoe on the ground or made some other noise by accident. The figure spun round, alerted by the sound. It was the new boy. *What was his name again?* Wee Mary wasn't sure. She thought it might be Andrew or Anthony. The little boy stood up and ran towards Wee Mary. She was a bit frightened but she froze, couldn't make herself move. He reached her and threw his arms round her and cuddled her. It was so tight, she said, still recalling it clearly a few years later. The boy stopped abruptly, pulled back and stared at her, then ran off without a word. She didn't tell anyone about it at the time. She hadn't known what to tell.

Teenage Cammy. Shelter Cammy. He denied it, swore Wee Mary had either made it up or else she was mistaken. Must have been someone else, he insisted. But Wee Mary was certain.

Primary Seven, first day back at school, parole rescinded after that glorious stretch of freedom. It didn't seem possible. You felt cheated because it was still summer outside. All that time, all those days and weeks that you had owned and now you had to hand them back. Yet in a way it felt good too. Everything was new. New blazer, still stiff and jaggy, new grey pleated skirt, new white socks, gleaming new shoes, new schoolbag. New classroom, new teacher, new pals who weren't really new, but you hadn't seen them all summer because they didn't live round your bit, so you felt shy around each other for a little while. At first, I thought *he* was a new kid, standing alone in the playground and so still. The bell went. He was at the back of our line with no partner, no one offering to hold his damp hand. Then I remembered he had started just before the end of P6. I couldn't think if I had ever known his name or if I had just forgotten it.

Our new class. We were going to be the biggies for a whole year. Top of the school, the rulers, heading for the high school next year where we would revert back to being the babies. As our first privilege for being in the top class, our new teacher, Mrs McDonald, told us we could decide where to sit ourselves. Choose carefully, she counselled, it's for the whole year. Wee Mary and I sat together, naturally, near the front.

Cammy didn't fool himself. He didn't hang about or wait for someone to ask if he'd like to share a double-desk. He made straight for the same spot, well, the equivalent spot, the place where he had sat in the tail-end of Primary Six. He was volunteering right away for solitary confinement and he might have stayed an outsider for the whole term, for his whole life maybe. But Mrs McDonald made him into a martyr, turned him into Jesus on the Cross.

Mrs McDonald was only a bit old, definitely younger than our Mums. She seemed nice at first as she took the register on that first P7 morning. She was friendly and made us laugh in a way that felt sort of grown up, told us she wanted to get to know us properly before we got down to all that boring work. Mrs McDonald said it was so lovely outside that we should all be allowed one extra day of school holidays before we knuckled down. She couldn't send us home, sadly, so we would do the next best thing. We would talk about the summer for the whole of the first day, talk about where we had gone on our holidays.

Looking back now, I suppose it was a pretty smart move. Maybe they taught you stuff like that at teacher-training college. Psychology. Let the kids settle in to their new class and their new teacher, make them feel relaxed and confident. This was a big year after all – the transition from primary to high school. Her suggestion would give her a chance to size up her new pupils at the same time. To identify the pushy kids, the confident kids, the articulate kids, the shy kids, the slow kids, the cheeky kids.

The holiday discussion. Hands shot up. A couple of boys talked about Butlins, in Ayr and Skegness, chalets and cheesy games. Another boy mentioned Blackpool, the tower of course. *It was dead dizzy up there, Miss, but it was worth it cos you could see for a hunner mile.* Two girls who had never really been friends before told how they had met each other, by surprise, in Scarborough. They hadn't known they were going to the same place. One of them talked about a cable car you could get from up a hill down to the prom. Sounded great.

It came to my turn and I talked about our two weeks away. Fair fortnight in Millport. We went there every year. I loved it. I used to think it was so far away, like being on a distant, desert island. I would imagine I was on the other side of the world. I was no Robert when it came to words so I didn't spellbind my classmates by weaving a tale. I just delivered a list of facts.

Bus into Glasgow, bags on our knees. The three of us, Mum, Dad, me. Central Station mobbed. Dad hauling a big wicker hamper with enough clothes to last a year never mind two weeks. Train doors slamming like rifles going off. Squashed up on the journey to the coast, then joining the trail of refugees dashing from the train station to the ferry through the quaint old centre of Largs where they actually had shops outside in the street, not all shoved together in a big boring town centre like Cumbride. The chaotic jostling at the ferry terminal, the sail to Millport, not on the car ferry, but the proper wee boat. It took longer but we preferred it because it sailed right into the harbour in the town instead of the ferry slip halfway round the island. I always wanted to sit up top, on the deck, even when it was raining, my eyes fixed on the tall church steeple in Largs, shrinking, shrinking, until it was the size of my finger, then finally disappearing when the boat turned the corner round the island.

Millport. Paradise. My Hawaii. The funny rock with a crocodile's face painted on it, the little park just up from the prom with trampolines stretched across a hole in the ground. Only time I ever saw trampolines. The fairground, dodgems, candy floss, the putting green. The little competitions we had, Dad giving us a stroke a hole then two strokes a hole but still winning every time. Crazy golf, with pink and blue rubbery golf balls that sometimes bounced right out on to the main road. The café, the Ritz, with a story cut out of a newspaper pasted on the window, saying it officially sold the best ice cream in Scotland. I read the story every year and believed it. Hot peas and vinegar, Sugar Sugar on the juke box. Mum said the ancient waitress was the same one who had been there when she was a wee lassie.

Mum and Dad were different people for that fortnight. Mum acted a bit like a girl. She blossomed in the white sea air and the seaweed tang away from the kitchen fog. She wore bright dresses and even shorts and white socks sometimes when it wasn't raining. Dad wore sandals without socks and he was clean, his face was shiny! When I was wee, he told me the oil and grime were stored away in our bathroom cabinet back in Cumbride, waiting for him to get home. Mum and Dad were playful, with me, with each other. Once or twice they even kissed each other outside and I'd get a beamer, but it was kind of nice in a way too. They went on a big swing like a rowing boat together. I stood and watched and shouted, *Higher, Higher,* and Mum screamed in terror but she winked to show me she was just pretending. One evening she had a go on the trampoline even though there was a sign up saying you had to be under fourteen. The woman in charge told her off but Mum made a joke I didn't understand about all that bouncing being good practice and she got to stay on. Another time, Dad stretched out on his back on a bench by the shore then took a bite out of a pokey hat at the bottom and sucked out the ice cream. He said he could do it all in a oner and we giggled when the sticky, melty ice cream ran down his chin and on to his neck.

THE FENIAN

During the day, Dad and I built sandcastles that grew into huge, complicated estates with walls and gardens and moats and roads leading in and out. We sometimes tried to dig a trench from the castle to the sea but we could never get the water to come all the way up. I had a ride on one of the sad, slow ponies on the beach but I didn't like its damp, fusty smell very much. I wouldn't let Dad walk along beside me. I was too big for that and I asked the girl not to hold the rein but she said she wasn't allowed. While Dad and I played, Mum sat on a towel, her back to the high prom wall, drinking tea from a flask and lighting one cigarette from the last. Every now and then, Dad said he was nipping to the shop for a paper and came back after ten minutes with hot, stinky breath but no paper.

We hired bikes from a shop on the seafront. A big red shop like an Aladdin's cave with spades and pails and fishing nets and dummy bleeding finger tricks and fart powder and kid-on sweets that made your tongue turn black. We rode the bikes right round the island. It took us all afternoon. Mum and Dad were on a tandem, Mum on the back, saying she was letting Dad do all the work, me on a two-wheeler by myself. It turned cold and bleak and a bit scary round the back of the island, far away from the houses and everything. I was always glad when the first buildings of the town came into sight again.

We stayed in a tenement just up from the harbour. It had somebody else's things in it and a door with a sign on it that said PRIVATE and we could hear voices. I always felt a bit like a burglar for the first couple of days.

In the evenings, we went to this club up a back street, Mums and Dads and children all together. Smoke hanging in the air in streaky blue clouds, overflowing ashtrays, traffic jam of glasses on tables, crisps floating on puddles of juice and beer on the floor. A man in a sparkly suit told jokes, mainly about someone called *me-missus* who he kept saying was *that ugly* or *that fat* or both. After each lot of jokes, he introduced singers and one night, a magician. At the end of the night, a really really old man with a miserable face came on and puffed out his cheeks while he played tunes on the accordion. The music made the Mums' and Dads' faces go as sad as his own. The man in the shiny jacket sometimes got people up from the tables to sing. My Mum got up one night and sang Once I Had A Secret Love in a low, husky trill. The place fell silent and her voice made me shiver. When I caught Dad smiling at her, with his eyes kind of watery, he made a funny face and said for *God sake pass the cotton wool.*

The other kids in my class laughed at the cotton wool bit.

Mrs McDonald said: 'Thank you, Lorna. That was very good.'

I sat down, pleased with myself, happy I had got it all out. Proud of our holiday and pretty sure I had done it justice.

I was the last before lunch. It got more exotic in the afternoon. A few of my classmates had been abroad and talked about the Costa Brava, Torremolinos, Majorca. Fabulous golden names like the titles of the pirate films we saw at the Saturday morning pictures. Kids exaggerated to make their points. *It was pure scorching Miss. Imagine the hottest, boilingest day here. That would be like their winter.* One boy had gone to France by car. He had stayed at a caravan in a place called Brittany that he kept stressing wasn't in Britain.

It all sounded wonderful and I asked my Mum later if we could go abroad one day and she replied: 'Sure thing, hen. Day after your Dad gets eight draws up.'

Almost everyone had a summer story to tell in class that day. Only one girl hadn't been away anywhere but that was because she had got a new wee sister during the school holidays. With Mrs McDonald's encouragement, the drama and excitement of the baby's arrival became her tale.

Then the babble died away and it was down to Cammy, the only one who hadn't put his hand up. He seemed so far away now, distant at his solo desk at the back by the window. He seemed smaller too, as if he had tried to make himself so tiny that Mrs McDonald wouldn't notice him, or maybe hoping she would forget about him. Cammy cringed, realising everyone was looking at him, waiting for him, and the ten-to-four bell hadn't gone yet. No escape.

Finally, glancing at her register, Mrs McDonald looked across at him and said: 'And what about you? Anthony, isn't it? You haven't told us about your holiday yet.'

There were lots of things Cammy didn't tell us, never told us. Things we didn't know back then, things we only learned later, drip-fed over the years by parents or brothers and sisters or pals, or from Cammy himself when alcohol unfastened his secrets.

For example, Cammy never told us that John the Bampot was his Dad. John the Bampot was what everybody called the dustcart man. His job title these days would be something like street cleansing operative. We would see John the Bampot next to the playground at lunchtime or on our way home, shoving his big bin on wheels, picking up litter and not complaining, which was how I'd remember him fondly years later when Dignity was playing everywhere. He was always grinning with his big bushy beard and cross-eyes that met in the middle. We called him John the Bampot because he had a picture of Jesus painted on the side of his bin, the picture with Jesus's heart showing. John the Bampot was friendly and chatty but never creepy. He would talk to you about dropping litter but he never gave you a row and he sealed his nickname with a stock of holy-holy parting shots.

THE FENIAN

Like. *Always remember, Jesus never dropped his rubbish in the street.*
Or. *The Lord preserve us...and turn us into strawberry jam.*
And his biggie. *Don't forget, there's always a welcome for everyone at the Baptist Church. Young and old, saints and sinners, Jesus loves us all.*

We never saw Cammy talking to him so we had no idea he was his Dad for years, until he finally ran out of excuses and took his turn to have a party for us, his shelter pals. We got to his house and there was John the Bampot sitting in the kitchen drinking tea like he lived there – and without his bright orange council jacket on.

Cammy was one of five children. We pieced that together. He had an older brother and sister and a younger brother and sister. But it was only much later that we found out that he had originally been one of seven. He'd had another sister and another brother who had both died. No, not just died, they'd been killed, separately, at different times. We never learned the details, like their names, or what ages they died at or anything, but we picked up fragments of information over the years. One of them had drowned in the bath at home and the other one had been knocked down by an ice cream van. Someone once told us they thought the sister who died had been Cammy's twin.

Cammy never mentioned them and I suppose we were too afraid to ask in case it upset him too much or just wasn't true. It somehow felt like something you weren't suppose to discuss out in the open. After my Mum died, I felt joined to Cammy in a way, because he had known what it was like long before me, known all about having someone living in your house for years who suddenly wasn't there any longer, who left a space and was never coming back. He had known it twice before he was ten and came to live in Cumbride and started at our school.

Now he was isolated as Mrs McDonald closed in. Cammy said nothing and refused to look up at her.

'Come on, Anthony,' she said. 'You've heard all about your friends' holidays. I'm sure they'd love to hear about yours.'

Cammy squeezed into himself, as if trying to make himself even smaller. He stared at his desktop. He stayed silent. Stalemate...till Mrs McDonald laid down a marker, an edge in her voice now.

'Right Anthony, on your feet.'

He stood up, well, half-stood, more of a crouch really. Still pulling into himself, refusing to look her in the face.

'Come on then, Anthony,' she said, a little softer. 'Don't be shy. Just tell us what you did. Where you went for your holidays. We're all waiting.'

Her patience slipped again.

'Now, Anthony.'

Cammy mumbled something, inaudible.

'Sorry Anthony, we didn't hear that. Did we class?'

'No Miss.' Twenty-odd voices in a sing-song chorus.

'Come on boy.' Mrs McDonald got tough. 'Try again. And this time, why don't we try opening our mouth when we speak.'

Now Cammy looked up, right at her and spoke in a small, whiny voice.

'Went to America, Miss.'

'You went to America?'

An echo, disbelief in the teacher's face.

'Yes Miss.'

'You really went to America, Anthony, or did you make a wee mistake?' She asked, gently this time, not believing it but giving him a chance to withdraw it and start again.

'Yes Miss.'

'And, eh, how did you get there?'

Cammy improvised.

'Em, on the Concorde, Miss.'

'The Concorde!' said Mrs McDonald. She threw him a snap test. 'And how long did it take to get there?'

Cammy hesitated, then said: 'Hardly any time at all, Miss. It's supersonic, so it is.'

'Uhu,' she said, and quickly lobbed him another one. 'Where did you fly to Anthony?'

'America Miss, told you.'

The teacher applied more pressure, certain she could crack him quickly.

'Yes Anthony, but whereabouts in America? Which airport? New York? Washington?'

'Er, New York, Miss,' said Cammy, warily, trying to spot the catch in the question.

'OK Anthony,' she nodded. 'New York it is. Now I'm sure the class can't wait to hear about America, so just you tell us all about it.'

'Ah, it was great Miss,' said Cammy, without enthusiasm. 'There's tons of skyscrapers and all the folk had American accents and everything, just like in the pictures.'

He made to sit down. No chance Cammy. As if Mrs McDonald was that much of a pushover.

'American accents? Well, isn't that a surprise.' Cutting, then sharp. 'Back on your feet, Anthony. We want to hear about all the places you went to. *Everything* you saw.'

Cammy had nowhere to go, no way out, so he started serving up nuggets of TV America.

'We went to the Empire State Building, Miss,' he said. 'It's massive. Easy bigger than the school. We saw the white house where the King of America lives but he wasn't in the day we went. Er, Las Vegas, we went there. Em, the, er, golden bridge, we crossed that every day. And, oh aye, the Rio Grand Canyon.'

Cammy paused, thinking hard, then he stumbled on.

'The Indian reservations, Miss. Where the Indians used to live. Er, er, and Hollywood. We saw the big sign and that.'

No grasp of scale, no clue about the thousands of miles or the different time zones. He had just reduced the vastness of the United States to a thirty-second sound bite. Not that any of us in the class knew better. All sounded pretty impressive to me.

'That's fascinating,' said Mrs McDonald, with undisguised scorn. 'And how long were you in America, Anthony?'

'Oh,' said Cammy, hesitating in case it was another trick question. 'A whole week, Miss. That was plenty – we'd seen it all by then.'

The teacher was right up at Cammy's desk now, breathing fire, swooping for the kill, but she was robbed by the ten-to-four bell. Cammy scooped up his bag and joined the rush to the exit. A reprieve, but only until the next morning.

About quarter past nine, Cammy's little sister came into our class with a message for Mrs McDonald from her Primary Five teacher. If we'd been old enough back then to be cynical, we might have thought it had been staged.

'You're Patricia, aren't you?' our teacher asked the girl, her tone friendly. 'You're our Anthony's sister?'

'Yes Miss.' Patricia was small and insignificant, just like Cammy, and when she spoke it came out as a faint squeak.

'And how did you like America, Patricia?'

'Pardon Miss?' Another squeak, confusion written on her face.

'America, Patricia.' Mrs McDonald said it slowly, savouring it. 'Anthony's been telling us all about your fabulous holiday. In America.'

'No Miss,' said the little girl, serious faced, a pawn in Mrs McDonald's justice game. 'We've never been to America. We never went any holidays.'

Mrs McDonald dismissed Patricia and got to her feet. Grim-faced and dressed in black, like a hanging judge, she marched slowly towards Cammy. He looked utterly crushed.

'Now then children,' said Mrs McDonald, involving us all in it. 'Who knows what we do with people who tell lies?'

There was silence but OK, I confess, we were excited. We were surely about to witness a public execution.

What her thinking was, I've no idea. Had she planned it at home the night before? Did she mean it as a genuine tough lesson or did she see it as comedy, a light-hearted way to send a message? God knows. Whatever her motive, Mrs McDonald hadn't expected an answer from us and she didn't wait for one.

'Little liars get pinned up on the wall,' she said. 'And their lie with them for all to see.'

We had seen classmates bawled out, reduced to tears by a screaming teacher. Once, in Primary Three, I was made to stand in the corner for twenty minutes for being a bold girl. I've never forgotten that phrase – *a bold girl* – and all because I was caught throwing a tiny ball of plasticine back at a boy who had tossed it at me first. On very rare occasions we had even seen kids getting the strap, but pinned to the wall? Wow! We couldn't wait.

Mrs McDonald made Cammy stand on an empty desk with his back to the wall. Sheepishly, he obeyed her instructions and spread his arms out. She got drawing pins and tacked the sleeves of his jumper to the wall, then the same with the tops of his socks.

She told him: 'Now don't you dare move from there. You'll stand there all morning young man, until you learn to tell the truth.'

We were open-mouthed. A few boys started laughing and Mrs McDonald made no attempt to quell them as she got a big sheet of white card from the cupboard, the kind we used for painting on. She took a felt-tip from her drawer and wrote something on the paper in big black letters. Then she pinned it up beside Cammy. It read:

ANTHONY CAMERON
THE BOY WHO WENT TO AMERICA

The class was in uproar and Mrs McDonald did nothing to stop it. So, this was his punishment then. Liars get found out. They become a laughing stock.

Eventually, the laughter subsided and we got down to work. I think it was English punctuation or something. But Mrs McDonald wanted to keep it going, the Cammy pantomime. She would show us something, like where to put commas, then she would ask questions and hands would shoot up.

But each time, she would say: 'I know, let's ask the boy who went to America.'

Or. 'I wonder if Christopher Columbus knows the answer.'

Then she would add: 'Oh no, I forgot, no point in asking him. He doesn't know how to tell the truth.'

It was funny her saying that. At least, it was funny the first few times, and it was funny too, what she had done, pinning Cammy to the wall like that. We would sneak glances back at him, standing there with that sign next to him. THE BOY WHO WENT TO AMERICA with his name above it. We would snigger. Then after a while, it stopped being funny.

It was tiny, the noise he made. A snuffle so tiny you could barely hear it. You had to listen hard to make sure you hadn't imagined it. But there it was again, like the briefest rustle of paper. Sob. Pause. Sob. Pause. Sob.

I saw a few others sneak a look. I sneaked a look. It was pitiful, heart crunching and sorrowful. Cammy was so exposed he might as well have been naked. Arms outstretched and straining, one foot resting on the other like he was really hanging there. All that was missing was the spear in his side. I couldn't bear to look again but that didn't stop me seeing him. The image wouldn't leave my head. I shifted in my seat, squirming. Around me, others were doing the same. It was like a contagious itch spreading from desk to desk then it was as if a vent had been opened and gas was seeping in, circling our feet then slowly rising, stifling us, poisoning us. We were too young to recognise the weight of guilt. So heavy, constricting and choking us. Breathing became difficult.

This guilt we hadn't earned, or maybe we had just by being there, by laughing, by joining in and consenting by not trying to stop it. The tiny sobs were screaming at us now, pounding on our backs.

I wasn't brave enough to raise my head above the parapet, to be first, to be the one who cried out, *Enough is enough*. It was one of the boys. I wish I could say it had been Ross or Cookie, just for extra evidence that our lot really had been something special. Truth is, I don't remember now who it was exactly but at least it was someone, some boy who stood up against persecution. An ordinary kind of boy, the kind of boy who maybe never did anything particularly special in his life again. He put his hand up.

'Miss, Miss.'

He caught Mrs McDonald's attention and spoke politely. 'Miss. Please may Anthony come down now?'

But Mrs McDonald was committed to it. She snapped at the boy with his hand up.

'Would you like to swap places with me? Would you like to come out here and teach the class?'

'No Miss, I was just saying….'

She cut him dead. 'Well don't then. When I want your opinion, I'll ask for it.'

Another hand, from the other side of the class. 'Miss. He's been up there an awful long time.'

Another one. 'I don't think it's really fair, Miss.'

And another. 'Please Miss, going to please let him down?'

The teacher was dodging bullets from all angles. She picked up her blackboard duster and brought it crashing down on her desk three times. BANG! BANG! BANG!

Battering us into submission.

'Silence.' She roared at us, her face purple. 'I will not hear one more word. Now get on with your work.'

Might is right.

A hush descended. Heads down. We were cowed, subdued.

Then the masterstroke. I remember clearly who it was this time. It was Charlie Canary, so called because whenever he spoke, his words were accompanied by whistling down his nostrils, like pan pipes. He always seemed kind of simple, a bit slow, but not this day. Charlie, who would leave the education system five years later without a piece of paper to show he had ever been there never mind passed a test or earned a qualification, stepped up to be a hero. He stuck his hand up but didn't wait for Mrs McDonald to acknowledge him. He just spoke and with his question he rechristened Anthony Cameron, handed him the nickname that stuck with him for life.

Charlie Canary said: 'Miss, if Cammy isn't allowed to come down, can I please go up there beside him?'

He stood up, ready to move. Before the teacher could answer, another boy got it.

'Yeah Miss, me too. Can I get pinned up as well?'

Then Ross, who had never given Cammy the time of day and snubbed him daily when picking football teams, weighed in too. 'Me and all, Miss. I want to go up there with my pal, Cammy.'

Six more, then a dozen. Boys, girls, even timorous little me. A peasants' revolt ambushing our new teacher and suddenly Mrs McDonald knew she was beaten, knew she had got it wrong. She had created a folk hero.

Chapter 10

August 2001
Perfect Gentleman – Wyclef Jean

IT was three days before I got another chance to go on the internet. Work had been busy. The summer was always playtime for the booze idiots. Then on the Friday, I got everything done by just after half-three. I had been giving it an awful lot of thought. Did I really want to read Robert's entry? Did I really want to know about this *Robbie* Kane and his wonderful wife/life? When had I caught this dose of self-punishment? Why should I even think about torturing myself? And why now? Why had his name come up again, twice in one week? First from Big Paddy, when I bumped into him last Friday, then on Tuesday, when I just had to let curiosity get the better of me and check out this Friends Reunited rubbish. Bloody Kath, encouraging me with her text the other day.

I tried to explain it to myself, the new Robert intrigue rattling about in there. Cause and effect. One wouldn't have happened without the other. If Big Paddy hadn't mentioned his name, planted that little seed in there, and we hadn't had the Friends Reunited chat in the canteen, maybe I wouldn't have been so curious, maybe I wouldn't have gone seeking him out.

But now, here I was, the choice in my fingertips resting on the keyboard. Did I really want to do this? What the hell. Internet explorer, click, Friends Reunited, click. No messing about. Don't even stop to think about it, don't give myself a chance to have second thoughts. Straight to St Joseph's Secondary, Cumbride, 1976. Robbie Kane. Double click on the envelope.

Two lines, a mere two lines! I didn't read his entry right away, I just kind of looked at it. Huh, is that it from our great storyteller? Is that the best you can do, Robert? Two lines? The great wordsmith Robert Kane, gone minimal.

OK. Here goes nothing.

One fine son, Jack, age 18. Worked in London 20 years. Back up the road in Scotland.

MIKE KERNAN

Love to hear from anyone who remembers me.
Not exactly the great autobiography. Instead of revelation, questions. That's all Robert had provided. He had told me nothing, he had just dumped a pile of questions on me.
Back in Scotland. What does that mean Robert? Are you on holiday up here and if so, when are you going back to London? How long are you staying? Or are you back for good, and if that is the case, since when? When did you get here? Where are you in Scotland exactly? Are you living in the next street or are you renting a remote cottage in Wick and working on Radio Sheepdip? What the hell do I care anyway? When did what Robert does with his life become my business? I twisted myself, felt my stomach tighten. I tried to discard bitter and petty. Back to Robert's words...
One fine son, Jack, age 18.
Typical. *Jack.* Mock old-fashioned and solid. A woodcutter's name. One of those trendy names trendy couples have revived, like Sam and Jacob, and stuck on their trendy kids. From nowhere, I conjured up personalised Christmas cards in my head. *Love and peaceful greetings from Robbie, Ruth and Jack.* The perfect little threesome. *Best Wishes Robert and Lorna.* Nah, too flat, much too ordinary for the great Robbie Kane and his family in telly-land.
But wait, there was no mention of ruthless Ruth. Why, and so what anyway? Just like how they came to choose their brat's name, what on earth did it have to do with me?
Worked in London...anyone who remembers me. Who are you kidding Robert? That was a bit like Madonna going on Friends Reunited and writing: *Done a wee bit of singing. Don't suppose anybody recalls me?*
Or was Robert just being modest? I mean, how could any of us have forgotten him? Because he was the one, our star. The one who made it from our wee crowd in the swing park shelter. The one who gave us a little bit of second-hand fame for a while.
See that guy on the telly? I used to snog him.
Fuck it. Be honest Lorna, just this once. No more pretending, tell it how it is.
Used to snog him? Used to love him. *Used to?*
Pathetic. Stupid. Useless. And now in need of a giant saucer of milk for all that bitchiness and venom I've been spitting. Who do I think I am? Well into my forties and alone with no life. Not much of a life anyway. Yeah, me. The one who made the golden boy weep because I turned him down and turned him down again. And look where it got me. Thanks a bunch, Mum.

68

Chapter 11

April 1974
The Entertainer – Marvin Hamlisch

R OBERT was always telling Jo that she should apply for Opportunity
   Knocks.
   'Can't be any worse than that Neil Reid dick.' That was Cammy's
eloquent and best attempt at weighing in on her behalf. 'Singing about his
maw in that shitey, whining voice. Needs his baws booted, so he does.'
   Just to show how much she appreciated the praise, however faint, Jo herself
would inevitably reply: 'And they mean that most sincerely folks...but
remember, getting the clap is just for fun.'
   Robert meant it, though, and he had a point because Jo was our one-woman
show, always animated, always making us laugh, always acting, always being
someone else. Sometimes it seemed the only person Jo didn't enjoy being
that much was herself.
   Jo was tiny. When she kept her mouth shut – and that wasn't often – she
could pass for an eight-year-old. The budding little bumps on her puny frame
were all that reminded us she was our age. But she had a kind of high-octane
mix of cute and bubbly and fun which made her irresistible to all of us and
attractive to the guys. She and Cammy had a kind of on-off thing for a while.
Robert and Ross were Jo semi-regulars too. The only one who seemed to
avoid her – as a girlfriend I mean – was Big Paddy. Oh, and Cookie of course,
but no one was ever sure if his apparent lack of interest in Jo – or any of the
other girls – was through choice.
   Jo and Big Paddy got on well enough, better than most in fact. But they
were probably only an item once – and definitely not for long.
   'Hey, don't get me wrong,' Big Paddy said to me, scrambling around to
draft an apology to the wrong person.
   I had been giving him a hard time for dumping Jo in record speed – an hour

and a half – which was even shorter than my infamous quickie fling/break-up with Cookie.

'Jo's pure brilliant,' he said. 'But it's just too much of a difference, our size, I mean. See when I was out with her that night? Walking about holding her hand and stuff? I felt like one of they kiddy-fiddlers. It was like winching a Primary Three, know?'

Big Paddy was taking this seriously. He did have a soul lurking in there somewhere.

Then he brightened and added: 'But see if I was stuck on one of they desert islands, Jo's the one I'd want for company.'

'Oh, thanks a lot Paddy,' I answered, mock upset. 'And there's me thinking we were big pals and all. I mean, who's ever been as close as us, eh?'

Ha, Big Paddy and me, we'd once had a bath together, dumped in the tub in my house when a five-minute neighbourly visit turned into a party. We were only little kids at the time but still, neither of us ever spoke of it to anyone else and he got a red neck at the mention of it.

'Shut it, and it's no' that,' said Big Paddy, still working out his guilt. 'It's just, if you got fed up, Jo would be like having the telly. Know what I mean?'

I did know what he meant. Jo had a gift for doing folk off the television, and the pictures. She picked up on voices and catchphrases and tossed them into our conversations.

When you turned up at the shelter, Jo couldn't be like the rest of us and just say: 'Hi, how you doing?'

No, it had to be: 'Hello, good evening, and welcome.'

Or: 'Shite to see you, to see you…' And, of course, we'd all shout the appropriate reply back at her.

When a couple of us made moves to start drifting home at night, she'd spring towards us, yelling: 'Boing! Time for bed.'

Or: 'G'night Ross Boy. G'night Grandmaw. Hey Cookie-Bob, what you doing in Karen's nightdress?'

Generous Ross would come back from the ice cream van, arms laden with ice poles and Caramacs. Shirley Bassey would greet him. 'Hey Big Spender.'

Robert would drone on about some obscure newspaper story he had read or a new album he was obsessed with. He'd be off on some baffling, marathon monologue, in love with the sound of his own voice and his own words. Jo would stop him in his tracks, fists clenched, stiff Gumby stance.

'My brain hurts.'

Jo had favourites. She did Cilla, Cliff, Kojak. She did cartoon characters like Muttley, Scooby Doo, Fred Flintstone. Fred's trademark *Wilmaaaa* became *Lornaaaa* bellowed from her little lungs whenever she spotted me approaching the shelter.

But Jo's biggie was doing us. Her party piece was to fade into the background at a party or round the wall at the back of the shelter. Then she'd re-emerge wearing someone else's coat, or jumper. The effect was immediately comical – and invariably ridiculous – because Jo was so tiny that everyone else's gear drowned her. Sleeves would flop beyond her hands, Big Paddy's denim jacket would be almost down to her feet. She would launch right into wickedly accurate mirror images, the voices pretty much spot on – not exact all the time, but close enough – with the mannerisms right on the money. No one escaped her deadly, piercing dialogues and no one was ever really offended because Jo's best trick, her gift, was teaching us to laugh at ourselves.

She would become Cammy, doing his moany, whiny voice and sticking one of her arms straight out to show us the plaster cast he invariably had on one of his limbs.

'Can't get my zip down with one hand…why's nobody volunteering to help us go for a pee?'

Wee Mary was next and Jo would fold her arms inside her jumper to create a freakishly huge, imaginary chest and thrust her bum backwards.

'You know, I just can't figure out what the guys see in me.'

I vividly remember us all cracking up the night we came back from the cinema after watching what most of us reckoned was the funniest film we'd ever seen. We were taking turns to repeat as many of the lines as we could recall when Jo climbed on to the bench in the shelter, puffed out her chest and flexed her arms like a bodybuilder.

'Big Paddy just pawn in game of life. Me knock out horse with one punch.'

In a beat, she switched from Mongo to an affected, effeminate version of Big Paddy's voice.

'Shame me have willy of hamster.'

She knew how to give me an easy beamer. She'd flutter her fingers, running them down the side of her face to paint my coal-black hair the way I wore it straight and long back then, so long I could sit on it. Jo would rattle out her exaggerated, triple-speed version of my nervy, typewriter way of talking, then – God, the embarrassment – she'd crouch in front of Robert and gaze up at him longingly, panting like a dog.

'No way do I fancy Robert. He gives us the dry boak. That's why I sit with my gob hanging open and jump up like a wee puppy the minute he's looking for someone to go up the chippie.'

Jo saved her Academy Award performance not for one of us, but for Karen's father. It ended with Karen not speaking to her for days and neither

Jo nor me able to face her Dad for months.

It was one Thursday after school. Jo and I had stopped at the shelter with a few of the others. She had recently taken up smoking, despite my nagging. *It's only the odd one*, she insisted. We met Cammy and they started to share an Embassy. Karen, who also disapproved, tutted and headed home. A little bit after that, Jo and I went up to my house to study for an hour for a big History test the next morning. But we'd hardly got our jackets off when I remembered Karen had borrowed my notes, so we dived round to her bit.

Karen's Dad answered the door and told us she had just gone out with her Mum and wouldn't be back till about half five. I told him what I was after and said I would come back. But I had been round there a lot and Karen's Dad knew me well enough so he said: 'Just pop into her room Lorna. Have a quick nose around. It'll be in there somewhere.'

Karen's Dad knew *me* but he had never met Jo. She had moved to Cumbride less than a year before so she hadn't been at Karen's record session. I thanked him and headed for Karen's room. I expected Jo to follow me but she didn't and instead went in the opposite direction – to the living room.

Karen's Dad was OK, though he could be a bit of a smoothy. When we'd arrived at Karen's that time for her party, he'd grinned as we trooped in and said: 'My God, will you look at all this talent in the one room. See if I was fifteen years younger, you lads wouldn't stand a chance.'

There is part of me wants to call him creepy, but cheesy is probably more accurate – a bit of a pain, but harmless, and no one took his chat seriously. Mostly he tried really hard to be trendy. He tried to keep up with *What you young folks are into these days*. He tried to have conversations with us *On your own level*. But he always just missed the point. He was always just out of date. But I'm being unfair. As adults go, he was OK, Karen's Dad.

I didn't want to ferret around too much in Karen's room. Sure, I was tempted, but I didn't. I had a quick glance *at* her schoolbag more than in it and scanned the desk next to her bed. I heard voices from the living room, and laughter. Then I spotted my History jotter on the floor, next to Karen's bed. I scooped it up and went to get Jo.

I walked into Karen's living room and Jo said something to me that I didn't catch properly. My first reaction was, that was quick, Jo and Karen's Dad must be getting on well because they're having some kind of a joke. I really thought they were kidding around because Jo was speaking in a German accent. It sounded pretty good too. Well, as far as I could judge from what I'd heard on telly. You know, Hogan's Heroes and stuff.

'Ah Lorna, mein wunderbar pencil friend,' she said. I just stared at her, confused.

THE FENIAN

Karen's Dad, his chubby face beaming, said: 'Heidi here's just been telling me about this exchange visit. Is it a school thing or what, cos Karen's never mentioned anything?'

All I could say was: 'Heidi???'

I kept on staring at Jo, hard, hoping she would read the *What the hell are you playing at?* in my eyes.

'Ja, zee schools,' Jo/Heidi ploughed on regardless. 'They are making zee arrangements. Lorna vill be coming to me next year, in Scheisseburg, ver I liff.'

I was speechless but Karen's Dad was lapping it up because Scots are such suckers for accents, American especially, but anything will do really. Anything that has the merest hint of the exotic, or just different.

I wanted to escape but Karen's Dad offered us a drink. *Tea? Coffee?*

I said: 'No. Thanks. We've really got to go.'

But Jo/Heidi was enjoying herself too much.

'I vunder. Do you haff any of zis ironing brew I haff been hearing about? Is it to give your fraus zee muscles for flattening zee close?'

Karen's Dad laughed again. 'Ah, you mean Irn-Bru. Yeah, I'm sure we've got some. Hang on a tick.'

He disappeared into the kitchen.

I turned on Jo and whispered: 'What the fuck are you playing at?'

A rare swear word, for me anyway – honest – but justified in the circumstances, I think.

'It's OK,' she muttered back. 'It's just a laugh.'

Karen's Dad came back and handed Jo/Heidi her drink. He was really getting into the spirit of it now.

'So, Heidi,' he asked. 'What do you think of Scotland then?'

'Ah, est schon,' said Jo. She had been doing German since third year – a little knowledge and all that.

'I am begging mein pardon,' she went on. 'Schon, eh, vot do you say? Beautiful. Just like my vater told me.'

'Sorry, your..?' Karen's Dad was clearly captivated.

'Oh, sorry very much again. In English, ja? Mein, eh, father.'

'Ah right,' said Karen's Dad. 'He's been to Scotland then? When was that?'

'No, not my father, he has not been coming here. Mein opa, pardon again, my, eh, father's father. He tells about your country when my father was just a boy and my father tells me ven he knows I am coming here. It vos many years before ven my grandfather comes.'

'Oh, right. And which part of Scotland was he in?' Karen's Dad asked. 'Do you know?'

'Ja, I try to remember,' said Jo/Heidi, really getting into character now. She held out her arms like aeroplane wings. 'Vot vos it again? Ah, now I know. Clyden-bank. Vood zat be right? Iss far from here, nein?'

Karen's Dad shifted his large frame in his chair, for the first time looking a little bit uncomfortable. I didn't get the connection but then I hadn't done the Second World War in History. Karen's Dad's knowledge was obviously better than mine and so was Jo's, apparently. He sensed a sticky moment and turned peacemaker.

'Ach well, that was a long time ago. Maybe you can go back and tell your grandfather what a friendly place Scotland is these days.'

Jo/Heidi let out a gasp, a loud sob which caught in her throat. I wanted to be anywhere else in the world at that moment.

She raised her voice and said: 'I cannot tell my grandfather any-sing. You killed him. Ze bombs. Boom!'

The last word was more of a sound effect and we both jumped, Karen's Dad and me. Now he was really struggling.

'Look, as I was saying, that was an awful long time ago, and I've, I've never killed anybody. I was only a wee boy, just like your father. And there's a lot...'

Jo/Heidi interrupted. 'Ja, of course. You are right. I am sorry. Very, very sorry. I must not be saying zees sings.'

I sighed with relief then caught myself. Christ, I was starting to believe it myself. I had sat through the conversation terrified to speak, unable to speak.

To my horror, Jo/Heidi wasn't finished. 'The vor. You vun, fair and skvare. Ve are freunden now, ja?'

Karen's Dad relaxed a little. It had been a bad moment but the worst seemed to be over – or so I thought. Jo/Heidi took a long swig of Irn-Bru then giggled.

'Ah, mein herren. I am sinking you are ze naughty, naughty man. Zis ironing brew, it is kratzten. Er, sorry, scratching. Nein, that's not right. Eh, eh...tickling, zat's it. I sink maybe you try to get me drunken. I sink maybe you are liking ze little frauleins, ja?'

I was already long past the aghast stage but even I didn't believe what happened next. Jo leaned over and she actually squeezed Karen's Dad's knee. He shot forward in his chair and I leapt out of mine. I grabbed the glass from Jo's hand, thudded it on to a coffee table and wrenched her bodily from her chair.

'Right, we're going. Now.' It was a command. Jo obeyed.

The fallout was heavy – predictable, but heavy. I was telling the guys about Jo's performance and they were falling about. Jo was basking in my description but nervous at the same time, knowing she had overcooked it.

Karen came storming into the shelter a bit later. If looks could kill, she was a mass murderer. Jo took one look at her and became Captain Kirk.

'Oh shit. Beam me up Scotty.'

Karen looked like she was going to hit Jo. Very hard.

'What the hell did you think you were playing at?' she raged. 'I've never seen my Dad so mad in my entire life, or so embarrassed.'

Jo had one half-hearted attempt at bluffing it out.

'Oh, thanks a lot Karen. You had to shop me, eh? Some pal you are and I don't think.'

Aye, very good Jo.

Karen was almost hysterical now.

'Are you serious? I walk in and the first thing he says is, *Hey Karen, you didn't tell me about your little German friend.* I didn't have a clue what he was on about. Then he described *Heidi.* The wee girl with blonde curls that Lorna brought in. That's when it dawned on me. What was I meant to say to him?'

I had tried to hide behind the guys but the mention of my name reminded Karen. She turned on me and waved a finger right in my face.

'And you,' she accused. 'My Dad's always thought you're great. Well, he did think you were great. You've known him since you were wee, Lorna. How could you let her take the piss like that?'

Jo stepped in. 'Look Karen, don't blame Lorna. It was all me, right? And I'm dead, dead sorry. Listen, I'll go and see your Dad right now. I'll apologise. It was just meant to be a wee joke but it kind of got out of hand and I couldn't stop myself. I'm really sorry. OK?'

'Don't you go near him,' said Karen. 'You've done enough damage, bloody *Heidi.*'

Jo didn't go near him. She didn't get an invite to Karen's next party and managed to keep out of her Dad's way for ages, right up until the big do at the hotel, in fact. Even then, Jo tried her hardest to avoid him and very nearly managed it, until late on in the evening. Then, a voice in her ear.

'Tanzen, mein fraulein?'

Chapter 12

July 2001
Nobody Wants To Be Lonely – Ricky Martin & Christina Aguilera

ROBERT Kane inserts the plastic card into the slot and shoves the door open. His sigh is heavy and audible. Christ, how he hates hotel rooms, like this one. He once tried to do a rough estimate of the number of nights of his life he has spent in hotel rooms but it very quickly depressed him and he stopped counting. He has stayed in hotel rooms all over the world. Countless sterile little sleeping boxes. Except this one is home, for now at least. Has been for three weeks, and God knows how many more weeks to come. He has to find a place and Jack is enough of an incentive. He knows he must force himself to make the time and the effort to get out and look for a new home. A proper home for himself, where he can try and have some kind of life outside of work, and a safe haven for his son. Then he groans again as he thinks of the realities of getting from here to there. The hurdles between this hotel room where he eats his room-service dinner off a tray every evening and gets clean socks from a suitcase under his bed, and that imaginary proper home with familiar photos and mementoes along with the bits of furniture retrieved from a cold storage unit somewhere. All that mass of stuff to get through. The wading through property pages, the viewings, the surveys, the haggling over whether the white goods are included, the bidding, the closing date, the lawyers, the building society, the calls to the removal company. Not to mention the remote dealing with the sale of the house in London. All the time and energy it will consume. Hassle, hassle, hassle. He shoves it all back into a corner of his head for the fourteenth time. Definitely make a start tomorrow…

It hasn't been a great day. Robert has not yet got to grips with being a boss, being *the* boss actually. Yes, he knows all the words, all the little mantras they teach you on the BBC leadership courses. Inspire, encourage, influence, decide, delegate, motivate, trust. That one at the end of the list, that's the key, he tells himself yet again. *Trust*. Remember, all these people know their jobs, they're all experienced professionals. Stop thinking you have to go checking up on them every five minutes. Stop thinking you'd be quicker and better doing the whole damn story yourself. Oh, and another thing. Robert orders himself to stop phoning the office after hours. Leave them to it. If there's something urgent, they'll call him.

Robert is convinced they resent him. Johnny Bigtime up from London. Especially his two inherited joint deputies who have both made it very clear, without a sliver of subtlety, that the job should have been theirs by rights. Well tough shit, he feels like telling them. I wanted the job, you wanted the job, we all put ourselves up for it, put ourselves out there, and I got it, so live with it. No, he catches himself, that's not good enough. *Give it time, give them time, win them round. I'll grow into it, they'll grow into me.*

Robert tells himself all of this every night. One night soon, maybe he'll start to believe it and then he might manage to go a whole evening without ringing the night news editor to see what's happening and advising him what to tweak – and how – for the late bulletin. Yeah, and when that happens, he might get round to house-hunting too.

Robert is not stupid. He is far from stupid. He knows what all the worries are really about. It's not really to do with his job. It takes little effort to turn all this self-doubt and attention to detail into a positive. These are exactly the foundations upon which he has built a successful career and enviable reputation. Same with the house thing. All it will take is to shut his office door for an hour and make a few calls next time it's property ads day in the paper. Then Jack will come up the following Saturday and they'll make a day of it, taking the piss out of the estate agents' fruit-and-vestibules jargon and inventing increasingly scandalous or tragic back stories for the house sellers.

No, it doesn't take the gift of insight to recognise what all the niggles and discontent are really about. He needs them because they save him from confronting the bigger picture, the bigger fear, that his life is pretty worthless and that the likelihood of doing something about it is diminishing by the day. Yes, worthless, he decides in those rare 3am flashes of stark, sleepless self-awareness. Worthless despite the numerous career highlights, the never-dwindling excitement of the exclusive, the promotions, the plaudits, the prizes. Worthless despite the casually and effortlessly accumulated wealth, which only greases the guilt trips. And yes, worthless even despite Jack. A bright and brilliant boy, a kindred spirit, a faithful pal – everything a father could want from a son. But he is slipping away. The kid on his shoulders, sharing adventures en route to a sneaky don't-tell-disapproving-mum ten pence mixture from the sweet counter, is now a distant though not fading memory. Inevitably and inexorably, the bonds are loosening, just as they should be, and Robert knows he has to let go. Of course, they will stay close and maybe one far-off day there will be a mini-Jack to let him reprise that golden time. But for now, he has to back off while his boy grows into his own man.

Which leaves...what? When he is honest, he knows the answer is a kind of emptiness. Apart from Jack, there's the job, of course. The new challenge which, despite all the teething problems, is interesting and will no doubt be rewarding in its own way eventually. But he has to dig deep for the hunger these days. He is haunted by a conversation he had with a psychologist a few years back. Someone he had just interviewed for background to a story and who easily saw through Robert's manufactured interest and a line of questioning designed purely to elicit a single, context-free sensational soundbite. The barely camouflaged nothing-matters-but-the-story attitude that had fashioned his career. When the interview was over and they were making polite small talk, the psychologist remarked that Robert came across as being ultra-driven and ambitious. He then explained how he volunteered at a hospice a couple of nights a week and tried to help people come to terms with reaching the end of their lives.

He looked Robert in the eye, laid a hand on his arm, and said: 'Interesting point, mate, is that folk who are dying almost always say they wish they'd spent more time with their wife, gone more holidays with their kids, seen more of the world, played more golf, read more books, listened to more music...that kind of thing. I've yet to hear one single person on their deathbed say they wish they'd spent more time at their work.'

So yes, Robert's nature means he will never give less that one hundred per cent from the moment he walks through the BBC's doors each day, but that sense of all-consuming importance has gone. His work no longer fills the major need in his life. Now he is getting to it, where all the fretting and the self-doubt is leading. This is what it all comes down to. The realisation that clichés become clichés because they are true. You only get the one life. This is not a rehearsal. None of us are getting out of this alive. Hackneyed and maudlin and trite, yes, but true nevertheless.

This is what he thinks about, night after night in his lonely hotel room, ashamed of his own mawkish self-pity. Here he is, just about at his mid-forties, his life at least half over, who knows how many more years of decent health – physical and/or mental – left to him. This is his reality and with it comes the question, the big question that always ends the self-examination. Where is she? Where is the person he was supposed to be doing this with?

THE FENIAN

The one who was meant to be sitting next to him, holding his hand, reassuring him, sharing the roller coaster ride.

For a while, he believed that person was Ruth. For a while, he was able to make a good fist of convincing himself all that other stuff was just childish nonsense. Ruth even looked vaguely like the real thing – willowy, dark-haired, a hint of bohemian fire and devilment about her. Their eyes met, they would explain sardonically at smart West London parties, across a crowded and smoke-filled conference room. They were both BBC newbies. He a young reporter tossed crumbs by the desk and lucky to get thirty seconds on screen on the rare days when he was able to snare a camera crew. She an intern looking up experts' phone numbers and fetching coffee and sandwiches for the Newsnight team. They began sparking off each other at the brainstorming story and idea sessions, backing up the other's ideas and ignoring the scowls at the temerity of such junior nobodies daring to open their mouths at all. Then, as Robert slowly graduated from the dregs to the odd mid-bulletin story, Ruth got her break at the end of another fourteen-hour day, thrust into the hot seat by a desperate and frazzled producer when the main presenter took violently ill twenty minutes before airtime and his understudy's taxi was side-swiped by a London bus on a junction as he dashed across the city. One eviscerating line was all it took to create Ruth's legend as she interviewed a smug and leering Tory politician who was about to regret lingering in the Commons bar for that extra snifter before going on air.

'Let me repeat the question, Minister,' she said, the camera a magnet on her cold laser eyes. 'And this time, perhaps you could try looking at my face rather than my chest while I ask it.'

She was an instant tabloid star, even if she never once graced them with a quote, let alone an interview. The sub editors had a field day. TV Totty Makes a Tit of Tory took the prize in the first batch of headlines. Within days she was routinely rebranded as Raunchy Ruth. The Sun ran a campaign demanding the Beeb boot out 'the most boring show on telly', and replace it with Nudesnight, starring – who else? – Randy Ruth.

While she seethed at what she called the cheap, sexist coverage, Robert delighted in winding her up by calling her things like *the beauty with brains AND boobs* in his best movie trailer voice. They had been dating for nearly a year by this time and without really knowing how it happened and definitely without anything in the way of hearts and flowers romance, he found himself falling into a wedding.

Not that he was complaining, because they came alive in each other's company, for the sharp wit and the spikiness and the endless fascinating shop talk as much as the fierce, blazing sex. If either of them had given marriage a tenth of the thought and attention they gave to their careers, they'd have realised it was a fire that would soon burn out.

Chapter 13

September 1967. March 1971
A Day In The Life – The Beatles

WHAT was it about Robert exactly? What was his Ingredient X, the vital component that made him the one the rest of us revolved around? What was it that marked him out as our star, the one who would carry the biggest dreams and take them way up there, way above us? What was it that made us all want to please him and be in his good books? He didn't act like he was aware of it. He didn't pick favourites or behave like he was anything special. He just was.

I've sometimes looked back and puzzled about what made him such a prize among the girls and elevated whoever was his flame of the moment. I know it definitely wasn't physical. Robert was kind of, well, all right looking, I suppose. He was probably average height and build, a bit on the scrawny side if anything. Certainly not hard and hunky like Ross or strapping like Big Paddy. The looks thing. He wasn't repulsive or anything, just, you know, stick him in a crowd with his gob zipped and he wouldn't stand out. But get him talking, switching on the charm, and we were putty.

So, what was it Robert had that took us all above the ordinary? That lifted nothing-nights and same-again summer days into events, that made you want to freeze time and stay there with him, hold on to him. Knowing that these were the days that you would talk about and that your time with him had a limit and that you should treasure it, cherish him.

Don't get me wrong, Robert wasn't some kind of superhuman. He wasn't some god walking among us mortals, gracing us with his very presence. Robert had his faults, of course he did. There were rows with him and about him, same as the rest of us. Big issues back then that seem so trivial now. But when arguments broke out, there was only ever going to be one winner because when it came to word combat, Robert was capable of shredding

81

MIKE KERNAN

anyone brave enough to go up against him. He could slice them open,
bamboozle them with language and sheer speed of thought. No matter the
opponent, it came down to the same thing. It was chess grandmaster versus
half-decent draughts player. Every time.

But the downside was that he often didn't know when to stop. Robert's
opponents could throw down their guns, run up the white flag, place their
hands on top of their heads like war prisoners, scream for mercy. But he
would drive on and on.

There was one time when he talked Cammy to a standstill. Can't remember
what it was about. But even when everyone else knew enough was enough,
Robert came back for one last hit, delivered quietly and with an unattractive,
superior sneer.

'Know what, Cammy? I envy you your uncomplicated life, your wonder at
simple things. Like a baby making the connection between switch and light.
That must be what it's like inside your head.'

On he would go, ramming his point home until someone else – usually Big
Paddy – intervened, by kicking a ball at him, hard, or shoving him into the
pool by the waterfall. Or by saying something like: 'All right, keys Robert.
You maybe know fancier words than the rest of us but your da' still works
for Avon.'

Then Robert would realise what he had done and he would be contrite,
mortified. He would spend the rest of the day/night trying to make it up,
siding with whichever poor sod he had just laid flat on the canvas.

Then he had these quirky days when he used to bug us all so much. Days
when no one else was allowed to be funny, as if he had appointed himself
the humour police. The rest of us could crack jokes or ping back what we
thought were dazzling one-liners, quips that would send the rest of us
rocking. But Robert would remain stone-faced, as if it was all beneath him
and he had weightier issues to concern himself with. These were the days
when the crown slipped, or maybe his own well had temporarily run dry.

The humour cop thing emerged a lot with television, which we spent a
disproportionate amount of time discussing. It was as if Robert believed he
was the one who should decide what was cool and what was uncool, what
was genuinely funny, and what wasn't. If you didn't agree, it couldn't be
down to anything as simple as a matter of opinion or taste. You were lacking
somehow, you were wrong, wrong, wrong. He was so dismissive of other
opinions and so utterly certain of his own.

Couple of examples. According to Robert, Monty Python, inevitably, was
tops and that was beyond discussion. It was radical and groundbreaking and
if you didn't get it, you were a moron, end of. Dad's Army was a classic piss-

82

take on the class system. Rising Damp was an amazingly clever satire about racism. On the other hand, On The Buses was cheap crap for the hard of thinking and easily amused and Are You Being Served was an insult to the intelligence and written for crass English folk with no brains. (Bit racist, Robert.) All the while there was hard-of-thinking little me assuming it was much more straightforward than Robert made out. If it made you laugh, it was funny. What was the big deal, it was only telly? First time I told him that, he started to explain, with a patronising semi-smile, that some of the shows he liked were probably over my head, but he stopped abruptly when he noticed the look in my eye and realised castration was a serious and impending possibility.

Yes, Robert had his flaws, like his dress sense, or rather, his complete and utter lack of dress sense. OK, call me shallow, but the rest of the guys at least made an effort so why couldn't he? Our shelter wasn't a catwalk, but it was a sort of matter of respect among the guys for the girls they were with, who *always* made an effort. But not Robert, with his long, untamed hair and jarring colour clashes. Mostly he dressed like he did it in the dark, like his wardrobe was a lucky dip.

Sometimes we'd get into a discussion about clothes, complimenting someone on something new or something revived, or some top that went really well with a skirt or a pair of new jeans. We would get right into it, all of us contributing – the girls *and* the guys. Except Robert. He would look distracted, as if it was all too trivial for him. Then you'd catch him glancing down, as if he had no clue what he was wearing and had to remind himself.

As the cravats and loopy shirts of third year were binned, Robert eventually adopted dark and moody. I think it was supposed to say, *Hey, look how introspective and rebellious I am.* For late-teenage boys anywhere, anytime, rebellious meant black. Black scoop-neck T-shirts, black jeans or cords, and a black – or maybe it was really dark navy – Army greatcoat. Robert rescued it from the bin when his grandfather was having a clear-out. You could tell he loved it and was proud of it. He thought it was so him and it was rarely off his back, even in the warmer months. His only concession to colour? Love beads! Yes, Robert actually wore love beads. Love beads that reflected his sensitive, creative soul. He actually told me that once and, unlike me, nearly kept a straight face.

It all changed when he got his first job, though. Trainee reporter on The Cumbride Courier, our local paper. He got his hair surgically cropped then dived into a phone box and transformed into Shirt and Tie Man. I got that from Paddy, because that was a version of Robert I never saw up close.

Robert was *always* going to be a reporter – a newsman, he called it – as if it was pre-ordained. Most of the rest of us talked about jobs, the more long-term thinkers about careers. But mainly our ambitions changed every five minutes, or else we didn't have any definite ones. Except Robert, oh, and maybe Fiona. She was always pretty certain about going to uni and studying law. Cookie mentioned vague notions about becoming some kind of engineer. But Robert was certain and told me he could pinpoint the exact moment when he first had the calling, or his vocation, as he described it. He could trace it back to an event that happened when he was nine, a year or two after his family moved to Cumbride from Glasgow.

There was some kind of official event happening at the top of his street – the opening of a new health centre, as he learned later. At the time, all it meant to Robert and his pals was a day off school and that in turn meant a day playing football in the swing park. (Yes, our swing park, where the shelter was. *Our* shelter. Only we hadn't moved in yet.)

Robert's recollection of that day was so vivid. His Mum had told him to be in for lunch by half twelve. Like all small boys, hunger was usually enough of a clock for Robert, but he got carried away in the football then had a sudden feeling he was running late for his beans on toast. He set off to sprint the hundred yards or so home from the park but found his way blocked by a mass of people in his street who were shouting, waving and cheering. Robert squeezed his way through the crowd only to find a rope barring his way so he ducked under it and came face to face with a woman. He was anxious about being late but remembered his manners and asked her: 'Excuse me missus, have you got the right time please?'

The woman didn't answer or else she didn't get the chance. A pair of massive hands grabbed Robert by the armpits and hoisted him back over the cordon. Robert stood stock still, shocked and frightened by what had just happened, as the woman and her entourage passed by.

A few seconds later, a man in a grey suit approached, keeping his eyes on Robert as he worked his way through the fast-dispersing crowd. The man crouched and leaned towards Robert and said: 'Hey sonny, what's your name and address?'

The man looked like authority, especially when he produced a pen and notebook, so solemnly, Robert gave his details and went home, too afraid to tell his Mum what had happened.

Later, just after teatime that same day.

Robert was playing in the street with Ross and a few others when his big sister Sandra appeared, bearing a smug *you're-in-huge-trouble* smirk.

She said to him curtly: 'You've to come in, right now. Dad says.'

No point in protesting or asking Sandra for a clue. They had been sworn enemies from the day, he claimed, she had swapped her newly dead tortoise for his all-singing, all-dancing one. Now he trudged home behind her, the condemned boy. He racked his brain. What had he done this time? Maybe it was something to do with that man, the one who had taken his name and address. Was he the police, or had someone told on him for talking to a stranger?

Robert got to the house and immediately, his worst fears were realised. The man was there. He *must* be the police. He was definitely official. He was still wearing the grey suit and he had his shoes on in the house. Mum always made them – Robert, Sandra and their Dad – take their shoes off at the door. The man had the notebook in one hand and his pen in the other. There was another man there too, lugging a silver box, and not as smartly dressed as Mr Grey Suit. He had on a shorter jacket, maybe leather, Robert thought. The two men were standing in the hall, talking to his Mum and Dad.

Robert tried to seize the initiative.

'Honest Dad, I never done nothing. Honest.'

But Mr Grey Suit was friendly and he only looked a *bit* old to Robert, not *really* old like his Mum and Dad.

He said to Robert: 'It's cool beans sonny. You're not in any bother. We're from the paper. It's Robert, isn't it, or do they call you Bob?'

Robert, still nervous, said to the man: 'Is it about the woman? Her in the furry coat?'

Mr Grey Suit said: 'Aye, that's right sonny, it's about the woman in the furry coat.'

He and Leather Jacket swapped grins.

Robert said to his father: 'Honest Dad, I was dead polite. Like you told me. I just said, *Have you got the right time please?* I did say *Please*. Honest I did.'

His Dad reassured him. 'It's OK, Robert. These men are just going to ask you some questions for the newspaper and take your photie.'

Mr Grey Suit asked the first question.

'What it was like sonny, talking to the Queen?'

Robert answered truthfully. 'The Queen? I never spoke to the Queen. I just asked some woman the time.'

Mr Grey Suit asked a few more questions but not really much else about what had happened. More about Robert, his age, what school he went to, what his hobbies were. Leather Jacket produced a big camera and took about twenty photos, Robert reckoned. Then they left.

Next morning, it was a huge event, and Robert was at the centre of it. His Mum went to the shop early, before he and Sandra left for school, and came back carrying about a dozen copies of the Daily Record.

Nearly eight years later, when Robert told me about his first brush with newspapers, it was clear the incident was a huge moment in his life and that much of it still rankled. He showed me the cutting one Sunday when his parents were out. He produced a cardboard box from the wardrobe in his room and sifted through its contents. It was stuffed with old photos, football programmes, a stamp album, a few foreign coins, some kind of small animal skull, school reports and battered jotters. Finally, he came across a folded-up sheet of newspaper and said: 'This is it, Lorna.'

Robert unfolded the cutting carefully and spread it out on the floor. The Daily Record. September 20, 1967. It was faded but still in good condition. Staring sternly out at Record readers was a younger, chubby-cheeked, freckly version of Robert, his straggly brown hair at least partially straightened with a watered comb. The story was on the front page, not the main item but a column down the left-hand side. I saw the headline in capital letters down four rows. Then that funny little photo, embellished with square glasses and a Hitler moustache in red ink. 'That was Sandra,' he snarled.

I started to read the article, but Robert jumped in and recited it without looking, word-perfect. God knows how many hundreds of times he must have read it over the years.

LITTLE
BOBBY
ESCORTS
QUEEN
By TOM BARR

WHAT do you do if you're a cheeky wee eight-year-old, just 3ft 9in tall, and you're desperate to meet the Queen?

Take a leaf out of little Bobby Kane's book, that's what.

Plucky Bobby found his way barred by crowds, barriers and police yesterday when Her Majesty made a right royal visit to his street.

The Queen – who will launch the QE2 at Govan Shipyard today – was in Cumbride to open a new health centre as part of her tour of Scotland.

But the sea of people who had turned out to catch a glimpse of HRH wasn't going to halt the determined little mite, who is a Primary Four pupil at St Jude's School in the New Town.

Brave Bobby didn't want to miss out on this once-in-a-lifetime chance to see the Queen up close.

THE FENIAN

He fought and shoved his way through the crowd, vaulted over the cordon...

...and found himself face to face with Royalty.

Bold little Bobby grinned at her and asked: 'Would you like me to show you round, Your Majesty?'

But her special police guard dashed in and whisked him away.

Last night Bobby, who lives near the scene at 3A Leeburn Road, Cumbride, said: 'I've always wanted to meet the Queen and she was as lovely as I thought she would be.

'And anyway, I knew she wouldn't scold me.'

I smiled warmly, part pride, part gentle amusement, as Robert finished his recital. But he shook his head dismissively.

'Total garbage,' he said. 'My Mum and Dad thought it was great. Mum saved a copy for my Grandma, and sent one to my Auntie Morag in Canada. Another copy went to some of their friends down in England.

"It was even read out at school. They had a special assembly for it and the headmaster kept repeating the bit about me being a pupil at St Jude's. That was about the only thing in the whole story that was true. The rest was a fairy tale.'

Then Robert produced something else from the same box where the cutting had been stored. It was a sheet of paper and I glimpsed small, neat handwriting.

'Have a look at this as well, Lorna,' he said, grinning. 'This'll give you a real laugh. It's a letter I wrote when I was 13 to the Editor of the Record. That story had been bugging me for four years by then. I never posted it, thank God. It's such a red neck when I think about it now.'

3A Leeburn Road,
Cardrum,
Cumbride,
14/04/1971

Dear Sir,
I enclose an article from your paper, dated September 20, 1967. I would like to draw your attention to a number of serious inaccuracies in this story.
1. The headline. I have never in my life escorted any member of the Royal Family.
2. I was nine years old at the time of the alleged incident, not eight as your story states.
3. I was not 3ft 9in at the time of the alleged incident. I was at least 4ft 2in tall.

4. My name is Robert. I am known to every person of my acquaintance as Robert and always have been. I have never been known as or referred to by the short-form Bobby. I did not give my name as Bobby to your correspondent.

5. At no time have I ever been desperate to meet the Queen or indeed any other member of the Royal Family. (Please note, we are still only on the first sentence.)

6. I did not fight or shove anyone during the alleged incident. In any case if I had been, as your article states erroneously, only 3ft 9in (which I was not, see Point No 2) then surely I would have been incapable of pushing a crowd of adults around.

7. I did not vault over the cordon. I ducked under it.

8. I did not offer to show the Queen, or indeed anyone, around during the alleged incident. Leaving aside the crucial point that the alleged incident did not happen, I have been taught never to go off with strangers.

9. I repeat (I refer you back to Point No 4), that I have never had any desire to meet the Queen. Furthermore, I did not even know the woman involved in the alleged incident was the Queen and made this abundantly clear to your correspondent.

10. Every single quote attributed to me in this story is a complete figment of your correspondent's imagination. For example, I have never used the word 'scold' in my life.

In conclusion, it appalls and saddens me to report no less than ten serious inaccuracies in such a brief article. I trust you will immediately dismiss the reporter concerned, and ensure that the rest of your staff are taught the importance of sticking to facts in the future.

Yours sincerely,

Mr Robert Kane

Robert shook his head wryly and said: 'What an obnoxious, pompous little twat, eh? The language, the alleged this and the alleged that. And apart from anything else, signing myself Mister? At 13! I still cringe when I think how close I was to posting that letter. And here's the real irony, Lorna. Do you know why I never sent it? Because I couldn't bear to part with the cutting.'

Robert might well have been saddened and appalled by his first contact with newspapers and newspaper people but, as he eventually acknowledged, he was also hooked. The thirteen-year-old Robert – if not the nine-year-old – was fascinated by the idea that you could do this as a real job. As in, go to people's houses and ask them questions then write it all down and see it in the paper the next day. I suspected that in some way he quietly admired what they had done to him – the *total bollocks* they had written.

He admitted as much to me the day he showed me the newspaper clipping.

'I kind of thought, wow, you could just come across something a wee bit different or a wee bit special. And the idea would come to you – the whole story in your head right away, just like that. You wouldn't let anything as trivial as the truth get in the way. All you needed was a name and a couple of bits of detail to make your story work, make it sound real. And if you're making folk famous, who's going to complain if you exaggerate a wee bit?'

The cutting explained one of Robert's more annoying habits in our shelter gang days – repeating stories from newspapers. He knew no one else really bothered about the papers, apart from the football pages (guys) and the showbiz stuff (girls). Robert knew we weren't really interested, but he would insist on telling us about these stories he had read.

Hey, did you read about that old man of a hundred and two in Ireland who hasn't stopped sneezing for thirty-four years?

See that story about the ten-year-old girl in Canada who was trapped in her house by snow for seven weeks and had to eat her pet dog and dead granny to survive?

Read the one about the cow that fell out an aeroplane's cargo hold and landed on a fishing boat and sunk it?

Yes, Robert had obsessions. Celtic was another one. Not that he was alone there – Big Paddy was just as bad if not worse and Ross and Cookie were the same with Rangers. Cammy claimed that he supported Motherwell but finally confessed it was because he liked a stupid joke that Jo had told him once. *Who made Rangers? God. Who made Celtic? The Devil.* (Or the other way round, depending on your persuasion.) *And who made Motherwell? The doctor.*

Robert's other big passion was music. He decided earlier than most of us that pop was just for kids and was something to scoff at. I think the rest of us eventually reached a similar conclusion but not to the same extreme. Chart stuff was fine for parties, but the rest of the time we switched to albums. An album cover tucked under your arm became a must-have fashion accessory. We liked to think we had moved on to *proper* music but unlike Robert, it didn't become an article of faith for the rest of us. He got heavily into one particular band. Can't remember which one now. Might have been Genesis or the one that sounded like a firm of accountants – Something Something and Palmer. Anyway, it was one of those big, flashy prog rock monster groups who were massive in the Seventies till punk came along and turned them into lepers. The thing about Robert was, he couldn't just be a fan, he had to be Superfan. He had to track down everything they had ever done and everything ever written about them – every single, every concept album, every bootleg, every magazine cutting. He couldn't just listen to the music either, he had to study it then lecture on it…endlessly. Their symphonies, their song cycles, their word-painting lyrics. *His words, not mine.* He'd put one of their albums on the stereo but wait, don't place the needle on, not just yet. He had to spend ten minutes telling you what to listen out for. That ten-second synthesizer burst six minutes and 42 seconds in, right after the fiddly drum and bass bit. Eventually he'd get round to actually playing you one of their songs, only he didn't call them songs. They weren't like the kiddie pop bands he sneered at. No, his favourite group *performed movements* – often a good 20 minutes' worth. Then Robert would settle in for a post mortem and be disappointed when he found no takers.

Mainly, the rest of us just wanted something with a beat, something that rocked. Music to dance to or at least tap your feet to. Brown Eyed Girl or Jeepster, that kind of thing, or else a snogging-with-the-lights-out backing track. Dark Side of the Moon did it for most of us, especially the long bit on Side One with that girl wailing like she's either in pain or having a really good time. But Robert would listen to something like that and want to write a thesis on it.

Hey, I'm getting really picky here. I'm just desperately trying to find holes, to knock him down a bit and stop myself painting this picture of perfection.

Because Robert did have...something. I never did figure out what exactly. I want to say power, or maybe I want to say charisma. But I don't want to create the wrong idea. He wasn't some crazed cult leader. It was nothing as heavy as that. If it was power – *if* – then it was gentle, benign, a way of coaxing us, calming us, bonding us. We looked to him for guidance because he was our centre. I supposed you could simply call it personality but that's too trite, too throwaway.

Robert had a way of looking at you, shining those deep-set brown eyes at you, into you. It was so hard to resist – or ha, maybe that was just me. Then there was the musical voice. Always the right words. Not just the catchphrases he coined, not just the lightning one-liners. Maybe it was what became known later as spinning, like it was some kind of trick. *Was it a trick?* He could put things in such a way, such an overwhelming, persuasive way, that it became virtually impossible to argue, almost impossible not to go along with him. Sometimes it wasn't even the words but the very sound of Robert, his tone, the melody of his voice.

Sometimes I get my timescales out of whack. (Yes, I admit it again, I do.) Sometimes I think this must have been something Robert learned, something they taught on newspapers. But Robert was like that at fifteen.

Bottom line, he was our special one, even then, and that's why it felt like it didn't fit, didn't make sense. *Robert and me.* Robert, our hub, the shining sun in our little universe. Him and little, quiet, nothing me.

I'm serious. This isn't me being modest, it's how I genuinely felt. I thought the rest of them all had *something*. Ross: his looks, his natural ability at just about any sport. Big Paddy: his physical presence and instinctive protectiveness. Jo: her addictive energy, her comedy. Kirsty: her sheer, unabashed sexiness. Even Cammy: his sorrowful, *aw there there, let me make it better,* puppy dog cuteness.

I couldn't see anything special about me. Sometimes I'd fret that the rest just tolerated me because I had always been there, because I had been a founding member. I couldn't see what I brought to the party. I couldn't see what Robert saw in me and yet, he turned it all on its head. He elevated me, he placed a status and a value on me that I had done nothing to earn.

Those months of fear when I thought he wouldn't notice me? He flipped that into a mirror image I didn't recognise. Told me he'd dreaded I would never take him seriously, that I'd always seen him as nothing more than the class clown. Robert said things to me that guys weren't supposed to say, words that overwhelmed me. He told me I was his whole world, the core of his life. Yeah, sounds corny when I repeat it now but back then, the way he said it, I took it seriously and at face value. He told me that everything he said, everything he did, he worried about whether or not *I* approved. Whether *I* was impressed. He called me his saviour, said I was this bar of gold he carried everywhere, a background lightness deep inside him, the salvation that got him through everything. I was his lifeline through every worry and problem – savage rows with his father, the constant threat of random violence at school, the dragging discipline and focus that didn't come naturally as he struggled through his O Grades and Highers. He told me *I* was the one who got him through all of that. *I* was the one who helped him survive. He told me that no matter how bad things got, how low and squeezed and drained he felt, it was OK, because he had something outstanding in his life, something bigger. He once told me something I have never forgotten. I can recall it word for word.

'I just think, what the hell. Let all this shite happen. I've got something nobody else has got. I've got you. That's what drives me on. Christ, most of the time it's the only thing that keeps me going.'

For that time – *our* brief time, our eleven weeks – I was utterly convinced I was involved in something so huge and so important, because that teenage boy gave me such a status, a worth that no one else has ever placed on me, an intensity of living I have never rediscovered.

Now that same memory makes me feel so small – the realisation that it was the best time of my life and it was there and gone so swiftly. Now, all those people and events and frittered years later, here I am, still waiting. Crazy, eh? My fortieth behind me, fifty the next biggie and yet I'm still waiting to feel and be felt about that way again but knowing with a certainty that I'm wasting my time, knowing it will never happen now. The truth of it is painful. The awareness that no one – and I mean no one – has ever or will ever live up to what we had, Robert and me, during that brief snapshot in our lives. No one has come even close to living up to it. Least of all, me.

Chapter 14

January 1971. August 2001
Breathless – The Corrs

YOU bastard Paddy. You big bad bastard. All those years, all those times we've bumped into each other, all those brief, snatched conversations. Me asking about your Mum and Dad, about your wife, about your kids. Lisa and Bobby – Christ, Bobby. Short for Robert? Me asking about your job, you asking about my work, about my Dad, about my husband(s).

Not once, never a mention, not even a hint. All you had to do was give me a single clue, Paddy. All you had to say one of those times was, *Remember Robert? We had some laughs, eh.* Or, *Mind that Robert Kane? He's coming up for the game on Saturday.*

That would have been my cue to say something like, *Tell him I'm asking for him.* You know, same as he told you to say to me.

But would Robert have got the message, Paddy? Would you have told Robert that Lorna from his faraway past wished him well? And how would he have reacted? Hmm, I bet at least a little more eloquently than me. I'm positive he would have come up with something a little more imaginative than my, *That's nice.*

But you didn't crack a light, Paddy. Not once. You just let me go on thinking Robert's out of reach. He's untouchable, he's a million galaxies from my world. You kept him all to yourself.

OK, got that out of my system. Sorry, Paddy. I'm so sorry. Honestly, I am. I owe you a full, unreserved apology because it's not your fault, not your fault at all. The blame is mine, utterly and completely. Because at what point over the years did I ever say to you, *Remember Robert? I saw him on the telly again the other night. Isn't he doing well for himself?*

That would have been *your* cue to let me know, to let me in on your secret

93

world. The secret world of Robert that used to be mine. So yes, I'm sorry, Paddy. But you have to see, I have to make you understand. The truth is, I'm jealous. I'm fucking jealous. There, said it. I'm so jealous that I'm ashamed. So, so jealous that you still have him and I don't.

That lovely boy, that teenager who gave me something no grown man has ever come close to touching. That closeness, our so-special closeness. It was once mine, Paddy, but now it's yours and it's been yours all these years. I'm jealous Paddy. I'm jealous of your trips to London. I'm jealous of you two sitting up long into the night, with your heads close together for long hours after your wives have gone to bed, with the lights dimmed, with your clinking glasses. Your shared past and your shared present, your shared future. Your long, long talks. Catching up, looking back, looking forward.

Why do you get to be the ones to keep alive the spirit of the swing park? Our youth belonged to me as well, Paddy. It belonged to all of us.

I'm jealous of your New Years, Paddy. Two kindred Scots among the Cockneys. I can almost hear your defiant *Flower of Scotland* – you two against the bewildered Londoners. I'm jealous of your airport reunions, your backslaps and your handshakes. Your football comradeship, your pre-match pints in some raucous, crowded bar near the ground, your shoulder-to-shoulders at the game, your shared worship of the Swedish guy the papers rave about. I'm jealous of your farewells, your till-the-next-time promises. Promises that you keep on keeping.

Paddy, you big, bad bastard. I'm jealous and I hate myself for it. That shameful, wasteful, bitter tumour of an emotion.

Wait till you hear this one. I'm jealous of your wife too, Paddy. The wife that you adore. A woman I've spoken to, what, half a dozen times in all those years you've been married? A woman whose life I only dip into second-hand for those few minutes whenever we bump into each other. Why has *she* got more of Robert than me? I was Robert's special one, remember? But she's had more of him than I ever had, so many more years of Robert than the three I had. Your wife has an ongoing stake in Robert. She has cradled his child, he has held hers. She hugs him, he kisses her cheek. Your wife is part of his life, but she wasn't the one who sat with Robert on our wall, learning how to talk, learning how to love.

You know what else Paddy? You know the absolute worst thing about this? You are innocent, your wife is innocent too. I like your wife, always have. Your wife is a kind, pleasant, friendly, shining person and she doesn't deserve this from me. She has done nothing to earn my rank, spitting bitterness.

But I can't help it. I'm jealous of all that stuff, Paddy. Everything. All that stuff I've just invented to go with this imaginary tirade I'm dishing out to you as I lie here in bed, not sleeping but lying wide awake. Alone.

Then, as sleep refuses to come and take away the bad thoughts, I start to wonder some more. About you and Ruth, Paddy. Don't get me wrong here, I don't mean anything complicated or more than friendship. I just wonder, do you like her, do the two of you get on? Is she an important person in your life, in her own right, I mean, not just as your best mate's missus? Do you get on the phone, the two of you, you and Ruth? Does she ring you and ask for ideas for *Robbie's* birthday? You know, trivial friends' stuff like that. Are you and your wife and Robert, sorry Robbie, and Ruth a tight, cosy foursome?

Then, of course, that gets me thinking about your wife and Ruth. Your strong, sharp, small-town wife, the one who loves you for everything you are and who always knew better than to try and tame you. I wonder about her relationship with Robert's wife, ruthless Ruth, with her big-time contacts in high places, her power-dressing, her she-balls, her need to stay on top and rule over her late-night sacrificial TV altar. What could they possibly have in common, Ruth and your wife? What do they talk about?

Yet that relationship, your wife and Ruth – whatever form it takes – couldn't be a stranger pairing than you two, Paddy. You and Robert.

I think about Robert's world. Airports, hotels, Prime Ministers and Presidents, TV studios, satellite links, camera crews, front lines and foreign capitals.

Compare that to your world. Petty crime and football and family, a cup of tea with your mum on Fridays, a few pints down the pub, still a PC in your forties.

I'm sorry, and let me be clear, I don't mean that to be condescending. If truth be told, I envy you that life, more than you could know. But come on, the TV high-flier and the beat bobby?

Then a flash and I sit up in bed. I was wrong about the first time I saw Robert on TV, and just maybe this ties in with you, Paddy, gives me a clue to your enduring friendship.

The exact when of this is all a bit muddled but at first I think it was before I got married, because I know I was watching the news on telly at home in Cumbride, with my Dad. But that doesn't fit because Robert was working on one of the big papers in Glasgow when this happened and I was married to Bill by then. Right, think about it, figure it out. Of course, there is a simple explanation. It must have been on one of my visits to Dad.

The background was that Robert had written a big story for whatever paper he was on. I can't remember the details but it was something to do with corruption in the police, possibly money changing hands to drop charges against somebody important. A few cops ended up in court because of it and Robert was summoned to appear as a witness. It came down to a leaked document or statement that he had gotten hold of. Robert sort of became the story because he refused to reveal who gave him the information – protecting his source, they called it. They said on the news that he could be charged with contempt and even end up in jail himself but he wouldn't give in and it became the talk of the steamie, the big issue for a few days. In the end, he didn't go to jail and it all seemed to fizzle out, as if some kind of deal had been worked out behind the scenes.

It was on the Scottish news and Robert was portrayed as a kind of hero for sticking to his principles. It thrilled me, probably because my memories hadn't been too soured or scarred by that time. I remember seeing him on the TV, coming out of the court, with people crowding around him and shaking his hand. In a small way, it felt like something to do with me because I knew him. Robert was talking about an important victory for Press freedom.

But my Dad gave a sarcastic laugh and said: 'Victory for Press freedom? Victory for Robert Kane more like. You watch, that'll be the making of the boy.'

'You think so?' I kept my voice neutral.

'Defintootly. You missed out there, Lorna. You should have stuck with that lad. Going places, so he is.'

Why didn't you tell Mum that, Dad?

I should have let it pass, but I couldn't. Because this was how it worked with us. It was never really brought into the open. The promise, the one Mum had made me make. The big, unmentionable Protestant-Catholic thing had become a conspiracy of whispers.

I tried to pick up little clues over the years, clues to the why, so I asked him: 'Would that have bothered you, Dad?'

'How do you mean?' He looked genuinely puzzled as if he had already left the subject behind and moved on.

'If I'd stuck with Robert Kane. You know, him being a Catholic.'

'Aw, was he?' replied Dad, then he either ducked the issue or told me an outright lie. 'Don't think I ever knew what he was.'

I pressed him.

'But would it, Dad? Would it have bothered you? What if Bill was a Catholic?'

He squirmed. He hated being put on the spot like this.

'Ach, it's a load of shite all that stuff,' he said and reached for his paper and tried to hide behind it, obviously wanting to get off the subject fast.

96

I persisted. 'But I thought you and Mum never approved. You know, mixed marriages and all that.'

'That was all your mother really. OK, it's maybe no' the best but it's no' that big a deal nowadays. No' really.'

I refused to let it go.

'So, what was Mum's problem with Catholics then?'

He hated this. That was obvious enough and I promised myself, this would be the last question because with the questioning came the guilt, putting my Dad in the witness box like this, and for what? To damn my mother, to damn his dead wife? He backtracked.

'Och, it wasn't really her either. More a family thing. Hers and mine. It's just the way things are, the way we've – they've – kept things. It doesn't really matter. It's no' something you want to get into, Lorna.'

You mean it's not something you want to get into, Dad. But OK, enough, I wasn't getting anywhere. I wasn't learning anything new, or else I didn't like what I was learning and maybe I hated the questions it made me ask myself. Was this all I had altered the course of my life for, given up Robert for? *A family thing.* A diseased hand-me-down? Where did that leave my Dad or rather, my sense of him? Was I left seeing him as some kind of fair-minded father content to let this heirloom of hatred dilute or even wither with him? Or was that giving him too much credit? Was he just speaking from a place of safety, a place where his only daughter was happily wed to a good solid Protestant? Or perhaps even that was too complicated and he was just a guy quick and willing to betray his wife's memory for a quiet life.

But then he surprised me by picking up the baton without a prompt and launching into what was probably the longest speech I ever heard him give.

'Look, Lorna,' he started, putting the paper down. 'Don't get me wrong. There's some decent ones. Frankie and Margaret, you know, the Allans. Helluva nice folk, brand new. We always got on fine with them. I still do. And there's one or two Celtic boys at the work are OK. Good for a bit of banter and that, nothing serious. But it's just, you know, Catholics in general. I could see your mother's point – and her family's. I mean, the reason they couldn't abide them. Thing is, they're a bunch of bigots.'

Wow, hang on, Dad, let me try and get my head round that.

'If that's what you think,' I said, feeling my way. 'Calling them bigots like that. Doesn't that make you just as bad? Are you not being a bigot by saying that?'

'Nah, you don't understand pet.'

I'd heard that before somewhere and yeah Dad, you're spot on, I don't. Explain it then.

'Thing about them is,' he went on. 'They glory in their suffering. They revel in it. Their wee sorrowful faces and their mortal sins and their penance. All this, poor wee us, look how they big bad Protestants have oppressed us. Makes you sick. Like they supposed oppressed murdering bastards bringing their bombs across the water. They poor souls in Birmingham and Guildford. But they'll no' be so brave or so daft as to try it up here. Aye, and we'll soon sort them out if they do.'

I'd never seen Dad like this before. My quiet do-as-your-told-don't-upset-folk Dad in full rant mode. And ready to take up arms! He raced on, pouring it all it now.

'I'll tell you another thing. Mind the disaster. At Ibrox?'

'Course I do.'

I was twelve when it happened. Day after New Year, 1971. A stairway collapsed at the Old Firm game. Sixty-six fans dead at the Rangers end. I remember my Mum and Big Paddy's Mum huddled around our telly, comforting each other as they waited for news flashes, anxious for word of their men. No mobile phones then, of course. Both had been at the game, separately, divided by the blue and the green. But as it turned out, both were safe, in other parts of the ground far from the carnage.

Now Dad had his own, righteous take on it.

'I was out with your mother no' long after it happened. Few weeks maybe. Down the pub. There's a bunch of *them* at a table near us. They start talking about it and they're no' caring who's listening. Now this is not a word of a lie, Lorna, but one of them goes, *Sixty-six? Wouldn't be enough if it was six hundred and sixty-six.* There. That's your goody-goody poor-wee-me Catholics for you.'

Dad shook his paper, moved it back in front of his face, and I thought he was done, but no, he pulled it down again. There was an encore.

'And how about they poor starving weans you did that sponsored walk for at the school, mind? Biafra, Ethiopia, whatever it was. The bones sticking out their skin. The Catholic Church is quick to sell them bibles and heebie-jeebie beads, but I didn't see their precious Pope put his hand in his pocket and give them a gold throne or one of his priceless paintings to flog for food.'

Dear me. I'd dowsed for clues and landed up to my neck in a mire of unfathomable bitterness – and all because I'd seen Robert on telly.

What had got me on to that, again, that memory of Dad's rant? Ah yes, Robert and Big Paddy, the enigma of a friendship that had survived the years and their far-distant, so disparate life paths. What age would Robert have been on the night my Dad and I first saw him on TV? Very early twenties, must have been. Had Big Paddy joined the cops by then? They said on the news that Robert had been *protecting his source,* so was there a debt lurking around somewhere in the back of their friendship? Was a debt like that enough to hang a lifetime friendship on? Even a big award-winning, career-making debt?

God knows, it wouldn't have been the first time Robert had owed Big Paddy in a big way.

Chapter 15

August 1974-September 1974
I Shot The Sheriff – Eric Clapton

OBERT was terrified. At best, he faced getting his head kicked in. At worst, he could be slashed, maybe scarred for life. The other guys from our school – Cookie, Ross, Cammy – did their best to ease Robert's fears. Not.

Cookie: 'He's the best fighter in the school by a mile. Everybody pure craps it from him.'

Ross: 'They say he hides a chib in his sock.'

Cookie: 'Aye, and a hammer up his jumper.'

Cammy: 'That's right enough about the knife. Stabbed a sixth year in the ear just for talking to a burd he fancied and that's far less what you done, so it is.'

Ross: 'Done the boy's da' as well. The man went to his house to complain and *he* came to the door. Stuck the head on the guy even though he was twice the size. Put him in the hospital along with his boy.'

He was Danny Lee. Dano. Born to be wild, bad and mad, with a reputation to match. Legend had it his malevolent side first showed itself as a six-year-old when, with a dull smile, he squeezed a kitten to the brink of death at a classmate's birthday party. More lately, he had graduated to punching random dogs in the street, staring down their owners and asking what the fuck they were going to do about it.

Now that trainee psychopath was coming to vent his violent craziness on our Robert. Yes, Robert, who had never met Dano in his puff, never even clapped eyes on him. But Robert, without knowledge or intention, had crossed Dano – and his crime was Kirsty.

Her favours had become famous all over our school and Dano had decided he wanted a piece of the action. He asked Kirsty out one Friday and she stalled but didn't turn him down outright. Everyone knew Dano was mental, bordering on the evil, but he was a name, a somebody. Jo said some people were claiming Kirsty had led Dano on. What, our butter-wouldn't-melt Kirsty? Surely not!

Robert knew nothing about any of this. It had happened at our school and Robert, of course, was at St Joe's, the Catholics. But he and Kirsty had got together at a party on the Saturday – the day after Dano asked her out. (Yes, we called them parties by this time because, obviously, we were so much more mature.) Robert and Kirsty had taken advantage of the party amnesty and who knows how, but word filtered back to Dano. He swore revenge and he was coming to our bit, to sort out *the bastard pape that stole ma burd*.

So maybe I was wrong then. Maybe religion did make its way on to our agenda, at least when outsiders intruded.

Robert was petrified. He was never a fighter. Words were his weapons. But he turned up as usual at the shelter on the Monday night after the party, caught between two fears – saving his skin and saving face. Maybe Robert thought he could negotiate with Dano, talk his way out of it. As if. Might as well try to bargain with a starving crocodile. Now he looked like he was sitting on death row.

Let me explain the geography. Our shelter was a kind of recess set in a high wall surrounding the swing park on three sides. You turned the corner from the shelter on one side and disappeared behind the wall into a short blind alley, which made it a convenient blind spot for snogging. But in the other direction, there was a footpath which led out of the swing park and rose gently. We could see it for about 30 yards or so until it reached a short tunnel, a kind of passageway under a block of flats. Anyone approaching the shelter had to come that way, so no one could take us by surprise. We were ambush-proof.

Tension. Eleven pairs of eyes took turns to glance up towards the underpass, watching and waiting. We were seriously afraid for Robert but at the same time, there was the sense of a tiny bit of bloodlust betraying the usual protective bond. It got to just after nine and Robert began to relax. The light had all but faded and already the yellow street lights were casting a glow across the swing park. Dano surely wouldn't come now and besides, Robert had stuck it out long enough to show he hadn't crapped out of it. He could find an excuse easily enough and go home. Cue himself an exit, like an essay he had to finish for school tomorrow. Most of us, I like to think, shared the sense of relief. But it was premature.

Ross said suddenly: 'Robert, you better shoot mate.'

We all looked up. There he was, the gunslinger strolling into town, his

101

ominous shadow backlit against the tunnel. Now he had his bearings and was striding confidently towards us. There was one escape route for Robert – an awkward clamber on to the slightly lower wall at the end of the snogging spot, then a dreepie into the street and a clear run for home. But Robert seemed rooted to the spot.

Dano got closer, no let-up in his pace. You had to give the guy his due. He was walking into bad odds – five-to-one against, or more for all he knew. But then again, his reputation had got here on an earlier bus. He was almost at the shelter now. Robert had turned white.

'I'm no' kidding Robert,' urged Ross. 'Run. He'll kick your head in or cut you open.'

Dano was only a dozen or so yards away. He wasn't a big guy but trailing from him was a fuse of violence just begging to be ignited. We could see his face now. Aggressive, sharp, feral, ice-cube eyes. Jo could never stop herself, whatever the circumstances.

'It's life,' she stage-whispered. 'But not as we know it.'

Robert, funnily enough, was not comforted by her flippancy and shook visibly. All the while, Big Paddy had been kicking a ball against the wall outside the shelter. Casually, he picked it up, sauntered inside, went up to Robert and said quietly: 'Sit where you are, don't move a muscle. And see just for once in your life…'

Big Paddy drew a zip along his lips then sat down next to Kirsty, right up close. Cammy, sitting on Kirsty's other side, slithered away from her.

The gunslinger marched straight into the shelter, hands at his hips as if ready to draw.

'The fuck's the Kane cunt?'

Just a snarl. No preamble, no build-up. This was business, serious business, no point wasting time on introductions. Dano, after all, was not here to expand his social circle. He planted himself, legs slightly apart, five foot six of bristling menace. Casually, Big Paddy Allan got to his feet. Six foot four of bristling menace.

He snarled back: 'Kane? That'll be me. The fuck wants to know?'

Dano's dead eyes bulged at this giant staring him down. He looked puzzled. This did not compute. He had obviously been given a wrong description. In an instant, a bottle crashed. Quietly, but not so quietly we didn't all hear it.

Then Big Paddy did an amazing thing. He handed Dano an out, and even with a little dignity. He strode over to the intruder, still bouncing the ball with one hand and actually placed his other great paw on Dano's shoulder. The rest of us sat, open-mouthed. Right at that moment, Big Paddy invented his hip-crouch trick and patented it.

THE FENIAN

He cracked his face a touch and said: 'What do you fancy, pal? Square go or a game of fitba?'

Big Paddy hadn't looked at Robert. Not once. Strange thing was, that night never made it into our folklore. That was one tale Robert never weaved. But to be fair, he took his turn at being Big Paddy's bodyguard, especially at school.

Fiona told us about one particular teacher at St Joe's. He was a priest, I think, only they called him a Brother, not Father. Maybe a monk, then. I never knew the difference to be honest. Some vague Catholic hierarchy. According to Fiona, he had a reputation as a cruel, cutting kind of guy and he wore a black robe in class. Sadist in a Smock, Robert called him, with his knack for catchphrases. He and Big Paddy got this teacher, Brother Bernard, for Religious Education.

Let me be clear about something. When it came to instinct or cool, Big Paddy had few equals. But he'd admit himself that he wasn't exactly cut out for articulating his innermost thoughts. Not back then, anyway. He didn't have the words which, honestly, is not meant as a slight. It's just the way he was, the way he was built. But Robert did and when the occasion demanded it, he had enough words for both of them. When Big didn't swing it, Robert's tongue was their shield. Not exactly Of Mice and Men but somewhere in the same postcode.

Anyway, this teacher, this Brother Bernard, was always giving Big Paddy a rough ride. He used Big Paddy to give the rest of the class time to work out their answers to the questions he always started his lessons with – the kind of questions that would make you examine your personal relationship with God. Fiona told us that and she almost managed to stop her sincere expression slipping.

It would be a question like, *You're on the bus home from school. God gets on and sits beside you. It's two minutes to your stop. You've got two minutes to tell God what's gone wrong with the world he created and what he should do about it. Now, what are you going to say?*

These Roman Catholic teenagers were supposed to be fascinated. They were supposed to look deep inside themselves at the whole me-God-creation-morality business. But R.E. was the last lesson before lunch and their innermost thoughts did not stretch much beyond whether to get a roll and cold pie or make do with a Mars Bar and two single fags.

For his part, the Brother didn't want wisecracks. He didn't want some little smart-arse winking at his mates and saying, *Sir, I'd tell God, how did you let Rangers beat Celtic last week? And then I'd tell him to destroy Ibrox with a bolt of lightning, Sir.*

No, the Brother didn't want that, didn't want his lessons wasted. The Brother wanted stunning, sparkling insights. He didn't expect them, if he was realistic, but if there was to be any chance of even a spark of wisdom being produced, it would take time. So, he gave the class time, and maybe he entertained himself a little too, by picking on Big Paddy. He had taken Big Paddy for English back in second year so he knew him and his limited capabilities of old.

The Brother would patrol Big Paddy's desk and say something like: 'Let's get a little help here first. Let's ask the Great Thinker. Let's hear what the class philosopher has to say on the subject.'

When, inevitably, he was met with silence, he would stand over Big Paddy and say: 'C'mon Allan. Can't hear you, Allan. Speak up laddy.'

Big Paddy would quickly sink into misery. He would squirm, defeated and humiliated, and everybody who sat behind him would know it because his ears would turn hot and purple. It happened the first time they got the Brother for R.E. that term. The second time, a week later, Robert was ready for him.

Sadist in a Smock had set the day's question with a smug grin.

'Cast your minds back to primary school. The very first question in your Catechism? Remember your Catechisms? Who Made You? That was the first question. And the answer? That's right, God Made Me. But tell me this, who made God? Where did HE come from? And when did he start?'

Pleased with himself, Brother Bernard left the others to figure it out and made a beeline for Big Paddy.

'Ah, Mr Allan,' he said. 'I'm sure your less intellectually endowed compadres here would all find it fascinating to hear your thoughts on...'

'Sir, Sir!'

He stopped and spun on his heels, aghast at an interruption to his rehearsed and honed taunting. Robert, who sat a few desks away from Big Paddy, had lobbed a grenade at the Brother's feet to draw his fire.

'Sir, Sir,' he repeated.

Or maybe it was, Brother, Brother? Fiona's admittedly second-hand account wasn't clear on the point.

Robert half-stood and put his hand up to get the teacher's attention. The Brother, clearly irked, said: 'Problem Kane? Not understand the question, laddy? Want me to try it again in Swahili?'

'It's not that, Sir.' Robert spoke slowly, politely and deliberately, almost dumbly. 'Just wondered if I could ask a question, um, about the afterlife Sir. It's something that's really been bothering me.'

The monk, in his short-lived innocence, was intrigued, a little pleased even.

104

THE FENIAN

What was this? A thinker, a self-starter, in this class of imbeciles?

'Go on then, Kane, let's hear your question.'

'It just Sir, well, I know there's life after death and all that. But is there, eh, sex after death?'

The Brother's eyebrows creased, first at Robert's question then at the handful of sniggers from around the class. Robert rushed on before he could be halted.

'It's just that I was thinking, Sir, about eternal life and everything. You wouldn't need sex to propagate the species, would you? In Heaven, I mean. But all those girls, them that don't stick to the rules – sorry, the Commandments – about sex and that. If they're all going to be in Hell, maybe that's a more attractive option. Just wondering what you think, Sir?'

The Brother's face matched Big Paddy's ears at critical mass.

'A more attractive option?' he bellowed. 'Are you seriously calling eternal damnation a more attractive option, laddy?'

The Brother's words were lost though. The sniggers had grown to uproar and Big Paddy was forgotten, for the moment at least.

It developed into a tactical battle. Every lesson, Brother asked question, Brother pounced on Big Paddy, Robert's hand shot up, Robert tossed another bombshell.

Big Paddy told us once about his favourite, the day Sadist in a Smock tried to nudge them towards a serious discussion/lecture on the evils of self-abuse without actually spelling it out. It just had to be Robert who got to his feet and asked: 'Sir, is it true that every time you masturbate, God kills a puppy?'

Then, finally, Robert being Robert, he had to go too far.

The Brother was in the process of pushing Big Paddy to breaking point, leaning over him, goading and taunting. Big Paddy's huge ham fists were bunched beneath his desk and he was trying so hard to keep them trapped under there. The class held its collective breath. They could see it coming. They were going to be witnesses to an assault. On a teacher! That would mean instant expulsion, maybe even criminal charges. Imagine the cops piling into the school and slapping on the handcuffs! It was going to happen any second because Big Paddy, his ears crimson and pulsing, was a volcano on the brink of erupting.

Then. 'Sir, Sir!' Robert was on his feet, shouting, one arm outstretched and pointing straight upwards. The Brother turned slowly.

'You again, Kane? This better be important, laddy. This better be very important.'

'Honest, it's dead important, Sir.' Robert looked serious.

'OK. Let's hear it.'

The Brother spun a look, all round the class, sparing nobody, a look that said, *One snigger, just one snigger and you'll sit there, every last one of you, right through lunchbreak.*

Robert launched in.

'Well Sir, I was reading that thing you gave us.'

Good start, because no one ever read the Archdiocese youth education pamphlets. The Brother was usually able to retrieve enough from the bins in the corridor to supply the next class.

'There was this article, Sir,' Robert went on. 'About priests being celibate and stuff.'

Robert kept his face straight, his voice earnest.

'And, apparently, there's some big debate going on. You know, about how can priests give you advice about marriage and, er, marital relations and stuff, when they don't have any experience of it themselves?'

The Brother sighed, already resigned. He waited for the punchline and Robert obliged.

'So, anyway, I was just wondering. If the Pope announced tomorrow that priests were free to marry, would you get the good suit and the aftershave on and go out on the randan, Sir?'

The class erupted. It was worth a missed lunch to see the bastard self-ignite and maybe, just maybe, Robert might have got away with it if he had known when to stop, known when victory was his. Known, like Big Paddy had known instinctively with Dano, how and when to end it. But Robert just had to go for the bonus question that would earn him four of the belt and a letter home to his parents.

'Would you go sniffing round the convent, Sir?'

Chapter 16

1983
Karma Chameleon – Culture Club

SOMETIMES Robert thinks he can pinpoint the downward shift in his relationship with Ruth to one word. It came up somewhere in the midst of that sickening, wounding, debilitating period when he – they – began to realise it was no longer working, when increasingly the spark had to be manufactured. It was a conversation they'd had just before Jack's second birthday and Ruth used the word *property* instead of home or even house for the first time. Hey, stop, it's no big deal, maybe it's an English thing, Robert would try and convince himself. But the word jarred and bounced around in his head. He liked to think of himself as politically a little left leaning, liberal with a small l, and had always assumed Ruth to be like-minded. But if Robert could have beaten the headline writers to coining the phrase, he'd have acknowledged that they were at least a little way down the road to becoming Champagne Socialists.

Ruth wanted to start buying up former council houses – or properties, to use the offending word – and renting them out. The tabloid fame she so despised had, ironically, earned her a regular presenting slot and a lucrative contract. Robert's career was on the move too. So even in prohibitively expensive London, between them they had a bit of money to spare each month. Robert, though, found it difficult to justify the idea to himself. They had always been steadfastly and vocally united in their contempt for Thatcherism, sick of the selfishness and greed her policies had allowed to soak into society. The low point, up till then anyway, was what he saw as the monstrous con of selling to the British public something that was already theirs. Yet here they were, ready to take advantage.

'It makes us just as bad,' Robert would say, as they rehashed the argument for the ninth night in a row. 'Who are we to be taking money off folk to live

107

in their own houses...and what, make a fat profit when we sell them again?'

Ruth would shrug and say: 'I know, I know, I don't like the thought of it either but everyone's doing it and we'd be crazy not to.'

'Everyone's not doing it, Ruth. Folk who haven't got as much dough as us can't afford to do it because we're charging them extortionate rents.'

Every single time, she would clinch her argument, ease him into submission, the same way.

'You don't have to like it, Robert, but do it for Jack then, so we can give him the best possible childhood...and education That's all that should matter. Save up for him and one day that money will put him through a good university.'

'Jesus, Ruth. He's hardly out of nappies and you've got him graduating. How about we actually let him have that childhood first?'

Robert would keep on arguing but deep inside he realised it was just for show. He knew he'd go along with it. The boy was everything to him.

Now Jack really is about to start university and Ruth had been right. If he lasts the four years and graduates, he will emerge without being saddled with a mountain of debt like so many less privileged students. At her instigation, she and Robert had recently sold a three-bed ex-council in Lambeth – bought in 1983 for £9,000 – for just under £600k. If Robert finds the figures obscene to the point of balking at checking his bank balance too often, he has to remind himself he has never been embarrassed enough to turn down his share. He salves his conscience with the knowledge that he was the one who took on the responsibility for the bulk of Jack's upbringing and has done his best to avoid spoiling the lad, though he hadn't always succeeded with that. How many students in Dundee would be driving to their lectures in a six-month-old Mazda?

Jack is the No1 reason Robert is back in Scotland, though he had been toying with escaping from London for a year or two anyway. The size and the speed and the vibrancy and the sheer being at the centre of everything that once so attracted him to London, have long since lost their appeal. He has grown tired of a city that takes itself so seriously, that sees itself as the nation's powerhouse to the extent it looks down its nose at the rest of Britain. He is weary of the relentless pace, the constant need to run ever faster on the hamster wheel, the way pausing and taking a breath is treated as a weakness in Blair world. Or maybe it's him, he acknowledges. If not exactly old and decrepit, he certainly no longer thinks of himself as young. He is no longer fresh-faced and eager to leap at every opportunity with spare fuel to burn. But whether it's London or whether it's him, the result is the same. He knew it was time to get out, time to go home, so it wasn't difficult to see as serendipity the happy combination of Jack being accepted on to the neuroscience course at Dundee and the big job in Glasgow coming up a couple of weeks later. Now Robert is close enough to be there when Jack needs him but not so close the boy will feel crowded and watched over when he gets up here in a few weeks' time.

The other big consequence of being back in Scotland, of course, is that it is more difficult to keep *her* out of his thoughts. If he is honest, she has never been far from his thoughts but now the sheer physical proximity means she looms larger than ever – the knowledge that he could bump into her in the centre of Glasgow any lunchtime, look her up in the phone book, be in Cumbride in half an hour. It excites him and terrifies him in equal measure. When he sits alone in his hotel room at night, or nurses a malt at the bar, he fantasises about meeting her and, by some miracle, everything instantly clicking back into place. Then he gives himself a shake. What is he playing at? He is a middle-aged, serious professional. A television executive. Get a bloody grip, son. Then his mind drifts back to her again. He can't help it, never could.

Robert is angry at himself, and a little ashamed if truth be told, for dragging Paddy into it. For turning the reporter's instinctive and insidious grilling on his lifelong pal, squeezing out as much detail as he can. He knows she has been married but isn't any longer – welcome to the club. He knows she works in Glasgow and has a house in Cumbride, but not whether she shares it with a partner or has a significant other elsewhere. He doesn't think she has children – Paddy is pretty certain about that. He shudders with embarrassment. What must Paddy think of him, coaxing him into behaving like they're back at school and spying on lassies?

And anyway, what is his end game here? What if Paddy does get her phone number for him or find out that she is on her own? Is he actually going to call her? And if he does, what is he going to say? Fancy meeting up at the monkey bars, Lorna?

He laughs. At himself.

'You're a clown, Robert Kane,' he says out loud to the greying reflection in the eighth floor hotel window. 'Time you grew the hell up and forgot about her.'

Then he thinks about her some more.

Chapter 17

May 1974
The Streak – Ray Stevens

THE Wee Mary Moment. The moment our boys realised what they were dealing with here. Not silly little lassies any more, but women. OK, trainee women, but women all the same. It was also the moment it dawned on the guys that they had better do some fast growing up if they wanted to keep pace with us. It happened at the swimming pool up the Tryst, the big sports complex next to the town centre.

Another Saturday was coming up, another possibility. We were always searching for something different, some new experience to try out, but ideas weren't exactly flying around. Robert suggested the pictures, which wasn't that different and certainly nothing new.

Big Paddy expanded on the idea and said: 'What about trying to get into an eighteen?'

We hadn't done that before. He fancied a new film some guys at his school were talking about, The Exorcist. Loads of them had seen it already, or at least claimed to have seen it.

'Sounds magic. Apparently, you absolutely pure shite yourself.'

That was Big Paddy's sales pitch. Who could resist after that? He was dead keen and he was confident we would all get in OK.

'Easy for you to say,' moaned Cammy, who was under no illusions. Next to Big Paddy, he was a wee boy. Well, up to that point anyway.

We all let ourselves fall into it with mixed levels of enthusiasm. The pictures it would be then, up in Glasgow on Saturday afternoon and OK, we'd try to get into an 18. No one spelled it out but we all knew what the real agenda was here. It didn't really matter what the film was. It was a test. It was a let's-see-who-looks-grown-up and let's-see-who-doesn't challenge. A sort of pact was attempted along the lines of, if we don't all get in, we'll forget it and do something else instead. But we couldn't agree on tactics.

'What if some of us have already paid and got in but the rest of you get a knock-back?' Good question Kirsty, obviously in no doubt which camp she would fall into.

'Easy solution,' chipped in Cookie. 'Let the youngest looking try first.'

'Two problems there,' said Robert, the pragmatist. 'First. Be honest, I know Cammy looks like he's hardly out the womb and got swapped with the afterbirth, but who's going to admit they're the youngest looking? And second, that might finish us off before we even give it a proper go.'

'That's right,' said Karen. 'Might be better if two of us more grown-up ones go in first. Say, Simon and me. Then they'll maybe think that if we're all together, the rest of you must be about the same age as us.'

'Aye, very good, you and Simon,' hissed Jo, who still had no problem getting half fare on the bus. 'I'll tell them you're my granny and granda.'

Wee Mary had a different kind of problem with the plan.

'I don't mind the pictures, but depends what time you're going. My swimming club's been put back to half eleven this week. Won't finish till about one.'

Ross was rarely our top ideas man but a light bulb flashed on.

'Heh, the baths,' he said. 'I've no' been to the baths for donkeys. Why don't we meet you up there, Mary? Anybody else fancy the swimming?'

Brilliant. Great idea. We certainly hadn't done that before, not all of us together anyway. It would be a laugh.

'Ah,' said Jo, tapping her head and turning slowly to Ross. 'Velly good Glasshoppa. Finarry you are rearning to think for yourself.'

You could almost touch the enthusiasm at Ross's big idea and it was fascinating right from the kick off, sorting out the keens from the not-so-keens.

Ross, obviously, and Big Paddy, both loved the idea. Jo and Kirsty too. No hesitation. So that was four in right away – the muscle boys, the show off and the stripper. Fiona said she would go. Me too. I hadn't been at the pool for ages – a few years probably. Yeah, I fancied it.

I used to go a lot when I was little, with Wee Mary and her Mum and Dad mostly. They took us every Saturday morning for a year or two when we were about halfway through primary. They did a lot of stuff like that, Wee Mary and her parents. You know, family things, and they included me a lot as well. Wee Mary was an only child, same as me. Maybe that was why we became such good pals. Who knows?

When I think about it, there were times when I felt more like part of *her* family than my own. We used to pretend we were sisters sometimes, Wee Mary and me. We went for drives some Sundays in her Dad's little light blue Ford Anglia. Having a car was still a bit special then. We went to places like Ayr for the day, or St Andrews, or Oban. Wee Mary and I were discovering Scotland, mostly through a rain-spattered car window.

Quite often they took us to the pictures, which my parents hardly ever did. I have a brilliant, vivid memory of the four of us driving back from Glasgow after seeing The Sound of Music. We were singing the doe-a-deer verse in the car and all starting at different bits and giggling as we tripped each other up.

One year, Wee Mary's Dad took us to the carnival – or *the shows* as we called it – at the Kelvin Hall in Glasgow. It felt like the real start of Christmas. We had these huge baked potatoes with loads of butter and burnt black skin that got stuck between our teeth for days. We ate them out of silver foil with little sharp wooden sticks.

It was just the three of us and I can't remember why Wee Mary's Mum didn't come. Her Dad played a joke on our way back from the Kelvin Hall, or at least we thought it was a joke. We were back in Cumbride, nearly home, and he stopped at a phone box a couple of streets away from their house and when he got back in the car, he said: 'I've told your Mum that's us just leaving Glasgow. We'll give her a big surprise.'

Wee Mary and I thought it was hilarious and we were excited about seeing the look of surprise on her Mum's face when we walked in. But it didn't work out like we hoped. Wee Mary's Mum didn't think it was funny at all and the two of them had a big row about it. They went into the kitchen and Wee Mary's Mum slammed the door behind her. We could hear them bawling at each other. The joke had spoiled the night and we felt like it was our fault because we had been part of it.

By that time, Saturday morning at the baths with Wee Mary's parents had become a regular event. She really got into it, trying out different strokes and doing lengths against the clock and learning how to dive properly and stuff. I never progressed much beyond learning enough to keep myself from drowning. Mostly I remember splashing about at the shallow end then after we came out and got dried, sipping hot chocolate from paper cups that were too hot to hold for ages.

I didn't do much of that family kind of stuff with my own Mum and Dad. My Dad always seemed to be working, except on Saturdays, and that was his football day. He would pace around the kitchen, shooting glances at the clock every two minutes. Then, finally, it was five to eleven and he was away, clutching his Rangers scarf in his hand, folded into a square like a hankie. A few minutes later I would hear the toot of Wee Mary's Dad's car horn and I'd be off to the baths. I wouldn't see Dad again till I was hiding behind the settee from the Daleks.

From what I can recall, Mum spent most of my childhood sitting at the kitchen table as if there was an anchor hidden under there. In my memory she is usually either lighting a cigarette, or stubbing one out. Oh, and drinking tea. Seemed like Big Paddy's Mum was there most of the time as well.

But yeah, the baths with our lot. I was all for it and most of the others were too. Cookie seemed keen at first, then he backed off a bit. The signals from Karen weren't positive.

She said to all of us: 'I don't know if it's really a good idea.'

Then to Fiona, Jo and me, in a low voice. Confidential.

'I'm just worried about Simon. You know what he's like. The rest of the guys are so immature. If they start staring at me and all that, you know, in my swimming costume, and making comments, he'll go mental.'

Jo stage-whispered back. 'Why don't you see if you can get one of those Jack Custard diver's suits, like on the telly? Probably get them in the catalogue.'

Karen actually looked as if she was considering the idea. Kirsty shook her head and muttered: 'Did they not say in biology it was the starfish that had no brain?'

Robert agreed on the baths with a kind of *suppose-so* shrug, probably miffed because it wasn't his idea. Cammy was the only serious objector.

'Ach, I don't think I'll bother,' he sighed. 'Don't really like the water that much.'

Big Paddy wasn't for letting him away with it.

'Nah, you'll be all right, ya mockit wee shite. It's baths, not bath, know? The water will be fine. There won't be any soap in it.'

'You're fucking hilarious, so you are,' grunted Cammy, just about the only one of the guys who could get away with cursing Big Paddy. 'Amazing they've no' snapped you up for The Comedians with your patter.'

It didn't really sink in until a bit later. We had got carried away with the idea and were all really looking forward to it, but then it hit us, me and the other girls. This would be like, eh, undressing, as in, taking our gear off. In front of the guys. What we'd just signed up for was a you-show-me-yours-I'll-show-you-mine exercise on a group scale. But still, no one talked about backing out and it was arranged. That Saturday. Ten to one.

Fiona didn't turn up. She phoned Karen on the Saturday morning to apologise and say she couldn't make it.

'It's her time,' whispered Karen, gravely. 'You know. Her period.' The last two words were only mouthed.

So, nine of us arrived at the sports centre from our various Saturday morning places. Ross battle-hardened from football, Robert and Big Paddy from their Saturday morning jobs as Cream Boys, lugging their plastic tubs door-to-door in brilliant white Bri-nylon jackets. Bit bright and uncool for Robert, now I come to think of it. Jo came from her Mum's hairdressers where she helped out most Saturdays. Karen and Cookie were dropped off by her Mum on the way back from shopping. The rest of us dragged ourselves away from labour-intensive Saturday morning Tiswas.

The boys all scrambled into the pool before us. They hadn't bothered about the little niceties, like folding their clothes and hanging them up carefully in the locker. Nervous, we headed for the water from the changing room in ones and twos, any chance of an elegant entrance killed off by the enforced fire walk through the freezing disinfectant foot bath. Straight away we spotted a row of five heads – the guys peering up at us over the side of the pool, waiting for us to emerge from the changing rooms like The Generation Game conveyor belt.

I had a rare attack of bravery or, more like, I decided to get it over and done with quickly. I went first. I stepped out in a black one-piece costume and bathing cap. I thought I looked OK. The guys cheered and I stuck my tongue out, trotted quickly to the shallow end and slid myself straight into the water. Ooft, it was cold, but hey, I was in, past the cattle judges with dignity more or less intact. I leaned back against the wall at the end of the pool and observed the rest of the parade. Karen was next. A costume quite like mine, but with flowers on it. She had a nice figure and the guys showed their appreciation. Karen tutted and turned to Jo, who was just behind her.

'Told you,' she said. 'I knew this would happen. They're all so bloody childish.'

'Morons,' Jo giggled. 'Probably keep the picture in their heads to help them sleep tonight.'

She sashayed past Karen in her tiny white one-piece like a model on a catwalk, not caring. The guys had a concentrated gawk and pleasant surprise registered, like they had been expecting a wee boy in a girl's costume. Yeah, Jo was a miniature but no question, she was getting there. Ross put his elbows on the side of the pool and hauled himself half out of the water for a closer inspection. He muttered something to Big Paddy, his stage whisper betrayed by the swimming pool acoustics.

'Sake, decent wee pair of paps on it, eh?'

Little Jo went straight for him. Dick Emery mince, the voice perfect.

'Ooh, you are awful.' She placed a foot on Ross's shoulders then gave him a shove and added the appropriate punchline. 'But I like you.'

The other guys howled as Ross toppled backwards with a splash.

Kirsty had clearly decided to give the lads a treat by saving the best till last. She tiptoed out in the tiniest bikini. The top made only a half-hearted attempt at doing its job, her high breasts jutting proudly like the last two cooking apples on the shelf. More whoops from the guys, then a catcall from Big Paddy, Mr Subtle himself.

'Aw it's you Kirsty, didn't recognise you with so much on.'

We messed around for a bit. Wee Mary's swimming club was still going on so about half the pool was roped off up towards the deep end. She was in the water. She spotted us, gave a wave, spread the fingers of one hand, mouthing: 'Five minutes.'

Robert and I were down the shallow end, chatting and flipping water at each other. Karen wandered a little out of her depth, faked girly fear and clung to Cookie's neck. Big Paddy and Ross staged a diving/showing off competition. Big Paddy belly-smacked into the water while Ross stretched and flashed his muscles before executing dives much sleeker than Big Paddy's. Jo and Kirsty provided the adoring audience. Not that Big Paddy and Ross needed one. They were loving themselves.

Or at least they were, until Cammy kicked sand in their faces. He had kind of slunk off into a corner on his own, shivering and obviously not enjoying this one bit. He clambered awkwardly up the rungs at the shallow end and sauntered off somewhere. To the loo, I presumed. A few minutes later he shuffled back, weedy and thin, his body the colour of John West salmon. There were no plaster casts for a change which was a brief respite for his limbs.

But it wasn't him we had noticed, not at first anyway. It was Kirsty, goggle-eyed and staring into the distance. We followed her gaze...to Cammy. He was standing at the edge of the pool, lugging an enormous, heavy weight in his swimming trunks, like some kind of deformed third arm strapped on to that scraggy frame.

The guys all reacted the same. They looked, what? Well, sickened, I suppose. Crushed. They hadn't thought it through, of course they hadn't. Guys that age don't. God, guys any age don't.

Lucky we never wasted our energy envying other girls with gravity-defying boobs or perfect bums or less flab. Thank God I believed the lies I told myself!

Anyway, back to that day at the pool. The other guys scowled at Cammy as he stood at the edge of the shallow end. But quickly they went into recovery mode and did what guys always do when someone else has something they don't have, or knows something they don't. They went on the attack, they took the piss, but they fell short and they knew it.

Ross: 'Sake, that where you're hiding your stookie, Cammy? Break your dick, ya dick?'

Big Paddy: 'What happened? You get a stauner looking at the kiddies' pool?'

· Robert: 'That you trying to sneak your wee brother in without paying?'

But Jo, our resident mimic, outflanked them and defused their mounting annoyance. She burst into song and excelled herself.

'I'm Jake the Peg, deedle deedle deedle dum, with the extra leg.'

Our laughter was interrupted by a piercing whistle blast. We all turned. It looked like Wee Mary's swimming club was winding up. The woman in charge was calling out instructions which we couldn't make out for the splashing and the echo of little kids' screeches bouncing off the big high windows. The woman was nodding at the swimmers – Wee Mary and half a dozen others – then pointing at the little diving plinths by the edge of the pool at the roped-off deep end.

We watched Wee Mary spring herself out of the water, her back to us, tight red costume, buttocks bulging. She turned round and stepped on to one of the platforms and just like Cammy a few moments earlier, she grew bigger before our eyes.

Everything seemed to fall into slow motion. Wee Mary rising on to her toes, sucking in her breath. Our guys' heads creaking round towards her, training their eyes on her, water spraying off their hair as they turned. The gaze of just about every other male in the place swinging round in unison too, then all the heads nodding in time to match her intake of breath.

I'm sorry, there's no subtle way to describe what we saw. *All* we saw. Big, big breasts, so expansive and deep, straining at the wet material. Slowly, slowly, she stretched her arms and that huge chest inflated some more as she breathed in, trailing her arms out behind her. For those few seconds, it felt like Wee Mary *became* her breasts.

Now she was crouching, then taking off in a slow-motion ballet. That mighty bosom took on a life of its own. Bouncing, bouncing. Up, down, up, down, the guys' pupils bobbing in a stunned, slavish synchronicity. Wee Mary was gliding through the air. So gracefully. So-o-o-o slowly. Then she was slicing into the water, soundlessly, endlessly, taking an age for her feet to complete the vanishing act.

From a few feet away, I heard Robert letting his thoughts escape of their own accord, speaking to no one in particular and as if I wasn't there.

'Christ, it's like a dead heat in a zeppelin race.'

THE FENIAN

Ross's reaction was so much simpler and from the gut but in its own way more eloquent. He articulated perfectly the expression on the faces of our five guys and most other males in the place.

He just said: 'Fuck sake.'

Then Wee Mary was coming towards us, gliding dolphin-like under the rope still strung across the pool and breaking the surface between Robert and me. Big Paddy broke the spell, jolted us back to real time.

'Heh Mary, you no' a bit old for water wings?'

Breasts? Yup, the guys had heard of them and knew we had them, somewhere, hiding out among our annoying layers and barriers of coats and anoraks and blazers and jumpers and blouses and cosy-tops. They spent an inordinate amount of time and effort trying to locate them. But until then, until the Wee Mary moment, it felt like there had been no quality control. Not that I could make out anyway.

It was as if they thought, breasts are breasts, they're marvellous things, but one pair/set is as good as any other. It was like they had a mission – a duty almost – to get their hands on them by any means possible. They'd send in a decoy paw and wait till you grasped it and shoved it away. Then wham, bandits at four o' clock, a new attempt from a different angle.

I don't really know how the guys saw us, how they looked at us, in pre-Wee Mary Moment days. How they decided which of us they fancied. I only got into their heads in tiny doses, via Robert mainly, and there were some things even he couldn't – or wouldn't – explain. Maybe it was as simple as looks, faces, what they judged to be pretty. Maybe they didn't see shapes at all before that day. Ha, maybe we *were* shapeless, maybe they just saw duffel coats and baggy smocks and ever widening bell-bottoms.

There was no pattern that I could figure out. Big Paddy would spend days pursuing tall, skinny Fiona. *It's not often I see eye to eye with a woman.* Then suddenly he was besotted with busting-out-all-over Wee Mary.

What about us? How did we choose? What standards did we go on? I don't remember ever pitting Ross's rippling six-pack against Robert's magical charm. I know I certainly didn't develop a sudden longing for Cammy after my first glimpse of his mysterious monster from the deep. I wasn't aware the other girls did either. Well, maybe Kirsty, but that was just Kirsty.

For what it's worth, I always thought it started as more of a pals kind of thing, certainly at first. You found yourself talking to one particular guy a bit more than usual, laughing with him a lot, maybe finding something in common, like a new telly show or a record you both liked. You were drawn to him and you sort of fell into it and became a pair for a little while, a couple. That's how I remember it anyway but possibly I'm giving us too much credit

– or maybe I'm just giving me too much credit.

But I do know the ground definitely shifted a bit after that day at the pool. The guys started to look at us differently, or perhaps not differently, but more carefully. I don't think they sat down and made a list or anything. I don't think they put us into any kind of order, with Wee Mary as the ultimate boobs benchmark and a line sloping down the graph to bony Fiona at the other end. I don't think they did. I hope they didn't. Mind, I could be way off though. Maybe they did see Wee Mary as something to aspire to and the rest of us as OK stopping off points along the way. I hope that is not how they thought of us. I hope I'm right to go on my instincts and memory. They were good guys, mostly, and I'd like to think I'm giving them a depth they deserve.

Whatever their response was, what I do know is that the Wee Mary Moment didn't change how I felt towards her. As far as the bust thing was concerned, I thought I was probably in the middle somewhere. The middle of this spectrum the guys didn't have! I was fine with that. I think I was happy enough with myself, my figure, how I looked.

Wee Mary and me. We had become close again, tight close. We had been best pals through primary but at high school we were put into different classes because of our surnames and I drifted to Kirsty for a while. Then when our lot, the shelter lot, got together, Wee Mary became part of it and we discovered each other all over again. We developed two friendships – one inside the group, another one outside. A bit like I had with Robert. Wee Mary and me grew back into sisters.

She put on a brave face when she broke her terrible news to me. It wasn't long after that day at the pool. She tried to give me the medical details, as if she was preparing me first, as if she knew I would take it harder than her. She had some kind of gynaecological problem. *Trouble down there in the lady's private area*, my Mum would have said. But I didn't pay attention to the technicalities, I only heard the bottom line. The doctors had discussed it with Wee Mary and her Mum and warned it was highly unlikely that she would ever be able to bear children. They explained there was nothing physically to stop her getting pregnant – unless she agreed to be sterilised. That is what they were recommending but Wee Mary turned them down flat. The doctors had been blunt about it because they said pregnancy could be dangerous to her, even life-threatening.

Wee Mary told me all this then shrugged and nodded downwards, towards her chest.

'Sod's law eh, Lorna? And me with so much to give as well.'

I cried for her because Wee Mary loved kids and was brilliant with them.

She was like a magnet to my little cousins when they came to visit and she had talked a few times about training to be a children's nurse or a primary teacher when she left school.

Despite all that, Wee Mary comforted me. *She* comforted *me*! I felt useless because I didn't know what to say to make her feel any better. Ah, we might have called her Wee Mary, but she was a thousand times bigger than me.

She shrugged and said: 'You never know, Lorna. I might get lucky and they'll figure out how to fix it. Maybe I'll get a miracle one day.'

Chapter 18

August 2001
Eternity – Robbie Williams

W ORDS were ganging up on me – Robert's written ones, such as they were, and Big Paddy's spoken ones. Tripping me up, messing me up, not allowing me to concentrate on doing nothing all weekend.

Now it was nearly lunchtime on Monday, a week and a bit since I'd bumped into Big Paddy at his Mum's front door. I was typing up a witness report about some poor guy who'd had the four wheels nicked off his car in broad daylight and found it up on bricks right outside his house. I shuddered at the hassle of getting the damage assessed and repaired, ordering new wheels, doing the dance with the insurance company. If that wasn't bad enough, a fortnight later the exact same thing happened again. Same place, same time of day. Some cases, like this one, were quite interesting, but mostly it was the same petty, sometimes nasty, stories again and again with only the names, dates and places changed. Repetitive as they were, they were doing their job of holding my concentration and I was content to let myself become absorbed in something that stopped my mind wandering to Robert. Then a message over the public address system.

Visitor at reception for Lorna Maxwell. Visitor at reception for Lorna Maxwell.

Really? For me? I had never been called to reception before, not in the nine years I had worked at the Fiscal's office. Curious, I peered across our open-plan office, perhaps unconsciously thinking I might develop a super power that would enable me to see round corners. Before I had time to think about it properly, Shirley at the next desk had her best crack at a Geordie accent.

'Lorna Maxwell to the diary room please.'

I acknowledged the effort with a small laugh. There couldn't be anything wrong, surely? If it was some kind of an emergency, they wouldn't broadcast it like that, would they? But who would come looking for me here? Not Dad, he never got much beyond the pub or the bookies these days. Hmm, there's a damning indictment of my life. How many people did I know? How few friends did I have that I was so surprised to have a visitor? I got to reception and PC 9043 was leaning on the counter, nodding when he saw me. Big Paddy, in uniform, chessboard cap tucked under his arm.

Jan, the receptionist, said: 'What you been up to, Lorna? Dodging your fare on the bus again?'

'Hiya Lorna, just passing.' He pulled a sheepish grin. 'Thought I'd pop in. See how this side of the operation's getting on.'

Big Paddy on the beat, me at the Fiscal's office – both on the same team, the side of the angels. What chance did the crooks have?

'Just passing?'

Pally enough back, maybe a little guarded. Big Paddy was a long way from home.

'Aye, just down the court,' he expanded. 'Witness, know? But the trial got canned. Some wee ned changed his plea at the last minute, as per. Waste of bloody time.'

'Oh, right.'

Still friendly, but not buying it completely. Thinking, funny that Paddy, you must have been at the court loads of times over the years – and the Fiscal's too. How come it's taken you all this time to find your way to my department?

Blank. Farmer's face. Not letting on if he'd spotted suspicion on my face.

He said casually: 'Anyway, you fancy a coffee or something? If they'll no' let you away, I could always take you into protective custody.'

OK, why not? I nodded back towards the office.

'I've got to get back right now, but I've got my lunch break in about ten minutes. Can you wait that long, or you got to shoot off?'

Big Paddy looked satisfied.

'See you in the canteen.'

I found him, hard to miss really. He was sitting at a table in the corner, plate in front of him containing a few remnants of pie crust, can of Diet Coke next to his hat. I placed my handbag on the table.

'I'll just grab a sandwich. Not be a minute.'

Big Paddy nodded.

Kath was following just behind me. It wasn't that unusual to see a police officer in our canteen, but she couldn't resist.

'Watch out for his handcuffs, Lorna,' she called after me. 'Dead kinky they cops.'

I survived the interrogation from the other girls in the self-service queue and went back to the table. As I sat down opposite Big Paddy, Kath passed again, with her loaded-up tray this time. I felt her curious, mischievous eyes on us.

'Whipped out his truncheon yet?' She smirked, wreathed in her own giggles.

Big Paddy, God bless him, actually blushed. A big lump in a cop uniform who took broken bottles from drunks and scraped people off roads, and he blushed at a Primary Seven joke.

'Sorry Paddy,' I smiled. 'That's my pal, Kath. Bet you never heard that one before.'

He shrugged and grinned, relaxed now, and started the Friday teatime doorstep routine. *How's the job going? How's your Dad keeping?* Blah blah blah. Except, I got an odd feeling he wasn't listening to any of the answers I muttered between mouthfuls of chicken mayo.

His next banal question.

'So, Lorna, you got any holidays planned yet?'

What is this, the hairdressers? Time for a little test, Paddy boy.

'Yeah,' I said. 'Going on an underwater basket-weaving break at the Fair. Me and David Beckham.'

Not a flicker from Big Paddy, not even at the football reference.

'Sounds good,' he said. 'Nice that time of year.'

You just failed, Paddy. I could see bubbles with my words in them, floating right over his head. *Why was I wasting my lunch break?*

I said: 'Something bothering you, Paddy?'

'Naw, nothing.'

Maybe a little flustered, but he gathered himself. It was almost imperceptible but he was in control again. Ah, here we go, time for business, PC Allan speaking now. But the calm front didn't last long.

'Er, Lorna,' he started, uncertainly. 'Been meaning to ask you. Em, how's your er... How's your, em...'

He spread his big arms on the table, leaned across and dropped his voice, almost to a whisper.

'How's your, eh, love life these days?'

What?? That wasn't a Paddy Allan question. Not the Paddy Allan I knew. I was rattled, must have sounded it too.

'What you on about, Paddy?'

'You know what I mean.' He suddenly had the look of a man who had wandered on to thin ice. 'I'm no' trying to be nosy or nothing but, you, eh, seeing anybody or anything?'

Now it was part shock, part horrible, serious, sick dread, and part deliberate tease. I looked straight at him and said: 'You asking me out, Paddy Allan?'

If his question had rocked me, my question horrified him. Big Paddy looked like he had just been hit by a truck.

'What?? Naw!' He glanced around, as if his wife might be hiding behind the soft drinks machine, eavesdropping. 'Christ almighty! Don't say things like that, Lorna. I'm a happily married man.'

Big Paddy was indignant, like I had just ripped off my top and leapt on him.

'Thanks for the compliment, Paddy,' I snapped. 'And don't worry, because if you were, you'd be at the end of a very long queue.'

We both let the lie pass. Ding ding, end of Round One. Retreat to our corners, tend to our cuts.

He squirmed some more and I decided, what the heck, it's only Big Paddy, let him off the hook, think of something to say. But I took myself by surprise and the wrong thing came out.

'So, Paddy, you seen Robert again lately?'

He blew loudly. I saw relief and he didn't try to hide it, like he was back on safe ground.

'Actually aye. Met him for a drink on Thursday. Going to the game this Saturday.'

Another question popped out from nowhere.

'Ah right, so is he up here on holiday then, or is it a work thing?'

'Oh no, he's moved back up for good, so he says. Got some new job on the BBC – don't ask me what it is exactly. He told me but I can't mind. Head of something. They seem to have that many different titles, I can't keep up when he's telling me. Worse than my lot. Some kind of big-time boss on the Scottish news, I think.'

'Oh, right,' I repeated, trying to contain myself. Robert, back up here, permanently. Close at hand.

'I assumed he was settled down there,' I said, with nothing whatsoever to back it up. 'Must be a lot of years since he went down south, is it not?'

Big Paddy was in full flow now. Did I detect the air of an agent who had botched his mission then unexpectedly been handed a second chance?

'Think he's been getting kind of fed up with it, London and that, know? And it's partly his boy, he's just starting uni up here. Well, Edinburgh...no, hang on, Dundee it is. Think Robert fancies being within reach but keeping his distance at the same time, if you know what I mean.'

Jack. Solid, trendy Jack, the student. Jack, aged eighteen, according to Robert's statement on Friends Reunited. I pictured Robert at that age. He wouldn't have wanted his Dad close. He couldn't wait to get away from Cumbride. From his home, his family, or so I'd always assumed. Now I thought about it, was there a chance his escape had been from me? Then I reprimanded myself for assuming I might have been that important to him. I was drifting and I realised Paddy was talking. Better pay attention, might learn something else.

'Aye, so then this job came up and it all seemed to tie in. Too good a chance to knock back, he reckoned.'

I should have left it there but the water wasn't quite deep enough to worry me, not yet. It still felt kind of pleasant, this little trickle of information lapping against me. I got more daring and waded out a little farther.

'Where's he staying then? Don't suppose he'll be coming back here. Sorry, don't mean Glasgow. You know, Cumbride.'

'Naw,' said Big Paddy. 'He's still looking for a place. Fancies the West End.'

That figured. Glasgow's West End – professional, fashionable, uni-land, luvvie-land.

Big Paddy went on: 'They've put him up in a hotel for the now. The Hilton. Just till he finds a place of his own. Tough life for some, eh?'

'Oh yeah,' I agreed. 'Suppose he's got his wife doing the house-hunting.'

The conversation had been rolling along fine. Why did I have to spoil it by bringing her into it? Ruthless Ruth.

But Big Paddy looked blank, kind of bewildered.

'His wife?' he asked. 'You talking about Ruth?'

My turn to look puzzled.

'You tell me, Paddy. How many wives has he got?'

'Naw,' he shrugged. 'Him and Ruth split up. Years ago, it was. Let me see, must be seven, eight year? Actually, probably more like ten or eleven now I think about it.'

Oomph, that was a big hit. A smack on the side of the head. The picture I had painted, the happy home I had constructed for cosy Robert, Ruth and Jack, the perfect family. The demolition squad had just moved in and flattened it.

I took another risk. 'He's never remarried then?'

I was trying so hard to keep my interest sounding casual. We were just having a throwaway little chat about someone – could be anyone – from our past, weren't we? Well, my past and OK, Big Paddy's past, but his present too.

'Naw.' It was becoming his favourite word. 'He went out with two or three women. After the divorce came through, know? Well-meaning pals and that, trying to fix him up. But nothing ever came of it and his mates down there just gave up. I could be wrong but I think he pretty much gave up as well. I suppose he must...naw, I really don't know.'

Robert. Big-time Robert, our success story, and alone, like me. Now the water was getting deeper, darker and murkier. But I was feeling brave, I wasn't quite out of my depth, not just yet. Maybe one more step then turn back, head for the safety of the shore.

'What happened? You know, with him and Ruth.'

Was that a question too far? Maybe Big Paddy would think it was none of my business – history and hurt for intimate friends only. But he didn't seem in a rush to change the subject.

'Och, I don't think it was ever that great to be honest. They tried. I'll give them that. They made a good go of it, especially when Jack was wee. Robert was great with him, still is. But you always sort of got the feeling Ruth was restless. Don't think weans and playing house were really part of the master plan – got in the way of conquering the universe.'

That sounded more like it came from Robert than Big Paddy. Too smooth, too well turned. The kind of thing the Robert I remembered might have said.

But what the hell, I'll take points anywhere. Thanks, Paddy. Must lick my finger later, draw a big tick in the air. I always knew Ruth wasn't Robert's type.

Hold on, what are you thinking about? Knew she wasn't his type! What, from seeing her on the telly? Get a grip – and shame on you too, Lorna Maxwell. Did I really wish that on them? On Robert...another love lost. On little Jack...a broken home. Did I even wish it on Ruth? What the hell did I really know about the woman anyway?

Big Paddy was keen to finish the story now. He picked up his cap and scraped his chair back, ready to dash for the exit and beat the traffic.

'I reckon they might have stuck it out,' he said. 'You know, for Jack if nothing else. But she left him in the end, thought there was another woman. Robert always denied it but Ruth was convinced.'

I didn't like this. OK, Robert and Ruth, the idea of them had never thrilled me, not that it was ever any of my business. But don't do this, Paddy, don't destroy my perfect boy. Don't let Robert be just like the rest – like Mark, my second husband, for example. Look, I'll take back all the questions, just pretend I didn't ask.

But no, I wasn't finished just yet. The water had reached danger levels so why did I feel compelled to take one more perilous step and go in out of my depth.

'And was there?'

Had to ask, sucker for punishment that I am.

'What?' Big Paddy played dumb, delaying the final blow.

'Somebody else,' I pressed. 'Was there another woman?'

Big Paddy stood, about to leave. He looked down at his shoes, anywhere but at my eyes.

'Aye, Lorna. I'm sorry to say there was.'

Robert, my beautiful boy. Charming, loving, trustworthy Robert, crumbling and falling to bits.

'Oh.' That was all I could manage.

Big Paddy went on, still not making eye contact.

'See, that was Robert's trouble, Lorna. There always was another woman...'

Now he raised his eyes and stared straight at me.

'You.'

Chapter 19

June 1974
There's A Ghost In My House – R. Dean Taylor

K AREN was dying. I cried in bed the night after she broke the news to us. I felt sorrow and guilt in equal measures.

Sorrow, because I was getting to know a little about illness and the toll it could take. My Mum was ill and though her suffering was plain for us to see, it was still in the early stages then. I had no inkling about how serious it would become, or how it would end. Back then, my Mum was in pain that was worse some days than others, and discomfort. The regular hospital appointments were starting. We, or maybe just I, assumed she was simply not very well and would get better. But my friend? Well, she was dying.

The guilt thing, though. I guess it was because I always found Karen the hardest to like out of all our lot. I called her a friend but sometimes I found myself wondering, was she worth it? All the hard work, the effort. Every so often I would come home fuming and rankled by her and try to figure out what it was about her that rubbed me up the wrong way so much.

I think maybe it was that she carried a kind of smugness about her, a doubt-free certainty about herself and her worth. The polar opposite of an inferiority complex, I suppose. Is there such a thing as a superiority complex? It was like she looked down on me, well, actually, on all of us at times. Sometimes Karen gave the impression she merely tolerated us and perhaps even pitied us in a way.

Karen was the best looking of all the girls in our lot. We knew that because she told us so often. To be clear, this was not about opinion, and certainly there was no air of conceit when she spelled it out to us. It was just, there were recognised degrees of beauty, she explained, and she had been born with just the right genes and, she conceded generously, a bit of luck. True, she was pretty in an almost classical way. She had a cat-like lushness, accentuated by a round, short, dark bob and stiff fringe, and a sensuous, soft mouth made for pouting. I remember one Sunday my Mum was watching an old film, Cleopatra, and she remarked that the main character reminded her a bit of my pal, Karen.

At the same time as being convinced of her own good looks, Karen never held back when it came to listing our faults and, in particular, our physical flaws. I didn't suit long hair – did me no favours because my face was long and thin. Jo was shapeless, like a boy. Fiona was Karen's closest friend, but that didn't spare her. She was harsh looking, a beanpole with no redeeming features. Wee Mary was top heavy and out of proportion. Kirsty was tarty – nice enough now and attractive on the surface, Karen observed, but she'd grow hard.

'Give her a few years and she'll be hatchet-faced and clapped out.'

Don't sugarcoat it.

Karen had another belief that filtered down through us – that there was a kind of financial and class gulf between her and the rest of us. She was well-off, we were poor. She was middle class, we were working class. Our families struggled while Karen's parents had everything. For all I knew, maybe it was true. Her Dad was a manager at the big machine factory where, it seemed, everyone in Cumbride either worked or knew someone who did. Big Paddy's Dad worked on the line and Wee Mary's Dad was his line supervisor, whatever any of that meant.

Karen liked to flaunt it, this wealth she hinted at. She had a special night for us girls one time when we were in first year. She kept us squabbling and anxious for ages about the ever-changing guest-list. The privileged ones who made the final cut were to come round for a look at her colour telly. It was the first one any of us had seen. Thinking back, the colours were too gaudy, like a child's first paint box, but wow, that did not stop us from being impressed. There was a Western on when we arrived and gathered round the new telly in wonder. We saw chocolate horses, orange-faced cowboys, a sickly yellow desert. Her Dad switched over to football when the film finished. Pillar-box strips and limeade pitch.

I'd never thought about rich and poor between my friends, at least not until Karen kindly pointed it out. See, one of the things about Cumbride was that there was a sort of New Town equality among all those families who had flocked to the land of the future. They had come lured by promises of urban living in the countryside. Bright open spaces with lush greenery, state-of-the art shopping out of the rain, modern schools with the latest equipment, clean air, freedom from the grime and the traffic. Safety was a biggie with all those footbridges and underpasses. I remember reading a leaflet, just before we moved, that promised: *You'll never have to cross a road again.* As I learned when I was older, there were plenty of jobs around too, both in the sprawling construction work in the rapidly expanding schemes and in the industrial estates sprouting up on the outskirts. So, although I obviously didn't understand all this at the time, there was a kind of a boom-town, land-of-opportunity feel about the place in those early days, and I certainly never had any sense of us being desperately short of anything. Mind you, I was only a kid so the financial realities were way over my head.

Down at our everyday level, there was something else that stopped us ever thinking about differences in status. We all lived in the same house – including Karen – or at least, the same type of house. Row after row of spacious, pebbledash hutches. OK, not identical, but variations on a very definite theme. These were Cumbride Development Corporation homes – council houses with a Sunday name, to be honest. Folk didn't really think about buying their own homes back then, well, not the kind who moved to Cumbride. Actually, now that I think about it, that isn't strictly true. We were always vaguely aware of a couple of streets that were different from the rest. Bigger houses not joined to each other but in their own plot of land. Little posh pockets, was how we thought of them. They were over on the fringe of our scheme next to the big park, the one everybody called The Fields. These were the *bought-houses*, as our parents called them, and they were strictly for the elite – the dentist, the GP, the headmaster. The private estate was part of Big Paddy's cream run and he used to grumble that they were the meanest when it came to giving out tips, both generally and at Christmas in particular. Robert would frown and nod sagely, as if this was some startling commentary about class.

Karen had her own property, of course. *Nice link, Lorna.*

I'm talking about Cookie. She was smug about that too – her future signed, sealed and already delivered before she was ten. No aimless drifting from boy to boy for her.

She told us one particular story, over and over again, as if we would eventually see the cuteness in it, as if it would help us understand the true meaning and depth of their love. Her words, I must stress.

The story was about her and Cookie. Karen and Simon. She was the only person who never called him Cookie. This was back when they were in Primary Five and sat at opposite sides of the class. She would catch his eye and give him a special signal and, simultaneously, they would push their pencils off their desks then lean over to pick them up, lock on to each other's eyes, and gaze at each other lovingly and longingly through a tangle of legs and white school socks and wellies and schoolbags, their faces upside down, their hair standing on end.

Karen saw something in Cookie that the rest of us missed. Cookie was OK. He could be pretty funny at times and he was quite clever and attentive. One night, when a few of us were discussing the guys for the umpteenth time, Wee Mary absently referred to him as harmless and we quickly agreed the word summed him up best. God, talk about damning with faint praise.

Karen said he was lovely, we said specky, a bit gawky. She saw something solid and sound, we saw marshmallow and skittish. Above all, Karen saw a future.

But now she had no future, and it had all happened shockingly fast. Barely a week and a half was all it had taken for her to plunge from healthy to no hope. Karen had gone to see her GP because she hadn't been feeling well, nothing more than that, just not feeling very well. But the doctor wasn't happy, arranged tests and something had shown up. Karen dropped the word tumour into her daily bulletins. Then came the bombshell. The doctors were saying it was too late to operate. The tumour was too far gone and there was nothing that could be done. It was only a matter of time.

I was wary of even having these thoughts, but there was something not quite right about this from the start. When was all this happening – these visits to the GP, these tests? Karen didn't seem to be around any less. She told us she went to the surgery right after school some days, but my Mum had to go to the hospital for her tests, through in Glasgow. Sometimes my Mum was away all day so if Karen was so ill, why wasn't she going to hospital? There was no point, she explained, she was resigned to it.

'I'm as well getting the most out of the little time I've got left,' she said bravely, her voice trembling.

I felt bad, worse than bad. I figured I must be evil for harbouring even the smallest doubts. This surely wasn't something you could make up. It certainly wasn't something you could put her to the test about. No, definitely not something you could interrogate a friend over, especially not a dying friend.

Karen's deteriorating health, her downwards spiral, it couldn't have come at a worse time for her. She had a rival for Cookie – a serious rival, she admitted – for the first time since they had met. Someone she thought could actually lure him away from her, prise him from her iron grip.

She was Allison and she was Cookie's cousin. Well, that's what he called Allison at first but after a while he explained she wasn't really his cousin at all. As far back as Cookie could remember, he had called Allison's Mum his Auntie Bev, but she was really just his Mum's best friend. The two women had grown up together in Glasgow, gone through school together, and they were still as close as sisters. When Cookie explained the relationship and how he had always called the woman Auntie, it made me think about Wee Mary and me. Would we still be best friends when we got to that age? But then, I thought sorrowfully, Wee Mary wouldn't be able to have any children who could call me their Auntie even though I wasn't really.

Cookie's Mum's friend was going through a divorce, we eventually learned. Divorce was a dark, whispered, grown-up secret in those days. She was having a tough time coping, was all Cookie had gleaned. (Hopeless at gathering gossip, our guys.) Cookie's Mum had offered to have Allison at weekends, to help take the strain off while her parents argued over the small print of their joint past and separate futures.

Allison was about two years older than us which, at that age, was a massive gap. We were still girls but she was more like a woman. Allison wore make-up all the time as a matter of course, not just for going out somewhere special. But even though she was that bit older, she started tagging along with our lot when she came for the weekend. I suppose she saw our company as not on the same level as her real friends back home in the city, but better than nothing. In retrospect, she probably quite enjoyed the status we gave her.

Cookie was in awe of her, that much was obvious. In fact, I think all the guys fell in love with Allison a little bit. We were all kind of jealous – the girls I mean – but only at first because Allison soon won us round. She was nice, she was cool, she explained things to us in ways that we hadn't got to yet. I mean about boys mainly, boys in general, what they were all about. Then a bit later, she explained things to us about our guys in particular, articulated some of the ideas we had maybe felt, but not quite been able to put into words. She seemed to suss them out pretty quickly.

Big Paddy was wild, a caveman, but also a rock, the kind of guy you could absolutely depend on no matter what. Ross was film-star handsome but dangerous. Cammy was hopeless but a heartbreaker. Robert was a patter merchant. Cookie was nice enough but a bit of a sap. These were all her words – Allison's words – and we got the message. She saw them as boys. From her lofty, grown-up eighteen-year-old perch, our guys were nothing more than kids, of no real interest or long-term use to her. We were safe. Allison wasn't even a tiny bit inclined to nick our guys. Well, with one exception as it turned out, and even then, only in passing and out of curiosity. Truth be told, Cookie was never at the races.

But it gnawed at Karen. The thought of this girl, this young woman, sleeping in the same house as her Simon. Even worse, in his room, in his bed. He had been relegated to a camp bed in the dining room at weekends. Karen couldn't see any other possibility: Allison must be after him.

Karen wanted us to freeze her out. Allison wasn't one of us, one of our gang, and she was disrupting things, Karen insisted. But we all liked her. She was like some colourful, interesting exhibit that flitted in and out of our circle. What's more, Cookie had delivered her to us. She was his invited guest and we couldn't find a reason to shut her out. So Karen started a propaganda war. She told us stories and tried to persuade us they were factual and had come from Cookie. The stories all started the same way, with the same name. Karen was clever like that. She planted a link in our heads. The name: Allison. The link: Cow.

PROPAGANDA BULLETIN No 1

Allison's a cow. She leaves the bedroom door open when she's getting changed for bed because she knows Simon has to pass the room to get to the loo.

PROPAGANDA BULLETIN No 2

Allison's a dirty cow. She sleeps with nothing on. Simon has to go into the room in the mornings to get his clothes and stuff. He knocks first and she tells him to come in, then she accidentally-on-purpose leaves the bed covers pulled back and lets him see everything.

PROPAGANDA BULLETIN No 3

Allison's a pure cow. The lock on their bathroom door's broken so she walks in when Simon's having a bath and makes out it's a mistake. Then she sits on the side of the bath and offers to wash his back.

Where was Karen getting this stuff from? Did she lie in bed at night, twisting and seething and imagining all this, or was she just straight out inventing it? We knew it was complete rubbish, of course. Grown-up, sophisticated Allison doing a big, unsophisticated seduction number on Cookie? No offence or anything Cookie, but come on.

Coincidentally, just before Karen was struck down by illness, she was hit with a new crisis. Two actually. In the long term, Cookie was talking about Allison coming to stay for the whole summer holidays. More immediately though, Ross had invited her to one of our parties, at Cammy's house.

I think with Ross, to give him his due, it was fifty per cent doing the decent thing. Allison didn't have any other friends in Cumbride, so it would have been rude for all of us to go to a party and leave her out. But I was convinced it was also fifty per cent Ross chancing his arm. OK, she was older and seemingly out of reach but a few drinks, music, lights out, and who knows? What a coup that would have been.

Karen was miserable. She knew Allison would be coming to the party with Cookie from his house. This called for desperate measures so she decided to enlist Big Paddy, only she didn't bother to tell him first. She made her big move about an hour into the party. The night was approaching the serious snogging stage but we still went through the ritual of making it into a game. Karen kicked it off.

'Why don't we play Chairs? With the guys sitting down.'

By then, you could play Chairs either way – with the girls doing the sitting and the guys squeezing on to the chair or sofa beside them, or with the guys sitting and the girls perching on their knees when the music stopped.

The game started, though a few folk hadn't joined in yet. Cookie was glued to Allison, which hadn't escaped Karen's notice. They stood chatting near the window and Allison had his undivided attention whether she wanted it or not. I was spare girl that night – or at least at the start of the night – which meant I was in charge of the music. I put on Queen which was usually guaranteed to get everyone in the mood. I had control of the light switch too. Not that the lights made much difference – it was the start of summer, still bright outside and the curtains at Cammy's were thin and only half-drawn anyway.

Karen made straight for Big Paddy who was sprawled on a huge old armchair in a corner. She planted herself firmly next to his chair and waited, signalling at me furiously. I was puzzled, but caught her drift so I halted Freddie abruptly in full flow. She dived on to his knee – and out-Kirsty-ed Kirsty.

Kirsty, it goes without saying, had been first to grope back. But even she hadn't gone beyond tentative caressing by that time – and strictly above trousers, at least as far as we knew.

It was common knowledge that Karen usually saved everything for Cookie, but she took Big Paddy by storm. She tore into him, kissing him hungrily and savagely. Big Paddy had his hands fixed firmly on the arms of the chair, which was standard Karen-mode for all the guys other than Cookie, but she lifted one of his huge mitts and moved it to her chest. Big Paddy didn't need asking twice. I saw all of this because you couldn't not see it, or hear it. Karen was noisy – loud, look-at-me noisy. She moaned, she wailed, she grunted. Then she went further, further than any of us had ever gone before. She let a hand slip into Big Paddy's lap and he instantly grew an expression like a pools winner. Then she unzipped him, squeezed in two fingers and he grinned dumbly. Karen groaned and spoke his name. Much too loudly.

'Oh Paddy, Paddy.'

It wasn't exactly subtle but it did the trick. I had watched her performance in shock, then I snapped out of it, flicked the light switch back on and let the needle bounce on to vinyl. Freddie ripped back into Keep Yourself Alive and Karen got up in a show of reluctance. The game did have rules after all. Big

Paddy, meantime, sat there in blissful shock and tugged a cushion on to his lap.

Karen purred at him. 'I'll be back. In a minute.'

But she didn't go back, not to Big Paddy. She didn't have to. Cookie wandered over to her, aware of the murmuring buzz her actions had sparked off.

'Eh, everything OK? Am I still getting you home all right?'

Karen glowed, mission accomplished. Mostly she clung to Cookie for the rest of the party. She spoke to me briefly while he was in the loo, asking me to pass on a message of apology to Big Paddy.

'Tell him I'm sorry. I don't know what came over me.'

Probably Big Paddy. Don't be so crude, Lorna!

I kept my thoughts to myself as Karen continued.

'I just don't how it happened. I really don't. I'm so guilty. I used him, I know I did.'

'Yeah, he looks dead upset,' I said. 'Probably feels really violated.'

Karen nodded back, gravely.

A little later, Allison developed a sudden interest in Cammy and they slipped into a private huddle. They talked, they laughed, he whispered something to her. She shook her head and looked disbelieving, but the pair of them left the party. Seriously, Cammy actually walked out on his own party. They convinced no one by declaring they needed to get some fresh air, even though it had started drizzling. They returned after about twenty-five minutes. Cammy was beaming from ear to ear and Allison had a look of stunned surprise on her face. Ross glowered and shot daggers at Cammy. But Ross got over it quickly, thanks to a consolation prize from Kirsty who had observed Karen's display with Big Paddy and determined to re-establish pole position – pardon the cheap pun.

The party approached winding down time and Cammy's parents came down from upstairs where they had been camped out. We were in decent shape and so was the house. Cammy's Dad – that's right, off-duty John The Bampot – popped his head round the living-room door and smiled.

'How's the prayer meeting going?'

Not pushy, not heavy, but we recognised the signal all the same. It was chucking out time. Cue the final pairing-off ceremony – last minute, rushed amnesties and walking home arrangements, maybe via the shelter or the sheds up at the primary school.

Meanwhile, all was right again in Karen's world, at least until Cookie fetched their things from the pile on Cammy's bed. Cookie brought back his anorak, Karen's coat…and Allison's jacket. He handed the girls their things.

'Need to just walk you straight up the road, Karen. Allison'll have to come as well. I can't go in later than her.'

Karen stormed out of the party like a character in a comic, like steam was rising from her. I imagined I could see the word FIZZING appearing in big bold letters above her head with five exclamation marks after it. God knows what went through her head that night. The awkward walk home, the three of them, none knowing what to say. Karen's performance with Big Paddy a blazing cross on the night, and no opportunity to explain it away to Cookie – if he had even noticed. Then his quick kiss on the cheek at her front door, Karen collapsing back against it once she was inside, shaking as she pictured the two of them, Cookie and Allison, still alert and buzzing from the party, walking off into the night together. Karen would imagine them holding hands and sense Cookie becoming heady, giddy, from Allison's scent. It was too much to bear.

It was just a couple of days later that Karen took ill and then went downhill at frightening speed. Just over a week later, she choked out the awful news that her illness was terminal and insisted Cookie wasn't to know.

'Promise me,' she gasped. 'Whatever you do, you won't say anything to Simon. He's not strong enough. He won't be able to take it. It'll destroy him.'

We heard. TELL HIM. TELL HIM. FOR GOD SAKE, SOMEONE TELL HIM.

Come to think of it, there seemed to be an awful lot of people that we weren't allowed to tell. Karen only let three of us in on it – Wee Mary, Jo and me. She said Kirsty couldn't be trusted and Fiona lived too close to her. Karen's Mum didn't want anyone else to know, apparently, so under NO circumstances were we to utter a single word to her parents because they hadn't come to terms with it and would break down if anyone spoke to them about it. Oh, and we weren't to mention it to our own parents either because they would be bound to phone her Mum. Not a word to the guys, either, just in case any of them accidentally let it slip to her Simon. Karen seemed to spend more time on this complicated web of no-tells than on the details of her illness itself.

I didn't say anything to Cookie and I'm pretty sure Wee Mary or Jo didn't either, but within a day or so, he somehow knew.

They hung around with the rest of us, Cookie and Karen, but pretty soon they were there, but detached at the same time, in a little private bubble. Cookie looked bewildered and afraid, as if this was all far too big for him to carry.

A few days later at the school, Karen had more gigantic, stunning news. She was excited and so, so courageous. She gathered us together in the girls' toilets, Wee Mary, Jo and me.

'We're getting engaged,' she announced. 'It's really Simon's idea. I tried to tell him there's no point, that he has to forget about me. He's got his whole life in front of him. But he wants to do this, for me. It's lovely, I can't believe it.'

As Karen hurried off to her next class – surprisingly sprightly for one so gravely ill – Jo screwed up her face and voiced the first tiny seed of doubt.

'You know, it's an awful shame about Karen. She could've had a great future writing crap stories for The Jackie or something.'

She had just opened a tiny crack in a floodgate.

'What's she doing at the school anyway?' snapped Wee Mary. 'What's the point in her being here?'

'Yeah, if she really is at death's door,' I added and tried to suck it back in again.

We glanced at one another then lowered our eyes, ashamed. Caught out in our little conspiracy of doubt.

Karen had a party coming up the following weekend. It had been arranged for weeks – long before she took ill. We all assumed she'd call it off, but she didn't. They had decided, Karen and Cookie, that it was to become a sort of engagement party – unofficial, of course, no family or anything, no need for a ring even. Cookie's paper round wouldn't stretch that far. It was just something they wanted to do.

'A little declaration of our bond in these final days,' explained Karen. 'Something we want to share with our closest friends.'

Shucks.

Karen plotted it with great care and skill. They wouldn't be announcing it till halfway through the party, so it would be a surprise for the others outside of Wee Mary, Jo and me. They would wait until after Karen's parents had gone out and, of course, better if no one outside our circle knew about it.

'That's why I can't invite Allison,' she explained. 'Plus, I don't want it to look as if I'm being over-dramatic or anything.'

Never crossed our minds.

Yes, it had been precision planning on Karen's part but Robert blew it apart completely. That's not fair. It was my fault in the first place, for breaking the confidence, for telling him. But then, I told him everything and it never felt wrong. I also told Robert about my nagging doubts, how the whole thing felt, well, not quite right. Karen didn't look any different to me, there were no visible signs of her being ill. OK, that was plausible because what did I know then about tumours, or how they affected you? But what Wee Mary said about Karen still coming to school, had stuck in my mind. And now the party. It just didn't add up.

For once, Robert didn't know what to say to me, or what to think about our misgivings. But he agreed on one thing. This was too big, we had to keep it to ourselves, these doubts could not be repeated. What if it was true? How would we live with ourselves?

Not long before, in the second half of fourth year, Robert had started writing a little column for the local paper, The Cumbride Courier. It was part of a school news round-up the paper had introduced. Robert didn't say it in so many words, but he liked to give the impression that he had been head-hunted, probably because he had come second in a national essay-writing competition and there had been a little bit about it in the wee paper, as everybody called it. But Fiona told us a very different version. The headmaster at St Joe's had asked at assembly for a volunteer to do something for the local paper and Robert had practically thrown both hands up in the air.

He could easily have posted his weekly report to them – his copy, he called it – but he liked to take it into the Courier office himself every Friday after school, and he would hang about in the office until they shut at five. He just wanted a taste of it, he said – *the buzz of the newsroom*. Yeah, Cumbride's own Daily Planet where they probably yelled *Hold the Front Page* for chip pan fires and chemist rotas.

I'm probably being too hard on Robert again. He simply wanted to spend some time with reporters, to see what they were like, to see what he was going to be like. From what I could gather, the reporters on the Courier seemed to take to him. I knew he'd be keen and likeable and I also knew he would ask them a lot of questions. He told me he always tried to take in at least one idea for a story, or a lead as he called it, on his Friday visits. He would scan the next issue when it came out and punch the air with a loud *Yes* whenever they followed up on one of his suggestions.

There was one young reporter in particular who took Robert under his wing. I can't remember his name, if I ever knew it at all. Robert got on well with this guy and they got into the habit of going for a coffee on a Friday after the office closed. Robert said the reporter told him loads of useful stuff, gave him pointers.

The day before Karen's party, the reporter asked Robert if he would be interested in doing a bit of sports reporting for the paper, covering the local junior football team. Robert lied and said he would love to. He'd never really fancied sports journalism but he was reluctant to show anything less than total enthusiasm. The reporter suggested Robert go with him to the team's game the following day, so he could show him the ropes and introduce him to some of the club officials and players.

Robert nodded without great eagerness, then asked what time they would get back. The reporter told him it was a cup game somewhere near Aberdeen, so they wouldn't return to Cumbride till late on.

'Aw, no, sorry,' said Robert, glad of a genuine excuse to get out of it. 'I can't go then, not tomorrow. Got a party on, an engagement party actually.'

He added the engagement bit so the reporter would get the message it was something important that was stopping Robert from grabbing the fabulous opportunity he was offering.

'No sweat,' the journalist said. 'Maybe some other time – there's plenty more games. So, your party. Big family do is it?'

'No,' said Robert. 'It's a pal of mine. I think you met him actually. Cookie. Simon Cooke. I brought him into the office once.'

'Oh right enough. Boy with specs? Couldn't make out a word he was saying cos his mouth was all frozen up?'

Robert was impressed that the reporter remembered little details like that. Sign of a professional, Robert concluded.

He had met Cookie one Friday up at the town centre just after school. Cookie had got out of class early for a dentist's appointment. Robert was on his way to the Courier office so he took Cookie in with him. I reckoned Robert was delighted at the opportunity to let someone see how familiar he was with the local paper office and the reporters, how they all knew him and how he was on first-name terms with them. Probably hoped Cookie would carry the word back so the rest of us would be impressed.

'Your pal,' the reporter said to Robert, casually. 'Who's he getting engaged to? Somebody at the High School? Might know her or a big brother or sister. I was there back in the day.'

'Yeah,' replied Robert. 'She is at the High. Karen her name is, Karen Hart.'

'Nah, doesn't ring a bell. But are they not a bit young for getting engaged? Your mate, he'll be about the same age as you, eh? What's he thinking about, settling down so young? No one told him the world's hoaching with women?'

It just slipped out. Robert swore to me it had.

'Oh no, they won't be getting married. They're just doing it cos Karen's really sick. Terminal apparently. Really sad.'

The reporter's eyes popped.

'Hang on, hang on. Let me get this right. They're what, fifteen-sixteen? Both still at the school?'

'Cookie, eh, Simon.' Robert nodded. 'Yeah, he's sixteen. Think Karen might still be only fifteen, though.'

The journalist galloped on excitedly, keen to stake a least a little ownership. 'And they're getting engaged because she's dying? School sweethearts! Fucking hell, Robert, that's a bloody great yarn we've got there. That's national paper stuff. Front page maybe. I could get us serious dough for this. We'll split it.'

Instant panic. 'Ah look, you can't say anything, right? They're wanting to keep it quiet. OK?'

'Sure-sure, no sweat. But can't guarantee somebody else won't pick it up.'

Robert learned a lesson that day, about reporters, about newspapers, about The Story. He confessed to me that night, racked with remorse for breaking our confidence and so, so angry. He swore he'd phone the reporter first thing on the Monday, when the wee paper office opened again, just to make sure he'd keep it to himself. But I'm convinced a major part of it was annoyance at himself for not getting there first and on his own. For not recognising a Big Story.

The party didn't happen. Fiona passed the word round that it was off. She had been at Karen's on the Saturday morning. They were in Karen's room and Fiona was helping her pick something to wear to the party. (No discussion of what Fiona was going to wear.) They were sorting out records when the doorbell rang. Karen's room was nearest the front door but her Mum called out from the kitchen.

'Stay where you are, you two. I'll get it.'

They heard a man's voice, sounded youngish.

'Eh, Mrs Hart?'

'Yes?'

'I'm really sorry to bother you, especially at this time and everything, but I'm from the, eh, Sunday Mail. Eric Clark's the name. I was wondering if I could talk to you? Just for a few minutes, if you can spare it.'

'The Sunday Mail?' Surprise in Karen's Mum's tone.

'Yip,' he said. 'As I say, I know it's a bad time and everything, a bit upsetting and that. But maybe just a minute or two?'

Karen's Mum's sounded baffled, concerned.

'Look, I think you've got the wrong person. I don't know what you're talking about. A bad time? Has something happened to my husband...?'

The man from the Sunday Mail was not fazed. Door-stepping was his craft.

'I understand completely, you not wanting to talk about it. Fair enough, and I really don't want to bother you, honestly. But just think about it for a minute. This might inspire other kids like her, give them some hope. We'll be dead sympathetic and er, we can help, with expenses and that.'

Dead sympathetic? Nice choice of words, Mr Clark.

Karen's Mum was getting upset now, and impatient.

'Listen, I haven't the first clue what you're on about. How do you mean, inspire other kids?'

In the bedroom meantime, Karen was hearing every word. Suddenly she looked like she wished she really was dying and that it would happen right there and then. The reporter continued, just the slightest note of panic in his voice. 'You are Mrs Hart, aren't you? Karen's mother.'

Rope, end of. Karen's Mum said: 'What's this got to do with her? What are you saying?'

The reporter was more assured now. At least he was at the right door.

'I'm sorry. Really, I do understand how upsetting all this must be for you. You know, Karen's illness, and it being, eh, you know, nothing they can do and whatever. Must be really hard on you. But her getting engaged, that's marvellous courage, a real inspiration. What's the boy's name again? Simon Cooke, isn't it?'

The mist cleared and in an instant, Karen's Mum saw the complete picture. She didn't mess about. She dismissed the journalist.

'I'm sorry, there's been a mistake. You've got it all wrong. There's no illness and there's no engagement.'

Fiona heard the door slam and a second later, Karen's Mum burst into the room. Her face was in flames but she spoke quietly.

'You better go, Fiona,' she said. Then to Karen. 'Right, my girl…'

That was the last Fiona heard.

Karen didn't show her face for over a week. This time she did stay off school. It was the last week of term anyway and the exams had finished. Then her parents took her away somewhere the start of the summer holidays, only Cookie didn't go with them as had been arranged for months.

Give Karen a little credit. She finally returned to the fold looking chastened. No one mentioned any of it at first – the illness, the party cancelled at the last minute, the non-engagement. Karen and Cookie spoke, quietly. It seemed no permanent damage had been done and Allison wasn't coming for the summer after all. It hadn't taken her long to outgrow us. A couple of hours later Jo, the smallest of us, plucked up our collective courage.

'By the way Karen, how you feeling? You any better?'

She tried to bluff it out and even knew the right word.

'I'm in er, remission. Looks like I'm going to pull through.'

Just like that, back from the brink of death. She had regained her health but lost a fiancé. Still, only another year, then she would get another crack at it.

Chapter 20

August 2001
Murder On The Dancefloor – Sophie Ellis-Bextor

NO chance Paddy, no way. Think you can just walk into my work, blow up my life then exit stage left leaving me in bits? Sorry, not allowed. What am I saying? I'm not sorry. This time I have nothing to be sorry for.

Big Paddy was already halfway across the canteen with those huge, loping strides of his, screwing his police cap back on. I got up from the table and took off after him, confused and raging. I was staggering, vision blurred, as if I was drunk. God knows what anyone watching me must have thought, but I wasn't caring.

My anger revved up, levelled out at grim determination, and I upped the pace. I caught up with him a couple of yards short of the lift. The door slid open and Big Paddy waited as two people got out. I squeezed past them, got in between Big Paddy and the lift door, then turned and faced him, my feet planted. I barred his way, my blazing glare daring him to walk round me. Words barrelled out in a rush.

'What the hell, Paddy?' I said, somehow manufacturing a sound so low-key and calm it bore no relation to the churning inside. 'You don't do that to a person...you just can't. You don't say something like that then walk away like it's nothing. No, not allowed.'

The laid-back colossus of a cop looked like he was now in severe discomfort, bordering on anguish. With the habitual grin suddenly frozen, he appeared severely constipated. Tough.

'I'm sorry Lorna,' he mumbled. 'Shouldn't have said it. I take it back. Just forget it, OK?'

Are you serious? No fucking chance, Paddy.

'Forget it?' I echoed. 'There's this guy I haven't seen in God knows how

141

many years. You stroll in here while I'm at my work and accuse me of wrecking his marriage...and bear in mind I wasn't even there! Then you tell me to forget it? Aye, sure, Paddy. No bother. What planet are you living on?'

My attempt at keeping it all on an even keel was coming apart. I suppose I must have started to sound a bit hysterical. Huh, a bit! People were staring at us so Big Paddy decided it was time to use his cop training. Take control, calm the situation. He went into the old half-crouch routine.

'Ssshh, take it easy, Lorna. I didn't mean it like that. Me and my stupid big gob. I'm sorry, OK?'

'No, not OK. A million fucking miles from OK. Not good enough Paddy. You say something like that, you owe me more. You owe me a proper explanation.'

Big Paddy was visibly anxious, as if he couldn't quite figure out how he had got to this place and would do anything for a way out. His face betrayed him. He was praying for the lift door to open again. He was desperate, but I didn't budge. I wasn't for letting him off the hook.

'OK, OK, keys,' he said. 'Hands up, you're right. But we can't talk here. Not right now.'

'You've got to talk sometime, Paddy.'

'All right, all right. Look, I could come round. To your place, I mean. You in tonight? About eightish? That any good?'

Did he think I had to check my social diary first? Did he think I had a social diary to check? But wait, sudden panic. Did I really want to hear any more? What was I letting myself in for? Maybe better to leave it, just forget it. But I heard myself agreeing.

'Fine, fine. I'll give you the address. I'm up in Westview now, you'll need directions.'

Big Paddy relaxed. A reprieve, for a while at least.

'I'll find it, Lorna. I'm maybe no Inspector Morse but I am a cop, remember?'

OK, but damn you, Paddy, you're not getting the last word.

'Right,' I said. 'I'll see you later...but as you were at great pains to tell me, you're a married man as well as a cop. Better get yourself an alibi.'

142

Chapter 21

July 1974
Kung Fu Fighting – Carl Douglas

THAT power Robert had, whatever it was, he used it with Ross. To haul him back from the brink when he looked like imploding. When it looked like we'd have to let him go, when it seemed like he was forcing us to force him out.

There was something about Ross, something wrong, something off. Or perhaps that's not quite right. Not with him or about him, but in him. Something buried, something stirring, simmering deep down inside him.

On the surface, Ross was brilliant. He was blond, a genuine high school heart-throb. The best looking of the guys in our crowd by a mile. Not that the rest of the boys would ever come close to acknowledging that, not even Robert when we got all deep and sensitive during our talks at the wall. But the guys did agree on one thing, something safer for them. He was the best athlete and, in particular, the best footballer of our lot, also by a distance. It wasn't just them that thought that. Ross was picked for our school under-sixteens when he was thirteen. People came to watch him play, scouts from some of the big teams. Cammy told us they used phrases like *naturally gifted* and *goal machine*. Ross was about average height but he was fast and tricky – like Jinky except he kicked with the wrong foot, Big Paddy said once. I didn't have a clue what he was on about. Football was Ross's big thing, his moment in the sun, his time to dazzle, his stage. On the pitch, Robert – our spiritual leader – bowed to Ross. On the pitch, Big Paddy – our physical leader – gave way to Ross.

We, as in the girls, didn't take much interest in football. But there was one game that stood out, a game the guys talked about for weeks after. A sweaty afternoon-long marathon in sapping heat. They limped and crawled back to us in the shelter, milking it like they were soldiers home from the Somme.

They were knackered but elated. They had been playing their arch-rivals, Brian Donnelly's team from a few streets away. They were reckoned to be untouchable but our guys had slaughtered them 26-5 and Ross, of course, was the hero. He had scored TWENTY-ONE of our goals. Ha, did I just say *ours*? The rest of the guys back-slapped him, shook him by the shoulders. They knelt down and worshipped at his feet. Ross's face, already burned red in the sun, glowed some more.

Cammy, who would have given anything to be a quarter as good as Ross, was delirious.

'Seven hat-tricks. Seven bloody hat-tricks. In one game. Amazing, Rossy boy. A-fucking-mazing. Dixie Deans couldn't wipe your arse, so he couldn't.'

Robert, over the top as usual, turned solemn. He had an announcement and, though he was obviously being tongue in cheek (or at least that's what I always assumed), he made it sound important and weighty.

'I'm going to write to the Guinness Book of Records. I'll post the letter on Monday. I don't think seven hat-tricks has ever been done before.'

Ross the hero, a legend in his own swing park. Maybe every class in every school has a kid like this, but we firmly believed it was his big chance, the football. His real opportunity to be somebody, to outshine Robert even. But it came to nothing because Ross let himself down, he blew it. He let himself go and started turning up late for football training, or skipping it altogether. He took up smoking and wouldn't give up even when his football coach pleaded with him. He boozed heavily on Friday nights and turned up for Saturday morning games like he'd been hit by a truck.

Ross had pressed self-destruct. We all saw it. Something there, something not quite right.

Robert did tell me some stuff about Ross's past during our nights at the wall. We didn't have to swear each other to silence. We could talk about anything and know it wouldn't be repeated. Not again, especially not after Karen.

Ross lived three doors away from Robert with his Dad and his wee sister, Trish. Robert said he was sure he could remember Ross's Mum being around when they first moved to Cumbride. He and Ross would have been five or six. But then she disappeared and it was never talked about. Not to them anyway, not to kids. Robert said Ross's Dad was a scary, sour kind of guy, wound-up and angry all the time.

There was one night that Robert had never forgotten. They all heard tortured screaming echoing down their lane and at first thought it was from someone's telly turned up way too loud. Then Robert's Mum poked her head out the back door and realised it was coming from Ross's house. Robert's

THE FENIAN

Dad and another neighbour went along and first chapped then battered at the door but got no answer. It wasn't locked – no one's house was back then – so they eventually barged in and there was a lot of loud, angry roaring and swearing. Ross and his little sister, Patricia, were brought out, tearful, in their pyjamas and stayed at Robert's house that night. He remembered some vague talk about Ross protecting his sister, but the episode was never discussed again. From then on, Robert knew never to go to Ross's door. He couldn't remember how he knew, whether his parents had warned him or he had come to the conclusion himself that it wasn't a good idea. He would always wait for Ross to come in for him instead.

Robert told me about another incident. He had become friendly with Paddy at school – St Jude's, the Catholic primary – and he had asked him round to his bit to play. This was before he was called Big Paddy. They were only seven or eight and he hadn't taken a real stretch yet, so he wasn't much bigger than other kids of their age. Paddy and Ross didn't hit off – a trace of mutual jealousy and rivalry possibly, over who was Robert's real best pal and who had the strongest claim. Paddy and Ross found an excuse to clash. They had a shoving match, a petty my-dad's-bigger-than-your-dad contest. Ross threw a puny punch and Paddy swatted him off. Game over. Ross cried – and in front of other boys too – then ran home in disgrace.

End of story? It should have been. It had been nothing more than a minor sparring, the kind of quickly forgotten squabble that happened in every playground ten times a day. But there was a sequel to this one. A few days later, Paddy and Robert were walking home from primary and passed Ross's house. Ross's Dad appeared, dragging his son behind him. Ross looked petrified as his Dad jabbed a finger in Paddy's direction.

'This him?'

He didn't wait for an answer but propelled his obviously reluctant son towards Paddy.

'Right,' he shouted. 'That's you claimed him. Get stuck in.'

Ross looked ready to cry again. For his part, Paddy was terrified of Ross's Dad, this noisy man with the wild, staring eyes who was yelling, louder and louder.

'Come on. Come on. Rip his fucking head off.'

Ross's Dad was in their faces and now the boys were both trembling but one of Robert's neighbours appeared, alerted by the disturbance. Ross's Dad cursed and stomped off with a parting shot to Paddy.

'This isn't over, ya wee fuck.'

Wind forward about a decade and Ross was a genuinely popular guy, close mates with both Robert and Big Paddy for years and a favourite with the girls. A big integral part of our shelter gang, a livewire always up for fun and a dare. But gradually, we became aware of another side to him. A kink, a lurking aggression waiting for an excuse.

He began to pick rows and become easily riled, far too easily. He was over-eager to get into a scrap – not with our lot, not at first anyway, but with interlopers, any rival stags who threatened to invade our patch.

There was one episode that Cookie told me about. Our guys were playing football against some boys from another part of the scheme, a return away leg to Brian Donnelly's mob, I think it was. As usual, Ross was our lot's main man and the other team put two of their guys on him, to mark him tight. They were tackling him hard, shadowing him, denying him space. Ross had his work cut out but gradually he was getting the better of them. Then one of their players shoulder-charged Ross heavily – for the sixth or seventh time. Nothing over the top, according to Cookie, just normal football stuff. But Ross turned on the guy, took off after him and recklessly kicked his legs away. The guy toppled over and Ross knelt down, punching at him, pounding on his back, blow after blow, till Big Paddy and two of the other team's players hauled him off.

Ross's moods became more blatant after that, as if he was surrendering control and making no effort to hide them. Dark, dark sulks. Sometimes without warning, he'd just walk away from us. We'd all be talking, a group of us. The usual inconsequential nonsense – laughing, joking, goading each other about nothing. Ross would be dishing it out with the rest of us, then one wrong word would set him off. I can't even give you an example because you could never predict it or work out later what the word had been, but Ross would just turn his back and storm off, raging, in a cloud of *bastards* and *sakes* and *fucking dicks*.

Then he would return the next night and no one would dare raise it or call him out because it would just be putting down a deposit on another sulk. We all sensed that one day soon, he would erupt and there would be no turning back, but when that day came, the target was the last person we expected.

He and Cookie had been great pals since the year dot, our primary's equivalent of Robert and Big Paddy. But somewhere, a little niggle was born. No one knew how it started, just some tiny seed of bad feeling that festered. Petty little taunts were swapped, I-was-sitting-there-first-no-you-weren't kind of rows, shoving matches where Cookie inevitably backed down. Finally, it boiled over.

It was one of those steamy, sweaty days in summer, a Sunday, two days after one of our parties. We'd trekked to our secret oasis – a waterfall deep in the countryside that Cammy had discovered years before on one of his solitary wanderings and shared with us as a gift. We couldn't wait. We were no longer shy after our day at the baths. The more organised forward planners among us had our swimming stuff on below our clothes, so we stripped off the moment we got there and piled into the deep pool below the waterfall, shrieking at the icy cold depths.

That brought home another quirk we'd noticed lately about Ross. He often held back on the riverbank but I'm sure it had nothing to do with the water. No, he just seemed reluctant to take off his T-shirt sometimes. It wasn't always like this – he'd had no hesitation that time we went to the swimming pool. But some days at the waterfall, he'd sit there alone on the edge, dangling his feet in the cooling current. He'd say he didn't fancy it that day or else he'd just have a fag first. Only one, then another, lit from the previous dowt. He would watch us messing about, letting us scoop spray at him and inevitably, the temptation would get too much for him. Either that or the teasing. He would slide his jeans off then cross his hands and grip the end of his T-shirt. He'd stay in that position there for an age, as if he was having a really good think about it, then he'd try and do it all in one movement – whip the shirt over his head, toss it on to the grass behind him, and slip himself into the water. He'd force himself down deep, crouching on the bottom if he had to, right in up to his neck straight away despite the chill of the stream which the rest of us took ages to get used to.

But no matter how careful he was, we still noticed, we still saw the shadows of the angry blue bruises rippling under the water, usually on his sides, around the ribs. We noticed, but we didn't dwell on it or comment. Bear in mind this was the Seventies. Child abuse hadn't been invented yet.

Back on that particular Sunday, Ross was on good form, on top of his game – chatty, smiley, playful, cheeky. Darting about, grabbing towels on the trek, inviting us to chase him like little kids. No delay at the waterfall – off with his stuff and straight into the river along with the rest of us. Then after, as most of us lazed on the bank, drying off in the sun, Cammy and Ross shared a smoke and skimmed flatties across the water, giggling like a pair of wee lassies.

Up to that point, it had been one of the most perfect days in shelter gang history. Then out of nowhere, Karen started sobbing quietly. Little sub-committees were convened. Karen and Fiona first, heads close, almost touching. Whisper whisper whisper. Karen still sniffling.

Cookie, trying to get Jo to do the Corporal Jones impression she'd premiered at the party, was wrenched from his ignorant bliss and summoned with a grave nod. More whispers then Karen, her mouth twisted, started nodding in Ross's direction. Cookie looked uncertain and unhappy. The story came out gradually in Chinese whispers. Ross had tried it on with Karen on Friday night.

The guys all knew the score. Cookie and Karen were our Mary and Joseph, our betrothed. Karen was strictly out of bounds. She would occasionally allow a brief, innocent snog but nothing full-on – and definitely no touching. She was claiming Ross had fastened on to her at the party, tongue, the lot, and had tried to force a hand under her top. She had shoved him off and he'd called her a tight, prick-teasing cow.

Now she was demanding honour. Her virtue had to be defended and Cookie was backed into a corner. He knew what was expected of him but he clearly didn't fancy it. He hoped, without believing it, that Ross would let him off the hook. He didn't have to actually say the S-word or anything. It was like, *Come on Ross, be a mate, just shrug and look a tiny bit embarrassed. Make an excuse, like you were wrecked, or Karen was looking so sensational you couldn't resist.* That's all he had to do. Wasn't too much to ask, was it? But Cookie knew he was dreaming. Karen sat back, head in the air, snuffling and haughty.

'Em, Ross, buddy.' Cookie tried for firm but conciliatory at the same time. It came out as a snivelling plea. 'You got a wee minute?'

Ross sent another flat stone bouncing across the river then turned happily, flicking the last stump of his ciggie after it. He sloped over, his face shining. It had been a fantastic day but it was about to be wrecked.

Cookie said: 'Listen pal, I think you should, er, apologise to Karen.'

In a beat, Ross turned into a different person. He bristled, his face contorted, and he dismissed Cookie with a sullen scowl.

'Sake, the fuck for?'

'You know, the er, the other night, at the party.' Cookie was squirming. 'What you said to Karen and that.'

In seconds, Ross had metamorphosed into a ball of ugly aggression, like someone had just done an eggy in his face.

'Kiss ma sweaty baws. You going to make us, ya dick?'

A Tommy Cooper moment, though anything but funny. Just like that, a fight was arranged. Our first proper fight…and between two of our own guys. It felt serious, and sad. I remember my illogical chain of thoughts. *We're too far away, they can't fight here, it's too far from home. What do we after it? With the winner? With the loser?* There would only be one winner, of course. Ross was giving away a couple of stones and maybe a head difference in height. But we all knew it, he would destroy Cookie, damage him even. Karen knew it too. She had known it from the start and prepared herself to weep over her fallen and wounded knight.

We edged back and created a natural boxing ring in the shade of the trees and held our breaths as Ross and Cookie began circling each other. I prayed it would be quick, and I knew I wasn't alone in waiting for the first sight of blood – Cookie's blood. We hoped that would be enough to satisfy Ross. Dread and fear and silence hung in the air. Ross wound himself up for the kill.

Then Robert turned it all into a daft game. The great showman had let us all go to the very edge before making his entrance. He sprang between Ross and Cookie.

'Hang on a tick,' he said. 'I've got a better idea.'

No chance Robert, I thought, not this time. No way his slick words would be enough to defuse the battle-ready blood lust oozing from Ross.

But Robert turned to the river and started marching away from Ross and Cookie, immediately dragging attention away from them. Robert waved a hand, hamming it up, and gestured towards the water with a flourish.

'Right,' he proclaimed. 'The great tree-trunk challenge. Or are you pair of shitebags too scared to accept it?'

Ross glowered and waved a finger at Robert's face.

'Don't you fucking well call me a shitebag, ya fanny pad, or you're fucking next.'

But he was already too late, just a fraction too slow, and he knew it. He felt the worm slide into his gullet and he was wriggling on the hook. Reel him in, Robert.

There was a fallen tree in the river which formed a dam, creating a pool which was the deepest part of this stretch, just along from the waterfall. The tree trunk was sometimes our diving board. Robert picked up a couple of poly bags which we'd used to carry our towels, and passed them to Cammy and me.

'Right,' he said, getting us organised. 'Everything we've got. Towels, T-shirts, socks, anything. Dump them into the bags.'

We obeyed, intrigued, caught up in it already. The bags soon bulged and Robert took them back from us and tied knots with the handles at the ends. He issued instructions to Ross and Cookie, making it sound all official, like a proper contest.

'OK, you two, bag each. Up on the tree trunk. Batter each other with them. First in the water's the loser. Best out of three.'

Cookie took half a second to agree. Anything was better than fighting Ross, who had clearly been itching to fire into him, to let it all out, all that poison, to let that tight ball inside him explode. But Robert had beaten him, turned the tables. He had thrown the challenge back in his face and there was no way Ross could back out of it.

Robert led the contestants and the camp followers to the river's edge, turning it into a show, reducing a serious square go to It's a Knockout. He was like a circus ringmaster, in complete charge of the entertainment while he made up rules and regulations on the hoof.

'Now listen,' he said. 'You've got to keep one hand behind your back at all times. No kicking, no using the head, no shoving, and you're not allowed to start till I give you the signal. Break any of the rules and you're disqualified.'

It was irresistible. Ross and Cookie clambered on to the trunk, each gripping a stuffed plastic bag. We formed a line on the riverbank, desperate to see this now. All the heat was gone, even from Ross. He was grinning again, despite himself, at the sheer daftness of it. Grinning at Robert too, grateful to his pal for saving him from himself, for pick-pocketing his dangerous, dark intent and replacing it with this farcical piece of theatre. Cookie, it goes without saying, was even more grateful.

When I think back now, it was ridiculous, the two of them up there, slithering about on the mossy trunk, their balance hindered by the hands stuck behind their backs as they laid into each other with the bulging poly bags. Cookie was bigger, a little bit naturally stronger too, but Ross was more nimble, more skilled at dodging the blows. They each learned their parts quickly and faked it, like the wrestling on the telly. Cookie let himself be knocked off first and went flying through the air like he'd been shot. He crashed into the water, handing Ross his triumph, letting us all see that our athletic ace had mastered it first, this new sport Robert had just invented. Ross got the idea too. Round Two. He quickly let himself overbalance. Splash, all square. Round Three. They swapped signals – *try to make it look more convincing this time.* They traded half a dozen swipes then Ross plunged, roaring with laughter as he hit the water, allowing Cookie to be Karen's champion. Honours satisfied all round.

But that wasn't the end of the tree-trunk challenge. *Hey, we all want a go!* So up the others went, in pairs. Big Paddy v Cammy. No contest. Cammy got a couple of swift soakings. Big Paddy looked disappointed that he had been denied an acrobatic death plunge, but Robert obliged with a quick, rule-breaking, pre-signal swipe and Big Paddy teetered on the trunk, clutching his heart before letting himself tilt over slowly, like a mighty tree crashing through the forest. We girls wanted a go too. Tiny Jo v lanky Fiona. Jo whacked the top of Fiona's legs, Fiona's bag swished over Jo's head. Kirsty, Karen, Wee Mary and me? We sulked because one of the bags had burst beyond repair. Match abandoned.

We didn't get a go that day but once we got over the disappointment, we all trailed home ecstatic, Ross and Cookie's conflict long forgotten. Our towels and tops were dripping, but no one cared. We analysed the tree trunk challenge like the World Cup panel on TV. Who had been best? Who had been fastest? Who performed the best fall? Who made the biggest splash?

It was a genius of a game, where losing was more of a prize than winning and more keenly coveted. There was frantic anticipation about the next time. We talked about refining it, making it a proper knockout contest. Let's bring bin bags, someone said. Better still, let's nick pillow cases from home and use more towels. Or why not just pillows? Then Kirsty had a brainwave – girls up on guys' shoulders. Brilliant.

I can't remember if we ever did play it again, maybe once more, I'm not sure. But I do know I was left with a big question. Why had Robert gone out of his way – and risked a doing from Ross himself – to save Cookie's skin? One day, he explained it to me.

Chapter 22

1982-1990
Owner Of A Lonely Heart – Yes

HE goes to the minibar with the tumbler from the bathroom, takes out a miniature of Scotch, and pours himself a drink, adding a splash of tap water. He desperately wants a cigarette. The argument with Ruth has taken its toll, as it always does. Her relentless, penetrating tone never fails to leave him feeling slightly nauseous and weakened. He knows how her victims, sorry guests, on Newsnight must feel. It's not his fault Jack isn't returning her calls. It's not his fault that Jack has chosen to stay with friends rather than her until he starts university after the summer. He's a big boy, nearly nineteen for God sake, so he can make up his own mind about these things and what does she expect *him* to do about it anyway? But if Robert scratches the surface of his conscience, there's a little guilt lurking in there too. He has been super careful to avoid speaking ill of Ruth over the years. Likewise, her new guy, though six years is hardly new, Robert reminds himself. He knows him slightly, an experienced BBC producer much older than both of them. Robert always considered him an unnecessarily brash pain in the arse and for years assumed he was gay, but what the hell did he know? He can tell himself, hand on heart, that he has never actively discouraged Jack from a close relationship with his mother but equally, he has never much encouraged it either. Perhaps he has been too quick too many times to offer Jack an out when he is looking for an excuse to avoid spending time with her. So yes, he is probably not blameless and once again frets that he has been unfair to his ex-wife.

Then, just as he is trying to work their debilitating conversation out of his system, Paddy phones about the game on Saturday and Robert can't stop himself. He asks if there is any update on Lorna. There isn't much of one. Yes, Paddy has asked her if she is seeing anyone and though he didn't get a straight answer, he is pretty sure she isn't. It is a strained and awkward end to the call and Robert knows that Paddy is far from happy doing this. So, he sits down cradling his drink, uneasy, wishing he could rewind a little and make things better with Paddy and OK, with Ruth too. Still, he can't help wondering how different and yes, better, life would have been...would be...with Lorna. Oh, for fuck sake, not this again. Get real and grow up, he orders himself.

A cigarette would fix it. He is sure of it. He hasn't smoked in seven years but he wants one now, very badly. The story they ran today has had the opposite effect from what it was supposed to have – on him at least. It has put him in the mood. He had made it the lead item on the main teatime bulletin. The first stirrings of moves to ban smoking – not completely, of course, but in public places. The health minister has hinted indoor Scotland could be ciggie-free in as little as five years, but Robert isn't so sure. What are they going to do, force smokers to hang about like lepers on pavements outside pubs and offices? No chance, never going to happen. But it's got him thinking about that delicious first draw. The sweet, brief, dizzying hit. Maybe he'll nip down to the machine in the foyer. No, maybe he won't.

He had been a late starter to smoking, and after slagging pals who did it when he was a teeenager as well. He took it up when he was a reporter on the Sunday paper in Glasgow and discovered fags were a useful opener with contacts, those dissatisfied guys he met in shady corners of gloomy, out-of-the-way pubs. Disgruntled men – and they were nearly always men – willing to reveal things about their work superiors or former pals. Seedy, overlooked blokes willing to snitch for a price on their bosses or colleagues or neighbours or former friends, who were usually footballers, TV actors, MPs, council officials, police chiefs, business leaders or clergy. Cigarettes and booze were useful for giving Robert and them something in common, something to put those guys – and himself – at ease with whatever shabby secret they were trading. Cigs were a valuable stalling tactic too. *Here, have another one before you go.* That was usually good for another ten minutes of murky revelation.

Ruth hadn't liked him smoking and she didn't hesitate to tell him so, like five or six times a day. Sometimes Robert thought it became a symbol of their marriage, his smoking, then other times he thought that was either way over-complicated or way over-simplified. But his smoking certainly was a convenient fire-starter, a burning red rag to wave in each other's faces. Ruth laid down rules. She told him he couldn't smoke in her home, *her* home, where he had moved in the day after they got married and for which he paid half the hefty mortgage. So, night after night, he would stand defiantly at the back door, in snow and wind and rain. OK, he'd be frozen, soaked or both and left feeling sheepish at best, downright foolish at worst. But to hell, he was making a point even if he was never quite sure what it was.

Ruth stamped her foot down hard when Jack came along. Fair play, because that's the hard truth about smoking: you can never really make a case for it. So, Robert stopped, or at least as far as Ruth was concerned, he stopped. He was a non-smoker until he drove round the first corner from the big lower conversion in Chiswick. Then he'd pull over, scrabble about in the boot and grope around the spare tyre until, sweet relief, his fingers touched the smooth, shiny packet with the chuckaway lighter wedged into the cellophane.

Weekends at home were bad enough but the cold turkey of holidays together verged on the unbearable. On the occasional weekend when he flew to Glasgow for the big games, he'd smoke his throat raw, burdening Big Paddy with another secret.

It went on for a whole year, Ruth praising his strength and willpower, Robert taking the credit but cheating on her all the while. Driving home with windows wide open even in the bitter depths of winter, frantically waving a Magic Tree around the car and faking another addiction to extra strong mints. On the odd occasions when she smelled stale smoke on his clothes, he'd moan about the colleague he'd given a lift to, or walked to the Tube station with.

'Yeah, bloody Sam. Bastard puffing away next to me, even lit up in the car till I made him chuck it out the window.'

The charade went on as the marriage gradually disintegrated. Home life had clearly become an inconvenience to Ruth's ambition. For Robert's part, it hadn't taken too long to suss that once the rush of explosive sex and smart banter had calmed down, there was little else between them. Well, apart from Jack, of course, and without really ever getting into it and spelling it out, there was a kind of unspoken acknowledgement that they had to have a go at making it work for the child's sake, even if the marriage was sliding into cold, sterile arrangement.

Robert kept his smoking secret until the chill reached freezing point and then one day, after a particularly ferocious row, he sniffed the ridiculous air freshener odour on his fingers, felt his teeth ache from crunching mints and took a decision. *To hell with this, who am I really fooling here?* He started smoking openly again and tossed another smouldering log on to the embers of their marriage.

That was when Robert thought he saw it. A simple equation. The smoking = the marriage. Battle of wills, laying down of rules, domination, defiance, deceit, guilty pleasure, capitulation, sneaking, cheating, lying. Fuck you. No, fuck you. Then one morning he woke up and realised that however real those things were, they had nothing to do with smoking at all. The truth came to him with the kind of jolt that makes you want to smack the heel of your hand off your forehead. It was even more simple than he'd thought. He had married the wrong person.

Now he hasn't seen Ruth in the best part of a decade. That is not strictly accurate. Of course he has seen her. They'd worked in the same building in London for most of that time, for God sake, and occasionally passed each other in corridors. On those occasions they had shown each other professional respect and courtesy. What he means is that he hasn't seen her in a personal setting for years now. They communicate formally about Jack and their joint property interests in strained, stilted phone calls and now, increasingly, via email which suits them both much better. It had taken little effort to forget they used to sleep together. If truth be told, he hadn't found it that difficult to get over Ruth and conceded that it had almost certainly been even less difficult for her.

The cigarettes had taken a few years longer to kick but by God, he feels like one now. Ruth was in the past, he has a present and a future to think about and a smoke would help relax him. But Robert has made a decision. He definitely isn't going to buy a pack of B&H from the vending machine tonight. He has done another reverse ferret, as they called going back to the original plan when he worked in newspapers. With or without Paddy's assistance, he is going to make one final, serious effort to see Lorna and, if his memory serves him right, she had hated smoking with a passion.

Chapter 23

Summer 1968
Simon Says – 1910 Fruitgum Company

ROBERT always had this big guilt trip going on about Cookie and, finally, he explained it to me at our wall one night. I have a feeling it might have been the same day Ross and Cookie had come close to fighting, or if not, shortly after. Robert reckoned what he had inflicted on Cookie years before was the cruellest thing he had ever done in his life, and the memory still shamed and haunted him.

It had been obvious to all of us that he backed Cookie up more than he should. We all noticed it. Robert stuck up for him loads of times when it was clear to everyone else that it wasn't the right thing to do. Robert would deflect, or distract, like if Ross was trying to engineer trouble or if Cookie was getting a slagging for something he'd done or something he'd said. Usually Karen was involved somewhere. Cookie would get ripped into for giving into her for the zillionth time or for going up the boring old town centre shopping with Karen and her Mum instead of playing football. Cookie got slagged rotten more than any of the others – and Robert seemed to see it as his job to defend and protect him. For example, Cammy would mock him for opting to spend a Monday evening studying with Karen, or helping her tidy up her room, rather than sharing a couple of cans left over from the weekend carry-out.

'Pathetic fanny. Sixteen and he's like an old married man, so he is.'

While everyone else nodded in agreement, Robert would fire back: 'Ach, at least that's something a scabby wee alky like you is never going to have to worry about.'

Robert stuck up for Cookie even when he was generally pissing everybody else off with his huffs. He sulked a lot. Not Ross kind of sulks, not menacing, aggressive sulks, but spoiled wee boy kind of moods.

THE FENIAN

Thing was, without spelling out in so many words, we had a kind of democracy we tried to maintain when we did stuff together. We liked everybody to want to go along with it, or at least not object too much. We didn't actually take votes or anything but we always tried to make plans by consensus. All of us accepted this, except Cookie. It felt like he learned emotional blackmail early on and used it to create disunity. We'd talk about going up the waterfall on a hot day, or into town to the pictures, or maybe the youth club at the high school on a Friday night. We usually shunned the youth club because, well, we reckoned we had one of our own but occasionally, just for a change, we'd grace them with our presence. We'd discuss it, the momentum would build and we'd all be up for it. Then at the last minute, Cookie would moan: 'Nah, don't fancy it.'

We'd try to coax him until someone, usually Big Paddy, lost patience and said something like: 'Aw, come on Cookie, stop being a knob. We're all going, we talked about it last night, mind? We all agreed, it'll be a laugh.'

But Cookie would play the martyr and start whining.

'Nah, you lot go, don't worry about me. I just don't feel like it.'

A bit more coaxing would follow but it would usually end in more self-pitying moaning.

'Look, I'll be OK. I'll maybe just sit here on my own for a while, pick the chocolate off my Mars Bar. You lot away and have a great time. Don't give me a thought. Seriously.'

We'd hear wailing violins and Karen, of course, would always crack first, or maybe she just spotted openings – an opportunity for some private life-planning, a chance to play houses. Then Fiona would weaken.

'Well, if Karen's not going either, I'll maybe just stay as well. Keep her company.'

Evening's plans wrecked, and that would inevitably lead to resentment and all-round bickering. After Big Paddy, Cammy was usually next to snap.

'All right Cookie, tell us your brilliant flash of inspiration. Or will we just sit around all night with our thumbs up our arses?'

But Robert would step in and deflect it.

'Know what, I don't really fancy the youth club that much myself. It's usually about as much fun as scraping dog shite off your shoe. Listen, I've got a better idea. We could always…'

Football was another sore point and again, Big Paddy was usually first to lose the rag with Cookie. The dispute was always the same. It was about going in goals. We – the rest of the girls and me – didn't get it. What was the big deal? But for some reason, the guys all hated being the goalkeeper. It was OK when they played among themselves, their casual two v three games.

They would take turns about at being keeper and, as far as I could work out, the rule was, you let in one goal and that was you back out again. Some incentive, eh? The team with two in it didn't have a proper keeper but something called a backsie which was far too much science for me.

But the argument got really heated when they arranged games against other folk – challengers from the outside, little teams from around the scheme. Then our lot had to have a proper keeper.

They would discuss the game in advance for hours – tactics talks they called it. They would think up moves. Who's going to mark the other lot's best player? Why don't we stick Big Paddy up front? That'll throw them because they'll be expecting Ross. Our guys would delay getting to the crunch issue for as long as possible – who was going in goal? It inevitably ended in acrimony. Cammy would start by trying to butter up Big Paddy on the basis his size made him the obvious candidate.

'You're a brilliant keeper, Paddy,' Cammy would say, then turn to the others for back-up. 'Mind they saves against Donnelly's dicks last week? Pure Gordon Banks, so they were.'

No chance. Big Paddy was having none of it.

'Aye Popeye. Last week. That means it's definitely not my turn.'

Robert was self-appointed team manager, or first team coach, as he called himself, but he would despair and turn nippy when the discussion came round to deciding on goalkeeper.

'You know what we need? A new guy. Some boy with no pals and a caliper who'd be grateful to go in goal. Heh Paddy, take Cammy up the mental school, see if you can do a swap deal for some spasmo with seven fingers.'

Did I ever mention how sensitive and politically correct our guys were?

It almost always came down to the same method: the short straw or, to be more precise, the short blade of grass. Robert would get four stalks, tear one in half and bunch them all up in his fist. Before choosing, the other guys would have a heated argument about who got first pick because it was better odds. Finally, they would each try to grab one at the same time and half-stalk went in goal. Only FOUR stalks, mind, because Ross was exempt. He was their star player and the game plan always revolved around him, so he was needed at the centre of the action. Big Paddy said Ross was their Pele. Pele, Jinky? Make up your mind, Paddy.

One time, Ross caught Cookie trying to discretely signal to Robert with squints and nods as he arranged the thin clump of grass in his hand.

Ross spat on the ground and shook his head in disgust. 'Sake, you really got to cheat?'

Cookie stared at his feet while the other guys hissed and snarled, then

Robert jumped in to deflect.

'Absolutely he has to cheat. He's the villain here, it's his role, he's got no choice.'

Cammy lowered his eyebrows, as if a little bell had gone off.

'What is that? The Animal Farm guy, or some Shakespeare pish?'

Robert kept a straight face. 'Dick Dastardly.'

The deal was that the guys – apart from Ross – would take their chances. If it was Big Paddy or Cammy who pulled out the short blade, or Robert who was left with it, the unlucky one would stare mournfully at the tiny stub of grass, as if they had just been handed a death sentence. But after a couple of minutes they would shrug and get on with it, even if it was with little enthusiasm.

Not Cookie though. If it was him, he would gaze at the scrap of grass, scrutinise it for a long moment, then announce: 'Actually, I don't really fancy fitba the day. Think I'll maybe just go up the road, listen to the new Genesis on my headphones.'

The other guys would seethe, because you just didn't do that. You didn't let your mates down. They desperately wanted to tell him to piss off, but they knew they couldn't do without him. They couldn't play a man short, not against Brian Donnelly's lot. That was kamikaze tactics and they would get torn apart.

Cammy would resort to begging.

'Aw come on, Cookie, you've got to. We can't take them on just the four of us. We'll get our baws mangled, so we will. That's a hammering, guaran-fucking-teed.'

Cookie, not being obvious or anything, would eventually say: 'Ach, I'm no' sure. I just don't know if I'm up to it. Think I might have a wee twinge in my hammy (a mystery injury learned through watching Scotsport) from the cross-country run. But I hate to let you guys down. I could maybe play at the back for a wee while, see how I feel and that. But no' in goal. That would cripple us, all that leaping and diving about.'

Cammy would now be close to boiling point.

'A wee twinge in your fanny, you mean.'

In that moment, they seriously hated him. They despised him deep in their guts and they should have chased him, they knew they should, but they couldn't. Right there, right then, they needed him much, much more than he needed them, and he knew it. Robert always knew how it would end. He would let Cookie stew right to the last minute, right up to the point where Donnelly's mob were already on the makeshift pitch, chanting and goading our guys, asking if they were crapping out of it.

Then Robert would say: 'All right, all right. I'll start off in goal and see how it goes.'

Several times I asked Robert why he did it, stuck up for Cookie so much, before he finally told me. In the early shelter gang days – before I got to know either of them that well – I thought it was maybe a mutual admiration thing, because Cookie often gave the impression he was in awe of Robert, so much so that at times he behaved like a kind of apprentice Robert. It was Robert's stories that did it for Cookie. He loved the way Robert told his tales. Cookie would listen with even more rapt attention than the rest of us and get so wrapped up in it that he'd turn flycatcher, his jaw sagging, mouth hanging open. I often thought Cookie would have liked to have brought a pencil and paper so he could take notes.

Occasionally, Cookie would try and do it himself, tell stories, I mean, as if he was Robert's understudy. He tried it mostly when Robert was away on his holidays or off visiting his gran in Paisley on a Sunday with his Mum and Dad and big sister. Cookie was OK and he got better as he went on, but he could never quite crack it. He was never spontaneous enough. His stories all came across as too rehearsed – and he chucked in far too many obvious Robert-isms to sound original.

It took Robert ages to admit it to me, the reason he defended Cookie so much. Finally, he told me of a cruelty that had lasted a whole summer. It had happened years earlier when they were still at primary school. A long, drawn-out series of acts of humiliation that still haunted Robert, never mind what it had done to Cookie.

Bless me Lorna, for I have sinned…

Robert reckoned they were all nine or ten when this happened because there were four of them that palled around together – him, Ross, Cookie and Big Paddy. There was no Cammy, so it must have been a summer or two before he moved to Cumbride. Cookie lived round the corner from Robert and Ross, Big Paddy a few streets away.

It was the school holidays which meant freedom, endless hours of roaming for miles during the day. Fishing at the canal, Open golf at the pitch and putt, Wimbledon at the school playground, one-man hunt – a kind of advanced hide and seek – all over the town. The kind of stuff parents still let their kids do back then and, funnily enough, they came to little serious harm. At least, little serious physical harm.

Robert and the rest were allowed to stay out till it got dark – and that could be half-ten – just as long as they were back within sight of someone's house before it got really late. So yes, absolute freedom for all of them. Except for Cookie.

THE FENIAN

The rest called him a pansy and a wee lassie because he had to be in by half past eight, every single night. Ross used to ask if it was to get his nappy changed. His Mum did nothing to protect his street cred. She would stand at her front doorstep dead on time and call: 'Siiiiiiiiiii-mon! Beeeeed-time!'

Three little horrors would crow it right back at her in an echo, and Cookie would trot home obediently while Robert, Ross and Big Paddy passed a happy few minutes congratulating each other on their own collective cleverness.

Robert had gradually shifted his gaze from my eyes as he filled in the background. He said to me: 'Lorna, about what happened next. In my memory I keep trying to shift the blame on to Ross or Paddy. But the trouble is, I know it was my idea.'

One night that summer, about five minutes after Cookie had been called in, Robert suddenly said: 'Hey, let's go in for him. See what happens.'

Ross and Big Paddy didn't get it, but they went along because Robert was always coming up with new stunts to make their lives more interesting and entertaining.

They got to Cookie's, halfway down a row of terraced houses. Each house had its own small walled, cobbled entrance with a coal bunker in the corner. Most folk called it their porch, even though it wasn't covered over. The boys turned in, heading for Cookie's door. From the porch, they had a clear view of his kitchen window and what they saw was a gift to warped young minds. From their angle, or more probably height, they could only see about the top third of Cookie above the kitchen sink at the window, but it was plenty. He was stripped to his vest and his Mum was dabbing at his face with a sponge. Already this was way more than they could have hoped for. She dropped the sponge in the sink, reached out of sight and produced a towel. Then she licked a corner, forming a point, and poked around in Cookie's ears. Cookie couldn't see Robert, Ross or Big Paddy because his face was hidden by the towel and his Mum had her back to them. They started sniggering.

But what they had seen so far was only the appetiser. It got much better/worse. Cookie's Mum dried his face then, obviously well practised, he raised his hands in the air. She pulled the vest over his head then helped him on with a pyjama jacket. A Rupert the Bear pyjama jacket. The sniggers turned to howls.

Robert's confession hadn't exactly horrified me...yet. There had to be more. There was.

'We'd got a right laugh out of it, Lorna. We should have ended it there and shot the craw. If that had been all there was, it would have been OK and Cookie would never have known a thing about it.'

But of course, they didn't end it there. Robert rattled Cookie's letterbox. A moment, then Cookie's Mum opened the door and smiled down at them, pleasantly. Robert tried to conjure up a face of innocence while Ross and Big Paddy stood behind him, still not quite sure what this was about but with their knuckles jammed in their mouths.

'Is Simon coming out, Mrs Cooke?' asked the bold Robert, the soul of politeness.

She was still smiling. 'Oh no Robert, Simon can't come out. He's ready for his bed. Look...'

The three of them tingled in warped anticipation as Cookie's Mum vanished for another moment.

They heard her call: 'Simon, your little playmates are here.'

Playmates!! Robert, Ross and Big Paddy went into fits.

Cookie's Mum reappeared, dragging him behind her, gripping his shoulder gently. Cookie was in the doorway now, his cherub cheeks still glistening pink from the sponging. He had a half-eaten custard cream in one hand, a glass of milk in the other, and looked horrified.

Cookie's Mum said: 'Look boys, Simon's having his wee biscuit and his wee drink.'

She gazed down at him.

'Then you're going up the wooden hill, aren't you, young man?'

Cookie's mouth dropped open and Robert, Ross and Big Paddy spied a gooey mess in there. Crumbs avalanched. A few clung on to Cookie's bottom lip for a moment, then gave up and floated down to the carpet. Cookie looked as if he was about to start crying. His so-called pals couldn't contain themselves. Robert convulsed, Ross laughed so hard he nearly vomited, Big Paddy thought his heart had stopped. Cookie's Mum kept a grip on him, preventing him from escaping his torment. She seemed oblivious to the spluttering coming from the three little boys on her doorstep.

'Would you all like to come in and have a wee biscuit with Simon before he goes up the wooden hill?'

Robert had tears streaming down his face now. Ross could barely stand. Big Paddy was grunting and snorting.

Robert admitted he was seriously tempted to go in for a wee biscuit with Simon.

'But we just couldn't, Lorna,' he told me. 'I seriously think one of us would have had a heart attack we were laughing so hard.'

The three boys pushed and pulled each other away from the door. Big Paddy somehow managed to get himself under enough control to make himself coherent and turned back.

'Naw, you're OK, Mrs Cooke. Thanks anyway, but we better not get too full up in case we can't eat our own wee biscuit when we get home.'

Round the corner, out of sight of Cookie's house, Robert was hysterical. Snot gushed from his nose. Ross collapsed on to his knees heaving while Big Paddy leaned against a wall, his stomach twisted and sore from laughing.

I had given up trying not to laugh at Robert's mea culpa. But there was real sorrow on his face, so I tried hard for gravity.

'Aw, that really is awful,' I said. 'But God, it was years ago. You were just horrible wee boys. All wee boys are horrible. You've got to stop giving yourself a hard time for it. Cookie probably doesn't even remember it.'

There was no comforting him.

'Naw, listen Lorna. That's not it. You haven't heard the worst bit yet.'

'Oh Christ,' I said. 'What else did you do?'

'I'm telling you, we were evil wee bastards. I've tried to convince myself I didn't start this next bit or at least we all did it together. But to be absolutely honest, there's a very good chance that I did.'

Still choking with laughter, Robert, Ross and Big Paddy staggered on blindly, half-shoving, half-towing each other along, until they found themselves at a fence. Cookie's back garden fence. By accident, Robert insisted.

It wasn't even nine yet and this was the middle of summer so it was still daylight. It dawned on the three of them that just a few feet away – right above their heads – was Cookie's bedroom. It had rained on and off that day but the air was warm and muggy and Cookie's bedroom window was open, wide open. Robert swore he couldn't remember who did it first but conceded again that it might have been him.

One of them called up, in a sing-song voice. 'Cookie's in his bed. Cookie's in his be-ed.'

The other two quickly joined in the cruel chorus but even then, they couldn't let it be. They had discovered an endless seam of sadistic amusement at Cookie's expense. Night after night, all through the holidays, the same routine. They'd wait five minutes after Cookie had been called home, then off they would go, round to his door, waiting desperately for the key phrases to trigger the convulsions – playmates and young man and wee biscuit and wooden hill. Cookie's Mum never let them down and she just kept smiling at them all the way through their raucous laughter. Then off they'd wander round the back for Part Two, gradually perfecting their timing, giving Cookie just enough time to get up the wooden hill, and each night they'd compose new, more outrageous variations on their cruel, twisted serenade.

Ross: 'You up the wooden hill yet, Cookie? You dreaming about your little playmates?'

Big Paddy: 'You better be fast asleep young man, or you won't get your lovely wee biscuit tomorrow night.'

Robert: 'Don't you be peeing yourself and getting they Rupert the Bear jim-jams soaked, Simon, or Mummy will have to come up the wooden hill and take that sponge to your willy.'

I was helpless with laughter now, just as Robert, Ross and Big Paddy had been on those Primary Five summer nights. Even Robert sniggered from the memory, but he fought to get his serious face back on.

He said: 'No, please Lorna, don't. It's not funny. Just think what Cookie must have gone through, lying there awake in his bed night after night waiting for it, dreading it, still light outside. That's what gets me. It was still light and us wee shits are outside yelling up all kinds of terrible things at him.'

'But did he not do anything the next day?' I asked. 'Or say anything to you? Or tell his Dad or something?'

'No, that's the other thing that gets me. He just took it all like the soft sap he was...is. Suffered it in silence, all those horrible, horrible nights. But the next day he'd be back out playing, never saying a word, as if nothing had happened. Cookie always was a crapper, even back then. For a while after it happened, I used to lie in bed at night trying to put myself in his position. Still do the odd night even now. And look at him, still can't stand up for himself. Karen's got him exactly where she wants him and that's him for life. He'll never ever have the guts to get out of her grip.'

Robert had a point, but he wasn't always right.

Chapter 24

August 2001
Stuck In The Middle With You – Louise Redknapp

I HAD been dreading Big Paddy turning up at my door. Even thinking about the trivial details niggled at me, like whether he would ring the bell or give it the big manly policeman's knock? Already I was regretting that I'd demanded an explanation, and gone along with his offer. From the moment the lift door shut on him in the office at lunchtime, I'd wanted to take it back. He had left my head swaying and I did something I've never done before in my working life – I faked sickness. Well, I faked physical sickness. I made an excuse, said I was feeling lousy and had to go home. Martin, my supervisor, was OK about it. He is a decent boss, though Shirley and Kath have taken to calling him David Brent after that new BBC2 thing. (I daren't admit it to them, but I thought it was yet another one of those reality shows and it was so uncomfortable to watch, I turned it off.) Whatever they say, Martin has always been good with me. He seemed genuinely concerned and offered to get me a taxi home or at least up to the bus station. I said no thanks because I just wanted to get outside, out of the office and into the fresh air. I needed to clear my head. I set off walking to the bus station and made it there by rote, oblivious to everything around me. A bit like the night my Mum died.

Then, I just wanted to be home, safe behind the front door of my little house, my cocoon, in Cumbride. I tried to convince myself, it's just another night, like any other night. Ha, I tried that once before. Correction, I've tried that many times before. *Come on, Lorna, give yourself a shake*. I'm home from work, as usual. I'll stick my Marks meal-for-one in the micro, eat if from a tray while Jackie Bird tells me what's happening in Scotland, watch Corrie or EastEnders or whatever other depressing trash I can bury myself in, then see what's on at nine. After that, I'll go to bed and read for an hour. Groundhog life. Dull, routine, safe, risk-free. Except I was expecting a visit from the police that night.

I was scared, no, I was terrified. Not just of what Big Paddy might reveal about Robert but what he might reveal about me. Did I want to hear it? Could I bear to hear it? But if I was honest, that was a higher level of fear. Down here, in my ordinary, real world, I was even scared of having company, someone in my home, a man in my little semi. I was scared of having my life invaded, scared of being reminded of how empty and solitary it all was. My life, I mean. The days ticking away, nothing to show for it, no personal goals any more. Two failed marriages behind me, no one else in my life. Well, not really. OK, as I might have touched on before, that was not strictly the whole truth and there was a possibility I could make that situation change. It was in my own hands. This time last week, I might have been OK with that, a little enthusiastic even and I promise, I will explain. Maybe. I don't keep *every* promise.

But Paddy...no, come on, be honest...Robert, had changed all that. Just as he had before.

So, face up to it, what did I have? There was my work, of course, and I did enjoy that. It was also my social life, more or less, because outside of the office, what else was there? An hour at the gym with Kath most Thursdays after work, occasionally a drink afterwards in the bar next door, but only if her Colin was working nights and she had no other plans. My other office pals? Oh sure, we had girls' nights out what, twice or three times a year? What else was there? Silly little dreams that resurfaced maybe once every five or six years, about a guy on the telly. A guy who had become a dot disappearing over the horizon, way way behind me in the far distance.

No one ever came here to my little cell. I didn't invite it, I didn't allow it. OK, be exact, be accurate, Lorna. Tell it how it is. Dad did come here very occasionally, about once every second leap year. I still saw him every week though, at his, ours, my old home, where Mum had been. Mum, another retreating micro dot. So that's my social calendar. Leotard and tracky bottoms for an hour a week. Fish and chips with Dad on Fridays. Huh, I didn't even own a candle, never mind burn one at both ends.

A large part of me hoped that Big Paddy wouldn't turn up. As it got nearer to eight, I prayed he would chicken out, or else the local teenage mobsters would stage a riot up at Scotland's most dismal town centre (official, it said so in the papers) and he would get called in and have to go and play Batman.

But another part of me knew that I had to face up to it. Face Big Paddy, face what he had to tell me. Hear it, deal with it, get over it.

When he did turn up, I awarded myself double points because I was kind of right on both counts. He knocked first, the solid policeman's knock I'd imagined, then he must have remembered he was off duty and rang the bell. I let him in and the house shrunk around me. My own home betrayed me, closed in on me. Big Paddy was too big and bulky for my poky little place. As I led him through, I had a vision of him having to bend down to avoid bumping his head on the door frames. I took him into the living room and offered him a drink. Anything he fancied, as long as it was red wine. I joked weakly that my drinks cabinet was away at the renovators that night. Big Paddy asked for coffee, followed me into the kitchen and sat down at the little table in there, uninvited, and took up residence. He must have decided, we'll do it here, I'm not getting cosy. Or perhaps he felt more comfortable in there because the kitchen was plain and a little more like the interrogation rooms he was used to – if Cumbride nick really had the kind of interrogation rooms I'd conjured up from repeats of The Bill on UK Gold. Maybe I should have fetched a tape recorder and sat it on the table beside him and brought in a world-weary plainclothes cop to observe.

I'd decided earlier that there would be no messing, not this time. None of that *How's your Mum, Paddy, how's the wife, how are the kids*? Don't hand him a soft option. Just give him his coffee and plunge right in, feet first.

'Tell me what you meant, Paddy.'

Simple enough? Straightforward enough?

Big Paddy was back in civvies – jeans and a thick V-neck jumper with no shirt underneath it, a couple of graying chest hairs poking out the top. Very working class, my snobby Aunt Irene would have said. He was facing me across my kitchen table, looking awkward. Tough shit. He was letting his hands burn on the coffee cup as if trying to turn it into his ordeal.

'Wish I'd kept my big bloody mouth shut.'

'Yeah, Paddy.' I was in no mood to take any prisoners or spin this out. 'You said that before and I wish you had too. But you didn't, and here we are, so get on with it.'

Tree trunk challenge revisited. Big Paddy looked like he was losing his balance, teetering on the edge, staring into the depths, knowing he'd have to jump sooner or later, but it was a long way down. Sooner or later? He was holding out for later.

'Christ. Robert would kill me if he had any clue I was talking to you about all this stuff.'

'Right, and I'll kill you if you don't.' Press, press, press. 'Which means you're a dead man either way, Paddy Allan, so either arrest me for threatening to kill a cop or get on with it. Tell me what this is all about and anyway, when were you ever scared of anybody?'

'It's no' that.'

Big Paddy was visibly troubled. He bunched his fingers together and squeezed his knuckles hard until the big flat tops turned white and the sides crimson. At least he didn't have Sadist in a Smock to contend with now. He sighed and continued.

'It's just, you know, you talk about things to folk. Over the years, know? You listen to all their troubles and you never think you'll ever say any of it. Repeat it, I mean, out loud, to anybody else.'

All right Paddy, since you're going for the Mr Sensitive route, I'll try the vulnerable wee woman card. I'll show it to you just the once, mind, and if you don't pick it up right away, the gun goes straight back to your head. I took the softer route.

'I understand all that. Paddy. I know, well, I know now. You and Robert, you go back all that way and I don't, but you've got to see it from where I'm sitting. You've just stuck your big Size Twelves, or whatever they are, into my life. My wee peaceful life. Come on, Paddy. Here's this guy, right? I haven't seen him since I was a daft wee lassie, well apart from on the telly. And this guy...I was his girlfriend for about five minutes a thousand years ago, so it's history, nothing more than a silly wee memory. Means nothing to anybody.'

I nodded at him and continued. 'Then PC Plod here strolls in and points the finger at me, tells me I wrecked his big buddy's marriage. What am I meant to do here, Paddy? Just say, oh is that right? Ah well, that's interesting. Then go back to my telly and my knitting. That's a joke, by the way. Get a search warrant if you like, you'll not find a single knitting needle in this house.'

Big Paddy capitulated, rolled over and held his hands up, palms facing me, a gesture I had seen from him before.

'OK, OK. Fair cop,' he said. Ouch, that's painful, Paddy. He was either oblivious to his own pun or he just had swapped roles with every two-bit villain he had ever lifted and questioned.

'I'll lay it out, right?' he went on. 'But Lorna, this has got to be just between the two of us, OK?'

'I'm hardly going to take out an ad in the wee paper, Paddy,' I replied.

'Naw, I know,' he said. 'I mean, I'll tell you about Robert and that's it. I'm not going through all this stuff again. I'll tell you it, the whole story as far as I know it. Then I'm going back to scraping folk off the motorway. A lot less traumatic. Oh, and it's Size Thirteen, know?'

OK, so that was the small talk out the way. Now Big Paddy climbed into the witness box, ready to give his evidence. Maybe I should have dug out an old bible. I made a promise to myself. Just listen, Lorna, don't interrupt. Listen, and save your cross-examination for later.

Chapter 25

November 1974
You Ain't See Nothing Yet – Bachman-Turner Overdrive

THE way Robert had with words, the way he was able to influence and carry us with him. I feel like I want to explain, so I think back to events. Minor ones in the great scheme of things, but major in our little history. I think of the night Big Paddy broke a rule, and Fiona broke a bigger one.

The thing about Fiona was, she always had such a huge downer on herself. She was clever, the most naturally intelligent of our bunch. The brains of the operation, Big Paddy called her, affectionately. But much of the time, it seemed she believed being clever was only a consolation prize and nowhere near enough.

Here is an example of what I mean. One day at Jo's house, not long before our prelims, Cammy came out with a simple but classic three-word phrase that became a kind of mantra for most of us whenever schoolwork was weighing us down, always delivered in an approximation of his whiny voice. He was staring at, rather than reading, a textbook – history I think – and after about half a minute, he let out a huge sigh, chucked it on the floor, and sighed: 'I hate knowledge.'

Most us laughed in a mixture of agreement and sympathy, possibly in a patronising way in one or two cases. But not Fiona. I caught a brief, wistful look, like she was letting her guard down for once.

She said: 'Yeah Cammy, me too.'

Robert was bright. From all accounts, he did pretty well at school and got consistently higher than average exam marks. But the way he told it, he achieved it with a flying-by-the-seat-of-his-pants smartness. He once confessed to me that he had never studied for an exam in his life but got results on memory and improvisation. He insisted he mostly made it up as

170

he went along by spinning a few headline facts into a lot of fancy words that made it seem like he knew more than he really did. Our other main contender at the upper end of the brainbox scale was Cookie. In contrast to Robert – and Fiona – his strength was careful, plodding logic. He was good at figuring out how things worked – cars, engines, electrical circuits, chemicals, gases. The kind of stuff that turned my head to mush. Cookie was good at being methodical.

But Fiona was study-it learn-it intelligent. French grammar, average rainfall in Somalia, X squared minus C to the power of ten equals do-re-mi. Her secret was discipline. She went straight home from school to do her homework and go over whatever she had been taught that day. She would hang about with us for a while after tea, but she was almost always first to head home from the shelter most nights for an hour's studying in bed. What baffled the rest of us was, this wasn't even homework she was doing, this was voluntary, this was over and above. This was school stuff SHE DIDN'T HAVE TO DO. Her nightly study hour became two or even three hours at exam times. Fiona wasn't trying to be boastful – it wasn't in her make-up – but she genuinely could not see any difficulty with school work. It came naturally to her. She saw it like this: someone told you something, or you read it in a text book and that was it, you knew it. It became a little file tucked away in the brain with so many others and when you needed an answer, you accessed the right file. What was the big deal? It wasn't unusual for Fiona to score one hundred per cent in exams, especially in the first couple of years at secondary.

'A hunner per fucking cent!' Big Paddy gasped when he told the rest of us about one of Fiona's test results. 'How the hell do you get a hunner per cent for anything? No way you can know every single thing about a subject. I'd be lucky to get a hunner per cent for counting my fingers.'

Robert said they'd be as well as giving Fiona her own permanent seat on the stage at school prize-giving. He usually got the English award. (Big Paddy once said Robert was like Brazil – if he won the English prize one more time, he'd get to keep it forever. I never knew what that meant.) But it was a bad year for Fiona if she didn't pick up at least two or three. Big Paddy used to moan that he felt left out on prize-giving night at St Joe's and joked they should give out one for height. At least, I assumed he was joking.

Despite Fiona's academic achievements and her prizes, she acted like she was inferior to the rest of us, the other girls. She envied our easy way of chatting to each other and to the guys. She rarely found casual conversation anything but painful. She'd lose the thread easily and end up standing around looking awkward and gangly, saying nothing while we batted all the usual rubbish back and forth.

Fiona also felt she was out on her own at the bottom of the pecking order with the boys. She was spare girl more than the rest of us and decided it was down to her looks. She was thin and long-limbed, third tallest of our lot after Big Paddy and Cookie. She had a shape like a big skinny boy, Karen would snipe, along with intense, jagged features. It wasn't just Robert being cruel those times we constructed the cast list – Fiona called herself horsey too. But sometimes, every now and then, she hit on a way of softening herself and producing a kind of sharp, sexy look. But that only happened when she could be bothered putting in the effort, which in retrospect was probably at the root of it. If it came down to a choice of learning something new or spending an hour in front of the mirror, there was never a contest.

Fiona's biggest problem, as far as I could see, was self-esteem, or the lack of it. Fiona was her own harshest critic. She put herself down, told us – and not in a fishing-for-compliments way – that she felt ugly, maybe rising to plain on good days. She told herself this so many times, it became a truth, an incontrovertible fact, at least to herself.

Her little brother hadn't helped. Greg was only about a year and a half younger than Fiona. Little Greg the money man, was what everyone called him after he stood up on his very first day at school and told his new Primary One classmates he was going to be a millionaire. He had a knack for gathering money and by the time he was ten, was already regarded as something of a tycoon. He was always on the lookout for get-rich-young schemes and poor Fiona was the victim of his second most notorious scam. (Second after his legendary Wacky Races betting syndicate.) Big Paddy heard about the one involving Fiona from his wee brother, Gerry, who was a pal, or as time went on, a client, of Greg's.

Fiona, who was twelve at the time, had developed some kind of infection and was prescribed Penicillin, which, it turned out, she was allergic to. She developed swelling and a rash all over her body and her face ballooned.

'Apparently her cheeks were all puffed up like a hamster and her face got absolutely massive,' Big Paddy recounted with colour and relish. 'Like a Hallowe'en Cake. Or one of they Aborigine masks like the natives in that book we saw in Geography. Mind, Robert?'

The doctor told Fiona's parents there was no real way of treating the allergic reaction but that the effects would wear off gradually on their own, probably in a week or so. Fiona was to rest and stay out of bright light until the swelling went down. Miserable, she confined herself to her darkened bedroom and waited for the blight to pass.

Which would have been unpleasant but fine, except that Greg the entrepreneur – though he had never heard of the word – spotted a window of opportunity. He waited until the Saturday afternoon when Fiona's parents went out on their weekly shopping trip. There was method in his planning – Saturday was pocket money day. Greg whipped up a tale and told it to as many gullible, pocket money-flush kids as he could muster. A curse had been put on his big sister by an old woman who lived alone at the top of their street and was really a witch.

'You must have seen her, staring out the window with her evil eyes,' he said. 'She's got a black cat and everything.'

Black cat? That clinched it then. Greg told the kids his sister had been turned into a monster by the wicked old witch and promised them a grisly peep show for threepence a head. Just three little pennies for a two-minute audience with Fiona the Freak. Greg knew he would only get one crack at it. He got a bunch of kids together, fourteen of them, which was a credit to his sales pitch, pocketed their coins and promised a full refund if they weren't satisfied. He double-checked his parents were out and put his finger to his lips, then signalled the trembling, awestruck tribe to walk on tiptoes and ushered them into his house. They gathered outside Fiona's bedroom.

'When I open the door, you lot pile in,' Greg instructed in a solemn whisper. 'If she comes after you, or even looks you straight in the eye, get out fast or else she'll pass the curse on to you and you'll end up looking the same as her. Anyone of a nervous disposition should back out now.'

Greg flung her bedroom door open. He flicked on the switch next to the door and light flooded into the room. He gave the order.

'Go, go, go.'

Fourteen children charged into the small room and Fiona, who had been dozing, got the biggest fright of her life. She sat bolt upright in bed and screamed. Fourteen youngsters shrieked and fled in terror, their little minds badly scarred, nearly as scarred as Fiona's. As a performance, it couldn't have worked out better. Greg got a tanking from his Dad but the change rattling in his pocket dulled the pain. Hey, three and six was three and six.

Maybe I'm making too much of it, but experiences like that, coupled with her lack of self-worth, must have been at least a contributory factor to the night Fiona broke a big rule. It was another party, at Jo's this time. We were well into fifth year by then, and booze had become almost routine and no longer a huge thrill for most of us, the exceptions being Big Paddy and Ross, who had grown into serious bevvy merchants.

The usual drill was this. We all chipped in and Big Paddy got the carry-out, which we would down between us at the shelter. Well, all of us except the one who was having the party. It was never that much to be honest. Drinking had already lost its shock value and had become more like doing something that was expected of you. We'd have a bottle or two of El-D and half a dozen Special Brews...between ten of us. Hardly what would qualify as binge-boozing a couple of generations down the line.

By the time we headed for the party, we'd usually be chewing on one of Cammy's Cures. (Robert's phrase, of course.) Cammy's Cures had become notorious. Each pre-party, he'd come up with something new, some fresh formula guaranteed to cleanse our breaths and get rid of the booze stink so we could pass the doorstep test. It couldn't be anything as simple as mints, of course. Over the months since we'd starting drinking, Cammy had got us chewing orange peel and cabbage, sucking teabags and swallowing spoonfuls of instant coffee. On one horrible, puke-making night, we even ate cold baked beans by the sticky, messy handful. Cammy was finally rumbled when he produced a can of dog food and even supplied the tin opener. He swore this would cast-iron, definitely, a thousand per cent guarantee to remove every last, lingering smell of alcohol. But he'd gone too far this time and we balked, rounded on him and threatened to make him try it first. Cammy made a full and frank confession. His breath-fresheners were based on no evidence whatsoever. He had just been curious to see how far he could go, to see what we were all daft enough to stick in our gobs. He was forgiven surprisingly quickly and as far as I can remember, it was just about his only deliberate, creative contribution to our folklore.

There was an unwritten agreement about boozing on party nights. We were meant to stay sober enough – or at least sensible and upright enough – to pass the parent-at-the-door test, and strictly no alcohol was allowed in the house. Mostly, our collective sets of parents played the game. They would count us in, giving us a quick once-over to check we were at least capable of standing up and unlikely to lapse into a coma in their living room. Then they'd clear off for a night of comparative freedom, little brothers and sisters already farmed out. Our part of the bargain? Don't deafen the neighbours, don't permanently disfigure the furniture, don't be sick on the carpets. Fair dos, because we valued our parties.

But Big Paddy was dangerous that night. He and Ross had already been hammering it in one of the pubs across town before we met up. Big Paddy had got a real taste for drink and he had the money to satisfy his thirst. He had just left school and was already making decent money labouring by this time. So he broke one of our rules. He joined us at the shelter to tan the booze stash, then slipped away as we dawdled to Jo's house and bought ANOTHER carry-out – and all that after his session in the pub. He came back with more beer, three bottles of wine AND a bottle of Bacardi. Ross had chipped in too. We got to Jo's but Big Paddy hung back and Ross headed straight for the loo and waited for the tap on the window. He opened up and Big Paddy passed in the booze. Ross stuck it under Jo's bed where it would stay planked until her parents went out. She panicked when she found out but quickly surrendered to the inevitable.

We all shared Big Paddy's drink. We swayed, we laughed, we got merry. But Fiona was the problem because she couldn't handle it. She was the kind who got tipsy and giggly sniffing a wine gum wrapper. (No prizes for guessing who came up with that one.) Normally she was the most sensible of our lot, to the point of being strait-laced and boring at times. Fiona's share of the shelter booze was usually more than enough for her and it didn't escape anyone's notice that she was always careful to drink less than the rest of us on each pass. She'd purposely avoid her turn sometimes as the cans and bottles were shared around. Where we took gulps and swigs, she took sips. No one complained because it was all the more for the rest of us. Fiona knew her limits, but she ripped them up that night.

She drained two glasses of Big Paddy's Bacardi quickly, far too quickly. Just two glasses, that was all, but it was more than enough and suddenly there was a stranger at our party, someone we didn't recognise. Fiona unleashed, Fiona frisky and wild. She started recklessly snogging any guy within reach. She groped wildly, she pawed at them, she tried to drag guys off to bedrooms – any bedroom and any guy. Fiona was insatiable and unstoppable. She even flung her arms round Karen and tried to kiss her and I mean, really kiss her properly. The guys loved it. Well, apart from Ross, who scowled and muttered: 'Sake, wummin poofs.'

But the rest of them egged her on and booed and hissed at Karen when she shoved Fiona away. Had the booze brought some buried urge bubbling to the surface? Nah, more likely she was too far out of it to know what she was doing, so we gave her the benefit of the doubt, on that score anyway.

Finally, she began to wind down. She disappeared into the loo, prayed loudly to Armitage Shanks, then returned and collapsed on the sofa in a hazy stupor. She lay sprawled like a discarded puppet and lapsed into an hour-long snoring session. Jo leaned over Fiona, studied her closely as she rasped and snorted, then turned to us and said solemnly: 'Gentlemen, we have the technology. We can rebuild her.'

Helpful, thoughtful Cammy chipped in: 'Probably needs a proper lie down. Me and Ross could pull her into your bedroom, Jo. Loosen her clothing a bit, so we could.'

Wee Mary and I had both drunk a fair bit, but we were in a just about sensible enough state to help Jo tidy the place up. Her parents were due back any time, so we got rid of the evidence of Big Paddy's misdemeanour, the empties carted off and delicately placed in a neighbour's bin. We marshalled the troops and got them into some kind of motley order as we passed round jackets/anoraks/coats. Then we roused Fiona, but that only sparked off a new wave of mayhem. She came round, batteries recharged, and was soon off again, falling about, knocking things over, grabbing at the guys. Way out of control.

We did our best to hide her when Jo's parents got home. We restrained her and propped her up in the middle of a huddle of bodies, then tried to smuggle her out, but she slipped the shackles. Disaster. She staggered towards Jo's Dad, tittering and slurring.

'Hey, you handsome fucker, you want a goodnight kiss, don't you?'

It wasn't even faintly alluring. The zig-zag trail of sick on her sleeve where she'd wiped her mouth did nothing to make her any more attractive.

Jo's face crumpled, all of our faces crumpled. Fiona wrapped herself around Jo's Dad and tried to kiss him. He pushed her off, more embarrassed than annoyed. Fiona stumbled and crashed into Jo's Mum. She was sick again. Colourfully, loudly, violently sick, all down Jo's Mum's good coat.

Fiona passed out once more and slumped to the floor. Looking back, Jo's Mum had no choice. She phoned Fiona's house and her Dad drove round, his face a ticking bomb. He and Jo's Dad carted Fiona to his car and poured her on to the back seat. We thought briefly about the old all-for-one...and legged it.

Next morning. God knows what state Fiona was in or what kind of interrogation she endured, what kind of torture. Thumbscrews? Racks? Whatever it was, she did the unforgivable. She squealed, shopped us, sold us out. Well, the girls anyway. Once she cracked, it all came tumbling out – the carry-outs, the pocket money and part-time job pay squandered on cheap wine, the booze sessions at the shelter. I never knew why she didn't dob in the guys as well. Best guess, it was a case of, *give 'em a few names, that might satisfy them, then they'll leave me alone and let me slip back into peaceful oblivion.* Or maybe Fiona's Mum just didn't ask about guys, didn't want to know. Maybe she didn't want to see boozed-up, horny boys as part of the picture, part of her serious, intelligent, ambitious, hard-working, prize-winning Fiona's life. But whatever the extenuating circumstances, it all came down to one thing. Fiona had ratted us out and that was the REAL big rule, never mind the trivial boyfriends-girlfriends thing. Loyalty. First, second, last. You didn't grass up your mates, ever ever ever, and she had gone and done it. She had broken the rule.

A little bit later on Sunday morning, Fiona's Mum got on the phone to our parents and emergency courts were convened in four kitchens across the Cardrum scheme. Our parents didn't even consider fair hearings or pleas in mitigation. We were guilty, convicted without trial. Karen got a prison sentence with hard labour – grounded for two weeks with hoovering and dishes every day. Jo was banged up too, for a week. Wee Mary and I got fines and probation. I was docked two weeks' pocket money and bound over for good behaviour, Wee Mary similar. No court for Kirsty though. She got off with a warning, her final warning – another final warning.

But Fiona's sentence was the stiffest, the one WE imposed on her. Instant expulsion, enforced exile. Cast out of the circle for life with no mercy and no remission. She was out for good. No time off for good behaviour, no parole, no appeal. Karen and Jo served their sentences, Wee Mary and I paid our fines. We were all so resentful and Fiona became our hate figure. She had done the unthinkable. How could she?

Big Paddy brought back despatches from St Joe's, sightings of our nemesis.

Fiona was alone. Tough, we stayed firm. Fiona was miserable. Good, we refused to budge. She deserved it.

Days passed. More bulletins. Fiona looked utterly wretched. One or two of us softened, just a tiny bit. Fiona was friendless and solitary. Another few weakened but no one would make the first move towards clemency.

Then Robert fixed it. He tapped into our feelings. He dipped a toe in the water one night about three weeks after Jo's party. Out of nowhere, he just said: 'Hey, let's go up for Fiona.'

Instantly, there was dissent in the camp.

Kirsty: 'No way. I'm never speaking to that grassing cow again.'

Karen: 'After what she did? Well, you lot can if you really want. But if you do, I'm out of here. You coming, Simon?'

Simon: 'Karen's right, Robert. Fiona dumped them right in the shit.'

Even me, usually so quick to side with him: 'Come on, Robert, she shopped us, so why the hell should we?'

He had bided his time, let us spend our venom. Unwittingly, I had fed him his cue and he spoke softly. Firm, but gentle. First though, he looked at each one of us in turn, into our eyes, into our souls.

Then he said: 'Because it's the right thing to do.'

Sorted, in seven words. It was that kind of statement. Devastating, simple, defining.

'About time and all,' weighed in Big Paddy.

Without delay, Fiona was brought back into the fold. Loved again, more than she had ever been. Smothered with forgiveness and understanding. The return of the prodigal sister.

Chapter 26

1984-1993
A Kind of Magic – Queen

BIG Paddy's witness statement: Robert told me he was going to marry you, Lorna. He told me that when he was fifteen. No offence, but I slagged him rotten. You must remember what he was like. He was always saying stuff, big things like that, to catch your interest in case you weren't paying attention.

It wasn't that long after he got to know you actually. We were on the bus back from St Joe's one day and Robert asked me if I thought you were good looking or hacket. Can't remember what I said. Convenient, eh? Then he just came out with it. He had it all figured out. You were getting married, the two of you, as soon as you were twenty. You were going to have three weans – a boy and two wee girls that looked like you. I told him to shut his piehole. I was probably embarrassed for him. I told him that was the kind of thing daft lassies said. But I remember I was dead chuffed when you two got together...finally. I used to watch you, you know, from my bedroom window. The pair of you sitting on that wall, laughing away, then sometimes going all serious, touching each other's arms and that, as if you weren't even aware you were doing it. I was always curious, wanted to know what it was you were talking about, how you found so much stuff to say to each other. Sorry, that must sound really creepy but honest, I wasn't like, a Keyhole Kate, or a stalker or nothing. I was just, I suppose, happy for you, the both of you, know?

Robert had fancied you for ages. Right from the start. Mind, when it was just me and him and you and that big doll Kirsty? He told me. Matter of fact, he hardly stopped going on about you. But you always seemed to kind of skip each other out at our parties and that. Then it happened that New Year, mind? It was like he'd been signed by the Celtic or something. After that, he used to boast about you at our school, tell the guys in our class about this amazing burd he had who was at the Proddy school. It was Fiona that told me. There were a couple of lassies in our school that had their eye on him but he kind of let it be known they couldn't compete or compare.

Then there was your Mum and everything. Sorry, didn't mean to bring that up. Then the wedding of course and er, Cammy. Christ, remember that carry on, Lorna? I'm not exactly sure what happened right after that. I've got this big missing chunk from around about that time. Reckon I must have spent about a year or more pished out my head. I remember you went away with…what's her name? Oh aye, Mary, wasn't it? I seemed to be either on a building site or in a boozer all the time. I didn't see Robert that much for a long while. He was still at the school but the odd time I did run into him, he talked about you non-stop, like he was making plans. Said he was just waiting for you to get back. Then you did come home but you were away again just as quick. Far as I remember you got married not that long after, Lorna, am I right?

A wee bit later, actually maybe it was a year or two, Robert and me hooked up again, at the fitba of all places. I actually met him at Parkhead one Saturday. Forty thousand folk and I bump into Robert. He was on the papers by that time and I was thinking about joining the Army. You believe that? I'd sickened myself with the drink and decided I better do something with my life. Get myself a uniform to go with my acne, as the Blessed Big Yin might have put it. Anyway, it became a habit, me and Robert, the Celtic. Every home game and some of the away trips as well – Dundee, Perth and that, know?

After we heard about you getting hitched, he never really mentioned you much for a long time. You always got the feeling he was desperate to get away. I know he never got on well with his old man so could have been that, or maybe he was just dead ambitious. I know he outgrew the Courier pretty fast. Anyway, whatever it was, he didn't seem to have much of a reason for sticking around our bit any more. Think he only stuck the wee paper about two year – if even that – then went to the Evening Times and got himself a little bedsit in Glasgow. Right dingy wee basement, so it was. He just, well, seemed in such a bloody rush, know? He was hardly at the Times, then he was on the Record or maybe it was the Sunday Mail, no sure. No long after that he was away to London, one of the big papers down there.

We did keep in touch, but not so much around that time to be honest. He still came up for Celtic games but gradually it got less and less and after a while it was just the big ones – cup finals, the Huns, sorry Rangers, European games. I went down there the odd time – London, I mean. Stayed with him, went out on the town, but we were both getting on with our own stuff. With him it was career, career, career. Me? I'd gone off the Army idea and joined the police instead – well, seemed like a good idea at the time! Robert still phoned regular, right enough. I mind him calling me once to say he'd got a job on the telly. I saw him a fair few times, on the news and that. It was weird. Your best buddy you sat beside in primary, the wee guy with the snottery nose, actually on the box, know? Sometimes you couldn't believe it was the same guy, gabbing about all that serious stuff and even looking like he knew what he was on about the odd time.

Then…let me work this out…this would be about six, maybe seven years after school. Early eighties kind of time. I hadn't heard from him for months, maybe a year even, then he calls us up one day, right out the blue.

He says to me: 'I'm getting married, Paddy. Three weeks on Friday. Any danger of you doing the Best Man gig?'

Of course I said Yes. Goes down the day before the wedding. I was dead excited, expecting an exotic stag night in the Big Smoke, know? A night on the town with all they glamorous folk off the telly. But it was just me and him, in his wee flat. We sat there and got hammered. Robert got in a right state, all kind of maudlin.

Then suddenly he goes: 'What am I doing, Paddy? What the fuck's happening here?'

Sorry Lorna, I'm quoting.

He starts saying he's making a huge mistake. It was all too quick, him and Ruth, know? They'd only been seeing each other a few month. Met when he went to the BBC – he'd just joined them from The Mirror, I'm sure. They hit it off, had the same big ideas about telly –great minds and all that. It had seemed the natural thing to do, Robert says. Getting married. Now he was thinking he couldn't go through with it. Now, I'm sitting there listening, Lorna. All the time thinking this was about her. You know, Ruth. And bear in mind, I've no' even met the woman at this point.

Then Robert goes: 'What about Lorna? What's she going to think?'

No offence or nothing Lorna, right, but I didn't have a Scooby what he was on about. I'd hardly seen you for years, mind, or even heard your name, no' even from Robert. Sure, I vaguely assumed you were still married. My mother gave me these occasional wee updates, but I had no idea where you were living or if you had weans or anything. So, as I say, I'm sitting there thinking this Lorna must be somebody else he'd been seeing down there. Robert must have clocked it – me sitting there baffled.

He gives us this look with his eyes all screwed up, so I says to him: 'Lorna who?'

And he takes this exasperated tone and goes: 'Lorna Ferguson. I'm supposed to be marrying her. Not remember I told you, Paddy?'

Don't forget now Lorna, we're both wrecked, so I'm thinking it's just the booze talking.

Well, I goes: 'What, wee Lorna from the swing park? Christ almighty Robert, you were kids. You weren't even shaving.'

But it all came pouring out. How he'd never forgotten about you, how he never stopped thinking about you. Swore he still loved you, said he'd never figured out where he'd fucked it all up. Pardon my French again, Lorna, but that's word for word. The guy was gutted, miserable. Honestly, I thought he was going to start greeting. Just like when we were younger on the school bus run, I was embarrassed sitting there listening to it, but it all kind of fizzled out after that. He went to the loo and that was the last I saw of him for the night. I don't know who crashed out first, whether he went straight to his bed or I fell asleep on the settee. But the next morning, he was fine, as if nothing had happened and nothing had been said. He's buzzing about, getting himself ready for the wedding, making phone calls, keeping busy and that.

Then the wedding itself. Listen, I don't know if you want to hear all this stuff, Lorna, so stop us anytime. But honest to God, it was the weirdest one I've been at in my puff. Robert didn't even have any of his family, just me and a handful of folk from down there. There was a few from the BBC and two or three from one of the big papers where he'd worked for a while. One of the guys took a few pictures. Ended up in the papers. No' cos of Robert, more that she had become a kind of a big deal on the telly. It was a registry office job, Robert in his good suit and Ruth in a red dress and a big straw hat. We went for lunch somewhere...can't mind whereabouts, no' important. Then she went back to her work. I couldn't believe it. On her wedding day! She had a programme to do that night. Looking back, don't think I spoke two words to her the whole time.

Anyhows, Robert had at least taken time off *his* work so we spent the rest of the day moving some of his stuff to her place in a wee van he hired, then I got the late train back up the road. It was unreal, the whole thing.

But they seemed happy enough and as far as I was aware, things were hunky dory. They had Jack about a year after they got married and me and Robert still phoned each other now and again. I'd got engaged myself by this time, so I was kind of busy concentrating on my own stuff. But then he came back up. Jack was still wee, don't think he was at the school yet. Came up for a big game and that's when it happened. He saw you, Lorna. Did his nut in all over again.

The Celtic were playing down in Paisley. St Mirren, and we had to beat them. I know it's boring fitba, Lorna, but it's important, to let you see the whole picture, to let you understand all this.

It was real Roy of the Rovers stuff. Last day of the season and we were behind Hearts for the league, so we had to hammer St Mirren and hope to Christ that Hearts shat the bed and got beat in their game, pardon my French again. As far as I remember, they hadn't lost for months and if I'm completely honest, they deserved it more than us. The papers never gave us a chance, but we all had a dead strong feeling about it. Sorry, sorry, Lorna, too much boring detail.

Anyway, I meets Robert in Central Station, off the train from London. The place was hoaching, green and white scarves all over the place. He comes bouncing down the platform, punching the air, then patting his gut and yelling at me.

'We're going to do it, Paddy. I feel it in here. We're going to do it.'

There was an amazing buzz about the place and like everybody else, the two of us were hyper. We were looking about, wondering if there was any possible chance of getting near a bar. Then he just froze.

'Fuck,' he says to me quietly. 'There's Lorna. With some guy.'

I spun round but I saw nothing, well apart from this heaving mass of green and white all heading for Paisley. Robert went from jumping up and down with excitement, to complete silence in the station bar and on the train down.

It was an unbelievable day as it turned out. Stinking weather, so it was, lashing down, but nobody cared because the Celtic were on fire. Four-nothing at half-time, five at the start of the second half. Then it all went kind of flat. No news from the Hearts game. All they had to do was hang on for a draw and the league was theirs, know? Time was running out, ten minutes to go or something, and it started to feel like we'd got tanked up for a special occasion, turned up in our best gear and sang our hearts out, only to be told the party was off cos the host had died.

Then it happened. It was all confused at first. Somebody in the crowd with a tranny shouted that the boy Kidd had just scored. But the thing was, Hearts had a player called Kidd so we all thought it must be him. So that was it definite, game's a-bogey. Good effort guys, but we're gubbed. Then it was like an earthquake. The ground began rippling. Sorry if I'm boring the arse off you, Lorna, but I've never known anything like it. It was a bushfire spreading through the crowd because the word was going round that it was actually Albert Kidd that had scored – a Dundee player. That's who Hearts were playing that day and they were one nothing down. Then it came through that the same guy, this Kidd character, had scored again and there was only a few minutes to go. I've got the video of that game now, Lorna. I must have watched it a hunner times. I know it's coming but I still get the shivers, every time, at the exact moment when the place erupts and the whole crowd behind the goal starts bouncing. I used to freeze the video and try and pick us out, me and Robert, but I never could.

Seriously, I'm sorry, Lorna, I'm getting carried away here. You don't want to hear all this rubbish. But the point is…Robert. Cos everybody, I mean everybody, in green and white is going berserk but he's just stood there like a statue, even when it sunk in Hearts had shot their bolt and we were going to be the champions against all the odds. I've got my arms round him and I'm lifting him off the ground and pulling him up and down, but he's a dead weight. It's like he doesn't have a clue what's going on or even where he is. And after, when we got back to Cumbride, there was a whole crowd of us down The Common celebrating. The big Celtic pub, know? Well, maybe you don't know. Anyway, everybody else is going mental but Robert just sits there no' opening his mouth. He sloped away early. No idea if he stayed at his mother's or got a late bus into town and headed back south or what.

He phoned me on the Monday, apologising, dead sorry that he'd spoiled it. Said spotting you was like seeing a ghost and he couldn't get the picture of you with that guy out his head.

Anyhows, once I got married, me and the wife both started going down to London. It was good usually. Ruth was all right, made us welcome and that, but you always felt she was a wee bit distracted, as if she was having to make a big effort to make time for us or even remember who we were. Maybe I'm being unfair to her. When I think about it now, she was always friendly enough. Things kind of rolled along for a few year. Robert and Ruth already had wee Jack of course, and then we had Bobby. Robert's his godfather, by the way. He always insists we named the boy after him but it wasn't that at all. Bob's my father-in-law's name.

Then, maybe ten year ago, another one of Robert's bombshell phone calls. He'd only been up here a few weeks before, never cracked a light or gave us a single clue anything was up. He comes on the phone this day, trying to sound dead cheery but I could tell, I knew it was an act.

'Guess what, Paddy?' he says eventually, without waiting for an answer. 'I'm a free man. Me and Ruth, our divorce came through today.'

I thought he was at the wind-up and probably muttered some pish at him, can't mind. Then he goes: 'You know what else? I'm an adulterer. Sixth commandment, remember? It's official, it's written on a bit of paper. Apparently I've been having an affair…with a woman I haven't seen for years.'

I knew it was you he was talking about again, Lorna, and I'm sorry, but you did ask. Robert almost came home then, after the divorce. He went after a couple of jobs up here but I was never convinced he was that serious to be honest. He admitted as much later that he was scared of getting too close. To you, I mean.

Anyway, he kept Jack which was dead unusual in they days, but Ruth never fought it. Robert changed his job. Well, he stayed at the BBC, but he stopped travelling so much. They were good to him, the BBC. They found him something where he was mainly in the studio, doing interviews and stuff and behind the camera sometimes, production stuff, know? But then I suppose they knew how good he was and didn't want to let him go. He organised his life round the boy, trying to work shifts so he could finish when Jack got out the school. I know he saw a few women from time to time, but it never really came to nothing. I could be massively wrong here, but eventually I think he just kind of packed all that in, women and stuff I mean, at least in any serious way. And he never mentioned you again, for years. Till a few weeks ago.

To put you in the picture, Lorna, you've been like this big conversation we've never stopped having, me and Robert, but with these massive gaps. Long silences in between, gaps that last years sometimes. Then he'll just pick it up again like it's only been five minutes since he last mentioned you. Now that he's back up here, he's started again. *Is Lorna still married? Is she seeing anybody?* Or, Christ, did you really think asking you about that stuff was my idea? So yeah, he's been talking about you, you and him. The rest of us as well, in fact. The old days. Only, it was different this time. He seemed OK about it.

Robert told me he'd always had this kind of fantasy. You know, daft stuff and I mean real daft, childish stuff. If-you-found-this-genie-and-he-gave-you-one-wish kind of thing. And he said he'd ask for a time machine and go back to that time. The swing park days and everything, back when we were at the school. He said he'd do anything for another go, to try and get it right or at least figure out how he'd screwed it all up. To see if there really had been any chance, you know, with you two. It was the most he'd ever talked about you at the one time. But as I say, it was different this time. He was calm about it, kind of accepting it almost.

Anyway, I says to him: 'So you've finally got all that sorted out? In your head, I mean. Lorna and that, know? Got her out your system?'

He goes: 'No chance Paddy. I'll never stop thinking I let the biggest, most important thing in my life go by me. But it doesn't matter anymore. I'm done with all that, I'm too old for her now.'

Here's the thing, Lorna. For a crazy minute, I nearly thought he meant it.

Chapter 27

1973-1975
Walk This Way – Aerosmith

S EX. Robert turned all serious, cheeks puffed out, eyebrows knotted tight. He was deep in thought for a long time.

Finally he said: 'With Kirsty, it's like, er, she somehow gives off sex.'

What the hell did that mean? I had asked him the question on one of those nights when we were sitting on the wall behind my house. Just the two of us, not caring about the smirry rain. I wanted to know what it was about Kirsty, why there was always a queue for her. Oh, and a few supplementary inner questions strictly for myself – what was my motivation, why did I want to know anyway? Did I want to be like her? Did I want the guys queuing up for me? No, surely not. Was it just plain envy then? Envy of all the attention Kirsty was getting.

Three months earlier, I could not have imagined having this kind of conversation, not with a guy, especially not with a guy. But by this time, we could talk about anything, Robert and me. We did talk about anything. There were no boundaries.

This was Robert's first reply to my Kirsty question.

'If you're asking me what the guys see in her, that's simple. Bit of a red neck, yeah, but simple. Thing is Lorna, we're not really in charge of ourselves.'

He nodded downwards in the general direction of his groin, quickly, but knowing I'd catch it.

'That,' he went on. 'Him, that, whatever you want to call it. It rules us. It's the simple truth...our horizons don't stretch beyond the end of it.'

I felt my face colour – pure ketchup. Shit, we all tried to be so mature, so grown-up and world-weary and nonchalant, and the one damn emotion you couldn't hide sneaked up on me when I wasn't looking. Robert either didn't

185

clock it in the semi-gloom of a drizzly dusk, or he was too polite or embarrassed to let on he had noticed.

Instead, he continued: 'It might be a terrible thing to say, cos she's your pal and that. But the guys all kind of know, with Kirsty I mean. There's always the chance, the possibility. If something's going to happen, it's probably going to happen with Kirsty.'

But that wasn't what I'd asked, or was it?

'Oh right, thanks a bunch Robert,' I said, trying to keep it light. 'Thanks for pushing the male of the species way way up in my estimation. But you haven't answered my question. What is it that Kirsty's got? Or what, you telling me she's just easy? That all there is to it?'

Robert shook his head.

'I'm sorry. I'm doing my best here to try and explain, Lorna. But you've got to remember, all us guys, our entire sex education is based on a nude book Fiona's wee brother Greg found under a bush and rented out till it could stand up on its own and the pages wouldn't open.'

'Puke. That's vile, Robert. Did I really need to know that?'

'Sorry, but you have to make allowances cos I'm one of that male sub-species. Anyway, if you're talking about Kirsty, I can only tell you how we doom-brain guys see her.'

'Well, that might be a start,' I smiled. 'But don't worry about it, I'm not planning to use your answer for my Biology O-Grade or anything.'

Robert and me, we had developed such an easy way with each other, a way of rolling the conversation along, bouncing it back and forward and all around – except when the topic was difficult, like now.

He was clearly floundering.

'I was going to say it's some kind of aura or, like a scent or something. But that's not what I mean at all. Christ, this is hard. Can you not just ask me some French verbs or something. With Kirsty, it's like, er, she somehow gives off sex. I mean...shit, I don't know. Christ knows what I mean. Maybe she kind of gives off sex, a bit like, like a female animal. You know, to attract a male, or...'

No. I didn't like that at all. It was horrible, especially from Robert who was usually so clear and clever with words. *Gives off sex?* It jarred. I slipped off the wall and faced up to him.

'Oh charming, Robert! You're basically saying Kirsty's a bitch on permanent heat then? Like, just gagging for it all the time.'

He covered his face with his hands.

'No, sorry. God, that sounds terrible. No, that's not what I mean at all. Honest, I take it back.'

THE FENIAN

His face was contorted in concentration.

'It's like, there's this dog, right?' He held up a hand, fingers stretched wide, to fend off the protest he saw coming. 'And no, I'm not back on the heat thing, this is different. Imagine there's a dog lives in your street, like the one next to Paddy, OK? It doesn't have to be the obvious fierce kind of thing. Not an Alsatian or anything, just this ordinary dog. But you know it's dangerous. You don't know why you know, you just instinctively do. You sense it. It doesn't even have to do anything. It doesn't have to bark, or snarl at you or anything. It could just lie there all day long, not even looking at you, but you're still wary when you walk past it because somehow you just know, you're aware it's capable of doing bad things. There's a kind of dangerousness coming from it, if dangerousness is even a word. Anyway, it's a bit like that with Kirsty. You know she's liable to do stuff – not bad things, at least the guys don't think they're bad things. It's just, you just sense it with Kirsty, you know it's there. A kind of danger that guys can't resist. And Lorna, I haven't a bloody clue what I'm talking about or if I'm making any sense whatsoever.'

I thought about it, then I decided it was all getting a bit heavy. Time to end it or at least, postpone it.

'Aye, very good, Plug, very deep and profound. But there's one major flaw in your grand theory...I'm not scared of dogs.'

Robert half-slid, half-jumped from the wall and faced me, up close, relieved to be released from interrogation. This was long before the New Year when we got together but for a few seconds, I was positive he was going to kiss me. But he laughed and then I laughed and the moment was gone. I couldn't tell if the relief was to do with closing down the subject or the non-kiss. Perhaps both.

'Ah, shut your face, Morticia,' he said. 'Or I'll pull the pigtails I bet you had when you were wee.'

Lying in bed later, replaying the conversation, I think I got what Robert was trying to say. Think I probably already knew it and understood, about Kirsty.

***

It goes without saying that it was us lot, the shelter gang, who invented sex. And Kirsty was our pioneer, our scout in all matters of the flesh. Always at least one step ahead, right from the start, right from her *You built in proportion?* crack to Big Paddy. It was the very first thing she ever said to him, bringing sex into it right away or at least, a tantalising hint of sex, a suggestion of it. She was, what, fourteen at the time, fifteen at the most?

Kirsty was the one who did everything first, the one who trampled down the barriers and cleared a path for us. More than that, she barged the barriers aside and dared us to follow.

The rest of us, we were just any girls growing up, from anywhere, any time. We explored slowly, we made small discoveries, then, gradually, bigger ones. We opened the book tentatively, we studied it, read meticulously, line by line, chapter by chapter. We never knew what would be on the next page and some of us were slower readers than others, always a few pages behind. Kirsty, though, read the book all in one go, from start to finish, couldn't put it down. She consumed it greedily and learned it off by heart while the rest of us were still timidly browsing the contents.

Yes, it had felt weird, talking about sex with Robert but then it had been strange too, discussing sex with the other girls, at least at first. We never let on to the boys. (To the guys, when we stopped calling them boys.) We never let on that we talked about sex, the way we knew they did. At first, we acted all coy and affronted when they mentioned it, or if one of them made some dodgy remark in front of us. But we would watch them playing football – or pretend to watch – and use that time to compare notes. It was fine at first when it was just snogging. Huh, not even that. When we first kissed, in those simple, childish games at our early parties, it was no more than a brushing of lips. So it was easy to talk about kissing and wondering which one of us – and which one of them – was first to believe Karen, about how you were supposed to open your mouth, about who was first to learn that your tongue was for more than licking stamps.

Groping/touching/fondling/feeling. It quickly became a contagious outbreak among the guys. Octopus disease, Jo called it. Enough to heat up our conversation by several degrees, especially after Wee Mary broke the ice. One evening, at the shelter, out of nowhere, she said: 'Think I might chuck Cammy. Can't keep his hands to himself.'

Must have been tough for her, right enough, because she had more territory to defend than the rest of us. Sometimes it seemed Wee Mary was expanding by the day. But that was it, someone had finally said it out loud and we sensed ice cracking all around us. Suddenly, it was open season.

Jo was next in the confessional. 'Robert's the same. I get fed up shoving him away so I let him sometimes…but only on the outside.'

Fiona looked a bit embarrassed and suppressed a smile. She had always been the straggler, up till then. She stared at her shoes.

'Don't dare tell the other guys but I let Paddy once. Inside my shirt I mean – but just two buttons and two fingers.'

Our eyes widened. Fiona continued, self-mocking as ever. 'Mind you, he's wasting his time. All he's feeling's the bones where my bust should be.'

We laughed, but kindly.

'Fiona-a-a-a!' Karen feigned shock then stunned us with a revelation of her own.

'I've let Simon touch my..' She dropped her voice to a Les Dawson whisper. '...nipples.'

Immediately, she felt obliged to qualify her bombshell in case we got the wrong idea.

'But only once and for two minutes because he'd been really, really nice to me.'

There it was again, that word that kept cropping up. LET. Was that how it worked, how you played the game? You eked out little favours, bit by bit? Always leave 'em wanting more! I said nothing. I had only just got to the outside-the-anorak stage, and only once, with Ross. Besides, it was my turn at spare girl. You didn't mention intimate stuff if it involved someone else's current boyfriend. Serious breach of protocol that.

Kirsty had sat through all of this, detached, as if she was barely listening, and occasionally glancing at us with condescending, smug smiles. No, sorry Kirsty, that's not fair. It probably was not so much smug as pitying. Then she annihilated us – all of us – with one shot.

'Ross's had my bra off.'

That was all she said, but boom! No hint of a *let* in there either. She had wiped out the competition, smashed us. She had allowed us, well the four others, to witter on about giggly little-girl stuff, tentative first fondles, daring little feels. She was talking flesh, bare flesh. Half-naked, exposed, full-frontal tits-out. We tried to pick up our jaws. My head whirred. When had this happened, where, how had she/they got to that stage without anyone noticing? Kirsty read our faces but let the unasked questions hang there. She perfected her timing then delivered the aftershock.

She nodded down at her chest and said: 'He sucks them.'

Not sucked. Sucks. What was she saying? That this wasn't a one-off but was happening on a regular basis?

Where did that leave us? Where did it leave me? Was it possible to dismiss or forget what she had said and carry on at my own pace? Trouble was, Kirsty had already drawn the picture, the graphic picture. She had drawn it and hung it up on our walls. It scared me, made me feel small, immature, like a silly little girl, but it excited me at the same time.

What happened now? Did I/we race to catch up, knowing we'd never catch up? Did we race to whip off our bras, grab the next guy by the ears, thrust his face to our bosom and issue orders. *Go on, start sucking. Faster, faster, so I can rush back and stick some points up on the board.* Or should we convene a meeting without Kirsty? Form a moral majority and decide she had gone too far too soon. She was in the wrong and we were the good girls. Of course we didn't. We didn't reach any consensus. How could we? We didn't even discuss what Kirsty had revealed. We each just stumbled on, each in our own way, groping around in the dark. Ha!

Down there. That was the next boundary. As usual, Kirsty went dashing on ahead and checked it out for us. We all saw it happen and it hit us like a newsflash. She and Ross, heavy and steamy, at one end of the settee during Cookie's party. The music restarted and the lights flashed back on but Kirsty and Ross flouted regulations. They didn't stop, too immersed to notice. No one bothered at first until Big Paddy called out: 'For God sake somebody chuck a bucket of water over that pair.'

We all looked over, laughing along with him, then we stopped laughing. Kirsty was writhing beneath Ross, his hand invisible from the wrist down while her tight, short white skirt was riding up. We saw the outline of Ross's knuckles under the thin material, circling and kneading. Another gate had just opened, maybe even literally. *Don't be so crude, Lorna.*

Then another stage, a second-hand, overheard revelation this time. It happened a week or two after we had spent that morning at the swimming baths, a morning that had changed the game. I approached the shelter on my own quite early one evening and heard voices, or mainly one voice. It was Cammy, excited and condescending.

'Fuck sake Robert, you never been felt? You'll be telling me next you've no' been near a tit since you were in nappies.'

So much to digest there, well, the first part of it anyway. I knew what Cammy was on about and I knew immediately, it had to be Kirsty. She had become more than a little obsessed with Cammy after what she had seen at the baths and made a beeline for him at the next party.

Now there was yet another big hurdle to negotiate – another hurdle after the one I was still struggling to clamber over. Now two whole new areas to think about. I hadn't let anyone touch me down there, as it was coyly whispered by the girls, or *fingered me*, as I'd heard Ross and Cammy put it a little less delicately. Big Paddy had tried one afternoon. He took a sudden, intense interest in my left knee and started worming his hand upwards, keeping his progress slow as if I might not notice, all the while talking to distract me. We had been sitting, half-lying on a chair at Wee Mary's. It wasn't a party, just a Sunday when she had an empty and one of the very rare times when we were an item. This crappy joke went through my head. I'd heard a guy telling it on telly. *Heh, tits first.*

THE FENIAN

I just said: 'Don't Paddy.'

It was enough and he pulled away, no protest.

Up top, as opposed to down there, OK. I was fine with that now, liked it a lot, if I'm honest. That sensation of something giving way, the almost unbearable melting when the toucher got it right. Yeah, breasts, I was OK with that – so long as the guy remembered they were actually attached. But now I was so far behind, with more worries piling up. What was the right thing to do? Play Kirsty's game of catch-up, or let myself keep believing/worrying the guys were calling me *Tight*. What were the other girls doing? What stage were they at? I wished somebody would instruct me, tell me what to do. But after a while, we seemed to shut down the sex chat. We pulled the shutters over because it had all become too serious, too personal. And when…if…I got over the down-there stage, what next? Feel them? Touch the guys? Where? Touch them down there? I was so innocent, such a baby, and I didn't want to be. I was scared stiff. But of course, I did get over it, eventually, like the others, like all the other girls before us. All round me, people were upping the ante and the pace was becoming frantic. It got more daring, more thrilling, more scary. Our parties sizzled now. Stroking, touching, under bras, up skirts, zips down. Eleven young bodies at boiling point.

But one thing kept niggling at me – an ethos the guys developed where they kind of demanded equal rights. They were obviously comparing notes and it was like, you let one go so far, that's it, that's what you do, that's how far you go. Maybe more, but definitely no less, as if it would be grossly unfair to deny the other guys the same. One of them got to unhook your bra for unrestricted access, then it was supposed to become a given, with all of them.

I finally got to the major (for me) down-there stage. With Cammy it was. We had been together for a couple of weeks, building up to it slowly. His hand was cool and sent a shudder through me. It happened at a party, but we were interrupted after a few minutes. We had gone back to our silly games for old times' sake – Chairs this time – and Ross moved in, squeezed up close to me. He didn't even kiss me but went straight for the main event. He tried to force his hand between my legs but I tightened up and pulled it away roughly. Ross looked wounded, insulted almost, and shot a furious glance at Cammy, who was already mobilising his forces for an attempt to scale Fiona. Ross's rage flashed up in big burning letters across the darkened room. YOU FUCKING LIAR CAMMY.

Slowly, slowly, we crept up on Kirsty but she felt us closing in and, naturally, needed to shock again, to grind us down. She needed to show us who was boss and she announced it at the shelter one early evening while the guys were playing football.

So matter of fact. Another we-interrupt-this-programme newsflash.

'Know what I did today?'

The superior tone had us all instantly on alert and – I can't vouch for the rest – set me on edge. I felt my heart thud as she prepared to reveal the grisly details. Even though I had no claim, I prayed her revelation wasn't about Robert.

Chapter 28

June 1976-June 1986
Love Don't Live Here Anymore – Jimmy Nail

S O, Robert had spotted me in Central Station, with *some guy*. I tried to do the maths. According to Big Paddy, Robert got married six or seven years after school and this had happened a few years after, but as clues went it was pretty much useless because those two hadn't left St Joe's at the same time. I left school in the summer of '75, Big Paddy sometime near the end of the previous year. Robert had stayed on another year after me so there was no way to be sure unless I went to the trouble of researching football records. Without a definite starting point, all I could do was place Robert's sighting sometime in the mid-eighties, in which case it could have been either one. The end of Bill, or the beginning of Mark.

Bill Harrison. I met him on a boat, the ferry from Calais, on the way home from my big trip – my travels with Wee Mary. We had run away together but I was heading home alone. She hadn't made it back all the way. She had bailed out in Italy after meeting some bloke – English, I'm sure he was. What was his name again? Digging deep for this one. Tony? Tommy? What I do remember is that he worked in one of the ticket offices at Punta Sabbioni, where you get the ferry across to Venice. This Tony or Tommy was almost certainly incidental and I never believed for a minute that it came to anything. But Wee Mary had been looking for a way out, an excuse, because she was too scared to go home and face all the crazy stuff. I'll explain that later.

I was sitting in the crowded ferry cafeteria, spinning out a mug of tea on the crossing back to Dover, when this guy ambled over carrying a loaded tray and asked if I minded if he shared my table. He was all fuzzy beard and glasses and he had an accent from home. I scrounged a slice of buttered toast from him and we got chatting.

So ironic. Ten months I'd been exploring the Continent, a handful of guys

193

along the way – French, Italian, a skinny Swede I met in Benidorm, one German guy I didn't really fancy but liked a helluva lot. Never anything that serious even though a couple of them wanted it to be. Around the World in Eighty Knock-backs. OK, it was only Europe, but it doesn't have the same ring. All those exotic foreigners and I finished up with a guy from Irvine. A new townie like me, about an hour away from Cumbride.

We hit it off right away. He was funny, he was good at listening, he was interesting, he was interested. He came across as sincere. Bill was a teacher, not long qualified, and French was his subject. He was a few years older – twenty-three to my eighteen. He had just completed a year's exchange at a school in a smallish city called Rennes, in northern France, and was due to start working at a secondary in Irvine after the summer holidays. It was all so easy, Bill was easy, and it got comfortable very quickly. He was a good talker – intelligent, down to earth, easy going, amusing, pliable, attentive. He reminded me of someone…

I got home and Bill was on the phone all the time. He got himself a sensible little car on HP and came up to Cumbride as often as he could. We went out, we stayed in, we sat at my Dad's and watched telly. He got on well with my Dad. Bill was steady and secure – a safe bet, my Dad called him. Bill always wanted to know what I wanted to do. Bill was Nice.

Nice. That had been one of Robert's hate words. He told me the word Nice was a death knell. You heard a girl use the word Nice, it meant you were seconds from being dumped. *Look, you're a really nice guy, but…*

We got engaged a year to the day after I got back from Europe and married another twelve months after that. It felt right and we did everything by the book. I moved down to Irvine to be near his work. We stayed with his parents at first but I got a job in a shoe shop and we saved up. Pretty soon we put down a deposit on a neat little starter home and got ourselves on the first rung of the property ladder. A modern, two-bedroom Barratt. We saved up some more and bought a newer car, another sensible, economical one. We booked a week in Menorca for the summer, self-catering to make it more affordable.

Bill and I made friends, mostly other teachers, and we visited each other's homes most Saturday nights on a kind of rota. We'd have dinner, with all the wives making a dish each, and talk about school mostly. Well, they did. I felt like I had hardly been away from school. It had been barely three years since I'd left Cumbride High and now I was back at school again, in mind if not in body.

I feel bad that the tone of this is already so sour and sarcy. In reality, our early years together were fine. We were happy enough and we did all the right stuff in the right order. We rolled along together well enough and Bill was pretty much the model, modern husband. Caring, generous, thoughtful.

He wanted kids, not surprisingly, and I sort of thought I did too at first because it was what you were supposed to do. The proper next step, right? But it didn't happen right away and I found I wasn't too unhappy about it. Bill didn't push it and I don't know why, but I went on the Pill. I didn't tell him and I was never quite sure why about that either. He just accepted it wasn't happening and didn't complain or question it.

Bill did everything right. He worked hard at school where he was building a good reputation. Without being pushy or overtly ambitious, promotion was bound to follow in time. He worked hard at home where he did more than his fair share of the housework. He was still attentive, he still wanted to know what I wanted to do. All the time. He was kind and generous and he just kept on being Nice.

I knew the truth of it then and I know it now. What went wrong in that marriage was my fault. My fault, because I eventually realised that Bill wasn't Robert and was never going to be. My fault too, for blaming him for that.

I could never quite square it with myself. Had I married a Robert substitute or was I trying to build myself a Robert clone? There had been obvious similarities from the start. The intelligence, the sincerity, the warmth, the humour. But gradually, I began to feel like I was married to a human duvet, a lovely big soft comfortable toasty safe security blanket. I kicked against it, I deliberately tried to provoke him, to see what was beyond the niceness, to see if there was anything beyond the niceness. I tried to noise him up but poor Bill, he took it all on the chin. The word *Sorry* came to him far too easily. He would apologise for anything, he would apologise for nothing and all the while, he kept thinking a great big hug could solve any problem.

I found myself – and I am sure Bill did too – being worn down by a repetitive cycle of misery. I would tell him I was bored, so he would ask me what I wanted to do. I would go all sullen and awkward and pouty, tell him I didn't know what I wanted to do and why couldn't he decide for a change? So, he would suggest something and I would accuse him of being selfish, of always wanting his own way. He would ask me what I wanted to do. And round and round and round. As I say, my fault.

Whenever he saw he wasn't getting anywhere, he would come over and try to give me a great big hug. *C'mere pet, let me give you a cuddle then you'll feel better.* The next morning, he would bring me breakfast in bed and leave me a little note on the kitchen worktop with the words inside a heart. *Sorry about last night. Love you XXXX.* Worst of it was, he never even knew what he was apologising for, or, more to the point, that he had nothing to apologise for.

I cannot make it any clearer. My behaviour was beyond the acceptable. I acted like an out and out Grade A bitch and Bill had done nothing to deserve it.

Eventually, I began to be unfaithful to him, with an old flame. Robert. He started to insinuate himself between us and he did it in plain sight. A couple of nights a week, he would stroll right into our living room while Bill and I were curled up at opposite ends of the sofa. Absolutely shameless. I'd be watching TV and I'd glance over at nice old Bill marking schoolwork and dropping another jotter on to the pile on the floor, his straggly beard needing trimmed, a smelly old sweater on. He would fart, he would apologise, he would sniff, he would snigger.

Then I'd glance over at Robert, who had crept in like a thief, but an intruder who couldn't help being a show-off. So cool and smart in his crisp white shirt, plain grey tie for gravitas, tanned face, hair perfectly groomed, brilliant blue sky at his back. Where was he coming from tonight? Washington? Rome? Sydney? Cumbride? I would hear his voice again and let it charm me like a musical box. I'd look into his eyes longingly and, for a second, believe I could reach out and touch him as he started spinning me a tale from the TV set. If Bill was really engrossed, his face buried in a jotter, I would sometimes sneakily touch myself then feel ashamed. Stupid, stupid, stupid.

Each time, after Robert had signed off, I would curse myself. Look at what I had – a good man, a safe man, a man who was going places, a man who could not have treated me any better. A nice man in a nice little home. NICE NICE NICE.

Back and forward, mood swings that endlessly patient Bill didn't deserve but kept on taking like a good-hearted, well-meaning softie for eight slow years until our marriage finally expired. A lingering, painful death from lethargy and neglect. His lethargy, my neglect.

But Bill couldn't stop being nice, even when I told him I was leaving him. Maybe he could have saved it, our marriage, even then at the eleventh hour. If only he had let rip, just one time. If only he had let rip and told me what a stupid, spoiled, ungrateful, immature little wretch I was. Or maybe he was more perceptive than I gave him credit for and knew that it was too far gone. Maybe he realised it, that I had been cheating on him – if only in my head – and that I had placed our marriage way beyond repair. Bill even offered to move out, the soft sod. But I was doing the leaving, so I went back to Cumbride, to my Dad's. Bill took care of everything, to spare me any hassle or heartache. I lost count of the times he used the word amicable in our final conversations.

Dad had a woman living with him by then. Sadie. Thin and nervy and edgy and a divorcee – like me (soon) – who worked at the bookie's. I didn't blame Dad. He was still a relatively young man after all. Who was I to even consider blame? Why should I have any say in it at all? Sadie didn't like me but that was OK, I didn't much like her either. She resented me being there, I was in the way. Tough, it was my home long before it was hers. Still, I told Sadie she didn't have to worry because I wasn't planning on hanging around long. I had plans, big plans. I was going to start over and do something worthwhile with my life. Then I bumped into a sex machine.

Chapter 29

1974-1975
Love To Love You Baby – Donna Summer

I HELD my breath as Kirsty, our sexual pioneer, our real physical education teacher, smirked and shook her head condescendingly. She prepared to reveal not just her latest exploit, but which of the guys had been complicit. There was one name I did not want to hear. We, the rest of the girls, had been chatting about our daring progress. The mutual touches, the hard-won opening of a button or two, the exploratory forays under outer garments. Kirsty sneered like we were babies taking our first footsteps and dropped her nuclear bomb.

'Gave Cammy a w**k today. Up at the waterfall.'

Hey, sorry, I'm not really Little Miss Delicate. It's just that word. I can say the rest, not a problem. Take my word for it, OK? It's just that one, the W-word, that I've got a problem with. I have a theory about my coyness over that particular word – and I mean the word, separate from the act. It goes back to when I was at primary and we used to go for Sunday runs, Wee Mary and me, in her Dad's car and he would make up word games for us. A-B-C was our staple. One of us would pick a simple subject, like animals or girls' names or countries, and we'd go through the alphabet, thinking up a word for each letter in the chosen category. It was just a game but thinking back now, it was smart of Wee Mary's Dad. He was stretching our little minds and our vocabularies, making us think about words and teaching us new ones when we got stuck. On long drives, when we got fed up with A-B-C, he'd invent other games, like Rhyming Target, where he would give us a word – simple ones at first, like hat – then set us a target of say, ten, and we would reel off BAT, CAT, FAT, MAT and so on. Gradually the words got harder and the targets bigger. It's strange the things that stick with you but I kept playing that game for years, in my head, sometimes in the class when the lesson was especially boring, or on the bus to Glasgow while Mum smoked or stared blankly out of the window, and Dad read his racing pages. So, when I first heard that word, the one I don't like, I went into Rhyming Target autopilot. I think I was twelve when I heard a boy at school not just saying it, but vividly simulating the activity in case anyone didn't understand. I couldn't help myself and I didn't like what I came up with. DANK, STANK, SHANK, RANK, LANK, SANK, (SEPTIC) TANK. Who says you can be logical all the time?

But Kirsty hadn't just said it, she had done it, and it felt like another huge, scary leap into the unknown again, despite all the big brave things I'd done. This sounded so close to real, actual sex. A step too far, a place where I didn't think I was ready to go. A couple of the other girls, Jo and Fiona, knew I didn't like the word so they tried to make a game of it, searching for alternatives, delaying the moment when we would have to start thinking about what it involved, never mind just saying it. Karen gave us our substitute word – or phrase – by accident. She had heard about Kirsty and Cammy and she knew Cookie had heard about it too. The guys were in a fever pitch, hating, admiring and envying Cammy in equal measures. Cookie was no different.

'I might give Simon one,' Karen told us, then screwed up her face in distaste. 'You know, a wank. Oh, sorry Lorna.'

Karen had stunned us. She was about to move only a couple of steps behind Kirsty in the big race, before the rest of us had given any serious thought to becoming runners. I couldn't help suspecting she would use it as another kind of power over Cookie. She saw the shock in our faces and felt she had to explain, or at least qualify.

'Oh, not right away. I was thinking maybe for his birthday.'

Classic Karen, but at least she had given us a new name for it.

All the while, Kirsty charged on, leaving us floundering in her wake, and rocking us again by handing out TWO birthday presents in the same day to TWO different guys, one right after the other and making an even bigger name for herself in the process. It happened at my house one Sunday afternoon when my folks were out. Cammy was first. He disappeared into my bedroom with Kirsty. It wasn't his first time so he knew what to expect. But then I noticed Ross lurking about outside the room. After about five minutes, Cammy trooped out, grinning, and nodded to Ross to go in, like the dentist. I don't know who else saw it, but it upset me for reasons I did not understand. I suppose I felt a little sick about it. Surely this wasn't what it was all about? So cold, so mechanical, so, *next please*. And in my bedroom! On my actual bed? Yuck.

199

After that, it seemed Kirsty couldn't stop herself, or stop talking about it. Her conversation had leapt galaxies from those innocent, giggly snogging comparisons. Now it was getting right down to it, comparing the guys, their size, staying power, sound effects. All in uncensored, graphic technicolor too.

'Cammy's easy the biggest,' she said casually, in connection with nothing, hijacking the conversation and leading us down the sex road again, just as we were doing our best to take a breather and stay off it.

Jo had been doing nothing more raunchy than analysing Rod Stewart's new hairstyle, but I caught Kirsty's meaning straight away, and I bristled. She must mean the biggest of three, four at most, I thought. Not Cookie, surely, and please, not Robert. Kirsty was in full flow, no stopping her. Once again, I said a silent prayer. *Don't let me hear Robert's name here.* I braced myself, but I was right, unless Kirsty was sparing my feelings – and Karen's, of course – which would have been uncharacteristically thoughtful. Phew, it was best out of three.

'Yeah, he's enormous, Cammy. Like a big, throbbing purple rolling pin. Wouldn't think it to look at him, would you? Well, when it's hidden in his trousers anyway.'

She sniggered and ploughed on.

'He can hold out the longest as well, nearly eight minutes. Big Paddy's the next longest and he's more light browny – like the colour of Jo's hair. Five minutes he does. Ross is thicker – than Paddy, I mean, not Cammy. He's done in two or three minutes first time, but he's ready to go again the quickest.'

Oh Jesus, thank you so much for sharing this with us, Kirsty, and what, are you actually timing them? Like, with your watch?

There was no stopping her.

'Big Paddy's quiet at first then he groans a lot like he's in pain. Ross is a shouter, like he's just scored a goal, and Cammy keeps thanking you faster and faster all the way through it.'

The action ramped up at a frightening tempo after that. Kirsty raced on recklessly, at full throttle, and somehow managed to raise the stakes yet again. Another party, another house. I was looking for my purse, worried I had left it lying somewhere, at the shelter maybe. I wanted to check my jacket pockets, so I knocked at a bedroom door where the coats were piled and walked in when I got no answer. Cammy was sitting on the edge of the bed, staring like a zombie and gasping out *thank yous*. His hands were on Kirsty's shoulders and she was kneeling, her head bouncing in his lap. At least, small mercies, Ross wasn't waiting outside for his turn.

THE FENIAN

It was only a matter of time by this stage and somehow, we all knew it without anyone coming out and saying it. It had happened. Real, actual sex. Kirsty, of course, but who with? She strutted around for days bearing a look of triumph, a look that said, no way, you'll never catch me now. Game, set and match to Kirsty, as if it had all been a competition which, perhaps it was.

Everyone knew it had happened, no question, but strangely, none of the guys was claiming the scalp, none of the usual bragging had filtered down to us. Maybe whoever it was hadn't lived up to Kirsty's expectations or, more painfully, his own. We guessed, we laid odds, with Ross and Cammy split as evens favourites, Big Paddy coming up fast on the rails and Cookie a decent dark horse bet. He was certainly the one with the most reason to keep quiet about it, we reasoned, and how Kirsty would have relished that victory over Karen. It couldn't be Robert. It couldn't be, could it? Was I fooling myself that he was different from the rest? I tried so hard to convince myself that he couldn't be in the running.

Because Robert was mine. Sex with Robert, making love with Robert, it was to be mine. I want to say it was our destiny, but that's much too Mills and Boony. We had been together nearly three months by that time – the longest of any relationship in our gang outside of Karen and Cookie. The heat had intensified as we advanced and made our own discoveries. We were so close, we were ready.

That Sunday, just two days before my mother died. We were alone in his house, in his room. His parents were off visiting somewhere, his big sister, Sandra, was out with her boyfriend. We both sensed it would go further this time, the full distance possibly. We kissed, softly at first, then savagely. We touched, awkwardly, like the rookies we were. We helped each other undo buttons and zips as we shed clothes. Suddenly, I was naked, we both were, and we lay still for a short while, trembling as we sneaked glances at each other. We were burning and terrified, well, I certainly was, and not really understanding what it was all about. But we were both ready and I knew it was going to happen. I wanted it, I wanted him, to feel him inside me. I needed him. He moved on top of me and I could feel him almost there. Yes, I was ready. He looked into me and spoke so gently, almost timidly.

'I don't have anything.'

'Just be careful, stop before…'

'You sure, Lorna?'

'Yes,' was all I said and closed my eyes, shaking, fearful, longing.

But then, a lightness. The very last thing I expected. At the last second, he had pulled away and rolled off me. I heard him stumble blindly then settle again. I looked up and he was slumped on the floor, sitting with his back to the wall, his hands covering his face. I was confused. I didn't understand and suddenly, I was hurting. My eyes filled, embarrassed in my nakedness. Robert took his hands from his face but avoided looking at me. He reached out, tugged his T-shirt over himself, such deep, shattering sadness in his face. I picked up my blouse and made a feeble attempt at covering myself. I didn't know what the hell was going on.

He just said: 'I'm sorry.'

'What for?' I asked, fumbling for an explanation. 'What, what's wrong?'

'I'm sorry,' he repeated. 'I'm just, so…so…scared.'

'It's all right.' Even in my confusion, I held up reassurance, offered it to him. 'I'm scared and all, Robert. It's my first time too. I hope you didn't think it wasn't.'

But I had misunderstood. Robert was in mourning, grieving a loss that hadn't happened. Well, not yet anyway.

'No, it's not that,' he said. My Robert, his face stricken, weighed down by emotions new and alien to him. 'I mean yeah, course it's my first time too, but that's not what I'm talking about. It's you, Lorna, I'm so scared of not having all this. Shit, fuck, I'm scared of losing you, Lorna. I'm scared of there being a time when I'll have lost you.'

A coldness, a tremor through me.

'I don't know what you mean, Robert,' I said. 'What are you talking about? Losing me?'

'Ah, come on, Lorna,' he sighed with such a deep hopelessness. 'Things this brilliant don't happen to me. I don't get this lucky. You're so far out my league and I'm scared every day's the day that fact is going to dawn on you. Fuck Lorna, I'm seventeen and I'm already terrified of a life that's not got you in it. What a fucking tube, eh?'

Powerful, soaring Robert. He had just placed himself in the palm of my hand, giving me the right to crush him if I wished. My love for him, right there, was undiluted, pulsing so strongly it scared me, as much as it apparently scared Robert. I don't know, maybe it was nothing more than childish melodrama but then, in that moment, it felt so real and so massive. I knew what he was getting at because I felt the advance pain too. I couldn't bear to think of a life without him. But surely it was down to us. Surely it was in our own hands not to let that happen. Why should it happen? Only, I didn't know it then. I didn't know it wasn't just Mum who was so close to death. I only had forty-eight hours to live too.

Chapter 30

1986-1988
You Give Love A Bad Name – Bon Jovi

I WAS twenty-eight, a marriage just behind me. I had plans, I was going to start again, go to college, find myself a flat, or even just a bedsit to start with. I was going to have a career, use my brain. Forget about men, or at least forget about serious relationships. Then I made a mistake. I was feeling wrung out after a session signing divorce papers in a lawyer's office up at Cumbride town centre, so I decided to splash out on a taxi back to Dad's instead of the local bus. Except I got into the wrong motor at the taxi rank. I got into Mark Maxwell's cab. By the time he dropped me home, I'd agreed to go for a drink later. By the end of the night, we'd had sex – twice – on the first date, in the back of his taxi. The teacher's wife and the savage.

Mark Maxwell. A good-looking, long-haired, mouthy, gallus, horny animal in a leather jacket.

With Bill, my first husband, sex had been the bonus prize, a pleasant by-product of being married. Bill had been slow, patient, gentle and sensitive. He always paid attention to detail and we always made love on my terms. He always tried hard to please and made me the priority. He always asked first and thanked me afterwards. He was always grateful and anxious to know if it had been good for me, or at least OK.

Mark, though, just took. It was rough, hard, sore, messy, loud, cramped, uncomfortable. And bloody brilliant. It was certainly nothing that resembled making love. It felt like doing sex and it was brand new, for me anyway.

After that first night, I couldn't keep my hands off him. I couldn't get enough. It was a filthy, frantic, fantastic, mucky whirlwind of sex.

We grabbed at it. I happily became the Martini girl...any time, any place, anywhere. He lived with his parents so we did it in his bedroom, his foot wedged up against the door. We did it at my Dad's house, when he and Sadie went upstairs to bed. On the settee or the floor in the living room or up against the bloody washing machine in the kitchen. We gagged each other with our hands to muffle the screams and the moans.

We got married within six months, just five weeks after my divorce from Bill was finalised. Naturally, I was wary – frying pan, fire and all that. Out of one marriage, straight into another one, two surnames in a matter of weeks. But Mark wanted it and what Mark wanted, he got. Most of his mates were married, both his younger brothers too. He was nearly thirty and felt he was falling behind. I always suspected it was the stag night he really craved – strippers and all that. It was practical too, getting hitched, because it still mattered with official stuff back then. We got a scummy, damp council flat without much trouble in one of Cumbride's less salubrious schemes, an early build fast turning tatty. But the surroundings were of little consequence. What mattered was that we had our own little fuck pad, a place to do it again and again and again with no interruptions or inhibitions. We had sex and more sex then some more again. We screwed this way and that way and upside down and back to front till I ran out of steam.

Then, without warning, I came up for air and regained consciousness. It happened one morning when I woke up about half eight and slipped out of bed quietly while Mark lay snoring. He worked nights in the taxi sometimes and didn't get home till four or five so he usually slept till about twelve. I waded through the wreck of our bedroom, stumbled into the shambles that was our kitchen and put the kettle on. Then it hit me and I panicked. I was trying to think of some garbled words Mark had mumbled in the early hours when he got home. Suddenly, I realised I didn't know what his voice sounded like and it scared the shit out of me. Would I be able to recognise Mark's voice if his or my life depended on it? If there was ever – and I know this sounds bonkers but I wasn't thinking straight – an identity parade for voices, would I be able to pick his out? As for me, I had become barely capable of stringing my own thoughts together, just a jumble of words scattered around in my head with no cohesion, making no sense. Something else dawned on me. When did I last have a conversation? I meant, an actual conversation beyond *fuck me harder you beautiful bastard*. I meant, a Robert conversation, a Bill conversation even. For God sake, any kind of conversation with anyone. I had known Mark more than eight months by this time, we had been married about two. But the more I thought about it, I couldn't remember ever actually speaking to him or him speaking to me, properly, I mean. Was this what I wanted? Had I really traded in nice, cuddly old Bill for a shagging machine? The truth of it filtered through me. Us, Mark and me, we communicated through sex. That's what bonded us, that's what we had in common and now I had this awful, dread feeling that it was all we had in common. There had to be more, surely? I would make there be more. Maybe things would settle down. Maybe this was the way marriage was supposed to be – a first hectic torrent of sex and passion. Maybe Bill's endless patient gratitude meant I had missed out first time round. I would make Mark take me out. I would make Mark talk to me.

He nodded and muttered *sure sure darling* a lot when I tried to explain it to him, sliding his hand between my legs as he did. Why was I surprised? Sex was Mark's life, his world.

We'd go to the pictures, on my suggestion of course, but he'd barely contain himself past the opening credits. He would take my hand and guide it to his lap where he would thoughtfully have his zip undone. He'd lean over and whisper: 'A fucking turn-on, eh, next to other folk in the dark? Just tease us, will you?'

Right, sure Mark, nothing I'd like better, this was exactly what I came to the cinema for. Silly me thinking we were here to watch a film.

On the way home in the car from the pictures or maybe a restaurant, I would wait for it. *His* hand this time, slipping across on to my thigh, gliding upwards. He'd start stroking me, like he had found the magic lamp. A few quick rubs and the genie would be begging to grant him more than just three wishes.

At my insistence, we started mixing with his mates down the pub, other cabbies and their wives/girlfriends. But Mark could never stay off the subject for long. He would nod towards me and whisper something to a pal. Chuckle chuckle. The pal would look at me, raise his eyebrows, take a sharp breath.

Once he'd stuck it out for an hour, hour and a half at the most, Mark would look at his watch and gesture towards me. He'd say something really romantic, like: 'Better be heading soon, I've got man's work to do the night.'

Or: 'You gonna try and keep your hands to yourself in the motor the night, Lorna?'

Or, worse still, he would pat a point just above his groin and say: 'Got to get home, the little lady'll be choking for her supper.'

Then he would give a big dirty wink and roar at his own dazzling repartee. The other wives/girlfriends would look at me and sneer down their noses. I could read their faces. They were thinking, *Slapper*, or, *Never last*.

Mark wanted sex on tap. No, not wanted, demanded. He would crawl into bed at four in the morning, cold from the night air, and from deep, deep in my sleep, I would feel him, pressing sharply into my bum, then his hand would slip round and start pawing at my breasts.

One time, after another small-hours session, he came up with what he called a brilliant idea that was absolutely classic Mark.

'Heh Lorna, why don't you start waking us up with a B.J.?'

I obviously didn't register enough enthusiasm so he winked, prepared to compromise, and demonstrated what passed for his sensitive side.

'All right, all right. If you don't feel like that first thing, I understand. Hand-job'll do then.'

He said he'd call it his alarm-cock, looking really chuffed with his own wit.

Don't get me wrong, it wasn't just Mark. Mostly, I went along, I was happy to go along. Our relationship might have had the depth of a teaspoon but there was still the sex and it was good. More than good.

Round about eight months into the marriage, Mark took me by surprise. He hadn't come near me in two days and for him, that was papal-level abstinence. Then he got serious and told me he thought our sex life had gone stale. After a few months? God help us in ten years! Mark suggested we try and spice things up. It was the usual, predictable stuff at first – stockings, suspenders and all that, stuff you could buy in Marks. He bought me stilettos and got me to keep them on in bed. Cost us two ripped bed sheets, that brainwave.

He always wanted to move on, to try something new. It was different positions next, more Twister or gymnastics than sex. I told him he should have married one of those wee Rumanian girls from the Olympics on the telly a few years back.

Mark kept on nagging. What about dressing-up games? Surely I must know somebody who's a nurse? Couldn't I borrow a uniform? I could tell her – this imaginary friend – that it's for a fancy-dress party, he suggested helpfully.

One night, or rather early morning, Mark got hold of a catalogue from another cabbie who had picked it up on a trip to Amsterdam. Mark phoned me at one in the morning. This was in the days before mobiles, so he actually stopped at a call box. He was breathless with excitement and I got into a state because I thought he had been in an accident or something, but he had woken me up to tell me about this catalogue. He finished early, rushed home and woke me again so he could show it to me. He perched on the edge of the bed, flicking through the pages in a frenzy, pointing out grotesquely large vibrators and other sex toys, hyper as a kid in Santa's grotto.

As for the dressing up, I went along with it for a while but it felt more panto than sexy. I couldn't stop worrying about what would happen if one of the other flats in the block went on fire and we had to dash out of the house and into the street in a rush. The neighbours in their dressing gowns or anoraks over pyjamas, me done up as a French maid or a nurse, or with a teacher's mortar board on my head and a cane in my hand.

THE FENIAN

Then, inevitably I suppose, came porn videos. Mark lapped it up but I couldn't get into it. Maybe it was just me, some kind of subconscious, prudish flaw, but I couldn't stop looking at the girls' faces and wondering what their mothers would think and what their names were. Not Candy Clit, or Little Miss Bighorn, but their real names. Surely they didn't want to be doing this? What had driven them to it? What desperate calamity had happened in their lives that had reduced them to making masturbation movies for money?

(See, despite shedding every inhibition I could think of and loads I hadn't thought of, I still couldn't bring myself to say the W-word even then.)

No matter how much I tried to kid myself, I saw the final straw coming. Monogamy had been a massive strain for Mark. He probably thought he had done so well too, that he deserved a Blue Peter badge for holding out so long. Just the one woman in more than a year. What a saint! He started coming home later and later, then some nights he didn't come home at all. Surely he wasn't picking up girls in his cab and screwing them on the back seat? What could possibly have put that idea in my head? I accused and his denials were feeble and half-hearted. I ranted, he shrugged. I wept, he stomped off to bed and said he needed to keep his strength up for the nightshift. At least he had the grace not to follow that up with his usual Monty Python nudge-nudge, wink-wink routine.

I wouldn't accept defeat. I wasn't going to walk out of two marriages in little over twelve months. I would hold on, I would try and turn a blind eye, I would wait until he grew out of it.

But the end came abruptly and when I think it through, I reckon Mark, in his own warped, misguided way, genuinely thought he was being caring and taking my feelings into consideration. Apart from an utter inability to see beyond the end of his penis – yes, just like the shelter guys in their teens, according to Robert – there wasn't really any badness in the guy so yeah, he probably actually believed his motives were sound.

After pacing the hallway a few times one morning, he marched into the kitchen, sat me down and confessed. He had been a bastard, there had been other women. He knew I must be feeling rejected, belittled. But the other lassies, they didn't mean a thing, he swore they didn't. It was me he loved and he was sorry, he would make it up to me. In fact, he said, he had given it long and careful thought and had come up with a solution, a way to sort things out and save our marriage.

A threesome.

'Aye, threes-up. You and another lassie and me like,' he explained, as if I couldn't count. *Oh right, Mark, not the two of us and that hunky hairy foreign guy from the flat upstairs. There's a shock.*

207

'It'll be great,' he assured me with unfettered enthusiasm. 'These three-ways – it's the future, the way ahead. And don't you worry about a thing. Leave it all to me, I'll fix it up.'

Mark walked out of the door to start his shift, cheerful righteousness spread across his face, leaving me open-mouthed and shell-shocked.

Two nights later. I hadn't believed he would actually go through with it. I was convinced it was just talk, another one of Mark's porn-fuelled fantasies which was supposed to get me in the mood. I heard the door of our flat open and smelled her before I saw her – cheap perfume, cheaper booze. I heard silly girly giggling.

Mark put his head round the living room door.

'This is it, Lorna,' he said, with only the faintest trace of uncertainty. 'The big night.'

He led her in. Bleached blonde, Tesco tan. She looked no more than twenty. Mark was a little apprehensive but clearly wildly excited.

'This is Angie,' he added. 'Angie – Lorna.'

Fuck you, Mark. Fuck fuck fuck fuck you. That's my mother's name. What my Dad called her. You despicable, degenerate creep.

I couldn't speak and Mark started to look a little bit twitchy.

'Er, tell you what, you two get to know each other, have a wee drink or something. I'll just go and jump in the shower.'

He walked out, then turned back, more confident now and taking my silence for consent if not outright eagerness. He was grinning – the little kid on Santa's knee was back.

'When I'm all ready, you can maybe put on a wee show for us like. But hey, don't start without us, eh? Unless you can't help yourselves, of course.'

His head was away with it. Porn logic. Mark had watched one blue movie too many and started to believe in it. You know, like when girl comes home, walks into bedroom, catches boyfriend in bed with some other Miss Big Tits. Does wronged girl throw tantrum? Does she yell and chuck stuff? Does she storm out? Does she get on the phone and sob, *I'm coming home, Mum, that bastard's messing me around.* Course she doesn't, not in Mark's porn-world. In Mark's porn-world, she is uncontrollably aroused and overcome with lust and tears off her clothes and joins in. The two girls put on a show for Master Prick.

Angie sat down opposite me, teetering on the edge of a chair, her head rocking slightly. Short skirt, flash of stocking top, high heels naturally, caked with make-up. For a second, I thought of Kirsty and the flashback saddened me. Angie looked over, unsteadily, trying to focus, as if I was far away. She was clearly drunk, maybe on some kind of pills as well. I was wearing one of

Mark's baggy sweatshirts, a tatty old pair of tracky bottoms and slippers, a towel wrapped around my head because I'd just washed my hair. Get the picture? The very image of a three-in-a-bed-romp porn star.

This Angie creature, she muttered: 'I like your curtains. They're nice.'

Nice curtains! Nice fucking curtains?

That's what did it. It came to me, I'm not an animal. Hold it right there. An apology to the animal kingdom. I couldn't recall ever seeing a couple of she-Alsatians getting it on while Mr Alsatian lay hunkered down, watching, panting, tongue lolling, waiting for his moment to show those damn bitches what they were missing.

I marched to our bedroom, took a hold-all from the cupboard, tossed in a few clothes and grabbed my jacket like I had done once before over another Angie. Mark came out of the bathroom with just a towel round the middle of his hard, muscled body, in a cloud of talc and reeking of too much Aramis, all set for his big entrance. He looked shocked when he saw what I was up to. The little boy all set for Christmas who's just heard Santa's sleigh has been involved in a pile-up en route.

'What you doing, Lorna?' he asked and nodded towards the living room. 'We've got a guest, where you going?'

I mirrored his gesture.

'Sorry Mark,' I said. 'You'll have to play one short.'

I opened the front door and headed for the stairs, his last words to me echoing along the corridor.

'But this was for you, Lorna. This was all for you.'

I have never clapped eyes on him since, and I can honestly say I have never missed him. Confession time again. I did miss the sex, which probably tells its own story. Truth be told, it took me longer to get over that than Mark himself.

Chapter 31

March 24, 1975
You're A Big Girl Now – Bob Dylan

MY Mum's funeral. God, I hated it. I mean, I know you're not supposed to enjoy funerals but I really really hated the whole thing. I hated the big cars crowding our street. Long, sleek, black and gleaming, with little kids gathered around them, staring at them and touching them, hanging about in anticipation in case there had been a mix-up with the occasions and there might be a scramble. I hated that the cars were for us. I hated the kid-on expensive, Mr Sheen smell from the leather seats on the drive to church. I hated that my Mum was shut up in that box, in that dark confinement in the car in front of us. All alone in that shiny, polished, cheap pine crate with a car to herself.

The church, Cardrum Parish. Modern, reminded me of the dinner hall at school. It was news to me if my Mum had ever been in this church before in her life other than for a wedding or somebody else's funeral. The minister? I didn't know his name but he knew hers and he knew mine. Who told him? I took objection to the fact that he was so familiar about my Mum and called her by her first name, Angela, as if he knew her. Mind you, he did know a lot about my Mum that I didn't know. Stuff about her childhood. He mentioned the Girl Guides. She had been a member, then a leader. No. My Mum? Really? Must have got her mixed up with somebody else. He talked about the biscuit factory in Govan where she worked after she left school at fifteen. I never knew my Mum ever had a job. The minister told how her father – my late Papa – had once warned her she would end up dead in a ditch because she messed boys around so much until she met my Dad. There was a whole life history there and I had only ever scratched the surface. How did he know, that man standing up there who talked about my Mum as if they were old friends? Who had told him all this interesting stuff and forgot to

210

THE FENIAN

tell me? Why did it take my Mum's death for me to learn about her life, or had I not been listening all those years?

Robert didn't come to the funeral. I never knew why for certain and I have thought about it a few times over the years. The best spin I've ever been able to put on it was that he had the sense to know this was too big a deal to risk us, him and me, being a distraction. But I never asked him and he never brought it up, so I suppose I let it slide. Fiona didn't come either. She was at a cousin's wedding, way up in the islands, whatever that actually meant, where her family were from originally. A wedding, a celebration, on the day we mourned. I found myself feeling strangely consoled by that rather than offended.

The rest of our lot were there at the church. My shelter pals. Big Paddy sat with his Mum and Dad near the back, in a suit that looked freshly off the peg but already two sizes too small. Big Paddy and Mr and Mrs Allan, three aliens in the wrong church. Cookie looked smart in a suit too, along with appropriate white shirt and black tie. He sat with Karen who was in a full-length, black, grown-up coat. Two kids playing at being adult mourners. Cammy and Ross were right at the back, schoolboy and workie, duffle coat and donkey jacket. The other girls, Wee Mary, Jo, Kirsty, sat with them in smart school blazers and pleated skirts.

Then the crematorium, just family. That was the worst bit. Why did no one think to warn me about the cruel melodrama, the haunting organ lilt as the velvet purple curtains were drawn, agonisingly slowly, the faint electronic whirr, then the curtains swishing open again and Mum's vanished, like a Paul Daniels trick. *You'll like this, not a lot.* Then outside the crematorium. Chill, rain in the air, a few people smoking as we waited for the cars to come round. More bastard fags. A kind of defiance. *You might have got her, you'll never take us.* But this day was about Mum, wasn't it? Were we really going to leave her behind in there? What was left of her?

The purvey was at the Labour club up the town centre. Watery vegetable soup, crumbly bread rolls, runny butter in wee foil packets that made your fingers greasy, lukewarm steak pie. Avon-scented aunts who held me in smothering grasps but said nothing. Nothing I heard anyway, well, beyond the occasional, *Aw, Lorna hen, come here.* There was a lot of stuff like that. Dad sheltered behind his big sister and my Uncle Tommy and Mum's lot, sipping away his pain.

My crowd had made it there from the church. Karen whispered non-stop in Cookie's ear. He kicked an imaginary ball while Ross and Cammy prowled tables, sneaking drinks. Big Paddy looked like he was trying to surround his Mum and Dad all by himself, shielding them from the glances, the stares, the

211

mutters. Shielding them from the wrath of my Mum and Dad's relatives. A circle seemed to open up around the Allans, like they had a bad smell. Could my Mum and Dad's lot see it stamped on their foreheads? *That's right, we're Catholics, we know we shouldn't really be here but Angela was our friend.* I saw my Uncle Tommy's face tighten into a scowl. He glared at them. I heard him mutter *dirty Hail Marys* under his breath and use other descriptions I didn't understand, like bog hoppers and tattie munchers. I picked up other random words and phrases. I heard tagues. I heard IRA. Someone said, *Pape soap dodgers, blood on their filthy hands. Remember Birmingham? Seventeen they killed down there.* Big Paddy defiantly stood his ground, staring them down.

Is this it, Mum, I found myself thinking? Is this the proud family honour you've made me promise to uphold?

Karen joined Jo and Wee Mary and they formed a league table of grief in the corner, comparing tears and red eyes for someone they didn't really know. I was being unkind. Maybe their tears were genuine, maybe they were really for me, their friend. Cookie wandered over to Ross and Cammy, joined them on the booze prowl, relieved to be off the leash. Kirsty copped off with one of my relatives. No one close, just a son of my mother's cousin, something like that. She was just turned seventeen, still at the school. He was mid-twenties. They disappeared for half an hour and I overheard him talking later to a few other guys – men, not boys. I picked up the word *nympho*. Kirsty! At my Mum's funeral too. But then I thought of Karen, Jo and Wee Mary again – the noisy choking, the tears, the drop-of-a-hat-grief. At least I knew with a certainty that Kirsty was being honest about who she was.

Then after, what was I feeling? Sometimes it was like it was all too big for me and the sheer size of it prevented me getting inside my head to figure out what it meant, my Mum's death. All the clichés piled up of course. Loss, grief, gaping hole in my life, etcetera etcetera.

The main thing was, I just plain missed her. The sarcasm, the secrets, the scorn, the sharing, the support. Other clichés crept in too – regret, anger, bitterness over Mum's weakness, her selfishness, her lingering forty-a-day suicide. *Why didn't you just jump off the Forth Bridge, Mum? That would have been quicker, less painful for all of us, you especially.* Mind you, knowing Mum, she would have drawn that out too. She would have stood there teetering on the edge, buffeted by the wind, flicking, flicking uselessly at her lighter in the gale. Still time for one final quick puff on the way down.

Robert was patient. All my friends were patient. They gave me space and time as I went into solitary confinement, self-imposed, in my bedroom, my punishment cell. The brief times I emerged, Dad and I moved around each other slowly, like chess pieces, quiet and courteous. After you, no, after you.

THE FENIAN

We never really got down to it, what it all meant. Just not his thing, I suppose.

So, I talked to myself. Actually, I tried to talk to Mum, but I could never quite reach her. What did I plan to say exactly? Sorry Mum? Sorry I wasn't more thoughtful? Sorry I put days and nights out with my pals before your last weeks on Earth? Sorry Mum, but I was in love and it's the best thing that ever happened to me? Sorry I didn't make your dying my top priority? But that's the thing Mum, I didn't know, I didn't understand. Was that the truth? Maybe I did know. Maybe I understood fine.

Maybe I wanted to reach her to say, Good luck Mum, wherever you are. Hope they've got good doctors there, hope they can take away the pain. Hope they've got fags there, your brand. They can't do any worse to you than they've done already so no point you stopping now. Or was it to say, wait Mum, you can't go yet, there's too many things you didn't get round to telling me, too many things you haven't explained? What do I do about Dad? What do I do about me? Am I doing OK? Am I the person you want me to be? Where am I going wrong? Point me in the right direction, Mum. I need you, you deserted me, you left me too soon.

Then, the other question. The one I put off facing up to a hundred times but knew I couldn't avoid forever. What about the promise? How's about it, Mum? You must remember it. I do. Can't get it out of my head. In fact, it's getting in the way of my grief. That promise you made me make, on the last day, after the eggs. Just tell me you didn't mean it. Please, Mum. Tell me you were sick, not of sound mind and all that. You were dying, for God sake, you didn't know what you were saying. Give me a sign. Absolve me from it, Mum. Let it pass. Please.

Never go with a Fenian. Never go with Robert.

He phoned the day after the funeral. Dad picked up but I shook my head. Dad said sorry, and told Robert I was still too upset to talk to anyone.

Finally, I went back out into the world, my world, back to the shelter. My friends were great, they gave me such a welcome, almost as if they had been rehearsing it. The guys clowned around, the girls fussed over my new jacket, the one I'd got specially for the funeral. The laughter was loud and raucous. They gave me exactly what I needed and I appreciated it.

Robert too, I appreciated him because he acted like a pal, just a pal, like he was just another one of the crowd. He wasn't pushing it, he was being patient. But I knew it wouldn't last forever. Gradually, he started moving closer, bit by bit, day by day.

Then, Big Paddy's party. I wasn't sure, worried it was too soon, but Wee Mary and Jo talked me into it. Our parties had matured by then. The Top Ten had all but disappeared, T Rex and Gary Glitter had become pariahs.

Chart singles were swapped for rock albums – Genesis, Yes, Led Zep, Sabbath, The Doors, Eric Clapton. The new, heavy-duty soundtrack to the drama of our lives. A tapestry of background music. The kids' games hadn't quite been phased out. We persuaded ourselves we still played them occasionally out of ironic nostalgia, but mostly we stood or sat around, drinks in hand, chatting and laughing, circling each other, dancing now and then and, gradually, pairing off. Then dimmed lights, hormone explosion, battlefield of bodies.

Robert came over and put his arm round me. I shuddered and gathered my defences. This was it. He spoke to me, up close.

'I've really missed you, Lorna.'

I stepped out of his hold and tried to make it look like an accident, as if I was turning to talk to someone else. He regrouped, got in front of me, two arms this time, bringing in the big guns. He leaned in to kiss me and I almost surrendered right away. I wanted so badly to surrender because all through the pain and the grief of my mother's death, it was my love for Robert – and his for me – that had sustained me, given me comfort. The very first wave of fire and I almost caved in, but I leaned my head back and took the easy way out. I played the coward's card.

'Just give me time, eh? Sorry, my Mum, you know? Please?'

I gave him no choice but to retreat, but I knew I couldn't hold him off forever. Truth be told, I didn't want to.

Chapter 32

MY fingers were cold. I became aware of them gradually, wrapped round my cup, my coffee untouched. Big Paddy looked uncomfortable, too big for my little kitchen, for my little home. He had talked about stuff that big hard policemen weren't supposed to talk about. Love and feelings and emotions and his care, his affection for Robert. He didn't know where to go from here.

A silence, awkward and heavy, hung between us. He had finished filling in Robert's life, post-me. He had bared Robert's soul to me, revealed to me the damage I had supposedly done to the man who grew out of the boy I loved.

My head was a mess. Big Paddy's recollections, the flashes of Bill and Mark, even his Celtic story. Now I was thinking about nothing other than Robert, listening for his voice, trying to conjure up his face. Words and pictures danced in my mind, thoughts and images from so many years ago, colliding, swirling around, banging into each other.

My first reaction? Put Robert out of his misery, absolve him via Big Paddy, his surrogate soul. Bit late though. If only I'd known earlier, years earlier. Finally, I broke the uneasy, fragile silence.

'Robert didn't screw anything up, Paddy. It was me, I screwed it up. Wrecked it for the two of us.'

Big Paddy knew his job, he knew the law. Anything you say etc. He hadn't read me my rights.

'Lorna, look, don't. You've got nothing to explain to me. This was a one-way deal, know? I just came here the night to tell you what you asked me.' He raised his big flat palms to the vertical again. 'I know, I know. I started it, saying to you about Robert and that, and I'm sorry, I should have kept my mouth shut. But I've got myself in way too far here. This really is none of my business.'

I didn't know how to go on. I was so confused. There was Robert, this mega successful guy, a son nearly grown, a big serious job, a top man at the BBC, sitting there in his fancy hotel, house-hunting in the posh West End. Was I really supposed to accept that his life was messed up because of such a little nobody, because of little, insignificant me? Believe me, that comes from a place of brutal self-realisation, not false modesty. I seriously did not know what to say, so I stalled.

'Christ, will you listen to us Paddy, this is ridiculous. Two supposedly grown-up folk getting in a state about bloody weans stuff.'

Big Paddy said nothing because he knew that if I really believed that, I hadn't been listening. Of course I didn't believe it. I was only playing for time. I played for some more.

'What's he like?' I asked. 'Now. As a person, I mean.'

'Who?'

'Tony Bloody Blair, Paddy. Who the hell do you think I mean?'

I wanted to start by asking him why Robert called himself Robbie. Trivial, I know, but it had been nagging at me. That was my real first question but I didn't want Big Paddy to know that I knew, that I had been giving Robert so much thought.

Big Paddy grinned, breathing a little bit easier now. He knew he had over-reached. He had taken the cap off the bottle and didn't know how to put it back on again or where this would end. But I knew he felt responsible, probably for the both of us. That was down to the basic decency that had guided this bruiser his entire life.

'Ach, Robert,' he said. 'He's still just the same guy, know?'

'Come on, Paddy, don't forget I missed the big picture. He's still the same as what? The guy you knew five years ago? The guy you knew when he got married? The guy that fell off a swing and cut his knee open when you were seven?'

'Naw, really,' said Big Paddy, earnestly. 'I know it sounds daft, but he's basically the same guy he always was. Maybe I'm wrong, maybe folk change out of all recognition and I'm just too thick to notice. But I don't think I've changed that much, for example. No' in here anyway.'

He tapped his head and continued.

'And Robert's like that. Sure, he comes across all confident – on the outside anyway. He can still talk the arse of a donkey and he still gets these big notions. He'll still argue his corner till you want to sever his vocal cords. But he was always like that, you must remember.'

I did remember and I tried not to smile. I just nodded, not wanting to stop him now that he was off and running again.

'I know you see him on the telly and he seems all serious and that, but when he's sitting right there and you talk to him, he's just the same as he always was. Maybe it's a bit like being an actor, know? The guy you see on the screen and the bloke you sit talking to over a pint are different folk. I know when we go to the football and we get into company in one of the pubs, he doesn't act like he thinks he's something special. Wouldn't get away with it with that mob. Naw, he's just like the rest of us, having a drink and a wee bit chat and a laugh and that. He's basically just an ordinary, decent bloke.'

Big Paddy fell silent for a moment. He looked at my ceiling. Then he let his eyes drift back to mine. He smiled and continued.

'One of the things I appreciate about Robert. He always lets me buy my round. I know that sounds daft, but it's a big thing to me, Lorna, and he understands that so it's never discussed, it's just the way it is. See, Robert's worth a packet. I don't have a Scooby how much he earns, don't want to know, none of my business, and I know he's got money behind him from some property thing he and Ruth did. Probably spends more on a pair of shoes than I make in a week. Motors – there's an example. It's probably my imagination, but it seems like he's got a flash new one every time I meet up with him. And you want to see the place him and Ruth had in London. But the thing is, he never plays the rich bastard, doesn't chuck it about. No' when he's with me anyway.'

Big Paddy looked suddenly embarrassed, as if he was taking the living eulogy too far, laying the paint on a bit too thick in this portrait of the all-round perfect bloke.

'Don't get me wrong, Lorna,' he said. 'Robert's no' a saint or nothing. I'm no' trying to sell you a second-hand motor here...no' even a flash one. Cos I tell you, he can still be an absolute Grade A pain in the arse. Like his latest, this *what ya gonna do* thing he keeps saying from some gangster show that's supposedly the best thing ever on television...you must remember how annoying he was when he got obsessed with something.'

We went quiet for a few seconds, each recalling, without much trouble, vivid memories of Robert's pain-in-the-arse moments. Then Big Paddy picked it up again.

'And talking of his dumb obsessions. It's still the same. All the things the rest of us grow out of? Well, he never. I mean, take the Celtic. I'm as daft as anybody about my fitba but I go to the game, have a good time, that's it. OK, I'll watch them on telly if I can't go, like Europe and that. But Robert? He tapes every game that's on, got all these boxes full of videos going back years. Says he's keeping them to show his grand weans. If he ever has any.

217

'And you mind these groups he liked? Pink Floyd and Genesis and Yes. Well, he still collects stuff, says the internet's opened up a whole new world to him. Spends hours searching for rare bits and pieces, lashes out a fortune on that ebay thing, buying up all these obscure, rare CDs from other anoraks like him. Concerts that folk taped on their cassettes, recordings of rehearsals, unlistenable junk like that. Just for the rarity value, he says. Rare because nobody else is stupid enough to buy it, know? I try to tell him music's moved on, that there's a whole new world of great stuff that's happened since the Seventies, but it's like he's stuck in a time warp.'

Big Paddy was in full rant mode now. If it was a magical rake through a secret box of treasure for me, it was a release for him. You could love someone the way Big Paddy obviously loved Robert, but that kind of closeness had its price too. Like a marriage, it meant exposure to all the little niggly flaws and foibles, and Robert's were tumbling out now.

'Know the worst thing? The thing that really drives me radio rental? Robert and his mobile bloody phone. It's like it's super-glued to his ear permanent. Sometimes he's doing that texting thing and laughing at the replies, and it's like he's having a parallel conversation that you're excluded from, as if your company isn't enough for him. Talk about rude? You should have seen his face the last time we were out. I meets him at his hotel and he's sitting in the foyer, right, on the phone as per. He gives me a two-minute signal and I'm left hanging about like a spare part, know? He finally comes off it and we head for the bar. Before we even get there, he's back on it again. Just phoning the office, he says, check what's happening. So that's another five minutes gone. I get the drinks in, sit down, starts talking to him and honest, he actually did this, Lorna. He put his hand up, like to silence me because he'd got a text and had to read it. So, I just reach over, grab his phone off him and drop it in his pint.'

'Oh Paddy, you didn't.' I had tried so hard not to interrupt, but this was too much. I really hoped it wouldn't put him off telling me more. It didn't.

'You want to see the look he gave us. You'd think I'd just shat on his living room carpet. But he got the message and anyway, he can afford a new one. Tells me in ten years we'll no' be able to live without them. What's the phrase he thinks is so clever...oh yeah, we'll have the whole world in our hand. Talking pish, I told him. Same as that stupid millennium bug he got all worked about. I mean, mobiles, it's just a phone, know? We've had phones all our lives. The novelty will soon wear off.'

Big Paddy saw me laugh, though it was more at the sheer euphoria of having this glorious delve into Robert's life. He switched tack again and I glimpsed a look of guilt, like he had been caught betraying his pal, his closest friend, in front of this evil witch who had cursed his big mate's life. He turned serious, sorrowful almost.

'But here's the really daft thing Lorna. Robert's convinced he's a failure, know?'

'Aye right,' I said. 'He's the one that made it, Paddy, remember? Out of all of us. Robert never failed at anything in his life, not that I know of anyway.'

'Aye, I know,' Big Paddy agreed. 'That's what I keep telling him. But that's not how he sees it. He gets these wee spells, these wee phases, where he just tells me he's screwed the whole thing up. And it's no' like he's looking for me to make him feel better, give him a gold star or nothing. I mean, I'm just his pal Paddy, the big daft polis.

'Lorna, this is the guy that's met folk we only ever see on the telly or in the papers. I mean, this is the guy that's had breakfast with Boris Yeltsin and sat at the same table as Bill Bloody Clinton. Oh, and a coffee with Neil Armstrong. Neil Armstrong, Lorna! First guy on the fucking moon...sorry, pardon my French again. I don't know about you, but these are folk that are so far removed from real life, so way above me, that they might as well live on the bloody moon.

'But you see what I'm saying here? See what I'm getting at? This bloke off the telly, this bloke you and me know, he sits there and tells me stuff about all the things he was going to do. How he's no' achieved half of them, how he's messed it all up. And as I say, he's no' looking for anything from me. I mean, I can't give him a pay rise, or a promotion, or a fancy new title or nothing. I can't wave a magic wand and give him his life over again so he can go back and do it all the way he wanted.'

I couldn't get my head round this. Robert the failure...at least to himself. This guy who looked so assured, so certain of himself. This guy I've watched countless times on TV, with the serious tie or sometimes, for rough and ready effect, the open-neck shirt. Right there among the blood and guts, gunfire in the background, soldiers dying around him. Staying calm, putting himself in the firing line to weave stories for us, to explain the world. This guy who knew everything, who could always find the right people, ask the right questions, gather the information, use the right words. This guy who could go to the top of the world, go head to head with terrorists and presidents and space travellers, and hold his own. I couldn't see where he had the capacity for ordinary insecurities. How he could do all those big things and still have room for a single fibre of self-doubt?

'I'm sorry, Paddy, I really don't get it. A failure at what?'

'Everything,' he said. 'Christ, you for a start. That's what he always ends up back at. But please, don't make me get into all that again.'

'No fears,' I agreed.

'His marriage,' Big Paddy went on. 'That was all his fault, as far as he's concerned anyway. He should have tried harder, he wasn't fair to Ruth, blah blah. Then there's his son, Jack. Robert worries all the time he's making a coo's arse of that as well. I'm telling you, Lorna, he's great with the boy, always has been. They're more like mates than father and son most of the time. But try telling him that. The way Robert sees it, he's either no' doing enough for Jack or he's doing too much. He's either neglecting him and not seeing him enough, or else he's smothering the boy, not letting him find his own way and make his own mistakes. Take this university carry on. Half the time Robert's convinced he's no' giving Jack enough support because he's stuck in that hotel and he's not giving the lad a proper base in case he has problems and stuff. The rest of the time, he's worried Jack'll think he doesn't trust him because he's moved up to Scotland to be near him. He's impossible, Lorna. You try and reassure him but you can't win with Robert because he can never win with himself.'

As revelations go, this was unbelievable. Robert the Anxious Dad. Robert the Guilt-Wracked Ex-Husband. Robert the Big Worrier. Maybe I was straying into territory I'd rather stay out of. Get back to the football and music obsessions, the mobile phone addict. There were laughs in there. That was more fun – and safer.

But Big Paddy wasn't finished. He was in full flow again, getting it off his chest, all this stuff Robert had laid on him. I wondered if Robert was Big Paddy's confessor too, the same way they used to be each other's bodyguards. Perhaps they still were.

'Then there's his work. Now I don't know nothing about that game. No' really. Journalists and telly and stuff. But I reckon it's like anything else, like the polis even. If you can't hack it, you don't last very long, know? And Robert's always been right up there, as far as I can tell anyway. He's always doing new stuff, bigger stuff and I know he's had offers over the years. There was even some American TV company wanted him to go to the States a few years back. But he's got this thing he keeps going on about. Getting found out, he calls it. Every time he starts a new job, or even if he's just been away his holidays, it's the same. Says he's terrified he'll go into his work and they'll have discovered he's been fooling them, getting away with it. Mind you, I think maybe that's why he does so well. He's spent all these years constantly thinking he has to prove himself, which is maybe no' such a bad way to approach it.'

Right there, right then, I wanted to be the one, the one who eased Robert's mind. Reassured him. I wanted to explain it all to him, to at least take away one of his doubts, the one that had lingered all these years.

'It was my fault, Paddy,' I blurted out. 'I mean, Robert and me. I know it's a lifetime ago but if what you're saying is right, Robert hasn't forgotten it. I haven't either. It's not the kind of thing you forget.'

'No listen, stop right there, Lorna' said Big Paddy. 'I've told you and I mean it. You've got nothing to explain, especially no' to me. This is Robert's hang-up, know? You've got your own life. Get on with it and forget about him.'

My own life? If only you knew Paddy. Just look around you. This is it, there's nothing more. What you see is what I've got.

I wanted to explain, to set the record straight. But I couldn't find it in me to dredge it all up. My Mum, the deathbed promise, Catholics and Protestants, Tims and Huns. Fenians. The Fenian. All that stupid, stupid garbage. I couldn't bear to pick at the scab of that ancient wound one more time. Too painful, much much too painful.

'Just tell Robert,' I said. 'Please. Tell him it wasn't him. He did nothing wrong. Nothing. Just tell him. That's all. Tell him it was me. It's all on me. And tell him I know it's a bit late, but tell him… just tell him I'm awful sorry.'

That reminded me. There was someone else I needed to say sorry to as well. That distraction in the background. That other man in my life.

Chapter 33

August 1975
I Can't Give You Anything (But My Love) – The Stylistics

THE wedding. That was the day it all ended. The day that should have been such a celebration. Our summit, a seal of approval on shelter world, our vindication. The barriers were being lifted and we were crossing the border, passports checked and stamped. We were being accepted into grown-up land. We were saying, *See, we told you. It wasn't just kids' stuff. There's two of us going the full distance.* But that's not quite how it turned out.

In all honesty, the cracks had been there for months. Kirsty had all but jumped ship already. She had climbed the age ladder and sniffed money, real money. Our guys couldn't compete with their couple of quid from the paper round or the cream, and an eleventh share of a carry-out on a Friday night. The prospect of a snog and a feel with a teenager behind the wall at the swing park had lost its allure. Kirsty still turned up at the shelter now and again, in shag-me shoes and too much make-up. But more and more through that final summer, it became a brief courtesy call, till a blast on a car horn whisked her away. Karen called Kirsty a big slut, Cammy called Kirsty a big ride.

Ross had been around less too since leaving school at the end of fourth year. He had been taken on as an apprentice plumber with the development corporation. At first, he had enjoyed impressing us by flashing his money around. He would splash out when the ice cream van stopped near the park. Bottles of Irn-Bru, Aztec Bars all round, a packet of fags and his very own refillable gas lighter instead of a single and a match. Then Ross's horizons broadened. He wasn't long past sixteen when he left school and, if anything, he looked younger, so baby-faced and fair he barely needed to shave. But his boiler suit became his passport to the pub and Ross swapped bottles of ginger for pints of heavy with his new workmates. Still, he would habitually

222

grace us later on after a session at the pub. He'd come and join us for a while after dark and bring along his beery breath, but it became hard to hide the impression that he was kind of embarrassed. A working man hanging out with schoolies.

Jo had started a hairdressing course at college in Glasgow after Christmas. The plan was that she would qualify then go and work in her Mum's salon. Little Jo was still very much one of us but she had new pals too – which wasn't a surprise given how naturally bubbly and friendly she was. She tried so hard to divvy up her time and herself. She plotted a merger, staged a joint party – her swing park pals and her college pals. It flopped. It was the worst example I've ever seen of an Us and Them party.

Big Paddy had left school, too, not long before Christmas – and in some style, according to Robert's account. One day he just got up from his desk without warning, right in the middle of one of the Brother's rambling God lessons. Big Paddy picked up his bag, walked to the front and tipped his school books on to the floor at the Brother's feet, then turned to the class and bowed.

'That's it, I'm rapping it. Had enough. But before I go, I'd just like to thank you all for your company over the last eleven years…it's been an education.'

Then his killer line.

'Monsieur Marsaud is leaving le fucking jardin.'

I hoped that really had come from Big Paddy and Robert hadn't added it when he told the story to the rest of us.

Claps and cheers, Sadist in a Smock stunned. Big Paddy walked towards the door then spun round, pointed a finger at the Brother and growled his parting shot.

'Two things to say to you. First, thanks for the strap all they times, cos you can rush to the bog and it doesn't feel like your hand, know? And the other thing, you better get down on your knees and pray I never meet you on the outside.'

Big Paddy got a job on a building site easily enough. Cumbride was one big building site back then. But he stuck faithfully to swing park life, as did the rest of us, right through fifth year. But end of term was approaching and there were big plans afoot, futures to map, separate paths looming up.

Robert was staying on for sixth year, so was Fiona. She was super smart and serious. She was talking about doing a law degree. Cammy was just rolling along with no real plan. *See what happens.* He never changed.

I hadn't told anyone my plans for after school, except Wee Mary, and she was sworn to silence. It was our big secret.

I stayed away from the shelter for spells during the weeks after my Mum's funeral, not so much to escape from my friends or to shun them, as to avoid Robert. The simple fact of it was, I missed him like hell and I didn't trust myself to keep the promise. Robert had tried gentle, he had tried upfront and every time, I had used my Mum to get out of it, not giving him an option.

'Sorry, Robert. I'm just not ready, OK?'

That was my line and I felt guilty for pushing him away and guilty too for using my Mum to keep him at bay, but then she was the one who had stuck the cross on my back. I tried pretending, to myself mainly. I tried making out that what we'd had was nothing special, Robert and me. That it had only been another swing park fling like the rest. I tried getting off with Cammy, then with Ross, sometimes even in front of Robert. It didn't work. We'd been over that tired old course too many times. It was starting to feel, I suppose, sort of incestuous. No, no, that's too strong. It was more like, with Cammy and Ross in particular, it had gotten to the stage where it felt like being intimate with somebody who, if not a cousin, was clearly a friend, nothing more. It no longer seemed appropriate somehow. Besides, the pain in Robert's face made it too difficult to bear.

He kept asking me: 'What happened, Lorna? Come on, tell me, please. What did I do?'

I tried gentle, I tried upfront, I tried staying away. Summer break was the hardest, our seven weeks parole at the end of fifth year. For most of us it was The End of school but somehow we felt we were still entitled to our summer holidays. *Then we'll become responsible adults, honest.*

Sometimes, when the weather was good, we would leave base camp and journey deep into the outback, beyond the valley of the dolls' houses. *Another Robert-ism, of course.* We'd take the snake bridge out of Cardrum, wander warily through other schemes, and across the ring road that led us out of the town itself and into a wooded glen and after-dark drinking den known as Fox Valley. Then we'd climb on to the pipey – a sewage duct next to a disused railway line – and follow it for a couple of miles before striking out into the hills to our secret haven, that waterfall of Cammy's.

Like before, we brought swimming gear when it was hot enough. We paddled, splashed, dived, swam. On one occasion we reprised the Tree Trunk Challenge for old times' sake. Generally, we just worked hard at playing and showing off, squeezing the few last desperate days out of kidhood. Then, late in the afternoon, we – they – would split into pairs and disappear into the woods. All that half-naked, still-wet, glistening flesh, all those throbbing hormones. The spare girl – when there was one – would be left to keep an eye on everybody's stuff. Then we'd wander home lazily. Five couples, hand in hand, and one spare girl trotting behind like a puppy.

Except, I'm wrong – it was only four pairs. There were three odd ones out that summer, three of us left behind to share guard duties on the gear. Spare girl, Robert and me. Robert had opted out of the changing partners ritual and I had too. We would sit in uneasy silence for an hour or more, listening to the river's relentless cascade, watching the reeds and the wild poppies sashay in the warm breeze, Mr Catchphrase finding our silence so hard, the court jester waiting for the rest to return so he could start up again.

Robert kept trying, I kept repelling. He tried again, I repelled again. A couple of weeks into the summer, I began staying away again. I thought it would be easier on both of us and that Robert might get the message. Then one night, about ten o'clock, I was in my room, miserable in my loneliness, lying on my bed flicking through Melody Maker without reading it, when I heard my name being called. I looked out of the window and there he was, the moron, standing in front of our wall waving a big white flag, a bed sheet pinched from his Mum's airing cupboard and tied on to one of his Dad's golf clubs. I smiled, I giggled, I couldn't help myself. I opened the window.

'Heh, hauf-brain, what the hell are you playing at?'

Robert shook his home-made flag more vigorously and called up to me.

'I give in, all right? I surrender. I'll stop…you know. I promise. But can we at least be pals again?'

A truce. Huge relief, but only kind of, because what I really wanted to do was defy my Mum, to give in. But Robert stuck to his word and within a day or two we were massive buddies again. We reclaimed the wall, we talked about everything, well, everything except what really mattered. He didn't push it any further, he stuck to his word. Till the wedding day.

Chapter 34

December 2000-June 2001
It's Raining Men – Geri Halliwell

OK, the whole on my own, no one else in my life business. Hands up, I've not been entirely truthful. Not that I've lied, exactly, except perhaps by omission. There is someone. It's just that it's kind of complicated because I have no idea if it – this thing, whatever it is – is going anywhere, or what it is really all about. Actually, it's probably not complicated at all and that's just my excuse for not dealing with it. Oh, and this other person who is kind of in my life but not really? He is hardly what you'd call new either.

I'd kept track of Bill over the years through Christmas cards, or to be accurate and fair, he kept track for both of us because certainly at first, my input was zero. He was such a good-hearted, decent guy. I'm tempted to say soft but I don't want to because it's one step from sap and that would be cruel and just plain unjust. It's simply his nature, same as how he offered me the house when I left and did everything in his power to make our break-up civilised and easy for me. So that first Christmas after I left him, when the card arrived, I shouldn't have been surprised but I was and anyway, I was so immersed in the bonk-fest with Mark that it barely registered and I definitely had no thoughts about sending one back. Huh, Mark and I never had anything as remotely organised as a Christmas card list and any we did get round to sending would probably have arrived about mid-January.

After that first year, his card would drop through the letterbox without fail in early December. Always a religious scene and when I picked it up from my Dad's house – because that's the only address Bill had for me – he would always say: 'There's your Merry Jesus card.'

A couple of years after I finished with Mark and got myself together, I made my own proper list and included Bill. I'll admit that whenever I got to writing

226

his card, I'd get a little nostalgic about our ritual. First Saturday evening in December, over a bottle of wine, we would go through his neatly typed list – with one or two extra names each year, handwritten at the bottom – and discuss each person or couple or family fondly for a minute or two before I picked something appropriate from the three or four charity shop packs. He would usually, but not always, agree with my choice. Not that he would ever say anything, but I could tell when he didn't approve, because he'd hold the pen still, poised a fraction above the card. Once we'd agreed, or rather, he'd chosen an alternative, he would write not just our names but a brief personal message in his precise script. When I was at the nit-picking stage with Bill, I'd call it unnecessarily fussy and a waste of time, but really he was just being thoughtful. Hey, I deserve a point there because I didn't use the word Nice.

For the first few years after our split, the card was just from Bill with, thankfully, generic messages like *Hoping Life Is Good For You* and *God Bless You And Yours* below his signature. Then, let me think, I'd just rented my own place after sharing for a while, so it would be a dozen years or so ago, when it suddenly became *Best Wishes Bill and Gail*. Over to the left, he used the blank side to fill me in briefly, not that he owed me any kind of explanation.

Dear Lorna, do you remember Gail? We got married in the Spring. All the best, B

I gave it some thought and yes, I did remember her. Geography teacher, I think. She came alone to some of our Saturday night dinners at the homes of other teachers and their partners who were sometimes, but not always, also teachers. From what I could recall, Gail was quiet, a bit reserved, but sincere and caring. There was something about her background that set off a little memory, something I identified with. It came to me later on the day I got their first card as a couple. Hadn't her parents been killed when she was very young? Some kind of accident – not car, but something outdoorsy like climbing or boating – and she had been brought up by grandparents. Above all, I remembered I liked her and out of all the wives and girlfriends and singles in that circle, I thought we could have become good friends, but she always seemed to hold back from that kind of closeness. I was genuinely happy for Bill, happy for Gail too, and could see how they would suit each other. Was there a little twinge of jealousy, or if not jealousy, regret? Perhaps, but it didn't knock me over and certainly didn't linger. I also didn't read anything into Bill's motive for telling me that he had remarried. I assumed he simply felt he had to explain the extra name rather than try to score a point.

A Christmas or two later, the Best Wishes section grew again, to *Bill, Gail and Crosby*. Like before, he felt obliged to provide a brief bulletin, though he did miss out a couple of crucial details or, more likely, the misunderstanding that followed was completely down to my denseness or at least lack of intelligent thought.

Hello L. Crosby came into our lives in March. We are blessed. B.

Confession time – and I cringe with embarrassment when I think about it – but purely from the name, I got it into my head that they had acquired a dog. It kind of made sense because it wasn't a stretch to picture Bill loping around a park, or the long stretch of beach at Irvine, in one of his outsized woolly jumpers and scarf, chasing after a big, loopy mutt. I could also imagine him smothering a dog with cuddles and showing it so much affection that he'd describe its arrival in that over-the-top way. I maintained the illusion for four years then sat alone in my kitchen with a full-on beamer – as we called it in swing park days – before howling at myself when his latest festive message cleared it up.

Hi L. That's Crosby started school. Where has the time gone? B.

Fine, not a dog – unless an exceptionally gifted one – but I then adopted the second misconception, without a shred of evidence, that Crosby was a boy. Don't get me wrong, I didn't deliberate on it or dwell on it or anything, it was just an instant reaction that took hold. In truth, I didn't give Bill or his little family much thought outside of the brief nostalgic reverie and genuine good wishes I felt for him for twenty minutes or so after opening his card each December.

Then, last Christmas, the Best Wishes grouping went into reverse. It shrank to just Bill and Crosby. Before turning to the now familiar update paragraph on the left, I had a fleeting stab of pain for Bill at the notion of another woman feeling suffocated by him and fleeing the nest. Knowing his character, he'd have been exactly the kind of guy to be happily and willingly left holding the baby, albeit a rather big one by now. But then the initial soreness I felt for him multiplied a thousand times when I read his words.

Dear Lorna, I lost Gail last February after a mercifully short illness. Best wishes, Bill.

Oh no, you poor sod. Bill didn't deserve that. He was the last person to deserve that. Whatever I felt about him in the end, I never doubted his sweet nature. I never doubted that pretty much all he wanted out of life was to find someone he could shower with love. Now, heading for his late forties, his relationship history consisted of one woman – yeah, yours truly – for whom that tsunami of affection and kindness was either not enough or too much, then another, his second chance, who had tragically died. Bill was blighted and blameless.

I hadn't sent my cards yet – don't be daft, I still had more than three weeks – so for the first time since our Christmas exchange started, I gave him back more than the terse *Best Wishes Lorna* in reply. The more defensive, OK, cynical person that I've become these past few years, would put my response down to a sense of duty. The right thing to do, as Robert would have put it. But I honestly felt deeply for Bill, an immense wave of sadness at the unfairness of someone with such good intentions repeatedly having them kicked out of him. I agonised over whether I should send a sympathy card instead of a festive one, but it had been ten months, so I settled for a bland, snowy countryside scene. The phrase *bleak midwinter* came to mind. I'm no writer – though I used to know one – so I kept it simple and brief.

So very sorry to hear this, Bill. I remember Gail as a lovely woman. I hope you and Crosby are doing OK and that you have the best Christmas you can. Thinking about both of you, Lorna.

So, for more than fifteen years, we had kept a faint line of communication open – ninety per cent him, ten per cent me, unless I'm being too generous to myself. Bill with his annual updates – and extra credit for starting it in the first place – and me simply by sending cards in return. Nothing more than a straightforward, polite, good-wishes swap.

But for him, my few extra words seemed to be like flicking a switch in the darkness. I'd forgotten that side to him. The way he would react to the tiniest encouragement like he'd just struck gold. Even in my darkest, debilitating sulks, one tiny smile or nod of approval and he would be bouncing and all was forgotten and forgiven. I used to despair of his blind optimism but, of course, the other way to put it was that he was just an out and out positive person. See, managed to avoid Nice again.

An old-fashioned, slow connection began. I hesitate to call it a relationship because to me, if it was anything that was taking shape, it was a sort of friendship once removed. Amidst all this marvellous whizz-bang technology that was apparently happening all around me and way over my head, Bill and I started sending each other olden-day, snail-mail letters. Well, a mid-January thank you card from Bill first, complete with a longer than usual message. Halfway down, he cleared up that other mistaken assumption of mine.

Crosby is a self-contained girl who does not show her feelings very much, but I try to be there to support her when she needs it.

If, in retrospect – and here's cynical Lorna rearing her head again – Bill was playing the long game, he did it to perfection. The letters continued for three months. His would arrive every couple of weeks, three or four pages long, and handwritten of course. I would type out a dozen sentences at work and sneakily print it off among the breaches of the peace. To his credit, he avoided turning his letters into a morbid homage to his late wife. He covered Gail's death factually in his first proper letter. She had been in hospital for a routine op – woman's troubles, he called it – and had picked up an infection that turned to sepsis and it was all over in four brutal days.

He didn't try to sell his kid to me either...God, I really am such a cynic. She popped up occasionally in mentions of things they had done together or places they had been, but only ever in passing. Mostly, it was everyday stuff with the occasional anecdote from our happier, early days. We had always watched a lot of films together so that gave us common ground, though our means of consumption was a little different now. He talked about buying DVDs, which were alien to me, while I was still such a Blockbusters video-rental stalwart that the spotty boy behind the counter referred to me jokily – at least I assume he was joking – as *the last customer*.

About three months in, Bill suggested, tentatively in a PS, that it would be lovely to chat and asked for my number. I couldn't think of a reason to turn him down without being rude, so the letters were ditched in favour of a half hour on the phone, at two- or three-week intervals at first, then every Friday evening. As summer settled in, he nervously mentioned in one call that school was about to break up and he was coming up to Glasgow for a few holiday bits and pieces, so did I fancy meeting for a catch-up and a coffee? Just as pals, he stressed, nothing more. You know what? To my surprise, it dawned on me that I did fancy it. The phone calls had been warm and amusing and interesting and, yes, it was once my hate-word, but they were nice.

You know that awkward moment when someone almost walks into you in the street or shop and you end up kind of dancing because you mirror each other's movements trying to get out of the way? It was a bit like that when I met Bill, outside the Costa just down from George Square. We must have looked like a couple of not very good mime artists, ducking and weaving and not knowing whether to shake hands or kiss cheeks or hug. In the end, he just opened the door for me and we got through the nervous opening scene by pretending the list of coffees on the wall was much more interesting than it really was. He hadn't changed much. Perhaps a touch more timber around the middle and he had let his beard grow longer, but the big round happy face was still his centrepiece. The only odd feature was the Chicago Cubs baseball cap. I couldn't remember him ever wearing any kind of hat – or being a fan of American sport, for that matter. I assumed he would take it off once we found a table in the corner and sat down. But he didn't, and as we talked trivia about our journeys to the city, I couldn't stop my gaze from wandering to the cap. He clocked it and somehow managed to let out a hefty sigh without losing the fun permanently fixed in his eyes.

'Huh, thought I might get away with a bit longer,' he groaned. 'But here goes. Prepare yourself, Lorna.'

He was completely bald, as in snooker ball under the lights bald. No, hang on, if you looked really hard – and sorry, but I did – there were tiny matching wispy tufts above each ear. Other than that, the top half of his head was flawlessly smooth and hairless. I had a flash of little Jo always keeping a lollipop in her pocket for added authenticity, before taunting any one of our gang who had just been dumped with a *Who chucked ya baby?* A much more polished Kojak than Robert ever managed.

All I managed was 'Oh', as I stared blatantly at Bill's shining skull. I know, I know, but come on, first the bushy beard then the naked napper? It was a bit of a shock.

He looked down at the table and said quietly: 'The kids at school call me Mr Upside Down Head.'

For a moment, I was appalled at the cruelty of children. Just for a moment, mind, because then I started laughing. I couldn't help myself and thought I'd better offer to refund him for the coffees quickly before he walked out, offended. Then suddenly he was laughing too and pretty soon we were both in hysterics. As ice breakers go, Mr Upside Down Head was Titanic level.

Look, there was no shiver down my spine when I saw Bill for the first time in so many years. My breath didn't catch in my throat. I didn't have to restrain myself from leaping into his arms and remember, this was not long before Robert came into the picture to further complicate matters and screw with my head. But I did feel, well, something, after that reunion with Bill. Maybe I simply enjoyed his company, the easy, pleasant company of a man that I liked. Whatever it was, it felt good. More than good. I'd never understood what people meant when they said they felt a warm glow inside, but I know I sat on the bus back to Cumbride feeling so much lighter, and smiling at nothing in particular. I also knew for definite that I wanted to see Mr Upside Down Head again.

Chapter 35

August 1975
It's In His Kiss – Lorna Lewis

COOKIE and Karen. They had been together forever. You could almost believe the spammy story about how their eyes first met as they swapped crayons at nursery. For whatever reason, for whatever tiny switch had been flicked in her fledgling brain, Karen had decided from the off, that's for me. Cookie had gone along with it all through primary, then high school, faithful through our pass-the-parcel days apart from his one tiny lapse with me, and how he had paid for that with days of tears and recriminations. Karen had developed a trick of arranging things months in advance, or getting her Mum to arrange things, arrangements soft Cookie couldn't or wouldn't break. Meals out with Karen and her parents on their birthdays, caravan holidays with her family. Cookie was so placid, so easy going, so anything-for-a-quiet-life.

University was Cookie's big rebellion. Karen had talked about them getting engaged – and without her having to fake her own death this time – but they/she decided they wouldn't make anything official until her eighteenth. Then Cookie would be *allowed* to go to university after sixth year, with a handcuff on his finger. Karen talked of *letting* him go to Glasgow, maybe Edinburgh at a push. She would try and get into a college near him or else get herself a job.

But all the time – unknown to any of us – Cookie had been quietly scheming, digging his escape tunnel. He didn't break the news to Karen until school broke up at the end of fifth year in June. No one knew he had even applied to go to uni that year, but he had received a conditional acceptance, a place on an engineering degree course somewhere in England. Cookie didn't specify where. He was sure his Highers had gone well, so why wait? That was how he explained it to her. Karen was distraught and outraged in equal parts. Her parents insisted she stay on at school for another year because she had struggled with her exams and anyway, it was too late for her to arrange a college place near his uni. But that wasn't the point. The point was, she had always been in charge, she had always made the plans and the decisions for both of them and Cookie had ripped up the rule book.

At first she tried to make the best of it and assured us nothing had really changed because Cookie would be back up home every other weekend and she would go down there for the occasional weekend too. He would only have three ten-week terms, so he'd be home nearly half the year anyway then, next summer, she would join him. Cookie didn't argue, he just nodded, but there was something in his manner that made us suspicious, not least the fact he had never let on which university he was hoping to go to. Robert and I saw it coming, I'm sure some of the others did too. The Great Escape.

We thought Karen hadn't clocked it. Yeah, right, she was miles ahead of us.

Cookie kept tunnelling furiously. He was beyond the guard post, under the barbed wire, just a little more digging and he would be out the other side. Free. Run and run and keep running, don't look back, and never go back. He was almost there, achingly close, then Karen hit the sirens, turned on the searchlights, manned the machine gun posts and did it all with just two words.

'I'm pregnant.'

She had foiled the escape and the tunnel caved in on Cookie. Karen wept but she was shining through the tears. This was her ultimate triumph. She confided in each one of us girls in turn, apart from Kirsty, but then she wasn't around much anymore.

'Please, please, Lorna/Mary/Fiona/Jo,' she would start, choking back sobs. 'Don't say a word to the others, I'm only telling you cos I've always felt, well, you and me, we've always been best friends, closer than the rest. It's just, Cookie can't bear the thought of us being apart. He doesn't want to wait. He wants us to get married, right away and, and, I'm going to have his baby.'

Cookie didn't argue. He just went along, resigned himself to it, and it was sealed.

The wedding was a whirlwind we all got caught up in – the excitement, the speed, the planning. Karen kept us informed in breathless instalments. The wedding's in five weeks. Five weeks!! Not a rush job then! It was to be at the parish church, where my Mum's funeral was, then a reception at the Osprey, the big hotel in the town centre. She and Cookie would stay the night there, then a five-day honeymoon at her Dad's caravan down in Portpatrick. Cookie was still going to uni, in Preston, but now Karen was going with him and they were getting a flat. Both sets of parents were going to chip in for the rent and the pram and the rest of the baby stuff. Karen would find a job and work until the baby arrived. She would save up, then they would just have to get by, somehow.

Cookie asked Robert to be his Best Man which put Ross's nose well out of joint at first because he and Cookie had always been tight pals. That was accepted, same as Robert and Big Paddy were best mates. But Robert was Cookie's banker. Cookie knew what he was getting with Robert. Ross sulked for a bit then considered it properly – the work, the organising, the speech – and decided he was well out of it. *Fill your boots, Robert.*

***

The bit I remember best, almost the only bit of the wedding day I can remember with any fondness, was Robert's speech. He was only seventeen, but he was ice-cold nerveless that day. He sat next to Cookie at the top table, both in kilts. Robert banged his glass on the table then stood up and dived straight in. Lights, camera, action.

He rattled off his opening line quickly.

'Apparently there's a legend in the Cooke family that the size of the groom's…er…equipment, can be judged by the length of the Best Man's speech.'

He sat back down, as if he had finished. It took a second or two for it to sink in, then Karen's Dad spluttered in his Champagne and Cookie's Dad chuckled. Disapproving looks from Karen's Mum, then a few throaty heh-hehs from the floor, from uncles and Karen's and Cookie's Dads' mates. The guests settled in, made themselves comfortable. He was only a boy but it looked like he was going to be a good turn. Robert was back at the shelter, weaving a tale, the audience in his pocket. There was colour, there was emotion, there were memories. Mostly, there were laughs as he walked a bad taste tightrope.

'Picture the scene tomorrow morning in the hotel room. Cookie, I mean Simon…sorry Mrs Cooke…Simon phones room service. Orders himself a full breakfast – bacon and eggs, sausage and tattie scones, toast and marmalade, pot of tea, the works. The girl at room service, she asks him, *And what about the lady, Sir?* And Simon says, *Just send up a plate of straw and carrots, I want to see if she eats like a rabbit as well.*'

Cookie leaned over and slapped Robert's arm in mock offence. Even Karen's Mum's face cracked, though she quickly covered it with her hand. Karen tried to manufacture a blush that didn't quite materialise. Robert was going down a storm. He had found the right balance – sauce with just the right helping of sugar.

'Bumped into Karen outside the church today, just before the ceremony. Now, me being Best Man and everything, I had to ask her, *How come you haven't got your wedding dress on yet? You not cutting it a bit fine?* Then I realised, it was her Mum. Could be twins, the pair of them.'

And he had the big finish.

'I'll sit down in a minute,' he said, pausing for the groans and ahs from the guests. 'But I'd like to get serious for a moment and tell you about something that happened this morning. I was with Simon at his house, waiting for the car, the two of us sitting there in our kilts. He turns to me, looks me straight in the eye and goes, *You know something Robert? I've finally discovered the true meaning of love and happiness.*'

Karen beamed up at Robert then leaned over and kissed Cookie's cheek, but she should have known better. Robert always had a punchline.

'Yes,' he continued, chequered flag in sight. 'Simon had a good look at me, sitting there in my short skirt, and told me he'd finally found true love. But of course, it was far too late to cancel the wedding by that time and he's not my type anyway, so I told him to get his hand off my knee.'

They loved him and he knew it. He milked it. A star was born and I couldn't keep my eyes off him all through the speech. I was so proud.

And yet, and yet, something gnawed at me, something just a little not quite right. Just a little bit, *Hey folks, the wedding and all, Karen and Simon and everything, great, let's hear it for them. But let's be honest, this is the bit you really came to see.* Maybe it was just me, but I wanted to say to him, *OK, Robert. That's your five minutes in the spotlight but remember, just remember, this isn't your day, it's not your stage, don't deflect so much.* Probably I'm being unfair again and it was just me trying to keep my sense of Robert in check.

A jolt. I was wrong. There was another bit that makes me smile, another glorious if bittersweet moment at Karen and Cookie's wedding. It was later at the reception when the ceilidh band was on a break. A tape was playing, and he was back from exile – Marc Bolan, Hot Love. One of our old standards from those early, innocent Record Sessions. Suddenly, we got all emotional and nostalgic. Us world-weary teenagers nostalgic for a time barely three years past. Nostalgic for those chaste nights when we dared to brush hands and lips. Three years ago, a lifetime ago.

Somehow, everyone else seemed to sense that this was our moment. The Mums, the Dads, the Uncles, the Aunts, the family friends, they all gave way, retreated to their tables and their corners.

And there we were, the eleven of us, the floor to ourselves. Dancing, swaying, linking arms, hugging, kissing, forming a fluid circle around Karen and Cookie, yelling out that never-ending Na-na-na-na-na-na-na chorus along with Bolan. For a brief moment, time stood still and we were invincible, we were immortal. If only we had known. It was to be our last stand. It would have been impossible to believe if someone had told us, but it was the very last time in our lives that the eleven of us would all be together in the same place at the same time.

Robert took his role so seriously that day, his Best Man duties. He tirelessly patrolled tables. I heard his patter-merchant gig in full flow. Awkward, reticent teenager? Not him.

You all OK over here? Enjoying yourselves all right? Karen was gorgeous at the church, eh? Awful warm in here, isn't it? The band's brilliant, eh? There's sandwiches coming later if anybody's a bit peckish. Anyone needing a drink? Any of you old dears fancy a two-minute thrill on the floor with a handsome young man in a dress?

Fine by me. It kept him at a safe distance. Because I wanted him. He was on fire that night. He was buzzing and I was aching for him. I wanted him so badly it was physically painful.

The band was back, playing slow, lazy ballads now. The lights were low. The night was at the winding down stage. The Gay Gordons and Canadian Barn Dance – with their raucous whoops and stamping feet and flying kilts – were a fading memory. Most of the guests were sipping shorts. Low, almost whispered conversations trickled across tables. One or two die-hard couples propped each other up and slow-motioned round the dance floor. I was sitting talking to Kirsty and Jo, trading memories and futures and dreams and ambitions and fears between long, easy silences. Then, without warning, Robert was there, standing over me, still going strong. Cheerful, hopeful, longing.

'Saved me a dance then, Lorna?'

Before I knew it, we were on the floor, and it was like I'd never been away. Guiding myself in towards him, playing it from memory, letting him hold me in tight, his cheek pressing into my hair as we exchanged warm, familiar scents. Suddenly he was sobbing, that star from the spotlight. Funny, confident, charming, everybody's buddy Robert, weeping, shaking on my shoulder.

'I'm sorry,' he whispered, and I felt his hot tears on the side of my head.

'It's OK.'

'I can't do this anymore, Lorna.' The words caught in his throat. 'I can't take it. What happened to us? Will you tell me for God sake?'

Then I was weeping too. I couldn't believe I'd done this to another human being, that I was capable of this. Damn you, Mum. Damn you. Damn you and to hell with your fucking prehistoric stupid promise.

'I'm the one that's sorry, Robert,' I whispered back. 'I'm so, so sorry.'

It was as if he didn't hear me. He pleaded again.

'What did I do, Lorna? Gonnae tell me? Just tell me the once and I'll walk away. I won't bug you anymore. Honest to God I won't.'

'You didn't do anything, Robert,' I said. 'You didn't do a single thing wrong.'

I held him tighter still, as if I could squeeze out the hurt that I had given him.

'Lorna, I love you.' He said it so softly, so gently. 'Do you hear me? Do you get it? I love you, that's all. You are the most important thing in my life and fuck all else matters.'

Right then, right at that moment, I was strong enough and weak enough at the same time to damn the memory of my mother's dying, to forget that promise and make things OK. For him, for me.

But Cammy screwed it all up for us.

Robert didn't kiss me, he was about a second too slow. I kissed him, homing in by instinct. We came together and it should have been long and definite and decisive and a permanent marker. But our little bubble popped before it even had time to fully form. A piercing scream shattered the moment.

Chapter 36

July 2001
All Rise – Blue

I T was the nachos that did it. Bloody nachos. Why did I even care about them? I've never eaten nachos in my life and, to be honest, I'm only vaguely aware of what they actually are. Some kind of crisp thing, right? But yes, it was nachos that tipped me over the edge and made me run for my life. Well, that and the briefest, barely perceptible look that she thought was too quick and sleekit for me. Oh yeah, plus the fact I felt I'd been tricked, though later I realised what had really annoyed me was that while that is what I instinctively felt, I didn't trust myself enough to believe it. Not of Bill, anyway. No, I couldn't believe that the Bill I remembered would have pulled anything as sneaky as that. There wasn't any side to him, you see, never had been. Despite how it had all ended between us, I'd never stopped believing that he was possibly the least complicated and most up-front person I've ever met, and I didn't imagine that had changed dramatically in the last few years. OK, now that I add it all up, I admit it probably was more than just the nachos.

It was to be our second...er, what was I calling it? Not a date, I don't think. It hadn't got to that stage yet and in any case, you don't have dates in the middle of the day, do you? (Huh, little did I know what was coming my way.) Our first meeting had been what Bill called a catch-up, which was pretty much accurate because that's exactly what we did. But that had only been two weeks or so before and certainly in my world, not nearly enough of consequence happens in the average fortnight to justify another catch-up so soon. The safest, most neutral way I could think of to describe our second meeting was that we were simply having lunch, though the cinema had been bandied around as a possibility in our woolly, inconclusive text exchange that had been in danger of slipping into the old familiar, *what do you fancy doing, no, what do you fancy doing?* So yes, getting together for lunch was a pleasantly neutral and appropriate way of putting it. We even had the same neutral venue again – centre of Glasgow. The subtext, I'm sure, being that if it turned sour or awkward or just plain dull, no one had to be evicted from the other's property.

My bus was almost in Glasgow when I got Bill's text. Still a good ten minutes at least from the bus station though, because there was always a bottleneck at the top of the town, around the Royal and the university. Hmm, that didn't give me nearly enough time to stew about his message.

Change of plan, hope you don't mind...had to bring Crosby.

What? No, you've got be kidding me. I was nowhere near ready to meet the daughter. Come on Bill, what happened to no strings attached? Your words when you first suggested meeting for a coffee, remember? It was supposed to be gently-gently, just old friends, let's keep it light. Now, without anything that resembled proper warning, it was suddenly playing happy families with the bereaved ten-year-old. I felt stitched up and backed into a corner. Of course I did, because what was I meant to reply?

Forget it, half-orphaned sprogs are just not my thing?

But I didn't want to believe that of Bill, couldn't believe it of him. Whatever problems we'd had in our marriage – and I probably should qualify that because the problems were all mine – he was never anything other than straight with me. But what was I supposed to think? I'd been landed in an almost certainly uncomfortable and difficult situation with no way out and no chance even to prepare.

Don't get me started on the name either. Crosby! In what world was that even a name? I understood Bill's explanation that it was in honour of his wife's granddad, who had virtually brought her up after the death of her parents. But how did that justify saddling a kid with some old bloke's surname as their first name? Nah, as far as I'm concerned, if you want to make that kind of tribute, stick it in as a middle name and bring it out on special occasions only, like criminal charges.

Hey, hold on. Stop right there, Lorna. Where's all this coming from? This hissy outrage. What does it matter to me? It was the same with Robert/Robbie's boy, Jack. It's got sod all to do with me. They're not my kids, so why don't I just stay out of it and keep my opinions to myself?

Except Bill had made sure I couldn't keep out of it, though my trepidation was softened a little when we met halfway – like some international diplomacy arrangement – between my bus station and his train station, next to the lions in George Square. He bared his teeth in a grimace and mouthed *Sorry* behind her back. She was quiet, obviously well mannered, but serious, unsmiling and dressed conservatively compared to a lot of ten going on nineteen-year-olds who it seems can't wait to chuck away their childhoods these days. *Huh, when was it ever different, Granny Lorna?* Crosby – oh, that name – had on a plain T-shirt and jeans and was carrying some kind of animal backpack with a hoodie over her arm. To my inexpert eye, she had long, straight, unstyled hair. She shook my hand formally when Bill introduced us and barely said a word en route to wherever we were going to eat. I wasn't getting any say in choice of restaurant either, apparently.

Oh give it a rest, Lorna, who's the child here?

I heard Crosby muttering something about pizza and that at least gave me the luxury of a little guilt trip as we walked in an uneasy silence in the direction of Argyle Street. There I was, seeing Bill – with no real idea why or where it might lead – yet it was Mark who popped into my head. I hardly ever thought about Mark anymore, but I suddenly remembered a stupid joke he cracked one night when we went for a pizza after a movie at the Odeon. It was Dino's in Sauchiehall Street. One of the original Glasgow Italians before all the chains took over. He'd ordered a big pizza between us and asked them to cut it up for us.

He said to the waiter: 'I was gonnae ask for ten slices but just make it eight...don't think we could manage ten.'

The downside of the gag was that once his laughter died down – probably when we were halfway back to Cumbride in his cab – he felt it necessary to explain it to me about four times. The upside was that it was possibly the longest conversation we ever had in our marriage.

Conversation had never been a problem with Bill and I in our early years, but it was now. He was keeping space between us but I still couldn't miss that look of hope against the odds that I remembered so well. God, he'd be offering me a great big cuddle next. Crosby, who I had already cruelly rechristened Bing in my head, dawdled a little way behind. I quietly seethed and determined not to let him off the hook easily.

Don't get me wrong. I have nothing against kids in general. I don't actively dislike them, I just couldn't eat a whole one. Seriously, children have just never been part of the picture for me. Sure, two of my cousins have got little ones that I see occasionally and yes, they're good, they're fine, they're fun in small doses. But as for having kids of my own, nah, it didn't happen and if I'm honest, it's never felt like a big empty hole. With Bill, a baby had once seemed like a solution, but then even the idea of it quickly turned into a chain that would bind me to a marriage that I knew was on borrowed time less than halfway through.

As for Mark, he gave the whole fatherhood question his usual deep analysis and delivered his eloquent, reasoned verdict as we walked home from his brother's on the evening he and his wife announced they were expecting their first.

'Weans, eh? Fuck that. Cannae shag for ages after you drop it apparently. Stitches and that. I mean, a chug's all right, but...'

So no, my objection to the place where I had been led unsuspecting by Bill, wasn't about children as such. I just didn't know what I was going to say to a ten-year-old girl who had lost her mum not so long ago and must be wondering why on earth this stranger from her dad's past had suddenly popped up in her life. What would she think of me, and hell, why should I even be put into a position where I was going to be weighed up and judged by a child?

Was I being unfair? Should I have been prepared for this? God, had I given it any thought whatsoever? I knew Bill had a kid, course I did. The extra name appearing on the Christmas cards had been a bit of a giveaway, even if I'd assumed Crosby was first a dog, then a boy. Bill had talked about her a fair bit at our first meeting, but we'd only been dipping our toes in the water, hadn't we? From my point of view, and surely from his, the likelihood was that we'd meet up a couple of times, exchange pleasantries, bury any old lingering hard feelings and move on. That said, I probably was at least a little open to the possibility of something more, but anything that involved his daughter was way way further down the road.

No, to hell with it, I wasn't in the wrong here, I was certain of it. I was confident my instinct had been right and we were a million miles from bringing his kid into it.

I wasn't paying that much attention to where we were going, but I know the place where we ended up was not far from Central Station. Some kind of busy, noisy barn of a chain restaurant. A Wetherspoons, possibly? I must have sighed a lot as I studied the menu with zero interest or enthusiasm, and at first refused to care about how Bill was coping with the mounting tension. It must have felt to him like having two sullen, fractious kids in tow instead of one. But I wasn't for budging. I was still waiting for an explanation. Surely I was entitled to that much, though in fairness, she hadn't been out of our sight since we met and I couldn't expect him to make excuses for being in his own daughter's company in front of her. Then it occurred to me that as much as his bumbling, unsubstantiated optimism was instantly familiar to me, the same, exasperating, sulky old Lorna would be nothing new or surprising to him.

Right, come on, Lorna, give yourself a shake. You're better than this. Give the guy a break and if that's too much to ask, at least don't let him see that you haven't moved on

241

or finally grown up. Besides, she's only a wee girl who has been through a really hard time and if anyone knows how hard it is losing your mum... OK, OK, keys.

'What do you fancy Bi...er, Crosby?' I asked brightly, reaching for a smile and, thankfully, finding it wasn't too much of an effort.

Bill, true to character – bless him – was happy to grab at the tiniest positive morsel and run with it.

'Ah, it's going to be great,' he beamed, suddenly so upbeat he might have been talking about our whole lives, not just lunch or the rest of the day. 'The food in here's magic. Big portions and great value too. Tell Lorna about that film you want to see...'

The girl's sigh put mine to shame and she made a noise that to my astonishment and horror, sounded like she was either clearing her throat or shushing him.

'Shrek.' Bill grinned, as he interpreted for the hard of understanding, i.e., me. 'Tell Lorna all about it.'

Another enormous sigh, then, in a flat, matter-of-fact monotone, she mumbled: 'Ogre has to rescue a princess.'

'Oh right,' I delved for enthusiasm. 'That sounds good. Who's in it?'

'Computer animated,' she mumbled impatiently, as if I was an idiot which, with each passing second, I was realising I probably was, just for being here if nothing else.

Bill raced to fill in the awkwardness hovering above the table.

'Right come on, don't know about you two, but I'm starving. What you girls having?'

'Hmm, I would really like the nachos,' said Crosby, diffidently. 'But I don't know, I fancy pizza as well.'

'Take your time,' said Bill, with a smile that was the definition of indulgence. 'Have whatever you want. What about you, Lorna?'

'Now you mention pizza, couple of slices would do me. I've not been in here before, can you do it like that? Or maybe I could share with...'

She cut in as if I wasn't there. What, was I invisible?

'Right, I know. I'll have the nachos for a starter then the four seasons pizza.'

I went to correct the obvious mistake and, innocently, started studying the menu again to help her out.

'No, you're looking in the wrong place, Crosby. The nachos is a main course. Where's the starters?'

'I know it is,' she said, firmly. 'I'll have the nachos to start with, then the pizza.'

I let a nervous laugh escape. What was she thinking?

'But the nachos come with chicken. It's a whole meal...you'll never eat that and a pizza.'

'It's OK. I'll just eat the nachos and leave the chicken. I don't really like chicken anyway.'

I realised that my voice was rising and tried in vain to bring it down a notch.

'You can't do that, it's such a waste.'

Then it hit me. Why was I even having this conversation? Why was no one else at the table, like eh, Bill, her dad, speaking? I turned to him, asked the question by raising my eyebrows. He intervened but neither his voice nor his words carried the least conviction.

'Lorna's got a point. Could you not have the nachos some other time, Crosby?'

'Dad.' She stretched the word out to three syllables. 'You promised me, you said just a minute ago that I could have anything to eat I wanted. Was that a lie?'

'Look, this is a ludicrous conversation,' I said, meaning it as the final word on the subject and not caring how she reacted. 'No one has two main courses, so why don't you just decide which one you're having.'

We both fell silent and turned to Bill, waiting for him to deliver the verdict. There was never an iota of doubt in my mind that he would cave and I took no pleasure in being right.

'All right, all right,' he said, softly and meekly. 'Special treat. Nachos and pizza, just this once.'

As he went up to the counter to give them the order, I caught it – the look she gave his back. The smug, scornful smile coated with a withering contempt which told me that the word respect played no part in their relationship, and that where Bill now lived was in the palm of his daughter's hand. The moment she realised that my eyes were on her, the blank mask was switched back on.

I felt like reaching over and shaking her by the throat, a part of me wishing I could shake myself by the throat while I was at it. Had I treated Bill that badly? I made do with shooting out of my chair, grabbing my jacket from the back of it, and ramming it against the table.

'Tell your Dad I'm feeling ill,' I said. I wasn't lying.

Chapter 37

August 1975
Send In The Clowns – Judy Collins

OUR wedding kiss was wrecked. Robert and I broke apart amid shouts, curses, hysterical cries and a stampede towards the hotel foyer. The colour drained from his face.
'Christ, what the hell's that?'
We joined the race and he grabbed my hand, towing me through the crowd.
'Best Man,' he kept repeating, like a doctor racing to a heart attack victim. 'Let us through, eh?'
Whatever had happened, it was finished. Only seconds had passed since that first, haunting scream but it seemed like it was over, or at least paused. The scene was like the aftermath of a car crash. Cammy lay on the floor, curled into a tight ball, hands clutching his face, head bathed in a pool of blood. So much blood. Most bizarre was the grubby surgical collar from a weeks-old neck strain. The injury had just about healed but the plaster had hung around, as if knowing it would soon be needed somewhere in the vicinity.
A man and two women – wedding guests I didn't know – knelt beside Cammy. The man turned, his eyes scanning the crowd.
He yelled: 'Somebody want to phone an ambulance, or are you all just gonnae stand there and gawk?'
Nearby, Ross sat on the floor looking, well, surprised, his back propped against a wall. He was staring at something in his hand, two of his teeth as it turned out. Big Paddy was restraining another man from behind, a huge arm locked tight round his neck. One of the hotel staff was in front of the guy, gripping him in a bear hug. Christ, it was Wee Mary's Dad and he was struggling, but in vain. There was so much to take in at once. Wee Mary's Mum was facing the wall, leaning on it, sobbing into her arm hysterically. In

244

the middle of it all, Wee Mary herself, bewildered and spent, desperately trying to make herself invisible. Then there was Karen, the battered bride, make-up annihilated by tears, dress torn at the sleeve, stiff wedding hairdo all over the place as if a dozen Kirby grips had been wrenched out simultaneously. Her Mum was trying to coax her away, an arm around her shoulder. Cookie was there too, bent double and gripping his face. Karen's Dad, blood streaming from his mouth, paced around the foyer, from Cammy to Ross to Cookie and back to Cammy. He leaned over each of them in turn, looking anxious and concerned – especially about Cammy – then he pinballed between Wee Mary's Dad and his own wife and daughter as if trying to restore order. Trying to figure out a way of turning the clock back – less than a minute would do it – to a time when this day hadn't been demolished.

Then sirens, blue lights flashing through the windows and a minute later, police piling in through the hotel entrance, ready for a Saturday night war zone. But they found a bloodied stage set with the drama over. Or nearly over. They saw Cammy lying prone, in the role of the corpse, plus a handful of walking wounded. They saw a rapt audience crushed into the reception hall's double doorway, jostling for a better view. An ambulance crew followed the police, then another. They focused their efforts on Cammy. Relief, I saw him twitch. He seemed to be responding.

Robert thrust himself forward and started talking to a cop, the one who looked as if he might be in charge. Robert was trying to broker a peace deal. He was Best Man, after all, but he had neglected his duties, taken his eye off the ball for a second and this had happened. Mayhem. Ha, my fault. Should have left well alone.

It looked like carnage to me but the cops didn't seem overly fussed. Just another routine Saturday night to them, probably. Robert began to look a bit more relaxed. He smiled for a second, the charmer back in control. Boss cop smiled too. The show was over. Move along folks, nothing more to see here.

As Cammy was eased on to a stretcher, Big Paddy and the hotel guy were, warily, little by little, relaxing their grip on Wee Mary's Dad. Karen and her Mum had decided to stick around. Karen was still sniffing. Then Cammy, the clown, let off a bonus detonator, a small attempt at revenge for his kicking and his pain. He shoved himself up on one arm and shouted towards Wee Mary's Dad.

'Heh fannybaws, your missus is some ride, so she is. Gives a great gobble an' all. Nearly as good as your daughter in fact. But you know that already.'

Cammy raised a finger and rubbed the plaster collar on his neck, then added way more information than anyone needed at that moment.

'Had her legs wrapped round my stookie for the fish course, so she did.'

Wee Mary's Dad took a lunge forward but Big Paddy tightened his grip once more. One of the cops instantly got between them and the stretcher. Wee Mary's Mum flew at the cop so another one got hold of her. Karen's Mum took the opportunity to lash out at Wee Mary's Mum. An encore! The audience loved it and were disappointed when the police sorted it out quickly.

The situation had exploded from uneasy peace to three arrests and two ambulance-loads. Two cops huckled Wee Mary's Dad out – now in handcuffs – and Wee Mary's Mum and Karen's Mum were also led away, separated from each other but still hissing like swans. Karen collapsed sobbing into her Dad's arms while Wee Mary was ushered away by Big Paddy. Cookie and Ross and Karen's Dad all shared an ambulance while Cammy got one to himself. His parents hadn't been at the wedding so Robert volunteered to go with him to the hospital. As he left, he turned, caught my eye, held an imaginary phone to his cheek. I nodded and got a lift home with Kirsty in the hotel assistant manager's car. At her suggestion, they dropped me off first. Kirsty had got chatting to him as the battle raged. Never one to miss an opportunity, our Kirsty.

***

Late morning Sunday, the calm after the storm. Big Paddy came along to my house and pieced the whole thing together for me from a combination of what he had seen himself and eye-witness reports. Ha, good cop material there. He started with a condition check.

'Cammy's got a couple of smashed ribs. Got a boot to the head but no sign of a brain never mind damage to one. Oh, and he needs surgery to reset his nose. Broken so it is. They should do us all a favour and amputate that knob of his while they're at it. Ross's lost a couple of his front teeth. What a shame, eh? Maybe improve his good looks, know? Cookie's got a stoater of a black eye. Karen's Dad's OK, just a burst lip. Looked worse than it was.'

'What the hell was it all about?' I asked.

'You'll no' believe it.' Big Paddy shook his head. 'Cammy and Wee Mary's maw.'

'No, you're kidding me.' I was truly shocked. 'I thought Cammy was just winding her Dad up. You mean something really happened?'

'Aye,' said Big Paddy. 'Out in the car park, on the bonnet of somebody's motor.'

'Oh, good God.'

246

THE FENIAN

I thought about Cammy, the no-hoper, the drifter. No ambitions, no plans, helpless and pitiful. He had played that role with us these past three years with his gypsy little-boy-lost face and mournful voice. All that, along with his freakish and now legendary physical attribute, had been a mix that had sometimes been irresistible or at least a curiosity that a fair number of girls had decided to check out. But Cammy and Wee Mary's Mum? Come on! She was mid to late thirties but looked younger. Short and Irish dark, lovely, all boobs and bum, a Wee Mary of the future. I had spoken to her at the reception and yes, she had been tipsy, but not falling down drunk or anything. I couldn't believe it of her.

'So what happened then?' I asked.

Big Paddy, as he would do in different circumstances years later, relayed his evidence. He told a tale of reactions, counter-reactions, misunderstandings and high farce. Domino collapsing on domino.

***

Wee Mary's Mum has been gone more than twenty minutes at the wedding. She'd told her husband she was nipping to the loo but as time goes on, he becomes concerned and goes searching. He spots his daughter and enlists her help, asks her to check the ladies. He goes to reception to see if his wife has left. Maybe she had taken unwell and got a taxi home without thinking to tell him. Unlikely, but a possibility.

Meanwhile, out in the car park...details supplied to Big Paddy by Cammy himself, grinning through mummy-like bandages in his hospital bed. Big Paddy pinched his nose to make it sound more authentic for me.

'Honest to God, Paddy, it was all her blame, so it was. Mary's maw I mean. She was all over us. I was dancing with her up on the floor, a slow one. I gets a root – no' my fault – and she starts rubbing herself against us, then she grabs my hand and pulls us out to the car park.'

Aw, you poor helpless soul, Cammy.

'She starts snogging us – tongues the lot, thought she was going to rip my tonsils out. I was pure chuffed, so I was. I mean, you hear about it, don't you? Older woman and that. It was dead obvious she was right up for it, so I slips the mitt, but I'm being dead smooth and polite and that. I'm giving it, *nice bit of tit, Mrs Webb.* Cos Paddy, I thought it'd be all saggy and wrinkly, her being decrepit and that. Then she pulls us over to somebody's motor and she's yanking at my belt and taking my zip down. I'm still being dead cool and that. I'm going, *thanks very much, Mrs Webb, this is brilliant, Mrs Webb, I never thought folk your age did this kind of stuff.*'

Big Paddy released his nose and I suppressed a giggle, because this was much too serious. He went on with the story.

Wee Mary's Dad is at the reception desk when his wife finally creeps in through the main hotel door looking all furtive. Eyes darting around, then head bowed. She is dishevelled, her usually perfect hair out of place. She is checking herself, fastening buttons. She sees her husband, panics, glances over her shoulder. Then Cammy follows, huge dumb grin, ear to ear – and he's fiddling with his trousers.

Big Paddy blew out hard, cheeks puffed, and said: 'Right Lorna, all that's the warm-up. This is where it really kicks off.'

WEE MARY'S DAD SEES: The whole sordid scene right away. He explodes and flies at Cammy, bullets him with his forehead. The blow smashes the bridge of Cammy's nose and blood shoots out of his nostrils in twin jets. His hands fly to his face. Wee Mary's Mum screams and her husband follows up with a boot to Cammy's groin. Cammy crumples, squealing, and Wee Mary's Dad rains more kicks, at least one directly to the head. Cammy, now on the floor, curls into a ball, his hands still trying to protect his face.

Enter Ross, from the gents.

ROSS SEES: His mate on the floor, splashes of blood, some bloke putting the boot in hard. Act first, ask questions later. Ross dashes over and leaps on to the guy's back, throwing his arms round his neck and trying to haul him away from Cammy. Wee Mary's Dad's head jerks backwards in a natural reaction as he is grabbed from behind. The hard bone at the back of his skull connects with Ross's face. Ross's mouth erupts and he bounces off. Fresh blood.

Pause, rewind, just a single frame. Enter Karen's Dad, bursting into the foyer, alerted by Wee Mary's Mum's screams and Cammy's squeals.

KAREN'S DAD SEES: Peter Webb, his workmate, his pal, occasional golf partner, in trouble. Someone is jumping on his back. Recognition. It's Ross, one of Simon's mates. What the hell is going on? Karen's Dad is vaguely aware of a bundle on the floor in his peripheral vision but his first instinct is to help Pete because he is the one under attack. He takes three strides across the floor, grabs at Ross. At the same moment, Ross is bouncing off Wee Mary's Dad and his arms flap wildly. One of his flailing fists catches Karen's Dad's face. Lip bursts. More blood still.

Back again, just half a frame this time. Enter Cookie in the wake of his brand new father-in-law.

COOKIE SEES: His bride's Dad grabbing at Ross, his best buddy. He can't be sure because it's so quick, but Ross seems to throw a punch and it catches Karen's Dad on the face. There's a spray of blood through the air. Oh, tough one. Where does his loyalty lie here? He has only a split second to think about it. Cookie compromises but for once doesn't crap out of it and launches himself between Karen's Dad and Ross. He is aware of more action in the background but for now he is in the middle of a tangle of arms and fists and an elbow whacks Cookie's face. He doesn't have a clue whose elbow, but the detail doesn't matter. The elbow catches him high on the left cheek and his eye howls in protest. Three walking wounded, each of them uncertain as to who is friend and who is foe.

Now, a big moment, here comes the bride. Enter Karen, elbowing her way through the throng. She is one of the principal characters so the audience that is gathering rapidly – already hooked on the drama – parts to let her through.

KAREN SEES: A guy in a white shirt booting something on the floor. What the hell? It's Wee Mary's Dad, but she can't identify the shape lying down there. Then she sees three punch-drunks wobbling around each other. It's her Dad and Ross...and oh my God, her Simon. The faces of her Dad and Ross are tattered and bloody and they are only now facing up to the reality of their pain. Cookie is the least injured of the trio and stands there sheepish and bewildered, rubbing his eye. So, obviously, Karen ignores her Dad and Ross, she ignores the main bout in the background, and starts wailing. 'Aw, Simon, what have they done to you?'

Then the United Nations peace-keeping force arrives. Enter Big Paddy, though he played down his own role in the action.

'I didn't really do nothing,' he told me. 'Just grabbed the guy till the troops arrived, know?'

I wasn't surprised to learn later that there was a whole lot more to Big Paddy's role. Wee Mary, tears half-blinding her, filled in the blanks later in bits and pieces...

BIG PADDY: Crashes on to the scene, has a quick scan around, weighs it all up and makes an instant damage assessment. He ignores the secondary stuff and goes straight to the heart of the battle. He throws an arm round Wee Mary's Dad's neck and hauls him backwards across the foyer. Big Paddy backs up towards the wall and Wee Mary's Dad wriggles like a fish on a very strong hook. Big Paddy barks an order to Cookie, Ross and Karen's Dad.

'You three, quit it, right now!'

They are happy to take orders and back off from each other. The hotel's assistant manager is on the scene now, alerted by the commotion, and he sees two strangers grappling. Two of the wedding guests, he figures.

With his free hand, Big Paddy points first at himself and says: 'Good guy.' Then he gestures at Wee Mary's Dad and adds: 'Bad guy.'

The assistant manager looks at big Big Paddy, then at Wee Mary's wee Dad, and makes an intelligent decision. He sides with Big Paddy and grabs Wee Mary's cursing, head-shaking Dad from the front. By this time, one of the guests has decided it's safe enough to offer a little audience participation and crouches over Cammy, looking concerned. Then two women join him. One of them announces that she is a nurse and studies and prods him with a more expert eye.

Back to Big Paddy's version. Enter Karen's Mum, squeezing her way through the throng.

KAREN'S MUM SEES: Utter confusion and madness. Various pools of blood on the foyer floor, a couple of streaks down one wall too. Karen fussing over Simon, who is still rubbing his face. Her own husband staggering and bloodied. Simon's pal Ross is dazed and he too is bleeding, from his mouth by the looks of it. She sees a body on the floor with three people kneeling or crouched beside it. Peter Webb is being restrained by Simon's other pal, Big Paddy, and one of the hotel staff. She screeches and asks perhaps the most banal question of her life.

'Oh my God. What's happened?'

Wee Mary's Dad gets in first. He is in a vice and has calmed down enough to realise that he is going nowhere, but he manages a nod towards his own wife, who is still sobbing in the corner.

'Ask that slut,' he spits. 'She's the one that's been humping your daughter's pal.'

He flicks his head in the direction of Cammy, who has not moved for the best part of a minute, though it seems longer, and adds: 'I hope he's fucking dead.'

Karen takes it in, begins to understand, leaves her wounded Simon and marches across to Wee Mary's Mum.

'You disgusting old whore-dirt-bitch,' she yells in her face. 'You've just ruined my bloody wedding.'

Oops, time for another rewind and yes, half a frame will do again. Enter Wee Mary, the last of the main characters in the drama.

WEE MARY SEES: Nothing else, just Karen ranting at her Mum, who is sobbing loudly. She catches Karen's fourth *whore-dirt-bitch*. Wee Mary is not having that and she stomps across the floor, screaming: 'Don't you dare speak to my Mum like…'

Karen spins, cuts Wee Mary off with a feral snarl.

'It's your fucking fault and all. She's your mother.'

Cool logic under fire was never Karen's strong suit. She takes a wild slap at Wee Mary then it's cat-fight time. Fistfuls of hair, the sound of ripping fabric. Karen's Mum makes a grab for Wee Mary. It's time for more audience participation. This is exciting. The girls/women are dragged apart and then

250

the cavalry weigh in with more handcuffs.

Big Paddy's story had come to an abrupt ending. There was so much to take in, but I couldn't help my first reaction.

'Em, sorry, whore-dirt-bitch? What does that even mean?'

'I know,' said Big Paddy, nodding. 'Dead exciting these grown-up parties, Lorna, eh? Never got any of this kind of stuff at our wee record sessions.'

***

Sunday lunchtime. Big Paddy had gone. Robert hadn't phoned me yet but Big Paddy had told me he was running around all over the place, hospital to police station, police station to various homes, back to hospital, round the houses again. It still hadn't clicked with him that Best Man was a one-day-only booking. He was officially relieved of his duties, he just hadn't realised it yet.

Wee Mary came round. She was shattered, her eyes red raw from crying. She was blazing at the world, the world that had collapsed around her. Raging at her Mum, how could she have done it? Raging at Cammy, how could *he* have done it – with *her* Mum? Raging at her Dad, that shocking violence. Raging at Karen and her Mum, their venom. They'd only had a wedding ruined, her life was in tatters. Wee Mary was hysterical, said she couldn't go on living at home, couldn't face her parents, couldn't stay while they fought to survive the lightning bolt that had just struck their marriage...if they did try to survive it. The alternative was just as bad – the recriminations and hostilities with her in a front row seat.

Her Dad was still at the police station. The cops had told Wee Mary that in all likelihood he would face charges but no, they couldn't tell her exactly what or how serious they would be. That was up to the fiscal, whoever that was. Her Dad was still being interviewed and they would be taking statements from Cammy and other witnesses later. They told Wee Mary her Mum would be released that afternoon. She and Karen's Mum might be charged with breach of the peace or they might get off with a caution if they were lucky. Ha, lucky.

Then Wee Mary brought it up. Our secret, our big plan. I'd been thinking about it too, since the night before, since that moment before the mayhem. Robert and me, our kiss. What had it meant? How much had I meant it? Where would it have taken us, and where did it leave that promise I had made to Mum? But this was a way out, for Wee Mary and for me. A way to avoid having to deal with all this or find any of the answers. Suddenly it looked very attractive.

Chapter 38

September 2001
The Way To Your Love – Hear'say

IT was Big Paddy's fault. That's not fair, not his fault. His doing then, at least partly, because he was the message carrier. But Big Paddy's intentions were good and true, or at the very least, backed by a sense of duty. I never doubted that.

It was a week or ten days after the night he had been round at my place. I heard the car horn as I stepped off the bus. Back from work, back from Glasgow and home to Cumbride in the drizzle. Only one other person got off at the same stop and we both turned, me and this other woman, and I saw a little car, white, no idea what make it was. I'm hopeless with cars, doesn't matter anyway. It's not relevant. I'm stalling, as per. It was parked just behind the bus stop, three-quarters up on the pavement.

'Somebody should report them to the police for illegal parking,' the other woman who got off the bus muttered.

But it was the police. Big Paddy got out from the driver's side and called out my name. I stared back, surprised but not displeased.

'You wanting a lift, Lorna? Save you getting soaked.'

'Yeah, sure Paddy,' I called back as I walked over and got in. 'I usually expect a police escort when it's raining.'

He was still mostly in uniform. No tie or cap though and it clearly wasn't an unmarked police car – no fancy extra radios or speakers or anything. I guessed he had just come off duty, or maybe he was just going on.

'OK, I confess,' I said. 'Slap the cuffs on, take me in, chuck me in a cell and throw away the key.'

I put my hands together facing downwards and thrust them towards him.

'My stash, the drugs, they're in the ice cream carton, in my freezer, next to the puff pastry.'

Big Paddy looked puzzled and faintly amused.

'What you on about?'

'Well, I'm obviously under surveillance, Paddy, or should I keep it official and call you Constable Allan? That's at least four times I've seen you in three weeks. About the same as in the last three years.'

Big Paddy tried for innocent but it didn't suit him.

'God sake. Can you no' give somebody a lift in the rain these days without them accusing you of police harassment?'

'Aye Paddy, and you just happened to know what bus I'd be getting off. The CID will be snapping you up any day now.'

The truth was, I was enjoying seeing Big Paddy again, as a friend obviously. I was enjoying the easiness, the gentle sparring, having a bloke in my life again, even if he was only borrowed, and probably temporary.

'All right, keys.' Big Paddy held up two outsized thumbs for a second then started the car. 'I'll tell you the truth. I just can't resist your coffee, Lorna – and there's something I want to tell you, OK?'

'There's a surprise,' I said. 'Right, drive on then, Taggart.'

Big Paddy had drowned me in revelations this past little while. Surely there was nothing else that could surprise me now? I was wrong, of course. He was back at the kitchen table, still too big and bulky for the place. He took one gulp of his coffee and cut to the chase.

'He wants to know if you'll meet him.'

My turn to play dumb in the face of the obvious.

'Who?'

Who else?

'Robert,' he said, flatly.

Oomph, this was it. This was the real deal. This wasn't reading a daft wee two-line message on a website on a computer screen. This wasn't discussing an imaginary friend across a kitchen table. *Play for time, Lorna.*

'Meet him? Meet Robert? How do you mean?'

As stupid, meaningless questions go, that was right up there.

'Er, just meet him, Lorna. As in, arrange a place and a time, go to that place at that time, sit down across from each other, have a drink, a coffee or whatever, and talk to each other. Kind of like what we're doing right now. Dead simple, know?'

I deserved that but hey, fight your corner.

'All right, smart arse. I mean, why? What for?'

I made an effort to sound exasperated, as if I had better things to do. As if. Big Paddy looked like he'd had enough.

'Christ, I don't know,' he sighed. 'Look, give us a break here, eh? I'm feeling daft enough as it is, like I'm running about carrying wee notes round the school.'

'I'm sorry, Paddy.' Not really sorry but editing as I went along. 'But you got me into this. I've been a Robert Kane-free zone all these years and you're the one that's dumped me right back in it, remember?'

'All right, fair enough.' He offered the palms-up gesture yet again. 'Here's the thing. I was talking to Robert last night. He phoned us up, just chatting and that, and he asked about you and I think I might have, er, kind of mentioned what you were saying.'

Panic.

'What did you tell him, Paddy? I mean, thought that was just us, you and me, talking.'

'Naw,' he tried to reassure me. 'Just what you were saying that night, mind? You said to me, tell Robert it wasn't his fault, it wasn't him that messed things up. You said to tell him.'

Yes, I had, hadn't I? So, had I assumed that it would never really happen, that my message would never actually get to Robert? Maybe I'd somehow thought my talks with Big Paddy didn't relate to anything real or, more likely, that we weren't talking about a real person. Maybe I'd somehow got it into my head that the guy we were discussing still lived in that imaginary remote galaxy and wasn't actually hovering close by in the background.

'OK Paddy,' I said. 'Not your fault. But why? Why does Robert want to see me? Why now?'

'I told you, Lorna, I don't know, and I'm not just saying that, I really don't. But I guess just to talk. You know, old times stuff, or maybe he wants to draw a line under things, know? Or maybe to see if there's any chance of you two being friends or something. How the hell do I know? He's my mate but I'm not a mind reader.'

It was ridiculous. I couldn't see it. Me, sitting in a bar, or the foyer of Robert's hotel – which one was it again? Oh yeah, the Hilton. Me in the Hilton, merrily chatting away with some guy I hadn't seen in the best part of thirty years.

'What have you told him, Paddy? About me?'

'Just what I said.' Big Paddy looked wounded, as if I didn't trust his word. 'Just what you said to tell him.'

'No, I mean, *about* me. What I'm like. You've told me plenty about Robert.'

Big Paddy switched tack, suddenly back to teasing and playful.

'Just that you're about twenty-three stone, hacket as ever, and toothless.'

I feigned hurt.

'Will they take your wee blue light off you if you get this cup of coffee all down your playsuit?'

Big Paddy relaxed. He liked this better – trading patter and barbs. He had made the effort, done his bit for his buddy, but he didn't really fancy himself much as relationship counsellor.

'Seriously Lorna, I told him you're great and just like I said about him, you're still the same person. No' too far gone for a forty-five-year-old either. Told him he won't get that embarrassed being seen with you as long as he takes you somewhere dark.'

Don't over-egg it, Paddy. This is serious, for me anyway.

'I just don't know,' I sighed. 'I just don't know what I'd say to him, Paddy. And it's forty-three, by the way.'

He caught the shift in my mood, the whiff of panic.

'Listen Lorna, it's totally up to you. Robert says to tell you there's absolutely no pressure. If you think it's a crap idea, forget it. He'd just really like to see you, that's all. Nothing heavy or anything but if you don't fancy it, he's not going to start stalking you.'

'Oh shit, Paddy,' I groaned. 'I don't know what to do. Really, I don't. I need somebody to tell me.'

'Huh, don't look at me,' he said. 'Just think about it, that's all? Look, I told Robert you get your lunch break at half twelve. That's right, isn't it? Anyway, he gets the subway into town from the BBC some days and nips into a wee pub-grub place called Rosie's, for a sandwich, know? It's in St Enoch Square, right across from the big shopping centre. Know where I am? Robert reckons it's only about five minutes' walk across the bridge from your place, the fiscal's I mean. Been doing his homework obviously. He'll be there Tuesday lunchtime. If you turn up, great. If you don't, no worries, he'll no bother you again.'

Tuesday! Five days away. At least that gave me time to mope around fretting while I decided whether or not to go through with it. Plenty of time to change my mind over and over again.

'Better tell him it's half-one for me next week...we're on a flexi-shift thing.'

'That mean you're going then?'

'I don't know, Paddy, I really don't and anyway, all those arrangements...sounds a bit lonely hearts, does it not? Is he going to be wearing a yellow carnation in his lapel?'

Big Paddy gave a short laugh, more of a grunt really.

'Seriously, there's no pressure,' he repeated. 'Robert said if it doesn't suit, he can make it any day or time or place that works for you. Says he can phone you first if you like. I didn't want to give him your number till I checked with you. Oh aye, and he told me to give you one of his cards, in case you'd prefer to phone him. Here, it's got his email as well.'

I picked up the card. *Robbie Kane. Head of News (Programmes), BBC Scotland.* Robbie!! That reminded me, I still hadn't asked about that. There was a list of numbers – work, home (temporary), mobile, two different email addresses at the bottom.

I said: 'Can't miss him, can I?'

***

I didn't watch telly or sleep much that night. I went to bed, got back up again, cursed Big Paddy out loud for using the last of my milk. Cursed him again for being at the bus stop, for giving me a lift home and interrupting my routine so I didn't get a chance to nip into the shop for some. So I made coffee, drank it black, and I hate black coffee. Yeah, that was going to help me sleep. I chased it all round my head, round and round and back again. I made definite decisions, I took a vote, I decided once and for all, then I changed my mind again and I changed my mind a hundred times more.

OK, I'll go. Why not, what do I have to lose, what's the big deal? He's just a bloke so what's the worst that can happen? We'll sit there, we'll have a drink. I'll just have a soft drink because I have to go back to work after. OK, it might be awkward and neither of us will know what to say but it won't last forever, nothing ever does. All things must pass. (Thanks George, my favourite Beatle, that has got me through a few sticky moments.) At some point my lunch break will be over and I'll be polite. I'll say, *Well Robert, it's been lovely seeing you after all this time. Must do it again sometime, maybe another twenty-five years?* Then I'll leave and I'll still be in one piece. I'll go back to the office, then I'll come home that night after work. My little house will still be here. My life will still be intact, nothing will have changed, nothing will be broken.

Maybe it will be fine, maybe it will be more than fine. Maybe it will be genuinely lovely seeing him again. Maybe one of us will mention something from the past, or someone from the past, like Jo and the day she pretended to be German with Karen's Dad, or that daft tree-trunk game he made up to stop Ross tearing Cookie apart, and it will trigger all these hilarious memories. We'll trade stories from those days and wonder what they're all doing now, the rest of our lot. Maybe one of us will mention Cammy and we'll go silent for a moment, but then we'll lighten up again and talk about the night Fiona tried to snog Jo's Dad. We'll laugh some more and my lunch hour will fly past. Before I know it, it will be time to go back to work, and maybe Robert will say, *It's been lovely seeing you after all this time, Lorna. Must do it again sometime soon.*

Maybe we will meet up again, maybe we won't, but I'll feel OK about it. It will give me a boost and it will last me a long time, that good feeling, and maybe I'll stop suffering from these occasional bouts of Robert Kane sickness.

Maybe, just maybe, he'll ask for my phone number. Not that I'll be desperate for him to do that or anything, but maybe I'll give him my phone number. Maybe he'll never call. So what, nothing lost. But maybe he will phone and we will meet again, we'll go out for dinner, or no, just a drink so we're not tied to each other's company for a whole evening. Who knows, we might become friends and start seeing each other on a kind of semi-regular basis – strictly as friends, of course. We might even have a night out with Big Paddy and his missus. Not as a foursome, mind, just as friends. That might make my life better, less empty. Get me out more and I'll stop dreading old age rushing towards me. Stop worrying that I won't even notice old age that much because it won't be so different to my life now.

Maybe I'll run with this fantasy just a little bit longer. Yes, maybe we'll start seeing each other, maybe we'll grow close and it will become a little bit more than friends. Maybe something will click between us, again. Maybe he'll think, hmm, she's not bad in a mid-fortyish kind of way. Ha, I once heard my pal Kath describe another woman at work as presentable, and even though she was damning with faint praise, the word stuck in my head and, if pushed, it is probably how I think of myself. Maybe he'll see that I've kept myself in reasonable shape. Maybe my self-inflicted torture sessions at the gym will finally pay off and he won't find me too repulsive. Maybe I'll be attracted to him too – again – and sex will stop being something I've decided I can live without. Maybe it will have nothing to do with twenty-something years ago and it will just be two lonely divorcees keeping each other company, filling in a vacant space for each other.

Or maybe, just maybe, it could happen. That million to one chance, that you can find the one – the one that is meant for you – at sixteen, and maybe you can turn the clock back.

Then maybe...maybe, I'll stop being so bloody stupid. *Get real Lorna, for God sake, get real and stop constructing a fantasy life out of a load of maybes.*

Chapter 39

August 1975
The Last Farewell – Roger Whittaker

T HERE was desperation in Wee Mary's face, pleading in her voice. She needed an escape from the carnage of the wedding.

'I don't know how I could go on if we weren't going away,' she said, when she came round to mine after Big Paddy left. 'Do you think there's any chance we could go sooner? Like tomorrow or something, or is that too bonkers?'

There it was. What I hadn't told Robert, or any of the others. The grand adventure that me and Wee Mary had been plotting for months. Our great escape, our crazy ambition. The reason neither of us had made any serious plans about finding a job or a place at college.

It had been my idea in the first place. A way to put distance between myself and, well, what exactly? Or, more to the point, who? My Mum? The memory of her dying? That stupid bloody promise I had made to her? Was it about place? Home, the shelter, school, Cumbride? Was location the problem, or did I think it was the solution? Was it about putting distance between myself and Dad? Or my pals, at least the rest of them? Or, OK, spell it out, distance from Robert? If I dug around even a little, that was certainly where the idea had first taken hold. It had been about getting him out of my system and keeping the promise at the same time, even though I cursed it.

I had decided to take part of my Mum's advice – the one useful thing she had said to me on that final morning. I would travel and I would do it now. See stuff, see places before I went to college or got a job, before I settled down, before I found that I couldn't find the time. Mum's life insurance had paid out. It had been my legacy turned escape fund. My share was nearly a thousand quid – a fortune to me – so I already had the time, the opportunity and the means. Now I had an urgent reason too – and a travelling companion. Wee Mary had fancied it right from the moment I first mentioned it. It had to be her, there was no one else. Karen was out, even if she hadn't been pregnant. She would never have left Cookie behind, of course, and besides, I'd have throttled her before we reached the border. Fiona, with her big ambitions, was staying on at school. Jo was already at college, well on the way to becoming a full-time stylist. Kirsty was too much in demand elsewhere. Not that any of those reasons would have made a difference because Wee Mary was my first and only choice, and she was perfect. She had the sweetest temperament and we had become so close again. We were sisters once more.

Wee Mary had been thinking about college, doing a nursing course, but the prospect made her miserable. Not the nursing part, she still intended to do that eventually. But the process seemed so depressing to her – out of one classroom, straight into another one. Surely that couldn't be all there was after all those years at school? Surely you had to do something, run up a flag on this bit of your life, achieve something, do something you could look back on in your old age. You know, memories for when you were like, thirty, or something wizened and elderly like that.

'It could become a thing,' Wee Mary said at school one lunchtime. 'You know, folk taking like, a year off, or a year out, before they get a job or go to college or whatever.'

My first remark about travelling, not long after my Mum died, had been little more than a throwaway notion. But Wee Mary had seized on it and her enthusiasm scared me a little, made me ask myself if I had really been serious. But in no time, it became a plan, a goal, a glorious diversion. We conspired, we got books about other countries from the library, we giggled in the little booth at the train station when we sneaked off to get our passport photos done up in Glasgow.

We decided that this plan, this adventure, was ours, it was just between us. Don't let anyone else mock it, don't give anyone else something to slag us about if it doesn't come off. It became The Big Secret.

The money I had would get both of us off and running and a fair way down the road. But Wee Mary was determined to pay her own way so she begged, stole and borrowed. She got herself a Saturday job at the big Woolco up the townie and we opened a bank account, a joint one, a travel fund. Her parents had a bit of money – her Dad had a decent job – and they agreed to lend her some start-up cash, long before all the wedding carry-on obviously.

By summer, we had scraped together more than enough to get us on the road and keep us going for a good while. We figured we would find jobs abroad if and when the money ran out – bar work, grape-picking, that kind of thing. In reality, we didn't know what we were talking about. We didn't have the first clue what awaited us or how we would go about doing any of that in places where we didn't speak the language or know our way around. But our plan sounded almost feasible if we said it quickly and didn't study it too deeply.

Now Wee Mary was depending on it. It was no longer just an escape for her, it was her salvation – and she was counting on me to be at her side and see it through with her. But what about Robert? Robert and me. Had I already scrubbed that vow from the records, the promise I had made to my Mum? Had I wiped it out with one kiss? Had Robert's tears on my shoulder washed it away? Had that kiss wiped out my reason for running?

***

Finally, he phoned me. Wee Mary was still there but she invented an excuse to disappear into the kitchen. Dad, who had been listening dutifully but half-heartedly to our travel plans, found something to do in the garden to give me space. Robert sounded anxious and exhausted.

'Sorry I didn't call earlier. Been all over the place.'

'It's OK, Paddy told me.'

I let him update me, even though I had already heard most of it from Big Paddy and Wee Mary. I made an effort to sound as if I was hearing it for the first time, mainly to delay the real conversation I knew I needed to have with him.

There was a little fresh information. Cammy was to have surgery the next morning – they were going to try and fix his nose. Ross was home, doped with painkillers and gumsy, our heart-throb disfigured. Like Big Paddy before him, Robert relayed that with what sounded suspiciously like relish. Cookie and Karen's Dad were home from hospital too, no serious damage. Cookie and Karen were still going to the caravan in darkest Galloway that night – best out the way, they and their families had agreed. Robert told me he hadn't seen Wee Mary. He had tried her house but no one was there. Without quite knowing why, I didn't let on she was here and felt guilty about it.

News bulletin complete. Here it comes. I braced myself.

'So, Lorna,' he said. 'Is it OK if I come over for a wee while? Or meet you somewhere. Really want to see you. We've got to talk, you know, about us, you and me.'

I bunched my fingers tight and rubbed one eye, then the other, as if trying hard to obscure my vision so I couldn't picture his face. The silence hung between us. I could hear his uneven breathing.

'Look, Robert,' I said, finally. 'I'm really sorry, but maybe we better just leave it.'

'How do you mean?' he asked. 'I thought, you know, last night and everything, before all the mental shit...'

'I know,' I went on, hating this. 'I'm sorry, it shouldn't have happened. I'm really sorry.'

Three sorries in ten seconds. Robert didn't understand and I didn't blame him. I was a long way from understanding myself.

'But it did happen, Lorna. Don't tell me I imagined it cos I know I didn't. It was real and OK, yeah, maybe we didn't plan it but it just happened and it felt right. We've got to at least give it a chance. Give us a chance.'

Come on Lorna, put him out of his misery.

'Robert, listen, there's no point. I'm...'

'Of course there's a point.' He leapt in, trying hard to keep his voice level. 'For Christ sake, I meant what I said last night. I love you, Lorna, and I think you love me or else you're one hell of an actress. And I'm sorry if I'm talking like a really crap, slushy black and white film here, but we can't let this go past us.'

This was so difficult. I said: 'I know you meant it. I know you did. But Robert, I'm, er...I'm going away.'

'What are you talking about?' He sounded frantic now. 'Going away where? When?'

'Tomorrow.' I broke it to him and surprised myself with the schedule at the same time. 'Me and Wee Mary. We're going away. I mean, away away. Out of Scotland. To Europe.'

There, done it.

Disbelief in his voice, then desperation, like trying to grab the wind.

'What, for a holiday you mean? Couple of weeks?'

'No. We're just going travelling, for a while. No, er, proper plan.' I used her, not for the first time, or the last. 'It's my Mum and everything, Robert. I just need to get away for a bit.'

He had questions, of course he did.

'For a while? How, how long? How long are you going to be away? And when did all this happen? I mean, how did you...when did you arrange it? Tickets, passports and all that.'

'Thought we might travel for about six months, maybe a year,' I said. 'We thought...'

He interrupted again.

'A year? Christ sake! Did you say tomorrow? Just like that? Fuck, you've got to let me see you before you go. Lorna, please.'

I couldn't do this, not any more. Not to him, not to me. I couldn't listen to his pleading. It was wounding me, plunging the blade in too deep. I know, selfish, selfish, thinking about myself.

'Listen, I'm sorry Robert. Really, really sorry, but there's just no point. You and me, it's finished, we're over, so forget it, OK?'

I put my finger on the little black button on the phone cradle, pressed down and held it there. I cut Robert off, cut him out of my life. I held the receiver to my face, a dam for my tears.

What the hell had I done?

Chapter 40

September 2001
Take My Breath Away – Emma Bunton

NO, I'm definitely not going. I don't need this, I don't want this. Meeting up with Robert Kane for a cosy chat in a bar in the city centre? Nah, the whole idea is ludicrous. I haven't seen him for what, twenty-five years? No, twenty-six to be exact – 1975 – and I've had a whole other life since then. So has he. I've got nothing to say to him. I don't even know him for Christ sake, and that works the other way round too. My life is OK. It's maybe not that exciting but it's fine, it's ordered, it's uncomplicated. I've got my little house and I don't have any big worries. I've got a decent job, it's steady and I could most probably stay there till I retire if I want to. My health is fine, touch wood. I've become quite an organised little lady in middle age so I don't have any money worries. I do all right, I don't let things screw up my life. I'm happy enough. I am, aren't I?

I made a big effort to get my life sorted and back on track after Mark. Just as I did after my first failed crack at marriage, I went back to Dad's for a while. He was on his own again. Sadie, the woman from the bookie's, hadn't hung around long, not once she discovered how little he had to say for himself and the penny dropped that the long silences weren't a front for hidden depths. Ha, good at this relationship stuff, my Dad and me.

I got myself on to a course for computer keyboard operators at a college in Glasgow, because everybody was saying it was the best thing to get into. Once I got the message that Dad preferred being on his own, I answered an ad on the college notice board and began sharing a grubby flat in Govanhill with two other women a bit younger than me. I found myself living like a slobby student ten years behind everyone else – and I didn't mind it one bit. Mind you, I'd had plenty of practice living in a guddle from sharing a home with Mark. Talking of ex-husbands, Bill, decent to a fault, sent me some money after selling our house in Irvine and deciding I was due a share. My pride made me hesitate about accepting – for about three minutes. So, his generosity, and a part-time evening job in an off-sales, helped me struggle through college. Once I'd qualified, I signed up with a temp agency for a few years before I got into the fiscal's office full-time. Steady job, flexible hours, good pension, decent bunch of folk to share my lunch breaks with. Suited me down to the ground.

I finally made my way back to Cumbride. Well, kind of, because Glasgow had virtually sucked it back in. The new town, built to ease city overcrowding, had been expanding over the years, gobbling up more and more countryside and farmland till it was almost back within touching distance of the mother ship. I saved up a deposit and took out a mortgage on a neat, new-build two-bed semi in Westview, one of the more recent estates and yes, it was called an estate not a scheme, like Cardrum where I grew up. The original, older part of Cumbride had not aged gracefully. It had grown seedy and rundown and wild, as tattered and worn-out and dangerous as the slums and war zones of Glasgow it had been built to replace. Some of the streets were reputed to be owned by gangs and druggies, especially after dark. Outsiders – and even some of the locals – now called the town The Nam, or Vietbride, or Scumbride, as Cookie had dubbed it in his Friends Reunited post. The newer, peripheral estates were decent though. Westview was probably as close to the centre of Glasgow as it was to the Cardrum scheme where my Dad still lived. Sometimes I reckoned I might be living right on top of Cammy's waterfall, but then geography was never my specialist subject. Anyway, whatever the exact location, I am settled and content.

OK, I don't have a man in my life. Well, not really. There is the Bill thing, of course, and yes, I suppose I have to deal with that, whatever it is, sooner rather than later. *Keep saying that, don't I?* The crux of the problem, what makes me put off figuring it out, is that I don't actually know what the Bill thing is. Or if it is anything at all.

He did the smart thing and backed off after what became known, at least in my head, as The Ludicrous Nachos Incident, when I'd done a runner from the restaurant and told his daughter I was unwell. I never did figure out if he was being naive or deliberately disingenuous when he texted that night to ask if I was feeling any better. My terse, *No, in bed*, did not exactly invite a reply or leave him room for manoeuvre. Likewise, my ice-scraper one-word answers when he phoned late morning next day, followed by my blanking his two follow-up attempts that evening.

I think it was a combination of still being angry at him for landing me, without warning, in a situation I wasn't near ready to face – might never have been, come to that – and the way he allowed Bing to take the piss out of him. The anger part first. It took me the bus journey back to Cumbride to not only calm down, but to work out that I was mainly angry because he had made me angry. That is really not like me, honest it isn't. I am not volatile, I rarely lose my temper, I don't even simmer to the boil much. My goal these days is pretty much to stay calm, to drift along on an even keel, to keep myself in check. Pretty boring, eh? So, for him to try and draw me into any kind of relationship with his daughter – unless I was reading too much into it – had riled me, upset the equilibrium, and sorry, but I don't allow that anymore, if I ever did. There was also part of me that resented Bill for not realising – or maybe not considering – how I would react. Not for the first time, I wondered if I was really that forgettable or dispensable.

As for Bing – sorry, petty and childish – Crosby, I was more concerned by what her actions said about Bill, not her. I'm sure this must sound harsh, but I had not developed any feelings about the kid. Wait, I am not made of stone. She is a little girl who lost her mum not so long ago and I, more than most, know what that feels like. I was only a few years older than her when it happened to me, after all. So yes, on that level my heart goes out to her, same as it would for any child in that situation. What I mean is, I felt no particular connection to her. She has been a name on a Christmas card once a year – a girl, not a dog, not a boy – and we had barely exchanged a word before The Ludicrous Nachos Incident blew up in our faces. If Bill imagined that some long-buried maternal instinct would kick in, then he did not know me at all and that lack of awareness was a wound that ran deep. More than that, the way he was so easily manipulated and belittled by a ten-year-old who then mocked him behind his back, screamed to me of a guy who had not changed one little bit. He was still the same mushy, eager-to-please pushover I had, ultimately, been unable to stay married to.

But wait, hold on, who do I think I am to judge? You can take my description, words like mushy and pushover, chuck them at a thesaurus (one of the teenage Robert's most treasured possessions) and call Bill an easy-going, unselfish saint who always puts others before himself. What say do I have in it anyway? I forfeited any right to have an opinion of Bill – or the way he goes about his life – the day I told him we were done. Probably long before that, in fact. More like I gave up that right on one of those long, boring, dark winter nights when I waited desperately for a glimpse of an old boyfriend on telly, and fantasised not just about his kiss and his touch, but about a whole different life. Ah Bill, you are lovely but so so soft. That, though, is not a fault and I have no right to condemn you for it.

I think I quickly came to the conclusion that this whole new thing with Bill was more bother than it was worth. It had started out as a pleasant little interlude, a few entertaining letters, warm Friday night phone calls, a cosy catch-up over coffee. But now it had become a wrinkle, a niggle in my life that I didn't need. Then, of course, in the midst of it all, an echo of our shared past, the spectre of Robert once more intruding on whatever it was Bill and I might have been building. This time round, he was an even more remote, background presence – almost spectral – appearing only in name through my conversations with Paddy, certainly at first, anyway.

I heard nothing from Bill until the school holidays were over, and when he started texting again, once every two or three days, there was no mention of Crosby. It was all very polite and general with bits and pieces of background news, the way it had been when our reconnection first started. *Hope you're well. That's me back at school. See the David Blaine interview? Felt sorry for Eamonn. What about Diana's butler? Did the butler really do it (haha)?*

Then, finally, the phone call. I can't say I didn't know it was coming...but the timing! I'd been thawing out gradually through our text exchanges. Bill was attentive and amusing as always and once more, I found myself starting to enjoy our, our – what was it exactly? Light, remote friendship? Suppose. Carefully, gently, he took it back up a notch.

OK if I phone on Friday?

Like before, I couldn't think of a reason to say No and actually, yes, when I thought about it, it was OK. The Friday night phone call had been part of our routine before the abortive day out with Crosby, and I realised I had been missing it. What I couldn't have factored in was that between times, I'd be ambushed by a cop with a second-hand invite from Robert. By the time Bill called – two nights after Big Paddy's latest visit – there was a fair bit of junk swirling around my head to say the least. So, the last thing I was prepared for was Bill baring himself to me like he had never done in eight years of marriage.

The conversation was innocent and inconsequential at first. He asked a few trivial questions, mentioned a new Ewan McGregor movie I might like, told me he had been encouraged to go after a deputy head's job but still preferred class teaching – the coalface, he called it. Suddenly, not sure where it had come from and with definitely no idea where I was going with it, I felt compelled to say something. Elephant in the room and all that.

'Look, Bill, that day with Crosby, I'm sorry if...'

That was as far as I got.

'No Lorna, it's me, I'm a fucking idiot.'

I nearly dropped the phone. I had never heard churchy Bill use a swear word before. I'm not sure if I actually got any words out or whether it was my sharp intake of breath he reacted to.

'Don't say anything, just listen,' he said, firmly. 'It's what I do. Screw it up every time. Least sign of encouragement and I see stuff that's not there and jump in without thinking it through and make a huge fucking mess.'

'Bill, stop...'

'No, you need to hear this, Lorna. Needs to be said.' He was speaking more forcefully and openly than I could ever remember. 'That day we met for a coffee, yeah? I loved it, loved seeing you again. And after, I was like some clown in a musical. Wanted to jump in the street and punch the air and run up the walls on the way to the station. But see any normal guy, they'd have kept their cool, been patient, waited a wee bit and maybe asked you out for a drink, then dinner the next time.

'Not me though, cos as I said, I'm a fucking idiot. I wasn't even home on the train that day and I had you and Crosby best pals, out shopping together, fighting to get in the loo. Us two getting engaged again. No, really. I'm not surprised you ran for the hills, Lorna. Scare the crap out of anybody with that kind of mentality. Hi, I'm Bill, your friendly neighbourhood stalker.'

How was I meant to react to that? I scrambled for words, but I needn't have bothered.

'Bill, listen, don't...'

'Let me finish. I know I was crap as a husband. Crap as a dad as well, as you saw with that stupid nachos thing. There's something missing. In me, I mean. Jesus, I wish I had more, I don't know, oomph or something. Get up and go, fire in the belly, whatever. And so thick I never saw it coming when I had you, never noticed you were miserable, and for that alone, I deserved all I got.

'But you Lorna, and God forgive me, this is nothing against Gail, God rest her soul... But you were always the one and I don't know, after I met you for coffee that day, I just got this mad idea. And I know, I know I'm not Mr Exciting, the great passionate lover. But I thought, maybe you and me, maybe you don't want to spend the rest of your life on your own either, maybe you'd like a bit of company too. And maybe we could be that person for each other, look after each other.'

I swear I could hear choking in his voice now.

'Except next time, in the next life or whatever, I'll remember and consult the other person first before I get carried away and start making plans for the both of us.'

Bill hasn't called or texted since and I have no clue what happens between us next, if anything. I know it's me who has to make the next move, if there is to be a next move.

It's only been a few days, mind, and I've got the small business of Robert to contend with. But hey, how the hell did this happen? How did I end up in this place after all those years of peace and quiet and solitude and safe existence? From nothing, from nobody, to suddenly two of them. Who needs it after all those years of no serious relationships? All those years when it hasn't bothered me, honestly, it really hasn't. If anything, it has made life easier – or at least simpler. No one in a position to hurt me or mess me about. I'm safe so why should I ever take risks again? Why should I even think about inviting risks again?

Because just supposing I do go along there on Tuesday and meet Robert. It could be a disaster. It could be embarrassing and painful. We might have absolutely nothing to say to each other. I might find him vain and arrogant, full of himself. Huh, he might have a right to be full of himself because look at all he has done with his life. When I think about it like that, I realise there is a good chance he will find me dull, ordinary and small and I might be left with a cold ache, a stone in my chest. Seeing this new full-of-himself, high-and-mighty version will disfigure the person in my head – the lovely guy I knew when I was a kid, the precious Robert I still carry about with me in a small secret file that clicks open from time to time. I'll be left with a horrible, sore feeling inside, the feeling that he thinks I'm a nothing and I think he's too much of a something.

Then of course, it could go a very different way. I might discover that the wonderful Robert that lives in a corner of my head sadly passed away years ago, and in his place is not an arrogant high-flier but a worn-out, self-pitying, middle-aged misery. And that might force me to look at myself and acknowledge that I am a worn-out, self-pitying middle-aged misery...and frumpy besides.

He might look at me and I'll read his thoughts. *My God, what has she done to herself? How could she let herself go like that?* I can't remember when I last thought about how men regard me...if men ever regard me at all. I haven't thought about all that stuff for years. All that stuff that's got nothing to do with me anymore. Why open that can of worms and risk letting it become an issue again?

Then I tumble down a different rabbit hole and wonder what happens if I do meet Robert and there are bigger feelings, but it's all one way. What if something stirs in me? What if I feel that I'd like to see him again, see where things go, but he shuns me, brushes me off, laughs at me? Maybe I'll deserve it. Yes, maybe he has a right to payback after all those years. Why not?

And what about Bill? I cannot pretend that he is not part of the equation. His proposal, if that's what it was – and no, I definitely don't mean it in the

THE FENIAN

marriage sense – was basically about two lonely people providing each other with a degree of comfort. I must admit there have been moments these past few days, my head bouncing around the Robert conundrum, when Bill's so-called mad masterplan hasn't sounded like the worst idea I've ever heard in my life. Certainly less complicated and an easy way of ducking out of making a decision about Robert. Ha, seen that, done that.

While I'm on the subject, does Bill have any bearing on what I do about Robert? Hang on, let me be clear here. Not for a second do I have such a high opinion of myself that I imagine I have some kind of choice here, or that there are two guys ready to draw pistols at dawn over ordinary wee Lorna. It's just, if I do decide to see one of them, is it going to be like, er, no, not cheating, that's ridiculous? Being sneaky then, that's closer.

Actually, you know what would be a whole lot easier? Forget the both of them. Yeah, as if. When I think about it that way, there is no question which one of them would be harder, if not impossible, to purge from my head.

There is something else in this messy puzzle too, and here it comes, hurtling towards me through the years just when I thought it had gone away. The promise. The cross-your-heart pledge I made to Mum. Does it still count after all this time, or is it like those criminals I deal with whose convictions are what they call spent, the bad deeds purged from their records after a certain period of time? In other words, is there a sell-by-date on a promise, even a promise you make to your mother on her deathbed? I was a different person then, just a kid, so surely I can't still be held to it?

Catholics, Protestants, all that rubbish. So many times over the years I have tried to figure it out – the ingrained, unconscious hostility. A hostility that no one has ever been capable of properly articulating to me in a way that justifies the loathing and the poison. Ha, and all of it based on some foggy history from centuries ago.

I keep coming back to the same questions. What does any of it have to do with the here and now? We all live the same lives, don't we? Catholics and Protestants, I mean. We all have the same goals, we strive for the same things – happiness, success, security, a decent home, good holidays, families wanting the best for their children. So I just find it all a bit sad, ridiculous even. Those misty-eyed, angry people who never see the inside of a church from one year's end to the next but keep on fighting hazy, ancient battles in their heads, with a pair of football teams on the frontline, a bunch of overpaid foreign mercenaries as their standard bearers. Sometimes it feels like religious supremacy in this twisted corner of the world is based entirely on the league table with the ironies conveniently shoved to one side.

It was Bill, such a fair man who never showed a trace of bigotry, who filled

269

me in on those paradoxes of the Old Firm's intertwined football histories. Celtic's heyday in the Sixties, champions of Europe, and led to those peaks by Jock Stein, a Protestant and an iron-willed genius ahead of his time who cut through all the religious crap. On the other side, Rangers, crowning their juggernaut, cash-rich dominance of the nineties with an Italian Catholic as their captain.

The way Bill explained it, I couldn't help seeing those fans on both sides, spewing their crap at each other, as nothing more than pawns in a lucrative, never-ending, tabloid soap opera. All the while, it seems to me that the tycoons and money men who run the clubs publicly condemn the extremists while quietly praying the hate never ends. They know the reality because they have a vested interest in it – bigotry is good for business. Bottom line? It's an embarrassment, this exclusive West of Scotland badge of shame.

I remember Martin, our supervisor at work, took us all out one evening just before Christmas. He's originally from the Midlands – Coventry, I think. We finished up in a bar in the city centre. It had been a great night, but our festive high spirits were scarred by a fight that broke out between two of our colleagues. A random, quick explosion punctuated by traded yells of *Hun prick* and *soap-dodging Fenian*.

If that particular F-word was a painful jolt to me, the whole sectarian explosion was an alien concept to Martin.

'Yeah, scrap over a bird, or because some tosser pisses on your shoes in the bog. But religion? Seriously? Who the hell cares?'

My pal Kath goaded him.

'Huh, wait till the rest of us start on you English!'

But really, Catholics-Protestants? It's nonsense. I try to tell myself it's never made a difference to me. Huh, apart from the small matter of screwing up my whole life. I try to pride myself in not letting it be an issue. I tell myself it wasn't an issue with Bill, or Mark. But of course it wasn't, and I can claim no merit points in either case. Bill got me off the hook right away within, what, five minutes of us meeting? He brought it up, about his Dad being a church elder and how he was heavily involved in the Kirk himself. There was no question with Mark either, though it was that other Kirk with him. The day after we met, he phoned me...*Oh for God sake Lorna, be honest after all this time.* OK, I phoned Mark because I was desperate to see him again. He told me, casually, that he might give me a buzz when he got back from Ibrox. He talked about the Rangers from the off, about Catholics too, and even made a joke of it after our first time in the back of his cab. An enquiry in his own delicate, subtle style.

'By the way, tell us I've no' just shagged a Provo.'

THE FENIAN

So what did that mean? Would I have gone on with them, with either of them, Bill or Mark, if they hadn't both made it obvious in their different ways? Was that why I avoided it now, the whole men/relationship thing? Was it really self-protection, a shield against failure and hurt – as I tried to convince myself – or was it to make sure the promise didn't become an issue ever again? Was that promise still lurking and if it was, could I really let it rule the rest of my life? Could I still be held to it? God, I really don't need this kind of brain ache.

That's it. I'm definitely not going to meet him. No way. What a relief that I've made up mind.

***

And then I was there, suddenly, outside that bar. Shit shit shit. I hadn't felt like this in years. Nervous as a kid on a first date.

Come on, go for it. Nah, run for your life.

I hesitated. All I had to do was open the door, and he would be there. I just had to march in boldly and say *Hiya, Robert*. I was about to meet my ghost. Come on Lorna, it's simple. Hand. Door. Push. OK.

Now I was looking at him for the first time in 26 years. In the flesh, I mean, as opposed to that disembodied reporter on the TV news. I spotted him straight away. I'd opened the door but stopped at the entrance, scanning the place quickly. It was pretty busy but there was no mistaking him. Robert, perched on a stool at the bar. BOOM. My chest thudded. Excitement. Terror. Panic.

Go on, state the obvious. He looked different.

I tried to recall the last time, the last time I saw Robert properly. Easy, Karen's wedding. Our dance, our kiss, his sobs, then all the chaos. My great love of less than three months way back in our school days, yet I could recall every single detail of our final moments together.

Now I saw him slightly side-on, his hair very short and speckled with silver. He was wearing a light blue shirt, sober burgundy tie, suit jacket draped over the back of the stool. He was talking into a mobile phone. *You can relax, Paddy, he did get a new one.* I couldn't hear what Robert was saying because I was too far away and the hum of the lunchtime conversation was too loud. I just saw his mouth working rapidly and it looked like a pretty one-sided conversation. He had a serious expression one moment, then a relaxed grin the next. I trembled, realising that even after all this time, the physical mechanics of his face were familiar, the way the smile grew out of his eyes. He had a glass on the bar in front of him, looked like fresh orange. A paper was placed on the bar, open and folded to manageable size. One of the big ones, The Herald or something.

I let the door swing shut behind me and took a step towards the bar. Robert turned his head towards me. He looked expensive, well groomed and assured. If he was anywhere near as nervous as me about our meeting, he was hiding it well. There I stood, ordinary, cursing myself for not making more of an effort with my appearance. You know, first impressions and all that. But then ten minutes ago, I still wasn't coming. Now Robert's eyes locked on mine, just for a split second. I didn't even know if he recognised me. I didn't hold his look because right in that instant, it struck me.

What the hell am I doing here? This guy is a complete stranger. I don't do blind dates.

I spun on my heels and turned to the door. I bumped into a couple on their way in but did not stop to apologise. I bounded down the two or three stairs at the exit as quickly as I could and got out into the street. I breathed in cool, fresh air as I walked away quickly and considered increasing my pace to a run.

Then I stopped again, abruptly. *What the fuck, Lorna? Are you a child? How are you ever going to fix this and move on if you don't face it?*

I sighed and turned back. Right, I decided, I would find some calm, invent it if need be. Walk in there, smile and shake his hand, tell him I'll have an orange juice too...and breathe. He's just another human being. What's the big deal?

I found myself laughing, at myself, at this whole absurd, childish nonsense. I got to the bottom of the steps outside the bar. OK, here goes nothing.

Then bang, the door was flung open again and this time it was Robert bursting through it, his face a grim mask, not even noticing me as I swiftly moved to the side to let him barge past. Unlike me, he really did break into a run, awkwardly climbing into his suit jacket on the hoof and making for busy Argyle Street. He quickly scanned the traffic, raised a hand and then I was watching his back vanishing into a black cab. He had taken about fourteen seconds to disappear from my life again.

Chapter 41

August 1975- June 1976
Happy To Be On An Island In The Sun – Demis Roussos

THE big adventure. I was barely home twenty minutes when Robert phoned. I never did figure out how he knew that I was back after all that time. Ha, that boy should become a reporter! Anyway, there I was, back after the best part of a year, running all over Europe with no pattern, no real aim. Trying to wipe so much from my mind, from our minds.

Wee Mary and me, we'd fled on the Tuesday after Karen and Cookie's wedding. The day before, we ransacked our savings accounts and packed in a frantic rush – just one haphazard rucksack each after all those months of talking in secret and listing the places we wanted to see, but never really believing that we would actually go. But we did and we left without saying proper goodbyes. I tried to explain it to my Dad on the Monday night but he was too busy watching telly, not really listening, not paying attention, so I left him a note in the morning before I left.

Milk in the fridge. Fish fingers for dinner, 20 minutes in the oven, gas mark 6, will do two nights. I'll be in touch. See you sometime. Love L. P.S Don't forget to turn the oven off.

Then we were away without a plan or a route. First bus out of town, ten past five in the morning, watery sun limping along the hills in the distance. Two seventeen-year-old innocents who had never been a hundred miles from home in our lives, and now we were fleeing the country. Coach to London, train to Dover, ferry to Calais. Dead easy when you put it like that. Thirty-six hours from home and we set foot on foreign soil burdened with naivety and ignorance. To us it was a bigger leap than Robert's coffee pal Neil Armstrong had taken.

For the first week we just kept running, jumping any bus or train we thought would take us further away. We were heading vaguely south, or so we

273

thought, our mode of transport determined only by whichever we found first – bus depot or train station. We traded lumps of our savings for handfuls of Monopoly money which we then dumped on counters and pointed to place names at random on destination boards, with only the vaguest notion where these towns and cities were. We'd hold up two fingers, not knowing if we were paying for singles or returns, placing blind faith in the honesty of the ticket sellers. We just kept running and looking over our shoulders. We were running from our ghosts – dead ghosts, living ghosts, ghosts of places, ghosts of events. At least we didn't once consider the old running-away-from-ourselves cliché. Nah, we could put names to who and what we were fleeing – my Mum, Robert, Wee Mary's parents, Karen, Cookie, their parents, Cumbride, the wedding, the carnage, the scandal, the shame. We were consciously putting distance between ourselves and all that.

We had been so excited when we first started talking about this – excited about seeing stuff that had only ever been black and white images on our telly screens. We wanted to see other countries, famous landmarks, how other people lived. It was supposed to be our voyage of discovery but it had turned into an enforced escape. The result was, we ended up letting our first foreign country slip by us in a blur. The cities and towns and landscape of France flashed past our bus and train windows. We touched down only in the dark, where we sharpened our instincts and became experts at finding cheap hotels and cleanish hostels, experts too at giving scary men a wide berth.

We kept up a frantic pace. Romantic-sounding place names zipped by – Lens, Rouen, Orleans, Troyes. With no knowledge to back it up, we convinced ourselves we were getting deeper and deeper into France, not realising we were zig-zagging and worse, going in a circle, plotting a giant Parisien city bypass. Through all those whirlwind first days of our trek, it never occurred to us, not once, that the key was there all the time. All we needed was a map but instead we just followed our noses, trusting an instinct we didn't possess.

We found ourselves in a town called Rheims and caught the first train back out again, bound for a place named Charleroi, which still sounded like France to us. The big signs announcing Belgique were a bit of a giveaway but it felt good – now three whole countries between us and home. Well, three if we counted England as a separate one which, of course, we did. We kept moving, clocking up cities, tasting their character and culture by peeking our heads out of train station exits between departures. Antwerp, Eindhoven, slowing down now, Rotterdam, Amsterdam. Then we stopped. We didn't need to discuss it or come to any kind of calculated decision. We just ran out of steam and knew it was right. It was time to pause, draw breath, rest, take stock. No sign of any posse kicking up dust in the distance behind us. A clutch of countries and two weeks' hard travelling from home – and still no map to show we'd kind of doubled back on ourselves.

That first taste of Amsterdam. We came across a square halfway down a big, broad main thoroughfare. The street was the Damrak. It's famous of course, but at the time it meant nothing to us. We'd had to cross a bridge over a canal next to the station – a real canal with barges and stuff, straight from third year geography – just to get on to the street. First thing we saw in the square – or heard actually – was a piper in full Highland dress. Kilt, sporran, skean dhu, the lot. Probably the locals' idea of Scotland – but not ours. We were new townies so the only pipers we ever saw were on shortbread tins or on the telly at Hogmanay. But we were weary and weak from trekking so we called it an omen and ended up staying for nearly three months before we headed south in search of some warmth. We decided to treat ourselves to a decent hotel for the first couple of nights in Amsterdam, letting the rhythm of the railway drain from our systems. As we queued for guilders at the bureau de change, I sighed and, with a prescience borne purely from impatience and exhaustion, remarked to Wee Mary: 'Why can't all these places just have the same currency – make life so much easier.'

With equally remarkable foresight, she replied: 'Aye, apart from ours obviously. Don't want anybody messing with our dough.'

But the wait was worth it as we checked into a hotel next to the train station and swapped cramped, upright half-sleeps for proper lie-down beds, appreciating properly for the first time in my life what a beautiful thing a mattress was.

Now I was back home in Cumbride, stretched out on my own mattress, my own bed, rucksack dumped on the floor, utterly exhausted.

Homecoming, inevitably, had been a huge letdown. Back on the same old 159 bus from Glasgow in the Scottish summer drizzle. For all I knew, the exact same lumbering blue bus, with its coughing diesel stink, that had carried us out of Cumbride all those long months ago. Last leg of the epic journey.

I don't know why I expected things to have changed but of course, it was all so depressingly familiar. The same drab, concrete mazes, the same houses with premature dampness creeping up their dull-grey, roughcast walls. The town of the future already showing signs of decay, descending inexorably into the kind of depressing, shabby slum our pioneer parents had left behind with such hope in their hearts.

Then another disappointment – no one home. I'd tried phoning my Dad the night before from London but got no answer, so I'd rung Big Paddy's

Mum instead and asked her to pass on the message, told her I was getting the overnight coach to Glasgow and would be home sometime late morning.

But there was no yellow ribbon, no Welcome Home banner strung above the front door, no Dad there to form a solo reception committee. Course he wasn't there. Why did I think for a minute he would take a day off work just to welcome his daughter back from her travels? By instinct, I lifted the doormat and yes, the key was still there where I'd left it. Probably hadn't been touched for the ten and a half months I'd been gone. Always was big on home security, my Dad! I let myself in and immediately, I shuddered. Mum was there, or at least her scent was. I felt her presence. Her coat was hanging there in the hall, her old brown coat, still reeking of fags. Dad hadn't got round to getting rid of it or, to give it a kinder spin, hadn't had the heart to chuck it in the bin. Bus-lagged, train-lagged, ferry-lagged, I felt Mum standing close to me and her name was half out before I caught myself. All those thousands of miles, all those months, yet her spirit, her essence, took two seconds to repossess me.

The house was dark and forbidding, like a museum after closing time, and just as I think I remembered it. But as I threw the curtains open, I sensed there was something not quite right. The place was too neat, too clean. On my regular guilt trips in various foreign beds, I'd pictured Dad spending his lonely evenings here. Sausage supper diet, slag heap of chippie papers growing on the carpet, him stretched out on the settee in his stocking soles, watching telly with a couple of empty beer bottles on the floor by his side, old newspapers discarded, left open at the racing pages. Letting mess and health hazards and chaos creep up on him like a sneaky assassin. I'd half expected to have to get my sleeves rolled up and go to work with the Flash as soon as I got back. But all was in order and it took me only a few seconds to work out the answer – Big Paddy's Mum. She would have felt she owed it to her old friend, to her dear-departed kitchen companion.

I also guessed Dad wouldn't have given her kindly intervention a thought or, perhaps, even have known a thing about it. It would never have crossed his mind to question how his dirty dishes magically climbed from the sink to the draining board each day, how his clever bed sheets folded back into shape all on their own, how his used underpants miraculously replenished themselves and found their way back to the bedroom drawer. I pictured my Dad just rolling along, accepting the solitude, knowing his place, not expecting much out of life. He'd still be loyally grafting away, day after day, with a little bit of lonesome comfort at nights in the shape of grub, telly, beer and the paper.

Still, I was disappointed that he wasn't there to greet me, that he couldn't find it in himself – just this once – to pluck up the courage and ask for a day off, for me. He had done it for Mum, when she was ill. *Come on, not fair Lorna.*

Then my heart soared. I spied a note on the kitchen table with my name at the top in Dad's laborious wee boy's scrawl. He had left me a note and it thrilled me more than it should have. But as I got closer, I saw just two words after my name.

LORNA
GET PIES

Was that what I meant to him after almost a year apart? His only daughter, his own flesh and blood, all he really had left after Mum. Was that all I was? Someone to save him a walk to the shop? But then, who was I to complain about that, or him not being here at all? Me, the dutiful, caring daughter who had left him home alone with his grief and his loss for all those long long months.

Later, after Robert's phone call, I did walk to the shop. The Mace. To GET PIES. It wasn't even ten minutes along the road but I dawdled, desperate to see a familiar face. A Ross, or a Jo, or a Cammy – someone, anyone – to let me know I was home, to let me know I really had been away. But I saw no one. My territory, my streets, my patch, they were empty and bleak, like some plague or chemical warfare had wiped out every last living soul and left the tatty, second-hand Lego intact. The woman in the shop, I thought, she'll know me, she'll remember me. She did. I took the pies up to the till and she reached under the counter. No preamble, no chat, just…

'There's that magazine you asked me to keep for you, dearie. You know, with that guy you said you liked on the front.'

She handed over an old Melody Maker, dated August 16, 1975, with Peter Gabriel on the cover, as if I'd ordered it last week. Had I really been away? Had I just imagined the last ten months? Me, this teenage, female Marco Polo who could order tea and a fried egg roll in six languages. Had anyone even noticed I'd been gone?

I tried to make Dad listen that night. So many memories I wanted to share with him. No great insights, mind, just snapshots. Like the morning I was ambushed by pigeons in St Mark's Square and Wee Mary said it was like that scary Hitchcock film. The toytown trams in Amsterdam with the lady at the back announcing each stop for you through a loudspeaker, as if you were her special traveller. The old bloke in Benidorm with the scary lizard the size of a dog that he took for walks on a lead along the busy front. The family of gypsies – or maybe they were refugees from somewhere – camped in the middle of a roundabout in France, the little waifs on the verge with their desperate faces, thrusting their hands out for coins chucked from passing cars and trucks. The one-legged street entertainer in a Rangers top in Amsterdam. Surely Dad would like this one? He'd been propped up on the pavement playing keepie-up when we first saw him, and was still nodding his ball in the air every time we passed.

But as if making a huge effort, Dad would drag his head slowly to look at me each time I started a new story and pretty soon he would stifle a yawn, his eyes would glaze over and I'd catch him glancing back at the telly or his paper. Eventually, I gave up and slipped out to the hall to phone Bill.

Three days later, I met Big Paddy and finally it felt like I was home. It was Sunday, nearly lunchtime, and Bill had just dropped me off. I had gone to meet his parents down in Irvine and stayed overnight – on my own in the spare room, of course. Bill's Mum and Dad were churchy, heavily involved in the local Kirk, good people. No worries about Mum's promise there. OK, I was weak, I admit it, but it was so much easier. Bill went off to take Bible Class that morning and I stayed upstairs while he was gone, listening to the murmur of his parents' voices down below and feeling awkward, like an intruder or a stranger. I stayed in the room till Bill got back. He had other church duties to attend to for the evening service, so he drove me home in his Dad's car. As Bill pulled away from outside my house, I heard my name being called. OK, bellowed actually. Then Big daft Paddy was lumbering towards me like a cartoon bear. He scooped me up and swung me round like a wee lassie.

'Parlez vous Cumbridy, senora?' he yelled. It felt brilliant. Big Paddy didn't give me a choice but dragged me off towards his house, just along from mine.

'You'll have to come in for a wee while, Lorna. My maw's been pure desperate to see you.'

They wrapped me up and swaddled me. So warm and welcoming round his Mum's kitchen table. Mugs of sugary tea with Big Paddy, his Mum and Dad, even his wee brother, Gerry, all of them indulging me for more than an hour, letting me have the stage all to myself. I told them silly things, inconsequential things. This wasn't Christopher Columbus new world discovery stuff, this was just odd little incidents transformed into memories.

Like the time at the shoe shop in Benidorm. We'd gone there in February, running all the way from surprisingly chilly Milan, well, flying actually – the only time we splashed out on a flight in the whole trip – in a desperate search for heat. Winter sun pioneers, me and Wee Mary.

I needed sandals for the warmer climate and studied the shelves and the prices, trying to do yet another new calculation in my head. We had switched currencies so often by then it was hard to keep up. The shop owner approached or at least, I assumed he was the owner. He was a balding guy who looked like he was in his thirties and I figured he must have heard us talking in English.

He said: 'Yes.'

I replied automatically, pointing quickly at my eyes, then the shelf. 'It's OK thanks...er, gracias...just looking.'

But then he grinned and added: 'No, Yes!'

I didn't understand until he pointed at the long, black, baggy T-shirt I occasionally wore as a summer dress. It was just something I'd thrown on that morning, borrowed from Robert at the waterfall one day and never returned, a souvenir he'd bought at a concert. On the front was the group's snaky logo amidst surreal Roger Dean artwork. I smiled back and the shop guy expanded.

'Yes! Reek Wekmin, Shon Endersun.'

Translation: Rick Wakeman, Jon Anderson, the keyboard player and singer from Yes.

Then he stepped back, put his arms out sideways and started swaying his hips and singing. More Julio Iglesias than heavy rock, turning Robert's prog heroes into a cheesy Spanish cabaret act.

'Kaaa-luss to thee ezh, dun ba a reeba...'

Translation: Close to the edge, down by a river. One of Robert's all-time favourite Yes songs. Oh, sorry Robert. Not songs, movements then.

Big Paddy and his family, bless them, they listened to my stories with endless patience, pulling amazed expressions, laughing at the right bits, making me promise to bring round the photos if and when I ever got round to taking the spools to the chemist.

A bit later, we took off, Big Paddy and me, wandering, retracing our steps. I needed to be brought up to date, to discover where our shelter crew were scattered.

Wee Mary I knew about of course. It was just a few days since we'd parted. Yes, she was lively and fun and capable of the occasional volatile outburst, but mostly she was the most lovable, calmest, best-tempered friend I've ever had. All those months of two on the road, of tight, closed, forced companionship and she made it so easy. She was so switched on and so sensible. The one who kept us organised, found us little jobs in shops and cafes here and there to keep our finances topped up and ticking over. I knew with a certainty that I would never have a friend like her again. Along the way we coaxed each other, nursed each other, tried to heal each other.

Not long into the journey, I told her about the promise – the only person I have shared it with in all those years since that morning when I broke eggs with my dying mother. I poured it all out one night, in one of those dark little

279

coffee shops off the Damrak where, though it wasn't legal just yet, blind eyes were turned to what you inhaled as long as you were discrete. We decided, when in Rome and all that – or Amsterdam in this case – and a little of the local weed helped unlock my secret. I nibbled daringly on a special cookie, as one of our Dutch friends called it, and it was my reluctance to smoke like most of the others that brought up the subject.

I told Wee Mary about Robert, about my Mum, the cross she had thrust on my back.

She never once mocked my feelings of guilt or tried to blind me with logic. Instead she supplied understanding and simple sense across a dozen countries and three hundred-odd days, drip-feeding me her uncomplicated message.

'Just remember, Lorna, you only get the one life. Don't chuck it away.'

I have never felt closer to a person. Not my two husbands and no, probably not even Robert.

But Wee Mary jumped ship just as we were plotting our course home. I understood. She wasn't ready, she was too afraid of what was waiting for her back in Cumbride, or what wasn't waiting. I left her behind in that little port after our day trip to Venice. I got on a bus, both of us too blinded by tears to look at each other one last time or even say goodbye properly. I've never seen her since and still miss her painfully.

As for the rest of the old gang, I'd got a glimpse of two of them so far, but both sightings had only gouged scars on my memory.

On my first night home, I'd given up on Dad and phoned Bill, arranged to meet him up in Glasgow on the Saturday and go meet his folks. I went to bed early, about half-nine, drained and weary, and conked out quickly. But I was woken up by moaning. It was a girl, wailing in what sounded like agony.

'Aw please, gonnae no, please.'

I pulled back the curtain a little, just enough to peek out. It was happening down at the wall – our wall, Robert's and mine. A girl was leaning forward, one hand against the wall to support herself. There was a guy hitting her, slapping the back of her neck, over and over while she begged him to stop. His posture, his build, were familiar and it was confirmed when I caught his face in the street light. I felt sick. It was Ross, our Ross, and he was pummelling the girl. Then he stopped, put his arm round her, helped her along for a few paces then started up again. Whack, whack, whack. I felt ashamed, still ashamed to my core even now, that overwhelmed by tiredness, I went back to my bed and did nothing.

Next morning, I nipped up to Galbraiths, the supermarket in the town centre. I needed to get stuff for the house, things Dad never thought about buying – Brooke Bond, Persil, Ajax, Right Guard, that kind of thing. Stuff that Big Paddy's Mum had taken care off in my absence, or in my Mum's absence to be more accurate. The depressingly desolate townie was busy, waves of people coming towards me. Suddenly, right in front of me, Karen, with her Mum – and she was steering a pushchair. Brilliant, Karen and Cookie's baby! But she blanked me, completely. I tried to tell myself I'd got it wrong, that she just hadn't spotted me among all the faces, but I knew she had. I had walked straight up to her, facing her and grinning, directly in her line of sight. She caught my eye for the briefest moment, then dropped her head and marched straight past me. I turned, saw her back disappearing into the crowd. I hoped Big Paddy would clear it all up. I needed to touch base.

'Where is everybody, Paddy? They all seem to have vanished.'

I told him about Karen, asked if she was back up from England visiting her family.

'No,' he sighed. 'Christ knows what the story is there, but Karen's been home for months. Keeping to herself though – and no sign of Cookie. For all I know he's still down there but I've never heard a peep from him and neither's anybody else.'

Four down – Wee Mary, Karen, Cookie and Big Paddy himself. Six to go. He did his best to fill in the blanks.

ROSS.

'He's been in the wars. Finished up in the hospital. Gerry was telling us, heard it from Ross's wee sister, Trish. Mind of her? Dead nice lassie. I've no' seen that much of Ross lately to be honest, but Gerry says he got a serious tanking yesterday morning. The brother and da' of some lassie he's been seeing, apparently. According to Gerry, Ross is talking about going down south, to England, to get work when he gets out. I know I should go and see him in the hospital, but everybody says he's a right twisted, angry wee bastard these days.'

JO.

'Aye, I bump into Jo now and again round here or up the townie and she's brand new. Kind of splitting her time between the college and working over at her Mum's, know? Always dead pally and got loads to say when I see her and goes on about us all definitely arranging something. But you know what's it like. She's kind of busy with her college pals and her own stuff. We all are.'

FIONA.

'Hardly seen her at all this past year. Head in her books, I imagine, same as ever. But Jo met her, says she's doing all right. Going to uni, Edinburgh, I think, and working dead hard for her exams. No' that she needs to with her brains, know?'

KIRSTY.

'Ach, she's long gone. Away up in Glasgow. Heard she's shacking up with some old bloke. And I mean, ancient – Christ, twenty-eight somebody told me. He's got a restaurant or a club or something and he's supposedly never out the papers, no' that I ever read them. Loaded, but a bit dodgy, so they say.'

Absent friends. I felt an overwhelming rush of sadness. Where was the good news? How had that group of pals singing T. Rex in a circle just last summer disintegrated so quickly and with such seemingly irrevocable force.

We had reached the swing park without realising it, drawn there like homing pigeons. We turned into the shelter, our shelter. Then a shock – squatters had moved in. Just little kids, fourteen-fifteen, proto-punks with torn tights, jeans ripped at the knees, even a spectacular Mohican in there. Designer scruffs, Johnny Rotten wannabes, and they had taken up occupation. They were standing around or sitting on our bench, staring with defiant, sullen faces and growling at us, unwelcoming and aggressive. I recognised Gerry, Big Paddy's wee brother. He must have gone a different way as we dawdled. Ross's wee sister Trish was there too, a pocket blonde bombshell. Good looks obviously ran in that family, I thought, then winced at the memory of Ross a couple of nights earlier. I spotted Gerry discretely let a ciggie drop from his fingers, trying to crush it under his Doc without his big brother noticing.

Gerry scowled and grunted: 'What Patrick? We're no' doing nothing.'

That was when I knew it was definitely over. It had been over for nearly a year but now I knew for certain. We were yesterday's news and there would be no encore, no reunion. Big Paddy was about to confirm that with a devastating finality. We drifted aimlessly, now only two names left that he hadn't mentioned. I already knew about Robert but hadn't let on to Big Paddy. That left only one other.

'So, how's Cammy doing?' I asked brightly, hoping he might have transformed into a superhero against the odds. 'You never mentioned Cammy.'

Big Paddy pulled an emergency stop, like he'd walked into an invisible brick wall. I couldn't read his face. Puzzlement? Shock? Definitely something close to disbelief.

'Lorna, you fucking serious?' he asked, his voice low.

Chapter 42

September 14, 2001
Act of Remembrance – The Proclaimers

RIGHT at this moment, there is nothing more important for Robert Kane than to speak to his son. Usually, when he is back in his hotel room in the evenings, they communicate by email. They both like it this way, keeping in touch electronically. It is part of the balancing act Robert works hard at. It is less intrusive than phoning, saves Jack the embarrassment of Daddy checking up on him if he is with his mates. Besides, his son has not yet completely grown out of that awkward teenage trait of never having much to say for himself on the phone beyond grunts and groans. So emailing is a useful middle ground. To Robert, it has become a thoughtful way of keeping in touch, like writing a letter but with the bonus of two-way interaction. With emails you can rattle off a message in two seconds, or you can take your time, consider what you want to say, read it back before you hit Send, and change things you're not happy with. The advantage over letters is that you can react and respond instantly just like, oh yes, a conversation. Jack's emails are pretty detailed, colourful sometimes, and Robert appreciates the care and time his son takes.

When he thinks about it, Robert finds it hard to believe it has only been, what, four or five years since emails became part of everyday life? Already he cannot imagine what it would be like without them. But then he has always been comfortable with computers, has always taken to new advances with ease and enthusiasm. He has grown up with the march of technology in his and other industries and has been quick to embrace and appreciate the benefits. Sometimes he finds it hard to take in how much and how fast it has all changed in a generation. In weak moments, he gets briefly nostalgic at the memory of feeding paper into his first Smith Corona on the Cumbride paper, and the legions of typesetters and compositors and machine operators that conspired to get his elegantly-crafted chip pan fire stories into print. But then he winces when he remembers clattering away on that same typewriter with the sticky F and having to X-out mistakes and the ink you couldn't get off your fingers for days after fiddling about changing the ribbon. Oh yes, and how photos – black and white, of course – had to be sent off and turned into wooden blocks 48 hours before deadline. Hmm, and not so long ago either.

It is so much cleaner now, smoother, more flexible. Some of his geekier acquaintances – and even a few professional media watchers – are predicting the internet will seriously damage print journalism and could even kill it off, maybe in as little as twenty or thirty years. He is troubled by this because newspapers are where he started and he still has a soft spot for them, even though he has spent most of his career in television. He conjures up reassurance. Cinema newsreels were going to be the death of papers, so were radio and television, yet here they were, still standing. Nah, he is confident they will reinvent themselves one more time and see off the internet too.

Talking of which, his server is up and running and the smooth, mid-Atlantic female voice informs him he has mail. He echoes his thanks out loud in a bad American accent. It is a silly habit and for a second he wonders if there will ever come a day when the machine will respond to his voice rather than the other way round.

It will probably be an email from Jack, or that American music rarities site if they have finally tracked down the old Pink Floyd live bootleg he has been chasing.

He will check later because he has an urgent need to phone his son, even if it does mean interrupting a night out with pals or that delightful Polish girl he has been seeing. Robert needs to make contact, to hear Jack's voice and risk embarrassing the boy by saying out loud that he loves him, to make arrangements to see him as soon as possible. He thinks he will give Paddy a ring later too, just to check in with him.

Robert has switched on the internet to check for updates, the same reason he has pointed the remote at the big telly in the corner of the room. He opts for Sky and feels traitorous but there is no getting away from it – nine times out of ten they are quicker and sharper than the Beeb's own rolling news.

This part of Robert's routine is not so different to the way he spends most evenings at the hotel. If there is no live football on, or it's not Sopranos night, his choice of viewing is usually between news channels. It is a sad reality, he acknowledges, but he can't help himself. He is a news junkie and he needs a fix. Tonight, though, he has an excuse and it is the same reason he is compelled to phone Jack. As the old newsroom saying goes, there is only one story in town. Only one story on the planet, in fact.

THE FENIAN

Robert had made it back to the office from the bar in the centre of town within fourteen minutes of getting the text about a plane hitting one of the Towers. He had immediately joined the throng around the monitor showing the live pictures, the feed he instinctively knew that virtually every TV news operation across the globe would be plugging into right now. This was horrifically compulsive viewing – an aircraft accident at one of the world's most iconic buildings. Or, as of 2.02pm, that is what everyone still believed.

A few of the staff acknowledged Robert and he nodded back without taking his eyes from the image of the flames and smoke billowing from the skyscraper. His first editor back in Cumbride had taught him to never be shy about speaking up when there was something he did not understand, and it was a lesson he had never forgotten.

To no one in particular, he said: 'It's hard to get a grasp of the scale. How many floors are we looking at here?'

Des, the bright young thruster who'd had the initiative to text him on his lunch break, replied: 'Aye, know what you mean. You'll see one of the news helicopters any second and that'll give you an idea. In fact, there's a plane coming in now...'

Use any cliché you like. Hairs standing up on the backs of necks, jaws dropping, scrotums shrivelling, a whole newsroom of experienced and cynical journalists stunned into silence then letting out a collective gasp straight from the pits of their stomachs. If it seemed to take an age for the second hijacked airliner to crawl its way across the skyline before smashing into the other tower block, it could only be that everyone's brain was taking so long to process it. The impossible, the incomprehensible, was happening before their eyes. The most horrific live reality show in history.

It was the senior of Robert's deputies, the one now beginning to show at least flashes of respect and co-operation, who spoke first.

'Put your feet up, folks. This isn't a fucking accident, it's World War Three.'

Robert knew what the guy meant on both counts even if he didn't like hearing it. OK, there might be no formal declaration of hostilities, no trenches, no fighting them on the beaches, no D-Day landings, but what they had just witnessed and what was to come in the following hours, was a clear signal of conflict ahead, a never-ending cycle of terror and bloody revenge and attrition and collateral damage. As for the line about putting their feet up, it might have been a cheap and tired quip from a seen-it-all hack, but it was essentially accurate. There was no question this was the biggest story of their lifetimes, but covering it would have little to do with the Scottish end of the BBC.

Even as the shock was setting in, Robert's brain was racing and he was up and running, rattling out orders to the news desk to start checking which if any Scottish companies had offices in the Towers, whether there were any events in and around the buildings which might have a Scottish connection. Was there any Scottish expertise that might be called upon in the hours and days ahead? By the law of averages, there would be the odd Scot in the buildings or the vicinity, but that was for further down the line. Yes, there was stuff to do but Robert knew that anything they managed to turn up would be a footnote, a brief sidebar to the real story.

Now he is back in the hotel, ready to have his first proper evening away from the newsroom in four days. He has returned a couple of times to shower and change, and get his head down for a few hours, but mostly it has been impossible to tear himself away.

After all, genuine Scottish angles had been emerging. Victims from Dundee and the Hebrides. A Glaswegian mum among the survivors. Scots fire fighters offering to fly out and relieve their heroic New York brothers. Yes, stories that had to be covered but Robert is wary of giving them too much prominence. His instinct tells him it's too much like putting a kilt on a massive global event.

Professional head or not, like everyone else he has found the events of the last few days momentous, terrifying in their scale, shockingly dramatic, almost unbearably moving. He felt himself buckling at the sight of the first jumpers, the office workers driven by ferocious flames to opt for one horrifying fate over another. Like many other journalists restricted to their own patch, he has also found the last few days incredibly frustrating. He has offered practical help and advice to his London and U.S.-based colleagues covering the unfolding story, opened up his contacts book from his stint in the States. He has done his best to check on old friends and colleagues he knows might have had a reason to be in Manhattan, the reality hammered home by watching distraught and disbelieving New Yorkers barrelling along Cedar Street past O'Hara's bar – an old haunt of his – to flee the rubble and dust cloud. All the while, he cannot shed the belief that he should be there, that he should have dashed straight to the airport and got on the first available flight. Envy is probably too strong a word, but he cannot deny a jolt of longing to be among the newsmen whose faces have grown familiar as they try to satisfy the world's never-ending appetite for the latest on the outrage. But he has to accept it. That is not the person he is any more.

In the last few years, he has found it interesting and not a little amusing to discover how quickly people forget you when you stop appearing on TV. He doesn't often get the looks anymore, the questioning, uncertain glances from strangers in hotel bars and supermarkets. Not that he ever got the Carol

Vorderman or Jonathan Ross-type instant recognition. He never thought of himself as a TV star and the idea of being called a celebrity would have made him cringe. When Robert was on screen regularly, you weren't really supposed to notice him, he was never what it was meant to be about. The important thing, the only important thing, was the story. Same as bylines in newspapers. Just as no one ever really noticed the reporters' names on stories in the papers except other reporters, Robert's policy had always been that if no one could recall his name ten seconds after the bulletin had ended, then he had done his job properly and kept the focus firmly on the story.

Thinking of bylines reminds him again of where *Robbie* came from. He had resented it at first, when a sub editor on the Record in Glasgow rechristened him Robbie and explained it was faster and snappier than Robert. Rob Kane was too staccato, Robert Kane was too much like a broadsheet windbag, the world-weary sub had explained. Now Robbie Kane, that had rhythm. So it stuck and gradually he got used to it. In a funny way it helped him jump into character at work then revert to the slower, more mundane pace of Robert with friends and family. Somewhere along the line the Robert-Robbie boundaries got blurred then faded altogether and now he answers to both without giving it a thought.

He allows himself a brief smile at the memory of the sidelong glances he used to get from folk when he was on the box every other night. He could tell some people were curious when they saw him at the cheese counter in Safeway, or at a petrol station, or in the pie stall queue at the football. They recognised him, they knew they did, but they couldn't place him. Occasionally, they would approach and ask him questions.

Sorry to bother you, pal, but I know your face from somewhere. Did I meet you at my brother Alan's wedding last year? You a mate of his or was it the bride's side or what?

Or.

Scuse me, my wife's convinced you were staying at the Jacaranda in Tenerife same time as us last October. That right?

Very occasionally, just for the hell of it, he says Yes, and sees how long he can bluff it out.

Of course, there is a tiny bit of a hangover from his sixteen or seventeen years as a bit-part player on television. Robert still gets the odd look. Ha, there was that woman outside the bar at lunchtime on Tuesday. Attractive, he seems to recall, though he only got the briefest glimpse. But she definitely stared for that short moment while he manoeuvred around her. Now he remembers something else. Even though he had already put his news-head on after getting word about the first plane, something about her made him smile as he jogged towards the road to grab a cab. About his age too, or more likely he is flattering himself. He tries to put it into context because life has been crazy these last few days.

Oh man! Oh fuck! He feels his scalp tighten, his stomach lurch. Lorna. Christ, of course. That's why he had been at the bar in the first place. He was supposed to be meeting her. The woman outside, at the door. Surely not?

Slowly, the pieces are starting to fit, now that he has put a little distance between himself and the nightmare of New York. Yes, he had been waiting for her, trying to keep a lid on the nerves. Convinced that she wouldn't show. Convinced she would prove what he has always known – that she was always so much smarter than him. Ha, worm, can of. What had he been expecting anyway, a miracle? Had he really thought he could roll back the years?

But now he is niggled by that moment of fleeting recognition, if that's what his memory really is telling him. Maybe it was the other round, so he desperately tries to bring the face of the woman outside the bar into focus.

So, what now? She is part of the reason he had been planning to call Paddy. Yeah, of course he wants to talk to his big pal for his own sake, same as so many other people have been desperate to connect with their loved ones after such a defining, off-the-scale tragedy. But he had also been intending to call off the dogs, to tell Paddy he is sorry for involving him in the whole crazy Lorna business and that he won't hear her name from him again.

Fuck. Maybe he is wrong, maybe it wasn't her at all. But what if...?

Come on, he tells himself, get your priorities straight. He phones Jack, but the boy is having a coffee with Katya and promises he'll call back later. Big Paddy isn't answering. Probably on duty.

His mind in overdrive now, Robert paces the room, fights the latest urge to nip out and buy a pack of fags. He checks his work messages and tries to concentrate on Sky News but it appears there is nothing immediately fresh happening, just the latest batch of talking heads searching for something different to say.

It will be a while until Jack returns his call, so he decides to check his emails – private rather than work this time. There are five new messages, one from Ruth and the rest from the same email address which he doesn't recognise: lmaxwell14@hotmail.com. He hesitates then starts tapping his mouse pad with two fingers. Wait a sec. Wasn't Maxwell what Paddy told him Lorna's married name was?

He panics, which is a very big deal indeed. Very rarely has anyone ever seen Robert Kane panic, especially not in his working life. Everyone who comes across Robert/Robbie has roughly the same image of him. To colleagues, friends and family, he is Mr Confident, the consummate professional. Calm under pressure, always making the right moves, always reliable and always delivering. If only they knew. Luckily for him, the jangling self-doubt has almost always stayed beneath the skin, even when he has had to wind himself up for another piece to camera. Another performance by that outwardly sure and steady alter ego.

But now, sitting alone, trying to bring himself down from the adrenalin binge of 9/11, staring at a bunch of emails from a distant lost love, he is utterly deserted by Mr Confident.

He hesitates. He is in a blind funk. Is this really the woman who ripped open that jagged hole that has never been properly mended? The woman who has stalked his thoughts for his entire adult life?

Yes. It is her. She has finally broken cover.

Chapter 43

June 1976
Heart On My Sleeve – Gallagher and Lyle

B IG PADDY stared at me hard, as if to double-check my question about Cammy was genuine. He saw that it was.

'You telling me you really don't know?'

I shook my head, not yet taking Big Paddy's build-up too seriously.

'Aw for fuck sake,' he groaned, the pain palpable.

'What?' I said, still no clue where this was going but suddenly realising, from Big Paddy's expression and tone, that it was major. 'What's he done? Not in jail, is he? God, he's not gone and got some lassie pregnant? Or, no, shit, wait, not Mary's mum? Tell me she's not had his...'

'Lorna,' he jumped in, turning his face to me and grabbing my arms tightly. 'Cammy's deid.'

The ground seemed to give way, like I'd stepped into quicksand I hadn't seen coming. The edges of Big Paddy's face shimmered. A heavy pulse pounded in my head and I felt myself start to tip over. Big Paddy's manacle grip was all that kept me upright. I couldn't take it in. Cammy. Our wee, helpless, wicked, lovely, pain-in-the-arse, whining, hilarious Cammy. Images flashed. The day at the baths when he cut the other guys down to size. Him spooning out beans to us, kidding on it would take the booze smell away. His small, cool hand touching me for the first time. He couldn't be dead. It was just, just, impossible. It didn't make sense. He was only young, like us. We were just getting started.

Then I saw Mum again, running across the sand in Millport, skirt swaying in the sea breeze, laughing with her witch's cackle, crooning softly in a halo of blue smoke, crushing a clenched fist to her chest as she coughed out pain, dabbing egg yolk from her ear lobe. Oh no, no, no, please, not more death.

'Last September it was, just a few weeks after the wedding. Fuck, how can you not know this, Lorna?' Big Paddy was clearly hurting at the prospect of going through it again. 'We're up the Stakis, in Ravenshill, know? Me, him and Ross. It's Cammy's round, well, the first round he actually ever bought, cos he was always bleating he was skint. So, this night, we're all pure rooked and Ross threatens he'll pick him up by the ankles and shake his scrawny wee carcass till the money falls out. Cammy finally comes clean he's got a wee bit left from his buroo. Fiddles about in his pocket and eventually puts a greasy fifty pence piece on the table with bits of oose stuck to it, and we chuck in our smash.

'Anyways, off he goes and gets the drinks in, and he's trying to juggle three pints at once to save himself a double journey back to the bar, lazy wee shite that he is. Me and Ross's eyes are fixed on the bevvy, in case the prick spills any and if he does, it's coming out his pint. Halfway to the table, we see the glasses and the beer suddenly fly up in the air, except it's all like, in slow motion. Then we realise Cammy's gone down and he's hit the floor like a pun of mince, so we're calling him all the stupid cunts – oh, sorry, pardon my French, Lorna – thinking the wee tube's slipped in a puddle of beer or something. But he just lies there, arms stretched out, staring up at nothing. Finally bought his first round and never got a sip of it. That doing he got, mind? From Wee Mary's old man, at the wedding...'

I was reeling. This was staggering, shocking, but it didn't make sense.

'No Paddy, that's not right. He was fine, he was OK before we went away. You told me yourself, he was sitting up in bed, telling you all about him and Wee Mary's Mum. Remember? Her and him, out in the car park. You told me, you told me...'

I was grabbing at a memory and trying hard to put my faith in it, as if the hard evidence I remembered so clearly could rearrange the truth and bring Cammy back to life.

'Naw, you're right enough,' Big Paddy nodded. 'He did seem fine after and aye, he was up and about in a matter of days. But turns out he had something wrong inside his brain, know? Can't remember what they called it. Some kind of weakness, like a brain thingwy just waiting to happen or something. Haemorrhage, think that's the word they used. I'm no' really clued up on the medical jargon.'

I thought back to the wedding night, the rage that had exploded, Cammy curled like an unborn baby as kicks rained in on his head.

'So what happened to Wee Mary's Dad?' I asked, thinking of my friend back in Italy and realising she didn't know the half of it. 'He must be in the jail then.'

'Aye, he is right enough,' Big Paddy muttered, darkly. 'Got four year.

Reckon he'll be out in two for good behaviour.'

'Four years for murdering Cammy?' I was incredulous. That didn't sound anything like justice. 'That all he got? How come?'

'Yeah, four year,' he echoed. 'Except, they didn't do him for murder. I went to the court and got kind of pally with one of the cops who was there that night. Decent bloke, know? Imagine that, eh? Chatting away with a pig and me thinking they're all wankers as well. Anyway, sorry, he explained it to me. They called it…hang on till I get it right…capable homicide, I'm sure it was. Kind of means Mary's old boy was to blame for Cammy's death…he caused it right enough, but he didn't mean it, didn't intend to kill him. The defence says this brain thing Cammy had could have happened at any point. A ticking timebomb, the lawyer called it. The kicking he got might have brought it on a bit faster, but nobody could be sure, nobody could prove it. Mr Webb got all kinds of good character references as well, know? Like Karen's dad, he spoke up for him. And he was full of remorse, mitigating circumstances, all that shite.'

In that single moment, it felt like I had lost two people for good. Poor Cammy, dead like his wee brother and sister. And Wee Mary. I couldn't possibly tell her this. If I did, she would never come home, I knew she wouldn't. But how could I not tell her? I had promised to write. What was I going to say now?

Actually, it was like I had lost three people in the short time since I'd got home. But suddenly, the whole girlfriend-boyfriend thing seemed so trivial and Cammy's death at least gave me some perspective.

Big Paddy seemed keen to switch the conversation. More a way of gulping down the loss of Cammy, I was sure. Knowing his character, his sense of loyalty, he would have felt it his duty to follow his pal's story to the bitter end and I wondered how many times he had gone over it since for the benefit of others. Perhaps I was the last and he could finally draw some kind of line under it.

'Oh aye,' he said, forcing a smile. 'You'll be wanting to hear all about the great Robert.'

Dredging up effort from somewhere, he started brightly enough but it soon became clear his heart wasn't in it.

'No' really seen him much either over the past year to be honest, but I bumped into him a couple of weeks past, up the town centre. Never recognised him at first. He walked up to us and for a second, I thought it was one of they bloody Jehovah's Witnesses. That's what I said to him – *stick your Holy Joe shite up your arse, pal.* I had actually realised it was him, by that time, but still. Anyway, he's got his hair all chopped off – it's all kind of short and neat – and he was wearing a suit for Christ sake. Said he'd just been for an interview...'

Big Paddy trailed off as if waiting for me to hit him with follow-up questions, but I didn't have to. The haircut was the only bit I didn't already know about.

***

As I said, a mere twenty minutes home from my big adventure and this love I'd run away from was back, on the phone, and sounding so excited, so joyous, like he was about to burst out of a box on a spring.

'Wow Lorna! Wow wow wow! Can't believe it, you're really home. How you doing?'

I'd been preparing for it, I'd rehearsed it, but now I'd forgotten my lines, my mind scrambled by his enthusiasm. I'd been so sure, I'd been so resolved. All I had to do was tell him about Bill.

Bill. Was he my easy way out? I wasn't sure how I really felt about Bill yet, how real it was. Robert's voice was all it took to send my doubts soaring.

I'd carried my virginity all over Europe – not without difficulty, I confess. I'd resisted Roland the charmer in Amsterdam, big sexy Gunter in Frankfurt and, especially, gorgeous, soulful Toni in Milan. All those miles, all those months, I'd been saving it, just in case. Then, with home almost in sight, I'd given it away without a second thought to a guy who lived an hour down the road from Cumbride. We'd both postponed our homecoming after hitting it off on the ferry and stayed an extra couple of days in London, the last of our cash – bar the bus fare – put together and splurged on a fleabag hotel in Belgravia. There had been no big fanfare, no tremors, just a gentle, quiet, coming together and it was over so quickly I hardly knew it had happened. Bill was so grateful, as he always would be, and guilty because he took these things so seriously. It had happened too easily and too swiftly for him and his religion was always there, watching over him and tut-tutting in the background. The Kirk, that had been established early on with the swift mention of his Dad being an Elder. And already, he'd invited me down to meet his parents. It was all so fast, as if there was an inevitability about the whole deal. But still, it would solve everything. No need to worry about my promise to Mum. An easy out with Robert too.

But now here was Robert buzzing on the phone – plus the echo of my assurance to Wee Mary that I would follow my heart and lay Mum's promise to rest once and for all. That had been fine out there in the sunshine, far away from home, when I was warm and mellow, when I couldn't hear Mum's voice – or Robert's. But now I was back and Mum's coat, still thick with the smell of her cigarette suicide, was hanging a few feet away from me down the hall.

This awful, awful decision. I was too young for the weight of it. My travels hadn't grown me the experience or the equipment for such a life-defining verdict.

Robert blitzed me with questions, his instantly familiar voice sang to me again and I wanted to give in there and then. I wanted it so much, wanted desperately to run to him. At the same time, part of me prayed – and OK, dreaded in equal measure – that he would let me off the hook by mentioning some amazing new girlfriend, though I knew instinctively it wasn't going to happen.

I stalled. When did I ever do otherwise?

'Slow down, slow down,' I said. 'Christ on a bike, you're a thousand miles an hour. Tell me about you, I want to catch up. I've missed so much. What's happening? You going to uni?'

'No,' said Robert, happiness in his voice. 'Can't be bothered with all that. I need to get out there and get on with real stuff. I've got a job on the wee paper, The Courier. Trainee reporter, start a week on Monday. College on block release next year.'

'That's brilliant.' I was impressed and so genuinely pleased for him.

He seemed physically incapable of slowing down and carried on talking at high speed. He was fired up, wired.

'So listen, you fancy meeting up? I could come round later...unless you're too knackered after all your travelling? Maybe tomorrow...'

Crunch time. Don't think about. Just say it. Huh, as if.

'Er, I am dead tired and I've got a bit of shopping to do, but yeah, if you like. I'll maybe collapse for a wee while this afternoon. Come up later if you want or I'll meet you at the shelter or something.'

'Fantastic.'

No, Lorna. You can't carry on like this, it's not right. Come on, do it.

So I did. It just came out.

'But Robert, listen to me for a second, OK? I've got to tell you something first. Thing is, I'm er, I'm sort of seeing somebody.'

'What?'

The last word he ever spoke to me. I kicked open the trapdoor and let him drop. 'Yeah, I've met this guy.'

The phone went dead. From his end this time.

Chapter 44

September 11-14, 2001
Turn Off The Light – Nelly Furtado

TO: kanerob@yahoo.com
FROM: lmaxwell14@hotmail.com
15:58. 11/09/2001

Hello Robert, it's been a long time. A very long time. (Sorry if you prefer Robbie but I still think of you as Robert.)

First, please forgive me for taking the coward's way out. Putting all this in an email, I mean, instead of telling it to you face to face. You see, there are some things I am embarrassed about, have been for an awful long time in fact. But I feel I owe it to you to tell you. These are things that I would find very difficult to say to you, so it's probably easier that I can't see your reactions. Well, easier for me. Selfish, I know.

Before I go any further, please go easy on me if what I write here doesn't make an awful lot of sense and comes out as a big jumble. I know words are your big thing, but I am just making this up as I go along and hoping that you can figure out what it is I'm trying to say. Also, this is my first ever email apart from ones at work – on my brand new email account which I have opened just so I could send this. (I hope you feel privileged!!)

I know, I know, I'm scrambling around here. I'm stalling. I bet you noticed. You were always quick to spot when I was playing for time. Remember? It's just, I don't really know where to begin.

All of a sudden I feel stupid because I'm supposed to be a grown-up and here I am acting like I'm all in a state about a daft wee boyfriend-girlfriend thing from my school days. Ach, what the hell, here goes.

TO: kanerob@yahoo.com
FROM: lmaxwell14@hotmail.com

MIKE KERNAN

Excuse the interruption. I'm in the big library in Cumbride. Not the one we used to hang about in sometimes when the weather was rubbish, where you and Cookie once thought it was a great laugh to tear out the last pages from books to annoy folk. Ha, Robert Kane the vandal. This is the new library that opened about ten years ago. Hey, guess who I spotted a wee while ago? Do you remember Karen, from the monkey bars? I'm sure it's her and I seem to remember hearing that she worked here. Anyway, it took me so long to set up the email and find my way around this keyboard that my computer hire ran out, so I had to go and buy a coffee to get change. (Why am I boring you with all this inconsequential nonsense? Playing for time again, I suppose!!)

Where was I? Oh yes, I was about to mention Paddy. I've been talking to him a lot these last couple of weeks and he's been telling me stuff about you. Don't be too hard on him. He's probably said more than he wanted to or meant to, but you can blame me for that. I put pressure on him. Turned the screws. (What was that thing you used to say? Oh yeah, I must have used my wicked womanly ways!!) Anyway, this whole thing, what I've got to say to you, is mostly about guilt and me taking the blame for stuff so I suppose a little more guilt doesn't make much difference.

Sorry, back to the point. Paddy has been telling me that you still think a lot about the old days, you know, when we were at school and hung around in that shelter in the scheme. I'm dancing around it again, aren't I? So let me get to it. Paddy told me you think a lot about us, you and me, and that is what I feel most guilty about. I mean, that you still blame yourself for what happened to us way back then, the way we broke up and everything.

So here's what I've got to tell you and I want to make it as plain as I can. IT WASN'T YOUR FAULT. Got it? None of it was. You didn't do anything wrong. IT WAS ME. IT WAS MY FAULT. ALL MY FAULT. Please believe it.

(Should I go back and change those capital letters? Does it make me look like a crazy person? Ha ha, maybe I am!!)

The only other person I have ever told any of this to in my life is Mary Webb. Do you remember her? We called her Wee Mary. It was when we ran away to Europe together after we left school. I told her then and now I am telling you.

What happened to us, to you and me, was to do with a daft promise I made to my mother. It was a promise she asked me to make to her on the day she died. Actually, she didn't just ask, she begged. I feel so ashamed and so stupid, writing this down now, seeing the words on the screen in front of me. You see, it was all to do with Catholics and Protestants. My mother wanted me to promise her that I would never get serious about a Catholic and definitely never marry one. Not that I'm saying we would have got married or anything. (Embarrassing moment!!) I just want you to know exactly what it was all about and I don't want to leave anything out. (If you are still reading this far!!)

You've got to believe me, Robert. All that stuff, religion, Catholics, Protestants, it doesn't mean a thing to me. Honest, I swear to you, it doesn't. I almost typed something daft, like some of my best friends are Catholics. But it's not even like that. It's the whole thing, religion. It just isn't an issue with me. My friends, the girls at my work – I couldn't tell you whether they are Catholics or Protestants or Muslims or Klingons or whatever. It just never comes up. I couldn't care less and none of the others do either. We don't even talk about it.

But I was just a wee girl and my mother begged me to make a promise to her and then she died, on the very same day. Just a couple of hours later, in fact. That promise was the very last thing she ever asked me to do – the single, final memory I have of my mother. Sometimes I think it wouldn't have mattered what the promise was. She could have made me promise to wear nothing but purple shoes every day for the rest of my life. It was just that, well, she asked me to promise her something just before she died and I didn't think I could say no, then after that, I didn't think I could go back on it.

That's it, Robert. That last sentence. The whole thing right there in a nutshell. I don't think I've ever spelled it out to myself as simply or as clearly as that.

The thing is, she went off and left me, without giving me the chance to talk it through with her. So whenever I thought about my Mum and about the day she died, the promise was there too. It was right there at the front of my head, this big thing I had to do. My mother's dying wish, for God sake.

I really really hope you understand. (Let me know if you do because I'm not sure I ever figured it out myself!!)

Thing is, what was I meant to do? Was I supposed to decide, my Mum only made me promise one single thing to her in my whole life, but what does it matter, she's dead, she'll never know?

I'm sorry, but I couldn't be like that and that was why I shoved you away. That was the only reason, nothing else. It wasn't anything you said or anything you did. I want to make that clear. Please, please believe that because I tell you, I hated myself for it. I wanted to give in so much because I did love you, Robert. We might just have been kids, but I did believe it was the real thing. (Oops, did I really write that? I am tempted to go back and take it out but I promised myself that I would be honest. See? I'm still good at keeping promises!!)

Paddy says you have never forgotten all that stuff and still think about it sometimes. OK, you think about it a lot, he says.

That's the bit I can't get my head round. I've watched you loads of times on television, Robert, and you're great. So clever, so confident. Honestly, I was so proud of you from the moment I first saw you on the news. (Actually, I was proud of you long before that.) But seeing what you became, that guy who could talk on the telly and interview all those big important folk...when I add that to the boy I remember, it doesn't add up. That didn't come out right – I don't mean how you performed on the telly didn't add up. What I want to say is, I would have thought you were too big to let all that old rubbish get to you. I just can't picture you getting hung up about stuff that happened when you were still at school. (Is this making any sense?)

But if it is true, then let me tell you this, you're not the only one. I've never forgotten about it either. You wouldn't believe the number of times I've thought about it, the promise, over the years, and hated myself for it. Hated my mother for it too. I mean, actually cursed my own mother, my own, poor dead wee Mum.

I've played that day back in my head over and over, and wished I could turn back time and go back there and do things differently. My Mum made me go to school the day she died. If only I had defied her. I wish I had stayed at home with her and talked to her, talked it all through, that promise she begged me to make. The number of times I've thought, why couldn't I have been stronger, even in the face of her illness? Why didn't I stand up to her and say, No, I can't do it, Mum. I should have said to her, sorry, but it's just not right.

But how do you do that, Robert? I didn't know how then and I'm not sure I would even know now.

Think about it. A woman is lying in bed dying, but not just any woman, your own mother. She is begging you to do something, just one wee thing according to her, and it's so easy to say Yes and so hard to say No, because whatever you think about what she is asking, it's someone you love and you know she is going to die. You know she hasn't got long. How do you refuse? How do you say, no, get lost, get stuffed, you're wrong, then turn your back on her and walk out of the house, knowing you will very likely never see her alive again? How do you do that?

I don't know, maybe other folk could, maybe you could Robert. Maybe it was just me and I didn't have the guts.

THE FENIAN

I couldn't kid myself on either. That promise wasn't some airy-fairy, hypothetical thing, about some situation that might or might not ever come up in the future. It was about you. You were the Catholic, Robert. Or the Fenian, as my mother so delicately put it.

But that was then and this is now, so what about now? Where is that promise now? Does it still mean anything?

I try really really hard not to think about it anymore. I haven't thought about it for God knows how long. Not until all this stuff came up again, talking to Paddy about you and everything. In fact, and this is dreadful, I don't even think about my Mum much these days. I sometimes go for years without thinking about her and then, when I do, I try so hard to remember all the great things about her. But the memories of all the good times are soured by the one she left me at the very end, on the day she died. I'm pretty sure that's why I try not to think about her. Why I block her out.

I know, I know. I'm ducking the issue again, the important one.

TO: kanerob@yahoo.com
FROM: lmaxwell14@hotmail.com
17:40. 11/09/2001

Sorry, I had to take a break. I couldn't concentrate for two folk near me raving on about planes crashing into buildings. Must be a new movie or computer game or something. They've gone, so it's quieter now.

So, back to that issue I've been dancing around. It's about that promise and what it means in the here and now. Would I break it? (Don't get the wrong idea. I'm not going to embarrass you, or myself, again!! I'm not talking about you and me, of course I'm not, just the principle of the thing.) The answer is, or the lack of an answer is, I don't know. I really don't know. I just try not to think about it. I can tell you that I look back now and it seems so, so stupid and petty. But now that it has all come back up again, it makes me wonder, would it be an issue, like, if I met someone else? Maybe that's why I don't bother now – seeing people, I mean. (Or maybe that's more to do with the fact that no one ever asks me anymore!! Or practically no one, but that's another story I don't need to bore you with.)

There you go Robert, you always had that knack, didn't you, that way of making people open up and tell you more than they set out to? Here I am doing it again – and we're not even face to face. Ha, it's Lorna Maxwell's true confessions via a computer screen. Is that what makes you good at your job? Or maybe you missed your true calling and you should have been a priest. You'd be good at confessions. (I can remember one or two things you'd have to confess yourself!!)

299

As I mentioned at the start, I have never written an email before that wasn't about work, so I don't know what the rules are or if there are any rules. Like how long they are supposed to be, or if you are allowed to spout on so much. I probably shouldn't worry, I'm positive you'll have got fed up and abandoned my rubbish ages ago.

Whether you are still reading or not, there is one more thing I have to get off my chest, one thing I am absolutely positive about. That promise about Catholics, it was nothing to do with why I didn't meet you today.

I did come, you know, to that bar. I was there. I stood at the door, I peeped in, and I almost marched straight up to you. I saw you sitting there – you look good, Robert! You suit the short hair. (Bit different from how I remember you!!)

I walked back out again. Stage fright, butterflies, call it what you like. I might have changed my mind though, and come in after all but I didn't get the chance because you took the decision out of my hands. I hung about outside the bar for a moment thinking about it. (Ha ha, that reminds me of the Lumberjack Song you and Cookie were always singing!!) Anyway, I was telling myself not to be so stupid, just to walk in and say Hello. I still hadn't made up my mind but then you came dashing out and rushed away and I figured you'd decided us meeting up was a daft idea, so that settled it.

But that's what did it, you see. Sorry, talking in riddles again. It was your hair. That was why I hesitated and turned back. It was the short hair and the fact it was kind of silvery. (I don't mean that in a bad way, honest, you really suit it!!) But I glanced over at you and it suddenly hit me that the person on that stool was not who I had come to meet and it made me feel ridiculous. I am a woman of forty-three, an office worker, a middle-aged divorcee, and I realised I had turned up for a date with a seventeen-year-old boy. I felt like some gruesome cradle snatcher, like I had turned into Mrs Robinson come to meet The Graduate. Sad, eh? I hadn't gone there for a reunion with this old friend Big Paddy has been telling me about. No, I came looking for a boy I know – or used to know – with his black T-shirt and his love beads and his straggly dark hair. I was probably expecting that old army coat of yours to be draped on the back of your chair, not a suit jacket.

I just felt so stupid. Again. Stupid and more than a wee bit embarrassed.

And what about you Robert? (Sorry, I just remembered you telling me that I should never start a sentence with the word and!!) Anyway, what were you expecting? A schoolgirl named Lorna Ferguson with shiny black hair down to her waist in a tank top and purple cords? I tell you this much, I'm not Geronimo's daughter any more. Remember you called me that once? (Not that I ever thought I was!!)

THE FENIAN

I can't help thinking, see you and me Robert, we're as bad as each other. If what Paddy says is true, then we've never really moved on properly since we were sixteen or seventeen and now our lives are half over – probably more than half over. It is long past time we both moved on but maybe we never will, maybe we've left it too late. I mean, what were we thinking? Did we imagine we could reach back all that way, recapture that time? Did we really think we could possibly be the same people, older versions of two daft kids who thought they were grown up and thought they loved each other? OK, I more than thought it, I know I really did, but it was an awful long time ago. (Sorry, I have no right to speak for both of us, so change the we to I!!)

Bottom line, we don't even know each other anymore. Yes, I know, I've seen you on TV and Paddy's filled in some of the blanks – and I'm sure that works both ways. But I don't know the person I saw in that bar today and you don't know the present-day me. We are complete strangers, Robert.

Look, maybe I've got this all wrong, maybe I'm reading way too much into all this and getting carried away. (See, some things never change – you used to say I had John Lennon syndrome, i.e., I was a dreamer!!) Probably these were just my silly ideas and all you wanted was a quick catch-up chat then walk away and forget about it. And yes, of course, it would be good to see you, to get together and talk about the old days and have a big laugh and a joke about it. Talking of old days, did you know that our wall is still there, amazingly enough, because so much else has changed in Cumbride? I saw it just last Friday when I was visiting my Dad. Do you remember our wall? Just down from Paddy's house, it was. There's another thought – maybe it would be nice to have a night out with Paddy and his wife. After all, Paddy is what we have in common right now. It's as if he is our link with each other. But it's a backwards link. It's two lines stretching way way back to a point in time that's so long ago it's maybe not even there any longer.

God, this is such a mess. So many strands and random thoughts. I hope you can understand even a little bit of what I'm trying to say here. (Good luck with that!!)

The thing is, Robert, I know hardly anything about you and what do you really know about me? Do you know that I was married twice? I married one guy because he reminded me of you, then I married another one because he couldn't have been any more different. (It took years for that to occur to me but I still haven't figured out the why!!) Talking of which, my ex has been back on the scene. My first one. We've even met up a couple of times. For a little while, I thought it might work out between us again, but I know now for definite that it's not going anywhere. Believe it or not, all this stuff with you has made me realise that it would have been for all the wrong reasons.

301

(Why am I even telling you this??)

I think that when I get right down to it, I feel a deep, aching sadness, a sense of loss for two people who don't exist, who never got a chance to exist. I mean the people we might have become – you and me, Robert – if things had been different.

Look, I've rambled on far too long and this is all becoming a bit heavy and I'm sure you've got better things to do than read all this garbage. Basically, all I want to say is this: If all that stuff, you know, you and me, if it really is still bothering you after all this time, then stop, don't let it. It's ancient history, just silly kids' games and I mean it, it was down to me, not you. All my blame. You're off the hook. End of story.

Look, Robert, if you still want, maybe we could meet one
oh my God I've just heard

TO: kanerob@yahoo.com
FROM: lmaxwell14@hotmail.com
09:02. 12/09/2001

I will make this very quick. I am so embarrassed. I must have been the only person in the world not to know what was happening yesterday afternoon. It's so awful. I can't get the picture of that plane from down below out of my head. Those poor, terrified people jumping.

I just, well, all I want to say is, please try not to think too badly of me. Honestly, I am not utterly self-obsessed, even though that is what you must be thinking. I took a day off work yesterday (yes, it was a big deal to me) and after you ran past me at the bar, I got the bus back to Cumbride and went straight to the library because I heard you can pay to use a computer there. I didn't even mean to send the last email. I was just so shocked when somebody asked me what I thought about the Twin Towers, then told me the news when I didn't know what they were on about. I was hitting buttons trying to shut the thing down. If I had known of a way to cancel the earlier emails, I would have, believe me.

I don't even know why I am telling you all this. It is of zero importance compared to what happened in New York. I just can't bear for you to think this is the kind of person I am, going on and on about something so trivial, going on about myself, while thousands of people were dying.

I will go now. You must be caught up in all this and very busy. I won't take up any more of your time. Please take care.

L.

Robert Kane leans back, swallows hard, then puts his fingers on the mouse. He has a straight choice. Reply or delete?

EPILOGUE

November 2001
Emotion – Destiny's Child

KAREN

Karen Cooke, nee Hart, still lives with her parents in Cumbride. She has worked in the library up at the town centre for more than twenty years in a career based on efficiency and reliability but little passion for the job and even less ambition. Karen has no contact with any of her old friends from her schooldays. In fact, if put on the spot, she would struggle to name anyone she could call a real friend.

Karen has had no significant other since Simon Cooke disappeared in 1976. Truth is, she is still waiting for him to walk back into her life. On good days, she is able to convince herself he will definitely return, tail between his legs, and admit he messed everything up, admit he made the biggest blunder of his life by leaving her, four months after their wedding, while she was carrying their child. Karen is waiting for him to knock on her door and beg her to give him another chance.

Karen is working on her latest Dear Simon letter. She has written to him – or at least people with the same name – in seven different countries over the past quarter of a century.

There was a period in the early years when Karen was able to worm Cookie's latest address out of his parents. She would spend weeks wearing them down until they finally caved in under the relentless pressure and gave up his details. Cookie's parents moved from Cumbride several years ago, leaving no forwarding address.

Karen stays after hours at work some nights because the internet is a gift from the gods and has opened up so many new avenues. She uses the library computer to go online and scour international telephone directories as well as Google searches. Nearly two hundred people across the world named

303

Simon or at least S. Cooke have received letters from her over the years.

Sometimes, when the trail goes cold, she wonders if it is too late to set the Child Support Agency on him. One day very soon, Karen will discover Friends Reunited and Cookie will have to withdraw his entry.

Karen's own parents are retired and take a lot of holidays. They spend most of the winter in Spain. When they are at home, they keep leaving items in Karen's bedroom, like schedules from estate agents and holiday brochures, but she never bites.

Karen has a twenty-five-year-old son, also named Simon. He left home at eighteen and got himself a job and a bedsit in Glasgow, then moved to Manchester, then London, and now somewhere in the Republic of Ireland. Karen tries to phone him at least once a week to find out if he has had any luck in helping her track down his father but annoyingly, he has a terrible habit of losing his mobile so his number keeps changing.

One night, about ten years ago, Simon junior met Big Paddy, although neither of them ever knew it. PC Allan was on foot patrol in the Cardrum scheme and popped his head into that old swing park shelter – the one where he used to hang out as a teenager.

A bunch of kids were in there, about fourteen or fifteen years old. A couple of empty cider bottles lay on their side in one corner, and the sweet, thick aroma of hash hung in the air. The teenagers were bothering no one so PC Allan gave them a half-hearted lecture about drink and drugs and told them to keep the noise down.

But for days it stuck in his head that one of the youngsters looked mighty familiar. Finally, it struck him. The lad was the spit of someone he used to run about with in his own youth and the memory hurt him.

Yeah, that's right, the kid was the double of his old pal. Cammy.

COOKIE

Simon Cooke is currently living in Los Angeles, in one of the more rundown, less glamorous parts. The kind of area where you get used to your sleep being broken by sirens and, not uncommonly, gunshots. So no, not exactly Beverly Hills, but Los Angeles nevertheless. He thinks of himself as living here *currently* because most of his adult life has been nomadic, as if he is constantly on the run.

His modest fourth-floor downtown apartment doubles as home and consulting suite. There is a small, home-made plaque on the door. It reads: Simon Cooke. Providing Genuine Scotch Holographic Energy to the Stars. He has a clientele of two *stars* at the moment. One is an overweight guy who appeared in an episode of Friends about five years ago, standing next to Joey in Central Perk, sipping coffee. The tubby guy calls himself a background artiste, not an extra. Cookie's other client is a thin, jumpy girl who once played a waitress with two lines in Sex And The City, though one was cut and she has never got over it. Cookie knows it is not much. But it is a start. He has only been here two months.

Cookie only ended up in Los Angeles because there were cheap flights going on the day he had to flee Sydney. His fourth wife, Wend, had found the letter from Karen. He had never told Wend about Karen, or about his son. How the hell had Karen traced him this time? And why did she always write in the present tense as if they still knew each other, as if he had just nipped out for a paper twenty-odd years ago and would be home soon.

That was only part of it, of course. Wend was twenty-seven, a fit and very physically demanding twenty-seven. It did not take long for her to start tiring of the Scot with the smooth, if kind of rehearsed-sounding, line of patter, especially when she discovered he mostly preferred to go straight to sleep at night. Then there was that childish, messy carry-on with the biscuit and milk at bedtime.

Simon has just updated his Friends Reunited entry for the umpteenth time. It now concludes: Currently sharing my life with Atlanta. She'll soon be Number Five, and this time it's going to thrive.

He knows it is reckless, describing his loves and his life on the internet so openly where Karen – and the others – could easily find him. But he cannot help himself and, if pushed, he might even admit that perhaps the risk and the chase are exactly why he does it.

Yet again, he tries to shove away the niggling fear that has hung over him all these years and, for a moment, he wonders how he would go about finding out stuff like statutes of limitations and what the jail sentence for a five-time bigamist might be in Los Angeles.

KIRSTY

Kirsty McIntyre dabs foundation on her cheeks, but only a spot. She has already applied the faintest smear of lipstick. No need to go mad. Alex will be home soon. Alex tells her not to bother with make-up, says Kirsty is perfect as she is. But Kirsty appreciates Alex too, so she always makes an effort to look her best.

Kirsty never imagined herself as a housewife, not until Alex, but she is settled now and content with her life, happy with herself too, mostly. Kirsty looks at herself in the mirror. She doesn't do that so much these days but she is OK with what she sees. The orange tan is long gone, the one she diced with skin cancer to maintain, or so the doctors on daytime TV tell her nowadays. Kirsty has let her hair fade back to mousy brown, the shiny blonde genie long left behind in the bottle.

Kirsty thinks her breasts are too large but hey, they're only breasts – and God knows they cost enough. Den paid good money for them all those years ago when he was big time, when he was on the verge of the Scotland squad and there was talk of one of the top English teams coming in for him.

Kirsty got paid for the breasts too, by a Sunday paper, after they split up. No one round here makes the connection, thank Christ. Must be fifteen years since she put them on public display.

SOCCER ACE BOUGHT
ME TWIN STRIKERS…
THEN GAVE ME THE BOOT

So embarrassing, her Christmas present tits spread across Pages Four and Five, not Page Three. That was just after the slide started and she needed the money. That was when she began dropping football divisions.

However much she flinches at the memory, Kirsty cannot deny it. She enjoyed it while it lasted. She had a good run, best part of ten years as a top footballer's bird. What the papers would call a WAG these days. The big house, flash cars, endless clubbing and parties, the lines of coke on demand, the reflected, second-hand fame. Pretending to be pissed off at the MacPaparazzi but smiling for the snappers all the same, flashing them a bit of cleavage. A life of laughter, laziness and lingerie until Den got bored with her. It was inevitable really and the oldest cliché in the book – swap deal for a younger, fitter model.

Kirsty stuck with footballers and let herself be passed from groin strain to groin strain. Down the leagues till she was thirty-five and got dumped for the last time by a thirty-seven-year-old has-been desperately fighting for one last contract from some no-mark Scottish second-tier team.

When she realised it was over, she only had one thing left to survive on, the only thing she'd ever thought she had – sex. She tried to hold out, tried to put it off but she got there, like gravity.

One chill October night, Kirsty bottomed out. Found herself in an office doorway at the top of Waterloo Street in Glasgow. Micro-skirt, coat left to flap open, goods on display. A huddle of other girls, hardened and unsmiling, eyed her warily from a few yards along the street. A canine-faced Eastern European hard case sat in a BMW across the road, watching over the other girls like he owned them and studying Kirsty with a business interest. A glimpse into her own future. She didn't even know how it would work, where she would go with the punters, how much to charge, how to protect herself if they turned violent. She lasted only two nights on the street. Then Alex rescued her.

Kirsty was sweating and disgusted – not from Alex but from the last guy, her third and final client. He'd pulled up alongside her, looked her up and down, wound down his window and snarled: 'Haun job. Much?' He'd driven her to a dark, unlit car park behind a bowling alley that had shut for the night. She gagged on the cheese and onion waft when he unzipped himself, and the way he clawed at her breasts made her skin crawl. And all for a tenner. She knew it would only get worse.

Kirsty's hand shook, machine coffee spilled from the cup. She was on the hard seats under the clock in Central Station, wondering if she really had the guts to step off a platform. Alex, waiting for the last train home, moved over and sat beside her, offered Kirsty a tissue to mop up the coffee she had dripped on to herself.

Alex taught Kirsty that she didn't owe anything, that Kirsty wasn't just her body, wasn't just her sex. Alex taught her that emotions and actions like affection, friendship and care, could exist in their own right, outside of sex. Kirsty learned that she didn't have to pawn sex for a fake closeness that would have to be traded in again and again until there was nothing left for her to barter with.

After only a few weeks, she moved into Alex's house, an old red sandstone lower conversion in a small town just outside Glasgow. Alex made no demands but gave without a price. It was five long months before Kirsty, shyly, went to Alex's bed. And Kirsty, who had screwed and sucked and sold her way to a kind of approval since she was fifteen, made love for the first time in her life.

Kirsty has been with Alex for nearly ten years now. Alex is the head teacher at a local primary and for that reason, they try not to show much affection in public. They don't hold hands in the street or anything but Kirsty has confidence and trust in their love.

Kirsty does more than just keep house for Alex. She does some voluntary work, three mornings a week at the local Citizens Advice Bureau. She helps people, helps herself at the same time, and in doing so is constantly reminded of the things that matter in the real world. Like the single mums trying to feed and clothe three kids on fifty-two quid a week and for whom, funnily enough, breast size is rarely a big issue. Likewise, the sad, third-generation unemployed young men who don't know where their next fix is coming from, never mind their next blow job.

Kirsty puts the kettle on. It's twenty past four. She can't help smiling with anticipation. Kirsty is waiting for Alex. She'll be home from school any minute.

ROSS

Ross McEwan also does a bit of voluntary work and he is happy too. More contented and at peace with himself than he has ever been in his life. In fact, he is happier than he thinks he has any right to be. He lives with his partner, Kate, and they share a small, cosy cottage in a hamlet called Foscote in rural Buckinghamshire. They might get round to marrying one of these days but there is no rush, no pressure.

Ross is especially happy right now because he is speaking to his twenty-year-old son Derek again. He dares to think they have become mates and Derek comes to stay for the odd weekend. Ross hopes his daughter Laura, who is sixteen, might come and visit in the summer. He has spoken to her on the phone a few times but they are taking it slowly. As Kate explained to him bluntly, the onus is entirely on him to do the building and repair work.

Ross tries not to think much about his ex-wife, Janice. He has taken the blame and he has written to her to tell her just that, to acknowledge the hell that was their marriage was of his making, and to apologise. That was Kate's suggestion too. He knows that simply writing the word down doesn't come near to making up for the bullying and the rage and the violence. But it is all he can do because the last thing Jan needs is him infiltrating her life just so he can feel better about himself. It has been nine years since the marriage ended in bitterness and acrimony – and a court appearance for him, for assault. It wasn't a first offence either and he spent six months in prison. But now Ross has moved on and he sincerely hopes Jan has too. He doesn't ask Derek about his mother but he genuinely hopes she has found someone who deserves her and looks after her.

Ross is settled and life is good. He loves Kate with an intensity that frightens him. He loves Derek too. The pair of them don't just love him back, they like him. Maybe Laura will also get to like him one day. He hopes so but he won't rush her and, in the meantime, he has more than enough.

Nice, happy ending then?

Well, not quite, because here's the kicker about Ross. He is in a wheelchair. He will never walk again. He smashed his spine six years ago, playing five-a-sides for his works team in Northampton. Some guy tripped him – no real malice, just a routine footie collision. Ross lost the rag, the red mist descended and he chased the guy, intent on brutal revenge. But he went over on his ankle, took a heavy tumble and crashed down hard on his back. He didn't get up again.

THE FENIAN

Ross spent fourteen months flat on his back, completely immobile in a steel cage on a hospital bed in the specialist spinal injuries unit at Stoke Mandeville Hospital. Kate was the nurse who sat with him through those never-ending sleepless nights, sat with him as he watched his own little patch of sky through that tiny, precious corner of window in his line of vision. Blue to black to grey to purple to blue. She sat with him through the seasons and after a while, she started turning up sometimes on her nights off. They talked out each other's lives, every detail, and Ross had to fight, night after night, to keep Kate coming back to his bedside because she gave him just one rule. *I'm only interested in survivors. I don't waste my time on victims.*

Derek calls his Dad R2D2 because of the way he scoots and spins about in his wheelchair. Ross is a sports hero again. He got into wheelchair basketball in a big way and now he is the main man at the local club – the David Beckham of wheelies, his team-mates call him. He is their ace.

Kate still works at the hospital and when she is on dayshift, Ross fills his mornings doing voluntary work. Counselling child abuse victims.

WEE MARY

Mary Vannuchi, née Webb, helps run a restaurant in Cavallino, Italy, with her husband Paolo. Tubby, jolly Paolo who drinks too much rough red wine on Saturday nights and, when he is drunk, sings Italian love songs to her in the pitch-perfect baritone that never fails to melt the heart of the wife he still calls his *Leetel Scottee.*

Mary has travelled less than eight miles, or twelve kilometres as she now automatically thinks of it, in more than twenty-five years. Twelve kilometres down the coast from Punta Sabbioni, where you catch the ferry to Venice. One short bus ride that was as far as she got on her journey home, before panic made her hesitate. She got off the bus, walked into the first restaurant she came to, sat at a table, ordered coffee and never left.

Mary Vannuchi has not been back to Scotland in all those years, not since the day she left to escape the scandal. Once a year, without fail, she writes a postcard, a plain postcard, addressed to her mother and father at the old house in Cumbride, and gets Paolo to mail it along the road in Lido. Mary only ever writes two words: *I'm fine.* She has no idea if her parents still live there, or if their marriage survived, or even if they are alive or dead. If they are, they will have long deciphered the postmark but to her knowledge, they have never come looking.

Mostly, Mary thinks of only one person from her past. Lorna. So sad that she only ever got one reply from Lorna, then nothing. Mary remembers their parting. The hugging, the crying, the mutual vows. At the bus terminal in

309

Punta Sabbioni, it was. Lorna was heading home but Mary stayed behind with that student she had met in Venice – Terry, the public schoolboy with the really posh English accent. But he had just been an excuse to delay her homecoming and it soon fizzled out.

Lorna had offered to stay too, but Mary had sent her home to mend things with Robert, to tell him she loved him.

A correction then. Mary thinks of two people from her past. She has long decided they did mend things, Lorna and Robert, and that it all worked out for them. Mary decided Lorna and Robert's love was the real deal. She has convinced herself they did get back together and they stayed together. She believes they are together still.

Mary often hears echoes from her past among the holidaymakers who crowd into this bright little resort on the Adriatic. Every year, from April to October, she serves tables and whenever she picks up a Scottish accent, she lapses into the Italian babble that now comes so easily to her. Just in case.

Mary dreams that one day they will walk into Paolo's Bistro by chance, Lorna and Robert. She is positive that she will recognise them – Lorna definitely. Maybe they will bring their teenage or even grown-up children with them. Mary Vannuchi loves children, always did, and shudders as she thinks back to the saddest day of her life, when a doctor gave her that grim warning about the deadly danger of falling pregnant.

Now Mary goes into her daily routine and counts them off on her fingers, trying to picture where they all are at this very moment. All boys, from Paolo jnr, the eldest at twenty-three and a student doctor, to Berti, the baby at seven. She ticks them off to make sure they are real and Wee Mary thanks God for granting her not one miracle, but five.

CAMMY
God rest his soul.

FIONA
Fiona McKenna, QC. A dazzling success, one of Scotland's top courtroom performers. She is formidable and the High Court is her turf, where she specialises in loosening the bowels of prosecutors with forensic skill and devastating persuasion. One day she might just say Yes to the overtures and move over to their ranks. But for now, she prefers to think of herself as being on the side of the angels. She has been consulted by the Scottish Executive who want her to help draft a new Justice Bill, with particular attention to crimes against women. Fiona's star is soaring, her path is up and up. She lives in understated style too – an exclusive townhouse in the Mearns, valued at

three quarters of a million at the last count, with an eight-month-old E-Class Mercedes in the underground garage. Fiona is still single, but she is fine with that because her adult life has been entirely career-driven. She is seeing a doctor these days, seeing as in going out with. He is a consultant and they met when she had a breast cancer scare three years ago. He is a widower in his early fifties with two adult children and even a couple of grandkids. As with other personal relationships, Fiona finds the whole extended family set-up awkward to negotiate, so they are all taking it slowly. The doctor stays at her place most weekends and this year they have moved things forward by going on holiday together twice – Caribbean by cruise ship, Chamonix for the skiing. It might become permanent and yes, she thinks she would quite like to fill that space in her life, but she won't fall to pieces if it doesn't happen.

Fiona McKenna is fulfilled. Life is as perfect as it could be. But she lives in permanent fear that it could all crumble in a single moment.

Fiona only lasted eight months at university first time round, in Edinburgh. By then she had met Eric. He was thirty-one, a mature student, a controller, and he introduced her to cannabis, then heroin. Fiona didn't resist and did everything he asked of her, sexually and beyond. But then he dumped her, just like that, when the fresh-meat intake of students arrived. Problem was, he didn't take the heroin hunger away with him.

Fiona's student grant didn't go anywhere near feeding her habit so she got a part-time job in a pub, behind the bar, and before long, she stopped going to classes. She earned a bit more by dancing topless in one of Edinburgh's go-go joints, even though she reckoned she still had no more than bones where her boobs should be. But the desperate hunt for cash was never satisfied and she soon began supplementing her income with fiver hand-jobs for the go-go customers under the table in a shady booth. Then one of her regulars offered her a hundred quid for a morning's work. It was too good to resist and she got herself fixed up before it. It was all a blur. A draughty flat somewhere, rough, dry, painful sex with two-three-four people, at least one other girl. She lost count of those who were touching or entering her body as a camera whirred somewhere in the background, and the air brakes of a double-decker whooshed at the bus stop outside the window. Hollywood this definitely was not.

Fiona got picked up by the cops a few times for possession but she was small fry and never got more than a caution. But a constable spotted her intelligence one night when Fiona, reading the charge sheet upside down across a desk, spotted two errors and warned the young cop she would get herself in bother. The WPC took an interest and, ultimately, saved Fiona's life. She tried talking her into rehab and at the second attempt, it worked. Fiona nudged her head above water, breathed in oxygen and hauled herself back from the brink.

She returned home to Cumbride and her parents were brilliant. They bullied her and they babied her in equal parts and a year later, she got back into uni, Glasgow this time. She stayed at home and got the bus back and forward each day. She walked it, graduated top of her year with first class honours and suddenly Fiona the career girl had her pick of suitors. She joined a big-name law firm in Glasgow who were offering court work, which was what she wanted. Even though it was minor, run-of-the-mill cases at first, she quickly gained a reputation as a tough, efficient and, crucially, successful operator, often against the odds.

She met a cop at the sheriff court, a detective sergeant. She was twenty-six, he was three years older, a graduate like her. A fast-track career cop and also, like her, ferociously ambitious. They hit it off, they dated, they got engaged, their life plan was laid out before them. Things couldn't have been better...until his stag night with mates from the nick and they ended up at some other sergeant's flat. Someone had blagged blue movies from the evidence store. Macho whoops and roars, applause and heckles. Then came the main feature: Thin Lezzy, soundtrack The Boys Are Back In Town, starring a scrawny, washed-out junkie the horrified groom-to-be recognised.

Fiona's fiancé was as decent about it as he could be. The tape got *lost* and the two or three close cop pals who had also recognised Fiona McKenna QC were sworn to silence. Her fiancé burdened himself with a mountain of owed favours he would be paying off for the rest of his career.

But on the advice of his mentor, a chief super who had been at the stag do, the wedding was off.

Fiona understood and she got over it. Her fears diminished as the years passed but they have never disappeared, not completely.

There is always the remote chance that there might still be copies out there, either on an old video or on some murky corner of the internet.

And one day some vermin might just recognise the face inside the wig.

BIG PADDY

Paddy Allan is stationed at Cumbride Police Office, still a constable at forty-four. He has just failed his sergeant's exams for the fifth time but he got a bit closer this time and, to be honest, he's never been that bothered about promotion anyway. He only takes the exams to stop the inspector nagging.

Big Paddy is probably the most popular guy at the station because he keeps morale up at even the most difficult times with his positive personality, permanent smile and fierce sense of loyalty. Pals at the station have a new nickname for him these days – The Pig With Two Dicks.

That's because his grin is even wider since his son Bobby, who has just turned sixteen, was asked to train with his dad's beloved Celtic. Big Paddy is not naive. He has been following Celtic all his life and he knows that the odds are stacked against young players going all the way. He has seen countless kids come up through the ranks, hailed by the pundits and the fans as the new Kenny, or the new Jinky.

They get on the big team bench a couple of times towards the fag-end of the season, get twenty minutes when the game's dead and, if they're lucky, get the chance to make an impact. The papers rave about them for a couple of days, give them daft nicknames like Kid Goals. Then, inevitably, the majority of the boy wonders disappear and resurface a year or two later at a Morton or a Rotherham or something.

But Big Paddy encourages Bobby to go for it, to chase his dream, as long as he sticks in at school and gets his Standard Grades first. There was another bonus – Big Paddy got to meet the Celtic manager during a special day at the ground for the youth players and their families. The Celtic manager even shook his hand and told Big Paddy he liked his boy and picked him out by name.

Big Paddy says sod an audience with the Pope, he can die happy now he's met St Martin.

He has a daughter too. He adores her, tells anyone who will listen that she is a smashing girl who is lucky because she takes after her mother.

Big Paddy has been married nearly eighteen years and is still mad about his missus, even if he is gobsmacked that they ever got together in the first place.

JO

Jo, aka the Karaoke Queen, runs her own hairdressers in Cardrum. She still worries, though not as much as she used to, that people might make jokes about her height so she tries to get in first. Take her salon, for example. She spent a lot of time on the name, trying to find just the right tone, something that linked her height with hairdressing so people can have a laugh about it right off, if they want to. Then, hopefully, they discover she is actually a pretty good stylist. Jo almost went for Half-Cut but she was scared customers might be put off by the idea of some pint-sized little drunk being let loose on their hair. She did consider her husband's suggestion, Trim Package, but in the end, she opted for Short Wave. Jo likes her work. She enjoys dipping in and out of the fringes (Ha!) of her clients' lives. She picks up conversations from previous visits, remembering who was about to go on holiday. *What was Cyprus like then?* Or recalling who was getting a perm for their nephew's wedding the last time they were in. *How did the big day go?* She's good at it — memorising details, storing them, so people feel they are more than just customers and, indeed, many have become genuine friends over the years.

Jo still does people off the telly. She still leaves herself behind, most Friday nights, some Saturdays too. Jo is a bit of a minor celebrity, at least in a handful of Cumbride's pubs where they always reserve the last half-hour on the karaoke for her. She tries to stay up to date, brings Madonna and Kylie and Britney into her act – but Lulu and Suzi Q and Donna Summer for a bit of nostalgia too. She escapes into it but now she knows when to put the characters back in their box and she can do that because she has got to like herself a lot more now.

The main reason for that is her husband because he has raised her value. He tells Jo all the time that he is her biggest fan, not just at the karaoke nights, which he tries to get to when work permits, but at home too. He tells Jo she is *his* trim package and that most of all, he likes Jo to do Jo.

Jo has two children. Her youngest, daughter Lisa, is fourteen and an extrovert. Her Dad jokes that she breaks into song and dance when the fridge door opens and the little light goes on. Lisa lives for school shows and Jo encourages her to think about drama college. Jo tells Lisa: 'Never know, we might finish up with two stars in the family.'

Jo will celebrate her eighteenth wedding anniversary soon. Folk call them the odd couple, Bashful and The BFG, or, more predictably, Little and Large. But it doesn't bother her. She is very happy and she loves Big Paddy as much now as the day he got down on one knee – and was still taller than her, she reminds him.

ROBERT
Nervous as hell but excited at the same time. Heading for a restaurant in town to meet an old friend for the first time in twenty-six years.

LORNA
Ditto.

Acknowledgements

There are a few people I need to thank who, unwittingly and otherwise, helped in the creation of this book.

The real-life shelter gang – though we never called ourselves that either – and other fellow travellers from Kildrum, Cumbernauld, and OLHS 1968-74, who inspired some of the characters and incidents.

Various teachers, relatives and other innocent adult bystanders who had to put up with our nonsense.

My brilliant daughters, Lynn and Laura, for the encouragement, suggestions and exploring Millport with me.

My son-in-law, Ryan McGinness, for the captivating cover, removing my technical fears and the best book review ever – 'I was worried it would be pish.'

My big sister, Barbara, for allowing me to mention the tortoises even though she still insists it isn't true. It is.

My early reader and friend of more than half a century, Carol Stobo, who was there for at least some of the story.

Above all, my soul mate, best pal and wife Margaret, who finally forced me to stop tinkering and get the damn thing published.

Mike Kernan, July 2020

Printed in Great Britain
by Amazon

24720170R00189